A t a dead run, breaking through into an open area of the forest with little ground cover among maple and birch trees, they abruptly ran up on a knot of half-naked people smeared with white ash, all hunched over around something on the ground.

They were Shun-tuk.

In the weak, early dawn light the Shun-tuk looked like ghosts. All had eye sockets painted with a black, greasy substance. Wide grins of teeth drawn on their faces completed the look, making them resemble skulls. Most of their heads were shaved, but some had a knot of hair remaining at the top that was tied up with strings of beads and bones to keep it standing up straight so that it resembled a fountain of hair.

Some of the men turned from their prey to look up in surprise as Richard bounded over a boulder and leaped in at them, suddenly screaming in rage, his sword held high in both fists.

In that frozen instant, Kahlan saw that the startled faces were dripping with blood.

The Shun-tuk had knives, but they remained in their sheaths.

Instead, they used only their teeth.

BY TERRY GOODKIND

Wizard's First Rule
Stone of Tears
Blood of the Fold
Temple of the Winds
Soul of the Fire
Faith of the Fallen
The Pillars of Creation
Naked Empire
Debt of Bones
Chainfire
Phantom
Confessor
The Law of Nines
The Omen Machine
The First Confessor
The Third Kingdom
Severed Souls
Warheart
Nest
The Girl in the Moon
Death's Mistress
Shroud of Eternity
Siege of Stone
The Scribbly Man
Hateful Things
Wasteland
Witch's Oath
Into Darkness
Heart of Black Ice

SEVERED SOULS

TERRY GOODKIND

Tor Publishing Group
New York

SEVERED SOULS

Copyright © 2014 by Terry Goodkind

A Tor Book
Published by Tom Doherty Associates/Tor Publishing Group
120 Broadway
New York, NY 10271

www.tor-forge.com

Tor® is a registered trademark of Macmillan Publishing Group, LLC.

ISBN 978-0-7653-6621-4

First Edition: August 2014
First International Mass Market Edition: February 2015

Printed in the United States of America

17   16   15   14   13   12   11   10   9   8

SEVERED
SOULS

B ring us our dead."

At the same time as he heard the voice, Richard felt the touch of an icy hand on the back of his shoulder.

He drew his sword as he spun.

As it cleared its scabbard, the blade sent its distinctive ring of steel through the hushed, predawn air. The power contained within the weapon answered the call, inundating him with rage in preparation for a fight.

Standing in the darkness right behind where he had been on watch were three men and two women. The dying campfire burning in the distance off behind him cast the faintest flicker of reddish light across the five stony faces. The gaunt figures stood passively, shoulders slumped, arms hanging limp at their sides.

Besides the hint of impending rain, the air carried the smell of wood smoke from the fire back at camp, the scent of balsam trees and cinnamon ferns growing nearby, their horses, and the musty smell of the damp leaf litter matting the ground.

But Richard thought he also detected a trace of sulfur.

Even though none of the five looked or acted threatening, having the crackling power from the ancient weapon he held in his fist thundering through him had his heart hammering. Their passive poses did nothing to ease his sense of threat or his readiness to fight should they make a sudden move to attack.

What concerned Richard more than anything, though, was that he had been watching and listening for any sound or movement in the predawn stillness— that was the whole point of standing watch—and he hadn't heard or seen the five come up behind him.

In such dense, uninhabited woods it was unimaginable to him that not one of them had made a sound by stepping on a twig or crunching any of the dry leaves and bark scattered about on the ground.

Richard was more than used to being in the woods and it was virtually impossible for so much as a squirrel to sneak up on him, much less five people. When he had been a woods guide he had played the game of sneak-up with other guides. He was well practiced at it and it had developed in him a kind of sixth sense for any living thing near him. People rarely if ever successfully snuck up on Richard.

Yet these five had.

The trackless wasteland of the Dark Lands seldom saw travelers. It was far too dangerous a place to take any chances. Any traveler would know that and not tempt trouble by sneaking up on a camp.

Richard was but one wrong word or sudden move away from unleashing his restraint. In his mind, the deed was already done, every move calculated and decided. If they did anything wrong he would not hesitate to defend himself and those in camp behind him.

"Who are you?" he asked. "What do you want?"

"We have come to be with our dead," one of the two women said in the same sort of emotionless voice as the man who had spoken first.

The gazes of all five seemed to be staring through him.

"Bring them to us," the second woman said in the same disembodied tone. Like the others, she looked to be little more than skin and bones.

"What are you talking about?" Richard asked.

"Bring us our dead," one of the other men repeated.

"What dead?" Richard asked.

"Our dead," a different man said in a voice equally devoid of emotion.

The circular answers were getting him nowhere.

Back in the camp behind him, Richard could hear a soft, calculated commotion as soldiers of the First File, awakened by the sound of his sword being drawn, threw off their blankets and sprang to their feet. He knew that they would be snatching up swords, lances, and axes at the ready near where they had been sleeping. These were men who were always prepared for trouble.

Without taking his eyes from the five any longer than necessary to snatch quick glances to either side in order to watch for other threats, Richard knew that the soldiers behind him would be giving hand signals for defensive positions. As distant as they were, as careful as they were, he could hear a footstep here, the rustle of leaves there, the squish of mud underfoot to the side as some of them moved swiftly through the forest to surround the strangers.

These men were the best of the best—experienced soldiers who had worked hard to join the elite corps of the First File. They all had seen years of combat. A number of their ranks had already given their lives after coming to the Dark Lands in order to help get Richard and Kahlan safely back to the palace.

Unfortunately, they were all still a very long way from home.

"I don't know who you are talking about," Richard said as he watched the distant gazes of the five people before him.

"Our dead," the first woman said in a lifeless voice.

Richard frowned. "Why are you telling this to me?"

"Because you are the one," the man who had touched him said.

Richard lifted his fingers one at a time, flexing them in a wavelike motion, readjusting his grip on his sword. He looked from one blank face to another.

"The one? What are you talking about?"

"You are *fuer grissa ost drauka*," another man said. "You are the one."

Goose bumps tingled up the back of Richard's neck. *Fuer grissa ost drauka* meant "the bringer of death" in the ancient language of High D'Haran. It was a name prophecy had given him. Very few people, other than Richard, knew the dead language of High D'Haran.

Perhaps even more disconcerting was how these five would know that it referred to him.

Richard kept the point of his sword toward the five, making sure none of them could approach any closer, even though none of them tried. He wanted to be sure he had fighting room should he need it.

"Where did you hear such a thing?" he asked.

"You are the one—you are *fuer grissa ost drauka*: the bringer of death," one of the women said. "That is what you do. You bring death."

"And what makes you think that I can bring you your dead?"

"We have long sought our dead," she said. "We need you to bring them to us."

"Bring us our dead," another man repeated, for the first time with a trace of dark insistence that Richard didn't like.

It seemed to make some kind of sense to the five people, but it didn't make any sense to Richard, other than in a decidedly perverse way. He knew the three ancient meanings of the term *fuer grissa ost drauka* and how they applied to him.

These five were using it in an entirely different way.

Behind him, he could hear Kahlan racing back toward him. He recognized the unique sound of her boot strikes and stride. She had been sharing some quiet time with him before dawn and had only moments before started back toward the camp. As she came rushing up behind him, Richard held his left arm out to make sure she stayed out of the way should he need to use his sword.

"What's going on?" she asked as she came to an abrupt halt not far away.

Richard stole a quick glance back over his shoulder. The tense concern of her expression did nothing to diminish the flawless beauty of her familiar features.

Richard turned back to the five to keep his eye on them.

They were gone.

He blinked in surprise and then looked around. He

had looked away for only a fraction of a second. It was impossible, but all five people were gone.

"They were right there," he said, half to himself.

There was nowhere they could have hidden in the brief time he had glanced back at Kahlan. The sloping, rocky ground where they had been didn't offer any cover. It was a few dozen feet to the closest trees. That was why Richard had picked the spot—it was open enough that no one could hide or sneak up on them.

He saw that the decomposing leaves and forest debris that had drifted in across the ground where they had been standing beside the exposed ridge of granite ledge looked untouched. He would have heard them move. They would have disturbed the leaf litter. They couldn't have taken a single step without making a sound, nor could they have gotten out of his sight and to cover that fast.

"Who?" Kahlan asked as she leaned to the side, peering around him.

Richard stretched his arm out, pointing insistently with his sword. "Only seconds ago there were five people standing right there."

The small bits of sky that could be seen through gaps in the heavy forest canopy were beginning to turn a leaden, muted gray tinted red by the approaching dawn. Kahlan knew better than to discount what Richard said he had seen. She scanned the near darkness to both sides.

"Were they half people?" she asked, the worry evident in her voice.

Richard could still feel the icy sensation from where one of the men had touched his right shoulder.

"No, I don't think so. One of them put his hand on

me—as if to get my attention. They didn't bare their teeth. I don't think they came to try to take my soul."

"Are you sure?"

"Pretty sure."

"Did they say anything?"

"They said that they wanted me to bring them their dead."

Kahlan's mouth opened in wordless surprise. Richard studied the place where they had been before again looking around for any sign of the five. In the gloom he couldn't see any footprints.

Kahlan hugged her arms to herself as she finally stepped closer. "Richard, there's no one there." She gestured off toward the trees. "And nowhere to hide until you get back into the woods. How could they have vanished?"

Dozens of soldiers of the First File, his personal guard, rushed out of the darkness to form a protective perimeter. Each of the big men had a weapon to hand, ready for pitched battle. It looked as if he were suddenly standing in a steel porcupine.

"Lord Rahl," one of the officers asked, "what is it? What happened?"

"There were five people here—just a moment ago." Richard gestured with his sword. "They came up behind me and were standing right there."

The soldiers briefly scanned the darkness, and then, without further word, at least a dozen men dashed away into the woods to search for the intruders. Although dawn was starting to bring a weak gray light to the quiet forest, it was still dark enough that Richard knew it would be easy to miss someone hiding in such dense woods. All the strangers would have to do would be to crouch in the darkness among thickets of bushes or saplings and they could easily be missed.

But he didn't think these five were crouching and hiding.

He knew otherwise.

He knew that they had vanished.

2

W hat is it?" Nicci called out as she pushed her way through the tight ring of towering soldiers. Her gaze quickly swept over his sword, probably checking to see if it was bloody. Despite the size of the men and their fearsome weapons, Nicci's gift probably made her more deadly than all of the men put together. Had his own gift been working, he would have been able to see the aura of her power shimmering around her.

"Five people came up behind me as I was standing watch," Richard told her as Zedd rushed in through the gap Nicci had created. "I didn't know they were there until one of them touched my shoulder."

Nicci did a double take. "They walked right up and one of them touched you?"

Like Nicci, the old wizard looked incredulous. Though Richard knew his grandfather well, from time to time he was amazed at what Zedd was able to do with his ability, as well as his uncanny knowledge about the most arcane of subjects.

"People?" Zedd peered to each side behind Richard and Kahlan. "What people?"

The young Samantha and her mother, Irena, rushed up behind Zedd. Despite only being in her mid-teens, Samantha had proven to have remarkable abilities as a sorceress. Richard didn't yet know much of anything about her mother's gift, but if Samantha was any indication, her mother was potentially quite formidable.

Despite the knowledge, abilities, and power of the people gathered around him, they were in a dangerous land that put all of them at risk. The fact that five people had been able to walk right up on them, and then vanish, only served to highlight the perils of the Dark Lands.

"Are you all right, Lord Rahl?" Irena asked with a look of concern as she reached out to touch Richard's arm.

He nodded as Nicci subtly but protectively stepped in close enough to move Irena aside.

"They snuck up behind you?" Nicci tilted her head toward Richard. "Five people snuck up behind you?"

Exasperated that he was being ignored, Zedd waved an arm. "What five people?" he demanded again before Richard could answer Nicci. "Where are they?"

Richard gestured behind in frustration. "They were right there, and then they were gone."

Zedd cocked his head as his bushy brow drew down. He peered intently with one eye. "Gone?"

"Yes, gone. I don't know where they went. I didn't see them come and I didn't see them leave. When I turned back around to keep an eye on them they were simply gone."

Samantha lifted her chin, sniffing the air. Her features had yet to fully take on the more sharply defined form of full adulthood. The soft contour of her nose wrinkled.

"What's that smell?" she asked, rather urgently, before Zedd or anyone else could say anything more. "It's fading now, but it seems like I remember it from somewhere."

Everyone looked around, distracted by the strange question and her tone of alarm.

Kahlan frowned. "Now that you mention it, I remember it from somewhere, too."

Richard methodically studied the shadows, still looking for any sign of the five strangers. "It's sulfur."

Samantha pushed some of the matted mass of her black hair back from her face as she peered up at him. "Sulfur?"

"Yes—the smell of death," Richard said, still gazing off into the darkness, still looking for any sign of the strangers.

"No," Kahlan said, tapping a thumb against the handle of the knife sheathed at her belt as she tried to recall. "The spirits know I've been around that stench enough. This was certainly unpleasant, but it's not the smell of death. It's something else."

"That's not what he means," Nicci said in a dark and disquieting tone as she shared a knowing look with Richard when he turned back to them.

"It's the smell of the world of the dead," Richard said in an equally somber voice to all the faces watching him. "Like a doorway to the underworld itself was briefly cracked open."

Everyone stared back.

"The underworld!" Samantha snapped her fingers.

"That's where I remember the smell from. It was when I was trying to heal you and the Mother Confessor. When I got near that poison of death deep in you both, I smelled that smell."

Irena, having moved around behind Samantha, put a hand on her daughter's shoulder as she leaned in. "Poison? What poison?" Her expression had turned suspicious. It was an expression that seemed to go naturally with the creases in the center of her brow and her mass of black hair. "What was my daughter doing anywhere near anything to do with the underworld?"

"Jit, the Hedge Maid, had captured Kahlan and me," Richard said, "but before she could kill us I was able to plug our ears with some wads of cloth and then break the restraints on the evil that resides inside her kind. When I did, she involuntarily let out a cry that called death to her. That was how I was able to kill her so that we could escape.

"Unfortunately, some of that sound was still able to get through. Now, that opening to the world of the dead is embedded within us. When Samantha healed our other wounds, she came near to that boundary rooted deep within us. That's what she is remembering."

"Samantha wouldn't know anything about such matters," Irena insisted as her gaze shifted from her daughter back to Richard. "She's too young. She has no business even attempting such things yet. She still has too much to learn before going near such dark forces."

As Samantha tilted her head back to look up at her mother, her eyes glistened with tears at the terrible memory. "It was the only way I could heal their wounds. I had to do it or they would have died. Lord

Rahl is the one meant to save us. He helped save many of the people of Stroyza.

"I had to do it or they would have died. He guided me in what I needed to do. It was then, when I was doing the healing, that I felt that terrible darkness of death deep within them. That's when I smelled that awful smell."

"She's right," Zedd grumbled unhappily. "I recall a hint of that same odor from when I started healing the both of them back before we were attacked and captured. I recognized it at the time as the stagnant stench of the darkest depths of the world of the dead." His eyes turned away. "I've encountered that singular smell before."

Nicci hooked a long strand of her blond hair back behind an ear as she scanned the darkness among the trees. She seemed lost in her own thoughts, or else she was using her ability to try to sense if someone or something was hiding out there.

"When you are near to the boundary to the underworld, when death is near," she said in a quiet voice that seemed to come from some dark place within her, "you could sometimes smell it, smell the world of the dead beyond the veil."

Irena glanced around at the grim expressions. "When death is near . . . ? The world of the dead? Here? Now? What are you all talking about? It's likely to be nothing more sinister than a sulfur spring nearby. There are a number of such places in the Dark Lands. Most likely the breeze carried a whiff of a sulfur spring in this direction, that's all." She cast a deliberate glance in Nicci's direction. "I think we're letting ourselves get carried away by groundless fears."

Nicci's flawless features took on a ill-humored cast

as her gaze settled on the woman. "I was once a Sister of the Dark. I suffered that stench often enough when the Keeper of the underworld visited us in our sleep, when he came to us to direct us to do his bidding. That's why the Mother Confessor thought of it as a memory from a dream. When she sleeps, the sights and sounds of the conscious world fade into the background. In that state, she is nearer to the boundary to the underworld now rooted within her."

Samantha's jaw hung open. "You were a Sister of the—"

"Hush," her mother cautioned from behind in a low voice as she put both hands on the young woman's shoulders to add emphasis to the order.

Samantha's mother looked shaken by the revelation that Nicci was once a Sister of the Dark. Richard knew that many people who lived in remote places, like Irena and her daughter, were superstitious and avoided speaking out loud of things they feared lest they call those mysterious dangers to themselves. There was nothing more terrifying than the Keeper of the underworld. Richard knew Sisters of the Light who called the Keeper "the Nameless One" for fear of calling him forth.

Richard also saw the shadow of suspicion in Irena's dark eyes. Women who had given themselves over to such dark forces never returned to the light, Yet Nicci had.

"Sulfur smells similar, but it's not exactly the same as the stench from the world of the dead. Considering my past allegiances, I could hardly mistake sulfur for the haunting stench of the underworld. When I touched Richard and Kahlan before, to heal them, I recognized all too well that death itself is growing in them both."

Hearing the unmistakable tone of authority and experience in Nicci's voice, Irena didn't argue.

The creases in Zedd's face drew tight as he looked around in alarm. "Where's Cara?"

Richard's grandfather knew that the Mord-Sith wouldn't be far when there was any sort of danger to Richard and Kahlan.

The words felt like a knife to Richard's heart.

"Cara is gone," he said in a quiet voice as he looked back into his grandfather's hazel eyes.

Zedd's brow drew down. "Gone? What do you mean, gone? She was here when we set up camp."

"She left earlier in the night."

When Zedd saw the look on Richard's face he closed his mouth, leaving his questions for later. Zedd had been there when Cara's husband had been brutally killed by the half people. Cara had been there as well. Richard could see in his grandfather's eyes that he suddenly made the connection to the reason she had left.

Irena eyed the dark shapes of trees emerging as dawn crept up on them. With the same wiry figure and the same mass of long black hair framing a face of delicate features, she looked like an older version of Samantha, if somewhat more tense. Samantha by contrast had faced terrible dangers with bravery and resolve. He knew that part of that was because she was young.

It occurred to Richard that, living in the Dark Lands her whole life and being an experienced sorceress, maybe Irena had experienced far more than her daughter and had good reason for being anxious. Irena would have seen things that Samantha had yet to see, understood things that Samantha had yet to comprehend. The older woman would have spent well over twice Samantha's years surviving the dangers of such a rugged and remote place.

Irena knew, too, of the barrier to the third kingdom being down. Being the sorceress of the village of Stroyza, she had been responsible for watching over that barrier in case it was ever breached and warning others if it was. She probably knew at least some of the terrors from beyond the wall to the north that her people had watched over for thousands of years.

Richard wondered just how much she knew about the barrier and the third kingdom that had for so long been locked away beyond, a realm where the worlds of life and death existed together in the same time and place. He needed to have a long talk with the woman to find out just what she knew.

"We should be away from this place," Irena murmured as she watched the shadows.

The mention of the half people had set her on edge, and for good reason. Her husband had been killed by the half people—devoured before her eyes in an attempt to steal his soul for themselves.

With the barrier to the third kingdom down, the unholy half dead—beings without souls—had now been loosed on the world of the living, attacking anyone they could catch, devouring their flesh in a deranged attempt to capture a soul for themselves. When that barrier had been breached after holding evil back for thousands of years, Irena had left her village to warn people of what was happening. She hadn't made it far. After killing her husband, the half people had taken her captive. After attempting to use her for their occult purposes, they would have eventually devoured her as they had so many others. Fortunately, Richard had managed to free her along with all the soldiers, Zedd, Nicci, and Cara before that could happen.

Unfortunately, Cara's husband, Ben, the general in command of these men, had not made it out alive.

Everyone turned to look when they heard a distant scream.

Richard pointed with his sword. "There!"

3

Just as Richard started out toward the source of the scream, Irena caught his arm.

"No, Lord Rahl—you can't. There could be too many of them. We must get you out of here."

Richard pulled his arm away as he heard another scream. "That's one of our men."

She pointed urgently in the direction of the cries. "But it's too late to save him. The risk would be for nothing."

"We don't know that." He swept the woman aside on his way past her. "We don't leave our own behind if there is a chance to save them."

Kahlan fell in close behind Richard to block the woman from interfering with him. It was not the time to debate the issue, but more than that, there was nothing to debate. Kahlan knew that as well as Richard. In situations like this, seconds could mean the difference between life and death.

Besides that, Kahlan could see the rage of the

weapon in Richard's eyes. He was intent on stopping the threat and he would let nothing get in his way.

She supposed it made sense for Irena to be concerned about Richard's safety—he was the Lord Rahl, after all, and the leader of the D'Haran Empire. In so many ways, everyone's survival depended on Richard. But Kahlan wondered how much Irena, being from such a remote place, knew of the wider world. Perhaps more troubling, she wondered how much Irena knew of the unique dangers in her birthplace. Kahlan had to push the issue from her mind as she rushed to stay close to Richard.

As the entire mass of men turned and raced after Richard, Nicci cut in front of Kahlan to stay close behind him. The woman's blond hair streamed out behind her like a flag as she followed the Lord Rahl into battle. Richard leaped over a wind-fallen spruce, charging off into the darkness of the dense forest as everyone else gave chase.

With Cara gone and the sickness of death preventing Kahlan's or Richard's power from working, Nicci was obviously intent on staying close to protect both Richard and Kahlan. She, perhaps better than just about anyone, knew how everyone's survival depended on Richard. Just as Cara would have done, she intended to make sure he was protected.

Kahlan was thankful that at least the power of Richard's sword worked for him. His gift didn't work any better than her power, but the sword had its own magic and he could still depend on that.

Rather than object to Nicci cutting in front of her, Kahlan simply followed behind the sorceress. She knew that in Cara's absence it made the most sense for Nicci to be as close as possible in order to protect them both. Besides, there was nothing more important to Kahlan than Richard's safety. More than his importance to everyone else, he was everything to her and if Nicci could best protect him, then Kahlan wanted the sorceress as close to him as possible.

Zedd followed on Kahlan's heels while Samantha and Irena were swept up and carried along with the tide of men rushing up from behind. Some of the men fanned out to the sides, creating protective wings around Richard and Kahlan and making sure that they weren't taken by surprise from an attack from the sides.

In the grip of the rage from the sword, Richard wasn't going to slow for anything and it wasn't long before he had outdistanced the rest of them. He ran through the woods, weaving his way among the trunks of towering pines, through thickets of brush, over rocks and fallen trees and streams with the kind of practiced abandon that the rest of them couldn't match. It was like watching an unstoppable shadow slip among the timber to be absorbed into the darkness out ahead.

More than that, though, the sickness she carried within her was hampering Kahlan's ability to keep up. It was troubling the way it sapped her strength, leaving her winded long before she ordinarily would have been. Richard had the same sickness of death growing all the time inside him, but it was more advanced in Kahlan. That death within would soon claim them both, but if not stopped it was destined to take her first.

The way that weakness swiftly drained her strength as she ran after Richard not only surprised her, it alarmed her. Zedd and Nicci had warned her how serious the situation was, and how the inner poisonous touch of death from Jit would steadily grow stronger. If it wasn't removed, neither Richard nor Kahlan would live much longer.

As she started losing ground to Richard and Nicci and struggled to get her breath, Zedd put a hand on Kahlan's back, between her shoulder blades. It was not merely meant to help her keep her balance. While he couldn't remove what was poisoning her, at least not until they could get back to the People's Palace, he was trickling his gift into her to add strength to the life within her still fighting for survival. That trickle of power was enough to help her keep up. She knew, though, that it wouldn't last for long.

From time to time Kahlan heard the soldier's screams out ahead of them. The sounds of those screams were getting closer. She knew it must be the half people attacking the man, but since they weren't making any noise she had no idea how many there might be. She hated running headlong into such an unknown situation, but there was no other choice except to leave the man to be killed, and that was not acceptable.

In the early dawn light, she saw branches sweep out of the darkness at her at the last instant before they whipped past. Sometimes she had to quickly duck to the side to keep from being hit in the face. Sometimes it was too late and she could only close her eyes. Other times, when they sprang back as Richard batted limbs out of his way, they slapped her shoulder.

At times, if the bough was too large to shove aside or avoid, Richard simply swung his sword as he rushed headlong through the dense woods, sending the limb sailing up and out of his way to come down among those following behind. The men shielded themselves with an arm whenever a branch came down among them. Kahlan struggled to regain sight of Richard as he vanished from time to time among the thick growth of spruce saplings and brush only to reappear again as he bounded up and over a fallen tree trunk or an outcropping of rock.

At a dead run, breaking through into an open area of the forest with little ground cover among maple and birch trees, they abruptly ran up on a knot of half-naked people smeared with white ash, all hunched over around something on the ground.

They were Shun-tuk.

In the weak, early dawn light the Shun-tuk looked like ghosts. All had eye sockets painted with a black, greasy substance. Wide grins of teeth drawn on their faces completed the look, making them resemble skulls. Most of their heads were shaved, but some had a knot of hair remaining at the top that was tied up with strings of beads and bones to keep it standing up straight so that it resembled a fountain of hair.

Some of the men turned from their prey to look up in surprise as Richard bounded over a boulder and leaped in at them, suddenly screaming in rage, his sword held high in both fists.

In that frozen instant, Kahlan saw that the startled faces were dripping with blood.

The Shun-tuk had knives, but they remained in their sheaths.

Instead, they used only their teeth.

Richard crashed down among the chalky figures, his fury at last unleashed. His blade swung around in an arc, lopping off a shaved head with startled, dark painted eyes. The speed of the weapon was so great that the tip whistled through the air even as the blade continued on to gash open the shoulder of the Shun-tuk beside the headless man, almost completely severing his arm. Richard immediately delivered a powerful side kick to the man rushing in on his other side.

As some of the half people around Richard toppled to the sides, Kahlan saw the soldier down on the ground under the white figures crowded around him like a pack of wolves in a feeding frenzy. Despite Richard killing several as he charged in, others only glanced sideways up at him, unwilling to relinquish the flesh clenched in their teeth. Others, lost in blood-lust, seemed oblivious of the danger to themselves as they tore flesh from the soldier.

Even with the half people piled in on him, the soldier still had his sword in his right hand and a knife clutched tightly in his left fist. He kicked and swung his sword past the bodies trying to hold him on the ground and at the same time used his knife to stab at others still trying to get in on the feast.

His screams were as much rage as pain. Wherever it was not protected by his leather armor his flesh was torn and bloody, but he was quite alive and full of fight.

It was clear that the soldier had fought fiercely, as any of the First File would have. A number of the white figures lay strewn along the forest floor, a line of bloody bodies marking a trail along which they had fought him to a stop.

A few of those downed Shun-tuk lying around the soldier were still alive and lay panting in agony as they bled out. Their wounds were clearly unsurvivable. Others, horrifically wounded from the soldiers' blades, writhed among the ferns and mosses at the side of a small brook as their blood ran down the rocks, turning the moss and water red. Some moaned, but none of them screamed in pain as did most of the wounded Kahlan had seen injured in battle.

The majority of the downed Shun-tuk, though, were clearly dead. The soldier had not gone down easily and the enemy had paid a heavy price to get him to ground.

The problem was, there simply had been too many of the half people for him to fight them all off. The danger to themselves seemed less important to these soulless beings than getting at their victim and having a chance to try to steal his soul.

Richard's sword arced around to cleanly cleave the head off a chalky figure rising up to grab him and try to pull him down with the soldier. A few others rose up, eager to rip into the new people coming their way in an effort to devour a soul for themselves.

To Kahlan's alarm, though, most of them charged Richard as if they recognized him and wanted him more than anyone else.

Before the Shun-tuk could overwhelm Richard and take him down under the weight of their numbers, the soldiers crashed into the pack of whitewashed figures, driving most back away from Richard. The half people, oblivious of the danger, immediately attacked the soldiers descending on them.

But teeth were no match for razor-sharp steel.

The terrible sight reminded Kahlan of blades scything down wheat. It was brutal butchery of savages bent only on murder.

None of what the soldiers did could match the violence Richard's sword brought to them. As half people reached for him, his sword took off fingers, hands, arms, heads, and split their bodies nearly in half. It seemed that his blade never paused and each time found its mark, shattering skulls and severing flesh and bone.

Knowing that the gift didn't work well against these half people, Nicci was at least able to use her ability to gather air into a powerful fist to knock back a number of them coming at Kahlan from the side. Soldiers hacked them to pieces as they stumbled back, trying to recover their footing. Kahlan used her knife to slash several of the whitewashed figures that got in too close to her. Their blackened eyes were terrifying up close, especially when they had their mouths open, baring their teeth.

Zedd, too, fought fiercely to protect Kahlan, as well as Irena and Samantha. Irena, though, broke away from Samantha's grip and Zedd's protection to run in toward Richard. She cast her hands out, clearly attempting to use her gift to protect him, but Kahlan didn't see that it was working at all. The half people saw her as an opportunity to have a gifted soul for themselves. Chalky white arms and clutching fingers reached out toward her.

Before they could snatch her, Richard severed their arms and cut down the ones racing in to dive atop her. As they fell, he circled an arm around Irena's waist and tossed her back out of his way and out of the way of immediate danger. Clearly relieved, Samantha clutched her mother's arm and tugged her back away from the danger.

Just as it seemed they were gaining control of the situation and putting down the half people who had attacked the soldier, brush and tree limbs shook as the woods came alive with Shun-tuk pouring out from the darkness all around them.

Kahlan had suspected that it had been a trap, with the soldier as the bait. These were predators and they were acting in a coordinated fashion to attract and then down their prey.

Back away from the battle, she spotted several of the chalky figures bent over the dead of their own kind. They weren't taking part in the attack, and the figures on the ground were clearly dead and not simply injured, so she couldn't imagine what they were doing. Their topknots waved around as they tossed their heads from side to side and moved their arms in a ritualistic fashion over the motionless corpses. They spoke words Kahlan couldn't hear.

As one of them finished his work and swiftly moved on to another body sprawled on its side, the first dead man sat up, then stood, rising to his full height as if brought back to life. His eyes, which a moment before had been glassy, now had an inner red glow. In the gloomy darkness it was difficult to see much of anything clearly, but those eyes pierced the gloom like hot, glowing coals.

Kahlan stared in shock as the dead man began coming toward them. He half stumbled as he stepped on his own entrails hanging from a horrific diagonal gash across his abdomen and dragging along the ground. He paused to see what kept holding him back at each step. When he saw the bloody viscera stretched from the open wound in his middle to his foot standing on them, he reached down and ripped his own guts away from his abdomen so they wouldn't interfere. Once free of the obstruction, he again started out for them.

Even as he hacked the living, Richard saw the dead man coming. His sword swung around and shattered the dead man's skull. An equally powerful blow on the return swing severed the dead man's legs at mid-thigh. As the headless corpse toppled forward, his arms reached toward Richard but missed. He landed hard on his chest. His fingers clawed at the dirt and clutched at a small brush to pull the headless, legless remains onward. Richard swiftly hacked arms from the torso as soldiers fought back Shuntuk to the sides.

Kahlan could see the chalky figures in the distance bending over and awakening other of their dead. She had a flash of hopelessness that even killing them was doing no good. Even in death they would keep coming.

Richard, too, saw what was happening. He pointed with his sword.

"There!" he called out loud enough so all the

soldiers could hear him. "Head for that higher ground at the base of that cliff. We need to get to a place where we're not surrounded so we can better defend ourselves!"

In a heartbeat, with no further orders needed, some of the men of the First File formed a wedge bristling with blades. It was a formation designed to punch through enemy lines. While it was not always the most effective battle tactic, in this case they knew from training and experience that it was what they needed.

Nicci and Zedd in unison laid down a blistering wall of flame to clear the way ahead of the soldiers. Some of the white figures, probably the same ones able to raise the dead, lifted a hand as if dismissing the threat. The fire parted, arcing gracefully away from the half people before it could engulf them. Others to the sides were not so lucky and were enveloped before they could turn the fire aside. Figures in flames stumbled blindly as soldiers cut them down. As the wedge of men rushed them, the half people in the way who had avoided the conjured flames were not able to avoid the steel.

With a backswing, Richard cleaved a slender, snarling figure almost in half at mid-chest. As the stricken man's legs buckled and Richard swung around with the follow-through of the powerful strike, he reached down with his other hand and clasped the forearm of the fallen, bleeding soldier. He pulled the man out from under several Shun-tuk still biting him. As Richard pulled the soldier to his feet, using his sword to chop the arms of half people away from the wounded man, he turned him toward their escape route and told him to hurry. Though covered with bite wounds

and blood, the soldier looked able to make it on his
own, at least for the moment, now that the weight
of all the attackers was off him.

Richard caught Kahlan around her waist to pull
her along with him and under his protection. "They
didn't kill him on purpose," he said as he bent close
to her. "They wanted him to scream. It was a trap
meant to draw us in."

She glanced up at the rage in his gray eyes, eyes that
at other times could be so kind and compassionate.
"I thought the same thing."

With a tip of his head he indicated the higher
ground. "We need to make it to that defensive position before they spring the rest of it on us."

"You think there is more to come besides this?"

"Absolutely."

With the man now rescued and the soldiers protectively surrounding them, they followed the wedge-
of-steel formation toward the rise of ground backed
by the cliff rising up among the hardwood trees. From
time to time Zedd was able to throw a flood of flame
out ahead of them. The blinding yellow light ignited
trees and lit the bottoms of the clouds. Pine needles
to each side flared as they ignited and went up in
flames, sending a cascade of fire up the sides of the
trees before they were turned to ash.

Any Shun-tuk unfortunate enough to be caught in
the blinding incandescence appeared skeletal for an
instant before even that much of their remains was
vaporized.

Kahlan thought the heat of it might burn away her
hair and eyebrows. She didn't know what kind of
power these half people had, but the flames were
doing more damage to the trees than most of them.

Fortunately, it had been raining so much and every-thing was so wet that the fire was confined to the immediate area and didn't set the woods ablaze.

While it didn't catch up as many of the half people in the inferno as they would have hoped, it at least helped scatter them out of the way. It seemed that the half people, once conceived with occult powers outside the Grace, were not affected by magic the way normal people would have been.

Kahlan saw more of the half people pouring out of the woods behind.

To her right, Richard tightened his arm around her waist to help her keep up, while on her left Nicci kept a hand firmly planted between Kahlan's shoulder blades not only to help move her as swiftly as pos-sible, but to give her strength. Kahlan hated needing the help.

Irena ushered Samantha along close behind them.

"Lord Rahl," Samantha called out, "what can I do to help?"

"Run faster," he called back over his shoulder.

Samantha and her mother obeyed as the troops fought the enemy off from the sides. Zedd laid down yet more fire behind them to protect their flank as best he could. Kahlan knew that using such power was difficult and exhausting. She knew that he wouldn't be able to keep up such an intense effort for long.

With the way ahead being cleared by the wedge of men of the First File, Kahlan was feeling more confi-dent that they could make it to the defensive position on higher ground up against a rock wall. Once they made it there, then they would only have to fight the half people from one side rather than from every direc-tion. In that way, they would be able to continually reduce the number of enemy and eventually, hope-fully, if there weren't too many, wipe them out.

Kahlan realized that she was falling, that one of the ghostly white figures had dropped from a tree onto her back, only when she felt the impact knock the wind from her lungs at the same time as she felt his teeth sink into the muscle at the side of her neck. She hit the ground hard, face-first, and went sprawling.

5

Gerald frowned as he straightened from his work of putting a sharp edge on his shovel. He let the ring of the file against metal fade away as he listened. He thought that he heard a strange, low rumbling sound.

He paused, motionless for a moment after the ring of steel had faded, the file in his callused hands still in midair, as he cocked his head to listen. He could feel the rumble in the dirt floor beneath his feet more than he could hear it. It reminded him of distant thunder, but it was too even, too unwavering, too continual, for it to be thunder. Still, more than anything, that was what it reminded him of.

He carefully laid the file down on the wooden workbench and went to the small window at the side that overlooked the graveyard. Beyond the far side of the sodden hayfields the woods that covered most of the Dark Lands rolled off into the distance, over ever-rising ground, toward imposing snowcapped mountains.

Gerald didn't especially like the woods. There were enough dangers in the Dark Lands without venturing too far into the woods. He had always thought that people were trouble enough without tempting fate with the things that lived in the woods.

Rather than brave the mysterious dangers of the trackless forests of the Dark Lands for no good reason, he preferred to stick to his work of tending the graveyard and burying folks who could no longer bring about any harm to anyone. People in the town of Insley didn't like coming out to where dead bodies rotted in the ground, so they left him alone, shunning him because he tended his garden of the dead, as he thought of it.

The dead left him alone, too.

The dead left everyone alone. People only feared them out of foolish superstition. There were plenty of real things to fear, like the dangers that lived in the forested wilderness of the Dark Lands. The dead never bothered anyone.

The job of burying the dead didn't pay well, but he had no family left and his needs were simple. Fortunately, most people were at least more than willing to pay him, even if it wasn't much, to put their kin in the ground. It was enough to afford him a small room in town, safe at night among the townspeople, even if they averted their eyes when he passed. He knew he would always have a roof over his head, a bed, and enough to eat.

One thing about his job, even if it didn't pay well and left him mostly alone in the world, was he knew that as long as there were the living, there would always be need of gravediggers to dispose of the newly dead.

It wasn't that people so much objected to digging a hole themselves—it was that the dead gave them the shivers, so they didn't want to dig a hole out in the graveyard and then have to handle the dead themselves. Gerald had long ago become numb to the dead. They meant he had steady work and they never gave him any trouble.

Most of his adult life, Gerald had had the dreary duty of burying those folks he'd thought highly of, as well as the privilege of putting people in the ground he hadn't much cared for in life. He'd often shed a tear over the passing of the first kind. The passing of the second kind brought him a grim smile as he went about the work of shoveling dirt over them.

He never smiled too much, though, since he knew that one day he would be joining them all in the underworld. He didn't want to give any of the souls there reason to bear a grudge against him. He tried to go about his work so as not to cause any of the living to bear a grudge against him, either.

Gerald swiped some of his limp gray hair away from his eyes as he leaned toward the small window a bit more, listening as he squinted into the distance. He noticed that all the cows in the grass fields had stopped grazing. They had even stopped chewing their cud as they all looked off in the same direction, toward the same spot to the northeast.

He found that unsettling. He stroked the stubble of his cheek as he considered it. There was not much to the northeast. The Dark Lands were desolate enough as it was with dangers not to be taken lightly, but to the northeast the Dark Lands were even less hospitable—mostly a trackless waste without any villages he knew of but one, Stroyza.

It was said that for as long as anyone knew, it had always been a wilderness and it always would be because there was terrible evil living off in that direction and anyone with any sense at all stayed away. It was general, if vague, knowledge passed down from generation to generation that there were wicked things off that way, even witch women, it was said. Everyone knew that witch women were not to be trifled with.

Most people didn't question, or investigate. Who wanted to go poke at sleeping evil? Or witches. What was the point?

Gerald had met a few traveling merchants who had been to the distant village of Stroyza, off in that direction beyond the looming range of mountains he could see to the northwest. He'd never met anyone from Stroyza, but he had talked to the few traders who had infrequently tried their luck off that way. There wasn't much to trade there and since the merchants returned with little of any value for the effort, it wasn't a draw for others. Stroyza was a small village of folks who lived in their remote, cliffside village, as he'd heard tell, and they kept to themselves. It was understandable that the people there would be aloof; strangers most usually meant trouble.

It was said that some who went off to the northeast to find their fortune simply never returned. Those who did return told stories of encounters in the dark of night with beasts, cunning folk meaning them harm, and even witch women. It was not hard to imagine why some had never returned. The ones who did never went back, instead going off to other, more well known places to try to make a living.

As he watched, Gerald spotted movement at the edge of the distant woods. It was hard to tell for sure, but it seemed like it might be one of the mists that would sometimes settle down out of the mountains and drift across the flatlands. He wondered if maybe he had been wrong and it really was some kind of strange mountain thunder he was hearing and what he was seeing was a mist leading the way down the mountains out ahead of a storm.

He shook his head to himself. It wasn't any kind of thunder he was hearing. He was just fooling himself to think it was. Whatever was making the low rumbling sound, he had never heard the likes of it before, that much was sure.

As he watched the relentlessly advancing mist, he wondered if it could be riders, a lot of riders, like maybe cavalry troops. Like everyone else in Insley he had heard stories about the recent war from some of the young men who had gone off to fight for D'Hara and came back to tell about it. They told stories about the vast armies and the thousands upon thousands of cavalry troops charging into bloody battles. He wondered if the haze could be a great many horses that were raising dust. Or maybe it was vast numbers of marching soldiers.

What such troops or cavalry would be doing this far out in the Dark Lands he couldn't begin to guess. Horse hooves galloping across the flatlands, though, might explain the rumbling sound.

He'd seen some of Bishop Hannis Arc's guards come through Insley in the past, but they didn't have large numbers of men. There had never been enough to raise a cloud of dust like he was seeing, or make the ground rumble.

He realized, then, that with the ground as wet as

it was, it couldn't be dust. It was far too muddy for there to be any dust. Yet the haze he was seeing seemed to be too dirty-looking to be mist.

Whatever it was, he was beginning to pick out a broad area of dots in that dirty, foggy cloud. Dots, like maybe people.

Gerald reached down, sliding his hand along the haft of a pickax leaning up against the wall, gripping it up near the head to more easily lift the heavy end. He didn't have any real weapons—never really needed them. Common weapons were really no good against such things as were to be feared in the Dark Lands, things such as the cunning folk or witch women. As far as anything else, well, most people, even when they were drunk, didn't want to have an argument with a pickax.

As much as he didn't like the idea, he headed for the door of the shed to go outside and see if he could tell what was coming his way.

6

Gerald used his free hand to shield his eyes from the gloomy, slate-gray sky as he stared off into the distance. In his other hand he gripped the haft of the pickax up near the head, letting the weight of it pull his arm down straight.

He had been right. It definitely was people in the distance. He could just make out the movement of them walking. But in all his life, he had never seen anything like the numbers he was seeing now. He had never even imagined that he ever would, at least not on this side of the underworld.

He knew from tales of merchants and traders, of course, that there were places with lots of people. He'd heard about a number of great cities far off to the west and the south, though he'd never seen them with his own eyes. There were also towns in the Dark Lands, mostly to the southwest, that were considerably bigger than Insley.

The biggest place he knew of was the city of

Saavedra, at the fringes of the most remote and dreaded areas of the Dark Lands. From the citadel in Saavedra, Bishop Hannis Arc ruled Fajin Province. Most people referred to Fajin Province by its ancient name, the Dark Lands. It was a name that had stuck, like the muck oozing from the dead that you could never get out from under your fingernails no matter how much you washed and tried to scrub it away.

Gerald had ventured to Saavedra once, when he was younger, but on the advice of those who knew the place he had made sure to stay well clear of the citadel. Those same people whispered frightening descriptions of Bishop Hannis Arc. There was nothing to be gained from tempting trouble, so he had heeded the advice.

He never found any work in Saavedra, but he had found a wife there. Being from a poor family with parents who could not adequately feed their children, she had cared more about having enough to eat than his occupation. Since it earned a living, she married him and they returned to Insley, and he to tending the graveyard in order to put food on the table.

She had long ago died when she had been with her first child. It seemed a lifetime ago. He never had another wife.

As he watched into the distance, watched all the people coming his way, Gerald had the decidedly uneasy feeling that it could be nothing other than trouble. He gave thought to running, but he was too old to run for far.

Besides, it was a crazy worry. What could they want with him? An old gravedigger was hardly worth ransom. He had nothing of value, really. The only things he had of any worth at all were a few tools and a rickety handcart that reeked of the dead, so unless they wanted to haul corpses and dig them graves, his possessions weren't worth much to anyone but him.

As he watched the vast numbers of figures spread out in the distance, his curiosity kept him rooted in place. Besides, where would he hide? The woods? There were things to fear in the woods that were likely worse than a lot of people passing through Insley.

The strangest thing, other than what looked like numbers in the thousands, was that the figures all appeared to be dressed in white. He assumed that, strange as it seemed, they must all be wearing white robes. As they got closer, and he squinted enough, he saw that he was wrong, they weren't wearing robes. Most didn't look to be wearing shirts or pants, either. They appeared not to be wearing much at all.

Their bodies, arms, and legs—even their heads— were a chalky whitish color, as if they had rubbed ash all over themselves. He had never seen such people in all his life. He couldn't imagine the purpose of rubbing white ash on themselves.

In the center, though, in the lead, were several darker figures. The contrast against the flood of pale figures behind them was striking and made them stand out all the more.

The dirty haze that Gerald had seen at first seemed to be something that enveloped the throng, as if it were being dragged along with them, or created by them. As they got closer it was an ominous-looking murk, an atmosphere of threat, oddly enough like they were inside their own dreary day and bringing it along with them.

Strange greenish luminescence crackled from time to time within that gloomy murk.

Gerald reconsidered his decision not to run. He

wanted to run, or at least walk away and maybe go visit the woods for a spell until all the people had gone on their way, but since the darker figures at the center were headed right toward him, he instinctively knew that running would be the wrong thing to do.

Running from a predator provoked them to chase.

Only then, with that thought, did he realize that he knew these were predators.

He decided that his best bet was to keep his wits about him, appear friendly, and maybe offer the approaching strangers any information they might want. He was obviously no threat to them, so his best chance was to be helpful and let them be on their way.

He knew well enough that folks kept you around if you were useful. Despite his having no real friends, and no one in Insley particularly holding any favor with him, they tolerated him with a brief smile and a passing nod because he was useful. He had survived a long time simply by being useful with onerous tasks.

He became more alarmed, though, when he saw that the darker figures at the lead were going to come marching with all those following them right across his carefully tended garden of the dead.

He could see that one of the darker figures had what looked like a faint, glowing, bluish green light about him—as if he were half man, half spirit. Beside him was a figure that was darker yet. That one wore heavy, black robes. From what Gerald could see of his hands and face, the man's flesh appeared dark with tattoos of some sort. Following behind him was another person all in red. He knew well enough what that had to be.

Gerald swallowed when he saw that the eyes of the man in the dark robes were fixed on him, and those eyes were red.

As he strode at a steady, easy pace, the spirit man walked with his arms down, his palms out. It appeared that he was the source of the dark haze, that it was being pulled along by the man's hands. It was like he was dragging the grim murk along behind him the way a boat dragged a wake along with it.

Gerald couldn't imagine what he was, other than one of the rumored beings from out of the darkest depths of the woods.

Against all common sense, Gerald finally decided to run. But as much as he intended it, his feet seemed rooted in place as both dark figures continued walking right toward him. He didn't know if it was something they were doing to him, some kind of magic, or if he was simply frozen in fright. Either way, he was unable to move and had no choice but to stay right where he was as he watched them coming.

As the darker figures entered the far side of his carefully groomed graveyard, with the mass of whitewashed figures dutifully following behind, Gerald could see the ground near them begin to move. It didn't appear to be the feet of the strangers causing the mud and clumps of grasses to shake and shiver. It appeared to be moving of its own accord.

It was then that he realized that it was not the ground in general that was moving. It was only the ground over the graves that was joggling, as if the dead beneath were agitated and pushing up at the soil from below.

All across the graveyard, as the dark haze dragged by the spirit man passed across the ground, the dirt over a number of the newer graves it touched began to heave and quake all the more.

Gerald looked up from staring at the incomprehensible sight and found himself looking right into the eyes of the two men who had by then stopped not far away from him. He didn't know which man looked more terrifying.

One of the two appeared to be a cadaver dressed in garments covered with dark stains that looked to be dried blood. Gerald had seen enough bloodstained clothes on corpses, but he had never had one of those corpses appear to be alive.

More frightening even than that, the cadaverous man had a bluish glow to him. To Gerald, it looked like nothing so much as a spirit in the same place as the corpse. At least a spirit as had been described to him—he had never actually seen a spirit himself. Until now.

Together, body and spirit, there was no doubt that the man was somehow alive and aware of everything about him. He looked out at the world both with the glowing eyes of the spirit and the eyes of the corpse beneath it. As cadaverous as the man's body looked, there was no doubt that he was looking, seeing, and comprehending.

Gerald did not think for one moment that this was a good spirit.

There was no doubt that the other man, the one with the red eyes and black robes, was living flesh and blood. His flesh, though, rather than being dried and dead, was covered with tattoos of strange occult designs. They were beyond counting. Every inch of the man, every speck of skin, was covered in the dark designs.

For years, Gerald had heard the whispered descriptions. He knew without a doubt who this man had to be.

Behind him stood a tall woman with blond hair pulled back in a single braid. Although he had never seen one before, he knew by her hair, her tight red leather outfit, and the cold look in her icy blue eyes that she could be none other than one of the notorious Mord-Sith.

Behind the three, the sea of the nearly naked figures, their flesh smeared with ash or whitewash of some sort to make them look intimidating and frighteningly like ghost men, had come to a halt and now stood with grim expressions, watching from black painted eye sockets.

"I am Lord Arc," the man in the dark robes said. When he held a tattooed hand out to the side, Gerald could see that even the palm was tattooed. "This is the spirit king, Emperor Sulachan."

Gerald had never heard of Emperor Sulachan.

"What is it you want?" he heard himself ask.

The spirit king's thin lips widened with the slightest hint of a smile. "We have come for your dead."

The sound of his voice sent pain tingling along Gerald's flesh.

y dead?" Gerald asked.

The spirit king's thin smile grew wider and his eyes more dangerous. "Yes, your dead. We have use of them. They are to become *our* dead."

With that, he lifted his arms. Far and near the muddy dirt a number of the graves began to churn almost as if it were a thick stew coming to a boil.

At the same time, the bluish, spiritlike glow of the spirit king changed to a disturbing greenish luminescence.

Gerald then saw an arm here and there push up through the ground. Hands of the dead beneath that ground wriggled and threw dirt aside. Feet emerged and kicked at the imprisoning soil.

The dead were escaping their graves.

The dirt churned and pitched in agitation, as if unwilling, or unable, to contain what was below. The whitish figures stood out of the way of the corpses twisting and pulling themselves up from the ground. It was as horrifying a sight as Gerald had ever seen, much less imagined.

Some of the corpses beginning to emerge were dark and desiccated. Their joints popped and snapped and cracked as they ripped at the shrouds cocooning them, tearing them away. Beneath the shrouds, the remnants of clothes had been stained with decay and then as the bodies dried and shriveled, the clothes bonded to the hardening flesh so that they were almost one.

Other bodies were slimy and bloated with decay, their clothes soaked through from the ooze coming from the breaks in their flesh. Their wet shrouds came apart like wet paper. In their struggle to pull themselves up through the ground, moldering flesh snagged and tore. Great wet chunks were pulled off them, leaving bones exposed.

Through splits in the flesh of some, Gerald could see gooey masses of maggots writhing beneath the blackened skin. Others of the dead were little more than skeletons with scraps and bits of sinew, flesh, and remnants of clothes holding most of the bones together. Some were so decayed that the effort of trying to emerge from the ground was too much and what was left of their bones crumbled in the attempt. Other graves were resting places where any traces left of the dead were beyond rising.

But a great many were sufficiently intact to emerge through the muddy ground. Many of those growled in anger at the ground trying to hold them back. They snarled with menace as they tore themselves away from the confinement of their graves, their eyes all glowing red. Gerald could only imagine that such a sinister crimson glow was the mark of an inner fire of occult powers animating them.

He stood frozen in fright as he watched the dead—the dead he had put to rest in the ground—leave their eternal rest and come back out of the ground. He recognized many of them, some by their faces, some by their clothes—remembered who they had been in life, anyway. Many were decomposed and decayed beyond recognition, so he didn't know who they had once been.

Now they were something else other than what they once had been. Now, they were the dead husks of departed spirits. Those husks were now somehow returning to the world of life. Gerald didn't think, though, that their spirits were returning as well. These seemed to be spiritless bodies driven by magic, not the power of the Grace and Creation.

For a moment, he thought that perhaps he had passed away and maybe he was actually dead, and he was at last seeing the mysteries of the underworld revealing themselves to him.

It was a fleeting thought, banished by the stench of the dead. He was all too alive. At least for the moment.

As the newly escaped corpses rose up they stood among the chalky figures, waiting along with them, staring with those terrible, glowing red eyes as the last of the dead were finally liberated from their graves. He noticed then that the dark painted eyes of the chalky figures resembled some of the dead, those who were little more than skeletal remains with their big dark eye sockets in their skulls, except the dead had a red glow back in those dark recesses.

"Lead the way," Lord Arc said at last once the

ground had stopped moving and all the corpses who could had emerged.

That's who the man had said he was—Lord Arc. Gerald had never heard him called "Lord Arc" before. He had always heard that the leader of Fajin Province was "Bishop Hannis Arc." It couldn't be anyone else. It had to be the same man.

As frightened as Gerald was, he was not about to question the change of title. "The way, Lord Arc?" he asked. "What do you mean?"

"Why, the way to Insley, of course," Lord Arc said. "I have yet to visit the place. Seeing as it is one of the towns in my empire, I thought it fitting that I visit it."

Gerald blinked. "Your empire, Lord Arc?"

The man lifted an arm toward the southwest. "Yes. The D'Haran Empire. I am assuming rule of the D'Haran Empire."

Gerald had heard some of the young men who had returned from the fighting talking about some of their experiences. They had said that since the terrible war with the Old World had ended and the world was now at peace, Richard Rahl was now the Lord Rahl ruling D'Hara. As far as Gerald knew, a Lord Rahl had always ruled D'Hara.

He swallowed, averting his eyes from the man. It was difficult for Gerald to look at the menacing tattooed occult designs covering his face and scalp, but more than that, it was unnerving to look into those terrible bloodred eyes.

"I deeply apologize for my ignorance, Lord Arc. I am but a humble gravedigger for a little town that is quite removed from the rest of D'Hara and we infrequently receive news here. I had always heard that Lord Rahl, Richard Rahl who led us in the war, was the leader of the D'Haran Empire."

Lord Arc smiled indulgently. "Yes, that was once true, but the House of Rahl no longer rules D'Hara, or anything else for that matter. His flesh has no doubt already been eaten off his bones by some of the Emperor Sulachan's half people."

Gerald blinked in confusion. "Half people?"

"The Shun-tuk warriors." A tattooed hand swept around at the chalky figures. "The half people. Ones without souls. Now, lead on, gravedigger, or you will serve us as one of the army of the dead."

Gerald had never heard of Shun-tuk or half people. He held an arm out, pointing. It took great effort to summon his voice as all the eyes stared at him.

"Insley is right up the road, Lord Arc. There is no road but this one, and no other town but Insley. It's not far at all. It lies just beyond a few bends in the road among the oak grove up ahead. You will have no trouble at all finding the humble town of Insley. I am sure the people of Insley will . . . welcome their new ruler's visit."

Lord Arc's disturbing smile returned. The spirit king didn't share in the smile, nor did the Mord-Sith or any of the sea of grim, chalky faces watching him. The awakened dead glared with glowing red eyes.

"I don't think they will be all that happy to see us."

Gerald was sure of the truth of that. He turned to look in the direction of town, wanting more than anything to be free of Lord Arc and all his people, to say nothing of the newly awakened dead. "But it's right up the road—a short walk. You don't really need me in order to find the place."

Gerald wished there was something he could do to warn the people of Insley. He wanted to tell them to flee. But there was nothing he could do.

"We don't need you in order to find the place,"

Lord Arc said with exaggerated patience. "Nor did I ask where it was, now did I? I asked you to lead us there."

"For what purpose?" Gerald asked, his fear of being with this nightmare collection of people and unholy monsters overriding his typical sense of caution.

The spirit king, rather than Lord Arc, spoke up. "We need you to bear witness," he said in a voice that burned painfully against Gerald's skin. It almost felt as if the hairs on his arm would be burned off.

"Bear witness?"

"Yes," Lord Arc said, "bear witness so that others, in other places, will know what will happen to them should they not bow down and welcome their new ruler and the new era he brings to the world of life. We are giving you the opportunity to help all those people. You are to be a messenger, bearing witness to what has happened here so they will have the chance to avoid the same fate."

Gerald swallowed. He could feel his knees trembling. "What is to happen here?"

Lord Arc spread his hands. "Why, the people of Insley failed to welcome me as their new ruler. That is an intolerable offense."

Gerald took a step forward. "Then please, Lord Arc, allow me to run ahead and tell them. Let me announce you. I know they will bow down and welcome you. Let me show you."

"Enough of this," the spirit king said in a low growl.

He casually pointed at the pickax still gripped in Gerald's fist at the end of his hanging arm. The handle grew hot and crisped to black. In a heartbeat it checkered into shriveling charcoal before turning to ash that crumbled away from Gerald's hand like dust going through his fingers. When it did, the heavy steel pickax head thumped down onto the ground and flopped over on its side.

Gerald stared in disbelief as, in mere seconds, the entire steel pickax rusted to crumbling, reddish fragments.

All that was left on the ground at Gerald's side was an ashen black stain that had been the wooden handle and unrecognizable reddish fragments that moments before had been the steel head of the pickax.

Lord Arc lifted a slender, tattooed finger, pointing it down the road as he cocked his head, staring at Gerald.

Gerald knew without a doubt that it was a command, and if he disobeyed that command or delayed another moment, he would swiftly regret it.

No choice left to him, he immediately turned and started for the road.

All the chalky figures, led by Lord Arc, his Mord-Sith, and Emperor Sulachan, along with the dead pulled up from their graves by the king of the dead, followed behind him.

8

The road curved several times as it wound its way among the grove of ancient oaks on its way into Insley. Because the massive oak trees grew together over the road, they closed off most of the churning, gray sky, making the day seem even darker, making the glowing red eyes of the dead stand out all the more. Gerald wished it was a lot farther to town, rather than a short walk.

He wished there was a way to warn people, but he could think of none. Even if he ran, Insley was so close there would be no time to explain it. Besides, had he not seen it, he doubted he would believe a story such as he had to tell.

Not far behind him followed the two emperors, Sulachan and Hannis Arc. The Mord-Sith shadowed her master, Lord Arc. Behind them came an entire Shuntuk nation of the half-naked, chalky figures with their eyes painted black all around them, making their eyes look like great, dead sockets. The sound of all those bare feet made the air rumble. The dark murk he had seen at first now seemed to envelop them all, like the air itself was poisoned by the evil of these people.

As the road made its way over a slight rise, Gerald glanced back into the distance behind and for the first time was able to take in the enormous numbers of half people. There were so many that he imagined it would probably be most of the day before the last of them passed the spot he was passing. It might even be well after dark before they had all passed that same spot.

Because of their vast numbers the Shun-tuk couldn't confine themselves to the road, instead surging across the landscape to either side, like a tide of ashen figures flooding the valley landscape and about to drown the town of Insley. In among the half people, the awakened dead lumbered stiffly along, like debris carried on that incoming tide.

It seemed that the garden of the dead that Gerald had tended for so long had finally been harvested by a spirit king come to claim them as his own.

As they rounded a bend in the road at the top of the slight rise, off between the oaks, the first buildings at the edge of town came into view. Gerald had heard of places where buildings were made of stone, but these were not so grand as that. They were simple structures made of wood cut from the ample supply in the trackless forests of the Dark Lands all around.

Most of the buildings of the small town were clustered along the road. Some of those were sheltered by big old oaks growing behind them. The dozen largest buildings were two stories, bunched close together on both sides of the single road, as if turning their backs on the Dark Lands behind them.

The bottom floors of some of those larger buildings provided workspace for leatherworkers, woodworkers, chair makers, or shops for the butcher, baker, and herbs. The families who ran those shops lived above them. There were a few narrow streets off to the sides but they were little more than footpaths. They led to small one- or two-room homes for people who worked the fields or tended to animals all around Insley.

Insley wasn't big enough to have an inn. When merchants came through, one of the shop owners often allowed the trader to sleep in a shop. Sometimes they slept in the barn at the opposite end of town.

Gerald had heard that in other places, mostly places much farther west and south, farmers who raised crops and kept animals had their homes out where they tended the land. That made it convenient for working, since coming to town was hardly a daily necessity. Most only needed to come to town on market days when they had goods to sell or when they needed supplies. People who lived on their land could watch over the land and they were always there for their work of feeding and caring for their animals, mending fences and barns, or tending their crops.

But in the Dark Lands such convenience was secondary to safety. In the Dark Lands most people, including farmers, usually crowded together in places like Insley, choosing to live close together for protection. Most folks didn't live off by themselves for good reason. Also, for good reason, most everyone shut themselves in at night.

Gerald knew that living close together for protection wasn't going to do them any good this time. Nor was daylight going to be any salvation. This time, trouble was coming right into town, into their midst, in broad daylight.

Gerald saw women off to the right behind a small home pause to stare as they hung clothes on a line. They quickly ran off to tell others of the approaching strangers. The sounds of life in town, everything from conversation to hammers and saws in the woodworking shop to chickens roaming everywhere, probably helped mask the sound of the horde coming their way.

Now that they were close enough, though, people started to take notice. Concerned people peered out from the narrow walkways between buildings, shopkeepers poked their heads out of doorways to look, and women stuck their heads out of windows. All of them wanted to see what the commotion was all about, much like Gerald had done when he had heard them coming.

When mothers called their names, children turned and ran for home. Chickens roaming the streets, pecking here and there and unconcerned by any of it, suddenly scattered when children ran through their midst.

As Gerald led the two emperors and their Shun-tuk army down the road and into the shadows of the buildings on each side, people started coming out of doorways and alleyways all over, dumbfounded by the strange sight, unsure what it meant. The vast numbers of the strangers were not yet quite close enough for the people to see and understand the terror of what approached. Even Gerald didn't understand what was to come, but he knew enough already to be terrified.

Out of the corner of his eye, off between buildings, he caught sight of the white figures. The Shun-tuk had slipped around to either side to surround the town so that no one could escape. Gerald hoped that some of them had already had the good sense to run before the town was surrounded, but by the numbers of startled people he saw, he didn't think that many, if any, had done so. After all, running would mean running off into the wilds of the Dark Lands. These people thought they were safer if they stuck together and stayed in the protection of the town.

Gerald knew that illusion of safety was a mistake.

A group of younger men, their sleeves rolled up from being at their work, emerged from between the buildings. They were big men, well muscled and young enough not to be easily intimidated. Most had fought in the war and were more accustomed to trouble.

Now they had gathered into a home guard to protect their town. They all carried weapons of some sort. A couple had clubs that they smacked in their free hands as an open threat. A few held axes or knives while a good number of them had swords.

Because of the rise behind, none of these men could see the vast numbers amassing behind Gerald just outside Insley.

One of the bigger men, one of the young men who had been with the D'Haran army in the war with the Old World, gripped a sword in his meaty fist as he stepped out in front of the others. It was a sword he had brought home with him from the war. The young man had used it to save his life in the past.

"Gravedigger, what is it these people with you want?"

Lord Arc stepped in front of Gerald before he could say anything. When he came into full view, some of the people in doorways shrank back a little. Some vanished entirely.

"The people of Insley have failed to welcome me as their new ruler," Lord Arc said. "They have failed to welcome me on bended knee. That is an intolerable offense."

"This is Lord Arc," Gerald hurriedly put in, hoping the men would realize who they were dealing with.

The young man nodded and then motioned to those with him. They followed his lead and all went to a knee. "Welcome, Bishop Arc. There, if it pleases you to see us kneel before you, then you have what you came for."

"Not yet," Lord Arc said with a grim smile. "But I shall."

The young man swiped his sweaty hair back from his eyes as he returned to his feet, the rest of the men rising with him. "We meant no offense and want no trouble. Now leave us and be on your way. We mean you no harm." He swept his sword around to point behind. "Go around our peaceful town and be on your way."

Watching with wide eyes, townspeople in doorways, those standing along the side of the street with their backs pressed up against shops, and those peering out from behind buildings all started melting back into the shadows, leaving the trouble to their young home guard to handle.

With a look behind him, Lord Arc met the gaze of the spirit king. "I think it's time to show them what they face."

A small smile seemed to be the spirit king's only command. With that small smile, the corpses freshly pulled up from their graves, and up until then out of sight among the closely packed, chalky figures, pushed their way out from behind and trundled forward. One of them bumped into Gerald on the way by, knocking him aside.

The young men looked as shocked as everyone else to see the corpses with glowing red eyes approaching, but they stood their ground and met them with the kind of fury and confidence that only invincible youth and simple ignorance could muster.

The young man in command who had spoken for the others drove his sword through the chest of the first of the walking dead to reach him, a putrefied corpse that smelled bad enough to gag half the men waiting to stop him. The sword jutted from the back of the dead man. The corpse twisted, yanking the hilt of the sword embedded through his chest from the young man's grip.

With surprising speed, the dead man seized the leader by the throat with one hand. With his other hand, he grabbed the young man's muscular arm and with a mighty twist tore it off at the shoulder.

Everyone, including Gerald, flinched in disbelief. It was an act of occult strength that no living man could perform.

Without delay, other men charged forward and drove their swords through the dead man still holding his victim. He soon had half a dozen more blades stuck through his chest to go with the first. None of them slowed him any more than did the first.

The dead man tossed the screaming young soldier down on the ground at his feet. Even as other men hacked at him with swords and stabbed him with knives, the attacker seized his one-armed victim by the ankle and threw him into the side of a building with such force it cracked the clapboard walls. The man fell unconscious at the edge of the road, bleeding his life away.

Others of the dead, from the dried and brittle to the slimy and bloated, advanced into the midst of the young defensive guard trying to keep them back. Axes driven by powerfully strong men failed to bring down even one of the dead. Confidence swiftly turned to terror and screams, both from the young men and from the townspeople watching.

The battle was as brief as it was one-sided. In moments it was over and any confidence or hope the townspeople had that their home guard could protect them was shattered. All of the young men lay bleeding, most of them dead, at the feet of the dead come back to life standing over them. And the Shuntuk had yet to descend on the town.

Lord Arc, the spirit king, the Mord Sith, and the untold thousands of half people waiting behind watched without reaction. The townspeople watched with unbridled terror. Some screamed. Some fell to their knees and prayed to the Creator to spare them. Some begged Lord Arc for mercy. Many tried to run and hide.

Then the king of the dead, the greenish glow wavering over his worldly corpse, turned back to the sea of whitewashed figures behind.

The spirit king said but one word.

"Feed."

With that single command, the silent Shun-
tuk instantly turned into a howling mass
of killers leaping ahead toward the townspeople. People screamed as they scattered in a panic
to escape, but it was too late. To the sides, a flood of
the half people spilled in from between buildings. At
the far end of town the road was inundated with the
half-naked figures. They poured around Gerald as if
he were a boulder in a raging river.

Some of the invading throng knocked into him on
their way past him, spinning him around, making him
stumble as he was buffeted first one way and then
another. They ignored him in their madness to get
beyond him to the people of Insley.

When they reached those frightened people, they
fell on them with the savagery of wolves taking down
terrified prey.

It was shocking how quickly the muddy road
through town turned red. Everywhere people shrieked

in panic. The Shun-tuk barged into buildings, going after people who ran inside seeking safety. People cowered inside, but Gerald could tell by the shrieks that there had been no safety in trying to hide.

In other places, people dove headlong out of windows on the second floors of buildings to escape those coming after them inside. Chalky white arms stretched out of those windows, trying to catch the fleeing people. Those who jumped escaped for only the brief moments they were in midair. Once they crashed to the ground, the Shun-tuk pounced on them, closing in so tightly that no more could get in on the ferocious feast.

Clothes were torn off to get at flesh. Teeth sank into victims. The howling, whitewashed figures strained, pulling their heads back with the effort of ravenously tearing off the stretching chunks of flesh. Others stretched in to lick at the blood gushing from open wounds. The chalky faces with the blackened eyes were swiftly stained a bright red.

It appeared to matter not to them what part of the victim they could get at. They bit into every part of their thrashing, suffering prey with equal intensity. Mouths of others opened wide as they tried to get in for their share. Teeth raked over faces, skinning off the features. Skin and muscle of legs and arms were pulled off in a savage feeding frenzy. As the soft parts of the bodies were torn open, bloody hands reached in and pulled the viscera out past those crowded in close so that they could get a bite of something for themselves.

Gerald had always thought he was numb to death. But now he felt like he was going to vomit as he stood watching, unable to do anything for anyone. He had never felt so helpless in his entire life. His whole body trembled. Tears ran down his cheeks as he panted in horror.

He didn't want to live to see any more of it. He would rather die. He wanted death to take him so he would not have to endure it.

The screams finally died out when there was no one left alive to scream, but the feeding frenzy continued. Every scrap of flesh was consumed, leaving only bloody bones. Those were pulled and twisted apart and taken by those crowded around so that they could be licked clean of the blood or bashed open to suck out the marrow. There didn't seem to be enough to go around, leaving the Shun-tuk who hadn't been able to feed to fight over any scraps that were left.

Gerald turned back to Lord Arc, rage filling his voice. "Why would they do this? There is no possible purpose for such savage murder!"

Lord Arc's face was shaded with a dark and terrible look.

"The Shun-tuk are half people. They look human, and in some ways they are human, but they have no soul." His calm voice seemed unaffected by what had just happened. "Having no soul, they feel empty and incomplete. They feel that those people with souls only have them because they were born lucky. They covet that connection to the Grace that a soul provides others. They are jealous. So, whenever they get a chance, they try to take a soul for themselves."

Gerald glared bitterly. "They think they can steal the souls of the people they eat?"

"That's right. They feel that the world has unfairly cheated them. They feel that they deserve what they covet, what others have." Lord Arc shrugged. "So they are intent on taking a soul, intent on having that which they want.

"They believe that the only way to get the soul they feel they are entitled to is to eat the flesh or drink the blood of those who have one and consume it before it flees the body on its way beyond the veil of life."

"You get a soul by being born human, through the Creator," Gerald insisted. "You can't get one by eating people."

Lord Arc shrugged again. "They believe they can, so they continue to try."

Gerald gazed out at the bloody scene. "Why have you not killed me as well? Why have you made me witness such evil?"

Hannis Arc spread his hands. "You, gravedigger, have the honor of being the first crier to announce me as the new ruler."

"The new ruler of the D'Haran Empire?"

"Yes, that's right, but also the new ruler of the world of life. You are to announce the beginning of a new era.

"Others will soon join you, but you are the first of many who will follow. Go from place to place and announce what is to come. Bear witness to the horrors you have seen with your own eyes. Let people know that those who do not bow down and swear allegiance in life, will serve me in death.

"The world of the dead, you see, will be joined with us in the world of life. Both worlds will be united as one.

"Since there will no longer be need for gravediggers, you have a new job. You are to go on ahead and tell those places before us that we come with our Shun-tuk warriors, and we come to rule the world. Give witness to what you have seen along with what others will see in other places that will also be taught this lesson."

Gerald's jaw was set with bitter determination. "I would rather die—I will kill myself."

The man's tattooed hand rose and he put a finger under Gerald's chin, lifting his face. "Then you will be responsible for a great many more deaths. If you warn people, if you convince people, then many will see how hopeless resistance would be and so decide to surrender to the inevitable. Those people will live. You must recount to people what you have seen, convince them of the futility of resistance.

"If you kill yourself, then you can't warn them and as a result you will be responsible for countless more people dying needlessly because you did not do your part to help them see what must be. If you die with that blood on your hands, then the spirit king will see to it that your soul is pulled back from the underworld and sent to wander the world of life, lost and unable ever to find peace, forever doomed to witness the suffering you allowed to come about by failing to do your part.

"Perhaps the worst of it for you will be the utter emptiness of your pointless gesture because, you see, you are not special. I can choose anyone to be a witness to warn the places that lie before our advancing army. If not you, then I will simply select others, in other places."

Gerald swallowed, now more terrified even than he had been, if that was even possible.

Lord Arc lifted Gerald's chin even farther, and reached a clawed hand out to push it against his soft middle. Gerald felt a pain such as he never imagined. It was a pain down to his soul. It was the pain of that man's occult power clutching his soul and threatening to rip it out.

"Do you now see the importance of your mission?"

Gerald nodded, as best he could with the finger still under his chin.

"Good." Hannis Arc smiled a deadly smile. "You see? I know what is best for people."

"Yes, Lord Arc," Gerald managed.

"Now, rush off on your way. Warn others what will happen if they choose to resist. As we visit other places, others will be enlisted to join you. Armies of criers will join you and help spread the word. Pray you all succeed. I will show mercy to none who think to resist."

Gerald wet his lips. "Yes, Lord Arc."

"And gravedigger," Lord Arc said as he leaned closer, his red eyes looking like coals burning in his soul, "you be sure to tell them all at the People's Palace. You tell them that I am now their ruler, and I am coming. You tell them there that we are bringing the entire Shun tuk nation with us, and that they had better welcome me on their knees. You tell them what will happen if they don't."

Gerald nodded. And then he was running. Running to warn people of what was coming—warn them to surrender and not resist what they could not stop or they would suffer an unimaginable death.

Lord Arc had said that he intended to unite the world of life and the world of the dead.

Gerald believed him.

10

K ahlan opened her eyes.

It was night. In the flickering firelight, as she tried to will her vision into focus, she saw fuzzy faces bent down over her. She felt as if she was a great distance away, and it was proving to be a long and difficult journey back.

As her focus began to resolve, she recognized Zedd's weathered, worried face bent over her. His wavy white hair looked more unruly than usual. The tips of his bony fingers pressed firmly against her forehead. That explained the persistent tingling sensation down her spine. Seeing Zedd, she realized that what she felt was the healing power of the gift.

She saw Nicci, then, kneeling down close to her on the opposite side from Zedd. The sorceress looked no less concerned. Nicci squeezed Kahlan's hand as she offered a reassuring smile to welcome her back from the dark world of the lost.

Samantha crowded in close behind Nicci, with her

mother Irena, leaning in over her shoulder, watching intently.

Then, in the fluttering light from a nearby campfire, Kahlan spotted Richard a little farther back in the center of the other faces. She saw the relief in his eyes as he let out a deep breath.

As soon as she saw him, Kahlan sat up and threw her arms around his neck, squeezing him tightly to her. She had feared he had been killed by the half people and she would never see him again.

Now that she had her arms around his muscular neck, her cheek against his stubble, she let the joy and relief of seeing him alive run rampant through her. She put a hand to the back of his head and held him to her, thankful that he was all right and there with her. She wanted to envelop him.

"It's so good to see you," she whispered privately in the midst of the crowd. When she held him, there was no crowd, there was only him. There was always only him in her heart and soul.

His arms tightened around her. "You can't imagine how glad I am to see you wake up."

She finally parted from him, holding his shoulders, and saw that he had cleaned off all the blood of the half people he had fought. She looked around at all the grim faces, their bleak expressions finally easing.

"Well," Zedd said, "it would seem that I have done it again."

Richard laughed. Everyone else looked like they had thought for a time that they would never smile again.

"What happened?" Kahlan asked.

"I healed you," Zedd announced, as if that should be explanation enough.

Kahlan waved a hand as she sat up the rest of the

way. "No, I mean what happened with the half people that were after us?"

She saw firelight from a nearby fire reflecting up the face of the cliff. As she looked around, she saw that there were two more campfires, one to either side of them, their light also reflecting off the cliff and helping to light the general area and the trees nearby. The men of the First File were close by all around them. The fires were large, meant to keep the darkness at bay so that no one could easily sneak up.

"Well," Richard said, "we made it here and we were able to fight them off. We set up camp with a tight defensive line. You were unconscious—"

"I healed you," Zedd repeated, apparently trying to get across how difficult it had been without complaining directly.

"Was it hard?" Kahlan asked him. It was dawning on her that he was trying to say something more without saying it. "Was it extra difficult . . . for some reason?"

Zedd leaned back on his heels. "Yes, it was hard," he confirmed with an earnest nod. He lifted one eyebrow. "Quite difficult, actually."

Kahlan decided to cut through the dancing and turned to Nicci. "Why?"

Nicci didn't shy from the question. "You were injured—one of the half people tried to steal your soul by eating you. The ever-present threat of death within you used that opportunity, when so much was going on, when you were weakened by the struggle, to try to pull you in. You were pretty far gone and it took all day and part of tonight, but Zedd managed to pull you back."

Kahlan put a hand up to the top of her shoulder and felt only smooth skin. She thought she remembered the pain of teeth sinking into her flesh there. She remembered the terror of it. Then there was only blackness and the terrible feeling of being forever lost to it.

She smiled at the wizard. "Thank you, Zedd."

Samantha leaned in, eager to tell the story. "Lord Rahl chopped the head off the man that was biting you so fast and with such power that I bet we were halfway here before it ever hit the ground."

"You were unconscious, though," Irena said, considerably more worried-looking than Samantha.

"Some of the men carried you," Samantha said as she leaned past her mother, eager to get to the meat of the story. "That way Lord Rahl could fight off the Shun-tuk. You were bleeding pretty badly. Lord Rahl and the men—"

"We made it here," Richard said, not at all interested in the drama of the tale. "Once we were here we were able to gain control of the situation and begin to reduce their numbers—"

"And then the Shun-tuk disappeared," Samantha put in, not happy with Richard's pace at storytelling. She snapped her fingers. "Gone, just like that."

"We set up a defensive position," Richard said, "so that Zedd and Nicci could heal you." The ghost of worry reappeared on his features. "Or at least heal your more obvious wounds."

Nicci laid a hand on Kahlan's arm. "You know we can't get the poison of death out of you, at least not here, or we would. We did the best we could to give you strength."

"It's getting worse, isn't it?" Kahlan asked.

Nicci nodded. "I'm afraid so. It was touch-and-go for a while, there. We were worried that this time we wouldn't be able to bring you back."

Kahlan nodded. "Me too."

"Ba," Zedd said with a dismissive gesture. "Nicci was afraid. I knew I could do it."

Nicci smiled at last. "Yes, Zedd, this time you proved yourself to be the wonder you have always insisted you are."

With a wave, Kahlan cut off the small talk. "What about the men? Are they all right? Were any of them hurt or killed? Did we lose any of them?"

"Surprisingly enough," Richard said, "we didn't lose a single man. The First File knows how to fight. Half people typically don't, although these are Shun-tuk, and they're more trouble than the other half people we've encountered in the past. They don't just attack randomly. They execute their attack accord-ing to a plan. That makes them more dangerous than the half people we've fought before.

"Worse, some of these obviously have an ability to use occult powers. We know how dangerous they are. After all, they've overwhelmed and captured these battle-hardened, elite troops and our gifted once before and took them beyond the barrier, so they're confident they can take us again. Even though we managed to escape, it wasn't before we lost a lot of men back beyond the barrier. It's pretty clear that the Shun-tuk don't give up."

"What about the man we went to help?" she asked. "Is he all right, too, then?"

Richard nodded. "While Zedd and Nicci were working on you, Samantha helped by healing some of the men who were injured. None of them were as seriously hurt as Ned, the man we went to help." He gestured to Samantha's mother. "Irena healed him."

"Ironic, isn't it?" Nicci lifted an eyebrow as she looked up at the other sorceress on the opposite side of Kahlan. "She healed the man she would have had us leave to be eaten alive."

Irena met Nicci's glare in kind. "These men are Lord Rahl's guard. Their duty is to protect him at all costs, even if that cost is their lives. That is their calling. They know the risks and accept them willingly. Yes, we saved him, but it was at a risk to Richard's life that was not the wisest choice. It could all too easily have turned out quite differently."

"And if we allow those men to be needlessly lost, then Lord Rahl loses their protection, now doesn't he?" Nicci asked in cold challenge. "They can't very well protect Lord Rahl if they are dead."

Irena had used "Richard." Kahlan noticed that Nicci clearly didn't think the woman was entitled to be so familiar as to call him "Richard."

Everyone but individuals close to him called Richard "Lord Rahl." To everyone else, he was "Lord Rahl." To some, it was a term of deep respect. To some, that name, attached to Richard, meant liberty. To others, it was tantamount to a curse.

Even Cara, his closest personal guard and close friend, had called him "Lord Rahl," not out of duty, but because he had earned her respect. The Lord Rahl before Richard had enslaved her into service to him as a Mord-Sith. Richard had freed her from that servitude, and out of respect for him she called him Lord Rahl. Even though it was the same title, it meant something unique when applied to Richard.

Richard had wed Cara to her husband, Ben. He had been there when they had lost Ben. And, he had been the last person she came to see before she'd left.

Richard was not only the leader of the D'Haran Empire, he had created that empire out of war-torn, fragmented lands in order to win freedom from a world falling to tyranny. He had become Lord Rahl in every sense of the term.

To most people, titles were important touchstones of power and widely employed as a mark of that power. Kahlan, as the Mother Confessor, was all too familiar with the power a title represented, and the fear it engendered.

Richard didn't do the things he did for a title to represent his power, or for power itself, or to impress anyone. Titles didn't really matter to him. While others concerned themselves with titles, Richard simply did as he needed to do. He judged people as individuals and by their actions, not by their titles, and expected them to judge him the same way, not by his title.

Nicci was one of the few for whom such familiar use of his name seemed to come naturally. To her his title meant something else. Kahlan wasn't exactly sure what.

"We lost the horses," Richard said, changing the subject. "One broke away and ran off in the confusion."

Kahlan was brought out of her thoughts. "What? How?"

Richard gestured vaguely into the distance. "When we went after Ned, some of the Shun-tuk used the opportunity to go after our horses. They want to slow us down. They drew us away so they could cut the horses' throats. One of the mares managed to get away and run off. We were able to get it back, but one horse won't do us much good."

Kahlan leaned forward. "Slow us down? You mean you think the whole attack was a diversion to draw us off just so they could get at the horses?"

Richard nodded. "I think that at least in part their

plan is to prevent us from being able to get to the People's Palace to warn them that Emperor Sulachan is heading their way with an army of half people.

"These Shun-tuk seem smarter than the ones we've fought before. Rather than simply relying on brute force, they're employing rudimentary strategy, such as killing our horses to slow us down. This attack was part of a larger plan and I'm not sure what the rest of it is, except that it is meant to have us all in the end."

"But they were trying to eat us in hopes of capturing our souls for themselves," Kahlan said, remembering quite well the teeth sinking into her neck. "That's what all the others we've fought before wanted."

Richard arched an eyebrow. "They didn't eat Ned when they had the chance. They wanted him making a lot of noise in order to draw us into coming to his aid, probably so that some of them could then get at the horses. Up until then the horses had been protected within our camp. We chose to try to save a life that was in immediate risk and that left the horses unprotected. Along with the horses, they also destroyed the carriage. All of that makes it easier for them to limit our ability to move swiftly.

"They're acting more like a wolf pack, working together to take down their prey. But once that prey is down, it's every wolf for itself."

Richard and Kahlan had both been riding in the carriage most of the time. With both of them weakened by the poison of death rooted deep inside them, the more of their strength they used up, the sooner death would take them. Riding in the carriage helped save their strength and thus prolonged their lives until they could get back to the People's Palace, where the poison could finally be removed.

Richard was right. Losing the horses would slow them down and make them more vulnerable. It also continued to leave the palace in the dark as to what was coming their way.

Before anyone else could say anything, a breathless soldier ran up to them.

"Lord Rahl!"

"What is it?" Richard asked.

"We got one of them."

"What do you mean, you got one of them?"

"We caught one of those pale bastards. We captured him as he was trying to sneak up to spy on our camp." He pointed off toward one of the other fires. "We're holding him over there for you to question."

11

As they made their way across the camp to one of the other fires where the captive was being held, Kahlan met the gazes of young men cleaning weapons, repairing gear, standing watch over the dark forest beyond, or having a bite to eat before bedding down. She returned hopeful smiles, easing their concerned looks, reassuring them that she was all right.

She knew most of these men by name. All had fought in the long and bloody war with the Imperial Order, a war they had won. Now it seemed that the victory and the brief peace that followed had only been an illusion, because the ancient events that had sparked that war had flared anew, as if leapfrogging across time to come after them.

It seemed to Kahlan that most of her life had been lived in one war or another, first with Darken Rahl, then Jagang and the Imperial Order, and now with the long dead Emperor Sulachan, come back to life to finish what he had started thousands of years before.

These soldiers had come to the Dark Lands to protect her and Richard and get them safely back to the palace. It should have been a relatively easy mission after Richard had defeated the Hedge Maid. It had turned out to be anything but easy.

As it turned out, the Hedge Maid had been a harbinger of the evil that had finally managed to escape its long banishment. Her deadly touch had taken Richard's gift and Kahlan's power. She ached for her ability every waking moment. Her Confessor power was who she was. She had been born with it. It was part of her. And now she was cut off from it.

The camp was quiet, with all the activity subdued so some of the exhausted men could catch up on needed sleep. From what Kahlan could see when she was able to get a glimpse between the soldiers in the tight ring guarding the prisoner, it was obvious that the captive wasn't going anywhere.

As they made their way to where the man was being held, she saw that the entire encampment was in a fairly tight but open space at the foot of a cliff. Since they were camped on what was mostly open ledge, it was free of trees and brush. Some of the closest trees beyond had been felled for firewood. Since the wood was green, it crackled and popped as it burned, sending snapping sparks billowing up in the acrid smoke.

With the cliff backing them, the enemy were able to attack from only one side. A heavily defended perimeter all the way around, from the cliff face on one end of the encampment to the cliff face on the other end, bristled with steel defenses. Having the men concentrated close together made it easy for reinforcements to move swiftly from point to point in the line

to fight off any sudden charge of the bloodthirsty
Shun-tuk.

Such a fortress strategy meant there would be no
guards posted at distant points beyond their perimeter as an early warning of an attack, nor any scouts
on patrol to gather information. Instead, all the men
were being kept together so they could all watch over
everything and one another.

While it did deny them advance warning of an attack, it also denied the enemy the opportunity to pick
off softer targets, such as outposts and patrols, in order to gradually reduce their numbers. They didn't
have a lot of men to begin with and couldn't afford
to lose any.

The fires lit their encampment so that they could
more easily spot anyone trying to slip into their midst.
They also lit some of the forest beyond. That must
have been how the men spotted and captured the
Shun-tuk trying to sneak in closer.

Such a tight layout was generally not the best defensive tactic for an encampment, since an enemy
force outside their perimeter could get in fairly close,
hide among the trees, and use arrows or spears to
pick off soldiers out in the open of the camp. While
the enemy could hide off in the darkness, campfires
inside the camp lit targets for them. But the half
people didn't have those kinds of weapons, so in such
circumstances a fortress encampment like this was the
safest way to prevent vulnerable lone scouts or small
groups of sentries from being attacked and killed, and
it made for a hardened defensive line that was extremely difficult for a lightly armed enemy to penetrate.

Some of the soldiers of the First File moved aside
when they saw Richard and the small party with him

approaching the prisoner. The captive Shun-tuk was on his knees, not far from the fire. He had a big soldier to either side of him, each man holding a well-muscled arm out straight and twisted so that he couldn't move.

A third, their even bigger commander, a D'Haran with closely cropped blond hair, had a boot planted on each of the man's calves, pinning his knees to the ground. Since General Meiffert, Cara's husband, had been killed by the Shun-tuk as they had escaped the caves, Commander Jake Fister was now the highest-ranking officer there with them. He had arms the size of Kahlan's waist and a neck like an oak tree.

Standing behind the Shun-tuk, the powerfully built commander, obviously not wanting to take any chances, held a razor-sharp knife to the immobilized captive's throat. Several other men kept nocked arrows pointed at the man.

Kahlan knew Jake Fister. He had served under Captain Zimmer when Kahlan had commanded the special forces in the war with the Imperial Order. Each morning Captain Zimmer would bring her a string of enemy ears collected the night before. Jake Fister, a sergeant at the time, had been one of Captain Zimmer's most trusted men, and had been responsible for more than his fair share of the ears they collected. Those men were proud of what they accomplished on their nightly raids, striking fear into the hearts of the enemy troops. Each ear represented the life of one less enemy who could harm them. Kahlan had always shown her sincere appreciation of their grisly trophies, which pleased the men no end.

It seemed so long ago. At the time, Richard had been held captive down in the Old World by Nicci, when Nicci had been fighting on the other side for

Emperor Jagang. With Richard gone, Kahlan had led the war in his place.

During his captivity, Richard had gradually taught Nicci the value of freedom and of her own life, and won her over. Few people valued freedom as much as those who had never had it, like Nicci, and had come to discover its true value in their own lives. Since that time, Nicci had more than earned her place as one of their most trusted and valuable friends.

Captain Zimmer was now Colonel Zimmer, serving in the First File at the People's Palace. Jake Fister had been promoted to a commander in the First File and was one of the men handpicked by General Meiffert to come with him to the Dark Lands to bring Richard and Kahlan safely home. It sadly occurred to Kahlan that with Benjamin Meiffert dead, Colonel Zimmer was likely next in line for general to command the First File. She knew he would find it a sorrowful honor. Ben had been his friend.

Despite the arrows aimed at the prisoner, it was obvious to Kahlan by the way Jake was holding the knife to the man's throat that at the first twitch of aggression, it was Commander Fister who would be the one to end it before an arrow cleared a bow.

The Shun-tuk prisoner wore only a coarse, bleached cloth wrapped around his waist and between his legs, as did many of his kind, including the women who fought with the Shun-tuk men. His legs, arms, and chest were bare. His mostly shaved head had a dense crop of long hair at the top, standing up like a sheaf of wheat at harvest. Strings of human teeth wound tightly around the bundle of hair kept it standing up straight.

Once she got closer, Kahlan could see in the firelight that his skin looked like it had been rubbed with a paste of ash, possibly mixed with something to make it stick better so that it wouldn't rub off easily when they moved through heavy brush, or wash off in the frequent rains. It looked like the man habitually rubbed the ghostly ash paste over himself, so that in places it was thick, crusty, and cracked.

Like all of the Shun-tuk she had seen, black grease smeared around his eyes mimicked the eye sockets of a skull. He glared out from that darkness. As was the practice of some of the Shun-tuk, the same black grease had been used to paint a skeletal grin full of teeth on this man's lips and cheeks to go with the skeletal eye sockets. Even held as securely as he was, because of the ghostly whitewash over his body and the skeletal face of a skull, the man presented a frightening, intimidating presence.

As Richard approached, the man's glare seemed to grow more menacing. Despite how helpless he was, his eyes were filled with hate and defiance, like those of a wolf caught in a trap. He did not look the least bit frightened by his helpless situation or all the big men towering around him. He wanted to fight. Kahlan thought that if nothing else, he would be wise to be more than a little respectful of Commander Fister's knife at his throat.

12

Kahlan waited a few steps behind Richard along with Nicci and Zedd. Irena put out a hand to the side, stopping Samantha farther back. She leaned close to her daughter and whispered instructions for her to stay where she was, safely behind the rest of them. Samantha's mouth twisted in disappointment as she folded her arms, but she accepted the order without a complaint.

She obviously wanted to go up closer to Richard and get a better look at the prisoner. She had fought these half people and she wanted to see what Richard might ask, but she always appeared respectful and deferential to her mother. Until Richard had shown up in Samantha's village of Stroyza, life had probably always been a constant, with clear-cut lines of respect, with Irena their sorceress and authority figure.

When the barrier holding back the third kingdom and the half people was suddenly breached, Samantha's mother had been captured by the Shun-tuk.

Everything in young Samantha's predictable, stable life suddenly changed. Her whole world had been turned upside down, and she found herself, young as she was, the only sorceress left in Stroyza. Richard had shown up in the middle of that crisis.

In their time spent together, Richard and Samantha had depended on each other for their survival as they went to the dangerous land beyond the barrier to rescue Irena, Zedd, Nicci, Cara, and the soldiers who had been captured.

Richard said that she was smart, and that she seemed to have a great deal of ability with her gift, although he wasn't sure of all that she was capable of doing with her power. Samantha didn't really know, either. Together, the two of them had succeeded in rescuing all those that the Shun-tuk had captured. At least, the ones still alive.

Kahlan could not help but notice that the young woman seemed to be infatuated with Richard. It was just a stage of youth, of growing up and discovering the wider world and the mysteries of the opposite sex. It didn't help that the object of her affection was Richard. He was an easy man to like, handsome and commanding, yet kind and considerate. Kahlan could certainly understand what Samantha saw in him, even if she wasn't particularly thrilled about it.

But Samantha respected Kahlan and did her best to hide her feelings, thinking that she did a good enough job of it that no one knew. Samantha undoubtedly realized that it was inappropriate and that nothing could come of it. Still, the heart wants what the heart wants and such feelings aren't so easy to turn aside.

Kahlan believed that the young woman was smart enough not to let herself get carried away and hurt, even if at times, when she didn't think anyone was looking, she did stare at Richard with unmistakable longing. Kahlan knew that it was best to let it die out on its own rather than say something and embarrass Samantha. Young women were easily humiliated in such matters, and Kahlan didn't want to hurt her. She liked Samantha. She just wished that Richard weren't the object of her desire.

Richard, of course, was oblivious of it. With so many more things to worry about, his mind was focused elsewhere and Kahlan was not about to bring it up. She, too, had enough things that were a great deal more serious to worry about.

Kahlan was taken by surprise when Irena abruptly left her daughter and rushed past the rest of them to grab Richard's arm.

"Richard, you must come away from this man." Irena tugged on his arm. "Leave these men to tend to it and come back with me. Come away right now."

Richard stood his ground and frowned down at the woman. "What?"

She leaned in close and turned her face away from the prisoner so he couldn't hear as she whispered, "He has occult powers. I must get you back away from him. Come with me."

Nicci immediately forced her way between them, breaking Irena's grip on Richard's arm. With a look from Richard, Nicci understood the instruction and towed Irena by her wrist back out of the way.

"Can you sense if the half person has occult powers?" Kahlan whispered to Nicci as she fell in beside her to escort Irena back away from Richard.

Nicci looked over out of the corner of her eye. "No. I could sense the gift in him if he had it, but he doesn't. I can't sense any other type of power in a person, occult or otherwise. Occult magic is an entirely different form of power. I suspect that you can only sense it if you possess it yourself, and while I may know a little about it, I don't have any occult abilities so I can't sense them."

"He has occult powers," Irena insisted. It was all too clear that she resented having been dragged away from what she had been doing. She was the authority figure in her village and was apparently used to people deferring to her. She obviously didn't appreciate having her word questioned or challenged.

"What are you talking about, he has occult powers?" Nicci growled through gritted teeth. "I am a sorceress with a great deal of experience." She seized Irena's arm and hauled her close. "If I can't sense any occult powers in the man, then how can you?"

Fuming, Irena yanked her arm away from Nicci's grip. Her expression had grown as dark as her mass of black hair.

"You don't need to be a sorceress or have occult powers to know that the man has such ability and that he is dangerous." She thrust out an arm, pointing back the way they had come. "Didn't you see some of those unholy demons during the battle when they brought the dead back to life?"

"What of it?" Nicci asked.

Irena leaned in closer. "The Shun-tuk didn't do such things by wishing the dead back to life, now did they? The gift can't do such things. They couldn't do such things without being able to wield occult sorcery. That's how I know he has such powers.

"It's dangerous for Richard to be near such a person. Richard's gift isn't working. He is naked before such dangerous occult abilities. He could be hurt or killed before any of us could do anything to protect him."

"She's right," Kahlan whispered.

Nicci pressed her lips tight as she glanced over at Kahlan. "Only some of them—not all—have such powers. This one has shown no indication that he has occult powers."

She finally gritted her teeth and turned back to Irena. "We don't know that this man is one of the Shun-tuk with those abilities. My gift works just fine. I am Richard's protection.

"Lord Rahl has a job to do. You let him do it. As the Lord Rahl he is doing what he has to do. He knows the dangers. You stay out of his way, understand?"

Irena looked shaken at being challenged. Before she could argue, Nicci grabbed the skirts of her black dress in both fists and rushed back to stand with Zedd, close behind Richard, where she could keep a close eye on the prisoner. Samantha wrung her hands, distraught at seeing her mother scolded. Zedd had been watching, too, but looked like he knew better than to get in the middle of quarreling sorceresses.

Kahlan joined Nicci at her side but didn't say anything. She knew Nicci's power was formidable, and if the knife the soldier was holding to the man's throat and the arrows pointed at his chest didn't stop him from harming Richard, Nicci surely would, even if she had to use her bare hands.

Kahlan hoped that Nicci really could stop him if she had to. She gripped the handle of the knife at her waist, making sure it was there if she needed it. She wished Cara were still with them. The Mord-Sith had always been Richard's protector, but now she was gone.

Kahlan's heart ached for Cara, for her loss. She could understand why she had left, but she missed her.

Kahlan couldn't imagine how she would feel if she lost Richard, or what she would do. Just imagining such a terrifying thing quickened her heart rate. Unfortunately, with the sickness afflicting them both, it was a thought that always haunted her and she couldn't entirely banish.

Richard looked back over his shoulder. "Everything all right?"

Nicci leaned closer to Richard and whispered so that he, but not the prisoner, could hear. "Be careful, Richard. We don't know what abilities this man might have. He could be a risk to you without him even having to touch you."

Richard rubbed his fingertips on his forehead as he shared a look over his shoulder with them. Kahlan could see by the reaction in his eyes, or rather, the lack of reaction, that he was already well aware of that danger.

"I understand. But we're running out of time. I have to find out what I can."

Kahlan understood what he meant. Death was coming for the two of them, and it was getting closer by the moment.

Nicci gave him a nod and he turned back to the prisoner.

13

"What's your name?" Richard asked the man on his knees.

The Shun-tuk glared without answering.

"Do you even have a name? Do any of your people use names?"

The man maintained his silent glare.

Richard clasped his hands as he looked down at the prisoner. "No name, no soul."

"We will have souls," the man said in a low growl filled with hate. Richard had touched a nerve. "We will have all of your souls for ourselves. They will be ours."

"It's foolish to even imagine you can get a soul by eating the flesh of people who have them. There is only one way to get a soul."

The man's brow twitched with the slightest bit of interest, but he would not ask.

"You can only get a soul," Richard finally said in

answer to the unspoken question, "by being born with one. It is forged into a person at their creation. It's an inherent part of them, a living connection to everything in this world and the next as shown in the lines of the Grace. It's their link to existence.

"Good or bad, kind or cruel, for better or worse, whether they want it or not, the soul they were born with is theirs from the instant of the ignition of that spark at their creation, through life, and on into the world of the dead. In the most basic sense, it is the sum of who they are, the distillation of everything they are. They can neither give it away or lose it nor have it stolen from them. That soul is a part of them and can't be separated from them, either willingly or unwillingly."

The man smiled. "If that were true, then how do you explain the existence of the half people?"

"You were born without souls."

"Not in the beginning. In the beginning the half people started life as you did, as people born with souls. Their souls were ripped out of them to create weapons, to create the half people—those without souls."

"Yes, but that was done thousands of years ago by Emperor Sulachan and his wizards, wizards who had powers none of us today have or can fully envision."

"But they did it. They took souls from people who had them."

Richard gestured to the south, toward the Old World, where Sulachan had originally ruled. "Sulachan's violation of the nature of life was depraved. It was not a simple plucking of a soul from someone. It entailed great effort of many wizards with long-lost powers and dedicated to Sulachan's perverted task.

"None of those original half people could give their

offspring a soul because they no longer had one. They had lost their connection to the Grace. Their offspring were born without a soul and can only bear offspring of their own without a soul.

"The only soul those original half people could ever have would have been their own, if Sulachan were to somehow reunite them. But those people are long dead and gone. Their descendants, like you, can't ever gain a soul by any means because none ever belonged to you."

"As those with souls die," the man said with confidence, "that soul flees the body as it begins its journey to the world of the dead. After all, the bodies that rot in the ground no longer have souls. Their souls left them. So, souls can flee the body of their host."

"That part of them that is their soul leaves them at death to go through the veil as the Grace shows," Richard said.

"And we can capture the soul by eating the living flesh that the soul is still bound into. If we consume the living, then at just the right instant, while their soul still resides in their flesh and blood, as they die we will have that warm flesh and blood inside us at the exact instant the soul departs the dying flesh of that host. Since we are living that soul that is within us will bind to us. It will have found a new, living host and we will then possess that soul."

Kahlan shared a troubled look with Zedd. It was about as sick a belief as she had ever heard.

Richard was shaking his head. "No, you can't. You can't, because that soul, that essence of who the person is, that spark they were born with, doesn't wander around looking for a new 'host,' as you put it. That isn't at all what happens. When that person dies, their soul, being part of the continuation of the gift, follows the lines coming from the spark of creation and passes through the veil into the underworld."

"Not if we capture it first as they are dying."

Richard watched the man without showing any emotion to the revolting idea. "It doesn't work that way. Someone else's soul—who they are—can't reside in you. It can't be trapped or take up residence in someone new. At death it is bound to the underworld."

"We will have your souls for ourselves," the man said with the confidence that only unshakable, irrational faith could provide.

While Kahlan wasn't entirely sure of what, exactly, constituted the soul, she knew enough to know that in these people wishing took the place of reason. It wasn't possible to reason with people who were irrational. That was what made irrational people so profoundly dangerous.

The half people had dreamed up an entire belief system around what they imagined a soul was, how it behaved, and how they could get one for themselves. They invented the entire belief system out of wishes. They wished it to work that way, and so they believed it must, simply because they wanted it to.

In a way, they didn't have the ability to listen to reason because they weren't human in the conventional sense. They looked more or less like normal people, but they weren't. They were a different kind of human. In some ways, without a soul, they had more in common with animals than people, with little more than the reasoning ability of a predator.

They were hungry, they hunted. They hungered for a soul, they hunted them. It was action based on need alone.

Richard stared at the man for a long moment before speaking. "And do you know any of your kind who have ever gained a soul by capturing it from a person they ate? Has it ever worked even once? Have you ever seen it actually succeed?"

He hesitated a moment. "I have not seen it yet, myself." His chin lifted a little, but not enough that Commander Fister's knife cut his throat. "If I had, I would have fallen on the man who accomplished it and I would have eaten him in turn to get that soul for myself. I need one for myself. I am entitled to a soul."

"Who sent you?" Richard asked, abruptly changing the subject from the dead end of blind belief.

The man's chest puffed up with pride. "Our king and emperor, Sulachan. He came back from the world of the dead. His soul returned. You are the bringer of the dead. Your blood brought him back. I was there. I saw it happen with my own eyes.

"If I do not first gain a soul for myself, our king will help us to be complete."

Richard folded his arms over his chest. "And how do you think he can do such a thing? How can he make you complete?"

"He is a spirit king," the man said, as if that said it all. When Richard only stared, he went on. "He can bridge worlds. He has proven that by returning from the dead. Now that his spirit has returned to the world of life, bridging the veil, he will bring the worlds together and unite them. The worlds of life and death will be together in one world—no longer separated by the veil. I will be complete when he does."

"How is that going to make you complete?"

"In life, you must have a soul to be complete. When life ends the soul continues on through the veil into the world of the dead."

He fell silent again, again seeming to think that should explain it all. Richard frowned in realization.

"I see your problem. The way things are now, after you die you can't go on to the world of the dead because you have no soul to go there, no soul to make that journey. Without a soul, there is no underworld for you, no going beyond the veil to the eternity beyond. Without a soul, when you die you will simply cease to exist."

The man stared off for a moment before answering. "That is why I must have a soul. Those with souls were born lucky. We are entitled to have a soul."

"So you think you are justified in killing people because you want their soul for yourself?"

"Of course. We need a soul, so we must kill to get one."

Kahlan was right. These half people were less than human. Without a soul they had no empathy for others. They didn't feel for their victims, or feel any guilt at killing. Without a soul they couldn't. They were predators, remorseless killers after prey. They felt no empathy for that prey, any more than a wolf felt sorry for deer it took down. It was simply prey.

She understood now that there was a larger purpose than she had thought behind the depraved desire to steal a soul. It wasn't merely a blind hunger for a soul to fill a void within themselves. It was a hunger to have a soul in order to do what humans could do—go on to the underworld after death.

Having no soul denied them the eternity of the underworld. The world of life was a brief spark in time compared to an eternity in the underworld. They were desperate to escape the fate of ceasing to exist at death. They invented a belief they thought would allow them to live on in the underworld, basking in the warm light of Creation. In a very real way, these people worshiped death because it seemed like a better world to them, a world without end. Theirs was, in a way, a religious quest.

Without a soul, they couldn't do any of that. Without a soul, death meant they would go out of existence like a candle flame being snuffed out. For the half people, having no soul meant that there could be no eternity among the good spirits. To the half people, having a soul meant gaining immortality.

In a way, she felt a twinge of sorrow for them, except that they were willing to kill to get what they wanted.

Kahlan knew that Richard didn't want her asking anything because it would draw the man's attention to her, but she couldn't help herself.

"Sulachan can't give you a soul," she said, "and without that spark of the gift within you, he can't take you to the underworld. You are bound to this world, but only for as long as you live. There is nothing there within you for him to take to his realm after you die. He can do nothing to help you after you die. So why would you follow him? What is it you think he can do for you?"

His dark eyes fixed on her. "Once our king unites the world of life and the world of the dead, there will be no need for a soul. Death will no longer be an end for us.

"Once you die, your soul goes to the world of the dead. In that way you are able to bridge both worlds. Without a soul we cannot go on to the world of the dead.

"But once the worlds are united into one, both worlds will be one, together, not separate. We will already be in the world of the dead as well as the world of life. All those like me will be able to exist in a single world of life and death bound together. It will be all parts of the Grace in one united world without end.

"Our king has promised that in such a world, once life and death exist together, I will be complete and have no need of a soul in order to go on to the underworld. I will already be there without needing a soul to make that journey, to cross over. There will be nothing to cross over to. We will be there.

"Once the worlds of life and death are brought together into a third kingdom, a kingdom of both life and death in the same place at the same time, Sulachan will rule over it all for all time in the eternity of that world brought together into one."

It was a profoundly disturbing concept. The very fact that after three thousand years Sulachan had returned from the world of the dead showed that the idea made a perverse kind of sense, at least to Sulachan and the half people.

Kahlan didn't believe that it could actually work, but she knew that they did.

It was troubling that it had been Richard's blood that had enabled the occult conjuring to work and bring Sulachan's spirit back from the dead.

But most troubling of all was that with such powers as Sulachan possessed, the very attempt to make such a delusional scheme work could very well destroy the world of life.

In that sense, there would be only one world.

An eternally dead one.

14

How did you find us?" Richard asked, changing the subject again.

For the first time a sly smile came to the man. "We tracked you."

"How did you track us?"

By his tone of voice, Kahlan didn't think these people read footprints on the ground. Apparently Richard didn't either.

The man's smile turned murderous "Some of us have . . . talents."

Zedd frowned, no longer able to contain himself. "Talents? What sort of talents?"

The man's eyes turned up to the old wizard. "Some of us are spirit trackers. It is an ancient ability passed down to us from the first half people that Emperor Sulachan created. Now that he has returned, he has use of us. He sent us to track you."

Richard paced as he thought about the unusual

claim. "You expect me to believe that you can track people by sensing their spirits?"

"I do not expect you to believe anything," the Shun-tuk prisoner said. "You asked, I told you. We are spirit trackers. It does not matter to me what you believe."

"So you're saying that some of you can track spirits," Richard asked, "that some of you have that ability to sense them and follow them?"

"The Shun-tuk are not all the same. Some of our ancestors were created with abilities forged into them. Among the Shun-tuk there is a variety of abilities."

"Abilities," Richard repeated in a flat tone.

Kahlan knew that such abilities created out of people were all too real. After all, she was a Confessor, an ability that had been created in the first Confessor, Magda Searus. That ability had been passed down to all the offspring of Confessors.

"Some of us were born with different abilities than others among us, just as some of you are gifted, while others of you are not.

"Spirit trackers can sense the presence of souls. Because we can sense souls, we can track them, much like a wolf can smell his prey and follow its scent. And like a wolf following a scent of a particular animal, we can distinguish between spirits. We can sense individual spirits and follow their essence. Once we found you, we did as we were commanded."

"Not exactly. You failed," Richard pointed out. "You failed even to kill the one man you had down and by himself. How does your spirit king treat those who fail him?"

"We did not fail. We tracked your spirits as instructed."

"Tracking us would only be part of your orders. I'm sure you were instructed to kill us or bring captives back, much as you captured all these people here once before and brought them to Sulachan.

"This time, you failed. You didn't kill any of us, steal any souls for yourselves, and you don't have any captives to take back to Sulachan. Knowing how he treats those who fail him, I would say that you are fortunate you will never see Emperor Sulachan again."

The man lifted his chin indignantly. "I will see him soon enough. When the world of the dead is brought together with the world of the living, I will be with my king again. In the meantime, the spirit trackers have not yet failed. We found you. We will continue coming after you until we succeed. We can fail many times and still keep coming. You can fail only once, and then we have you.

"Sooner or later you will be ours. We will have the souls of those with you, and bring you back so that Lord Arc can send you to the world of the dead with his own hands."

"Lord Arc." Richard frowned. "So you were instructed to bring only me back with you?"

"That's right, our king sent us at the request of Lord Arc. But he sent us to bring back only you, for Lord Arc."

"So you are not to bring back any other captives?"

The man looked over at Kahlan with lust in his dark eyes. "No. Just you. The rest he no longer needs. The rest we can eat. We can have their souls for ourselves."

He smiled up to Richard. "Your soul belongs to my king and Lord Arc to do with as they will. That is their business, not ours. Our trackers are free to do what they will with the rest of your people."

"And where are your spirit king and Hannis Arc? Where were you to bring me?"

The man's brow lifted with a dismissive expression. "They head to the southeast."

Kahlan didn't like the sound of that. By the look Nicci and Zedd gave her, neither did the sorceress or wizard. The People's Palace was to the southeast.

"Where are the rest of your trackers?" Richard asked. "When are they coming back to attack again?"

The man stared off without answering. It was obvious enough, now, that they would return, and keep returning. Kahlan knew that the only way to stop them was to kill every last one of them.

"It seems to me that it is in your best interest to cooperate in order to stay alive, since if you die without a soul you will not be around for the time when your king unites the worlds of the dead and the living."

The Shun-tuk frowned. "What do you mean?"

"The longer you cooperate, the longer you live. Who knows, you might live long enough to see the worlds united.

"But if you don't cooperate, then you are of no further use to us. Why would we want to keep you around, take you with us, watch over you? Like a wolf in our midst, your existence will have to be extinguished. Then there will be nothing left of you, no spirit, no spark of anything to live on in the united world of the third kingdom. For now, death is the final end for you."

The man tried to shift his weight, but with big soldiers to either side holding his arms, and Commander Fister standing on his calves, he could move little more than his head, and that was limited by the knife at his throat.

"If you kill me, then it cannot matter to me, because I will not exist in any world. I will be no longer."

"But you would rather continue to exist, or you wouldn't be trying to steal these souls," Richard said as he gestured around at all the people watching.

The Shun-tuk looked at the people surrounding him with the eyes of a hungry wolf.

"Now, what are their plans?" Richard asked in a quiet, deadly tone that made most people tremble, making it clear that the man was running out of time. "What are your spirit trackers planning to do next?"

The man, staring ahead for a moment, finally looked up at Richard. The unshakable resolve was back in his eyes. "It can make no difference for you to know what we will do. Knowing cannot help you because you will not be able to do anything to stop us, or to stop our king.

"So there is no point in me telling you."

The man lifted his chin and fell silent.

I think there is a very good reason for you not to tell me," Richard said. "I think you don't want to say because you fear that I really can stop them." Richard spread his hands. "After all, if what you're saying were true—that the spirit trackers will have us sooner or later—then why would you be so afraid to tell me their plans?"

The man frowned. "I am not afraid."

"The only reason for not telling me has to be because you really do believe we can prevent them from capturing me and having all the rest of us. You're afraid that if I know, I will stop them and you will have none of our souls."

The man frowned as he thought it through. Finally, he decided to speak.

"Your spirit"—he tilted his head to indicate Kahlan—"and hers, are touched by death. We can feel it, sense it, like the smell of death. The spirit trackers can sense that sickness darkening your lives. You are like wounded animals.

"We can sense those times when that weakness comes over you and makes you lose consciousness. That is when your people are vulnerable. Without you, they cannot fight us off.

"After all, we captured all of them and more once before when you were unconscious. Had Sulachan's spirit already returned and used his trackers, we would have known that you were among the others, but unconscious and hidden. Sulachan had not returned from the dead, yet, so that time you both escaped.

"This time, the trackers will again attack, but they will do so when they know that you are weak and vulnerable. We attacked earlier, when we felt your woman drifting closer to death. When we sensed her weakness, we came for you all.

"Sooner or later that will happen to you, and we will know. When it happens, then we will have you all.

"Even now, we can sense your spirits losing the battle for life. You do not have long to live. Soon the time will be right and the trackers will be all over your people while you lie helpless. They will tear them apart and have their souls.

"Then we will capture you and take you to our king."

Richard shrugged. "If what you say is true, I may be dead by then. If I die, your plans will be ruined."

He looked disinterested. "If you should happen to die before we can take you back, that will satisfy Sulachan just as well. Either way, we will win in the end. You have no chance."

"If he wants me brought to him so badly, then how can he be satisfied if I die first?"

The man smiled again with the kind of arrogant smile that put Kahlan in mind of so many killers right before she had touched them with her Confessor power. No matter how self-assured they were, no matter how superior they behaved, no matter how dismissive and arrogant toward her, no matter how tough they thought they were, once she touched them with her power all that ended in an instant and each and every one of them confessed their crimes to her, no matter how vile those crimes might have been.

"Sulachan does not care if you should happen to die first," the prisoner said, "because he already has plans for you in the underworld."

Richard planted his fists on his hips. "What are you talking about?"

"Sulachan is called the king of the dead for good reason. He has infinite patience that only the eternally dead can have. He has been there a long, long time, working on his plans for his return, for his revenge.

"Sulachan was there in the underworld when the scream of death that escaped the Hedge Maid's lips claimed her and pulled her through the veil. Sulachan knows that the same poison that took her touched you two as well.

"Like Sulachan, the dark ones he commands in the underworld recognize that taint of death on your souls and know that you do not have long to live. Those demons stir, restless in that realm, the world of the dead, eager to have you.

"When you die and your souls cross over, those eternal, dark demons will be there at the veil, waiting to latch on to both of you and drag you each down into the deepest, darkest depths of the under-world where you will be forever lost.

"Lord Arc would like to kill you with his own hands, to look into your eyes and watch you die, but he deals in occult powers and so he knows very well of the demons Emperor Sulachan has waiting for you when you cross over. He would like to kill you and personally send you into the clutches of those dark ones, but if you should happen to die first he wants us to bring him your head so that he knows that your soul is in the hands of those dark demons, suffering worse than any worldly horror he could inflict on you. So, you see, either way, he gets what he wants."

Everyone watching seemed to be holding their breath.

The man looked around at his captors, "Know that when that taint of death touches your leader—sooner than you think—we will have all of you. We will hunt you down, eat your flesh, suck the marrow from your bones, and steal all of your souls for ourselves."

He looked deliberately at Richard and then pointed with his chin at Kahlan. "Our people will devour the living flesh and drink the warm blood of your woman. We will enjoy her helpless screams as we rip her apart. Some will lick up her tears as others drink her blood."

Richard made an effort of not showing his feelings but Kahlan had no trouble reading the anger in his body language. "You just said that your spirit king has dark spirits waiting for our souls, so your trackers can't have any hope of having hers."

The man smiled in a way that revealed his darkly determined, inalterable nature. "The trackers know that they cannot have your woman's soul. They know it is promised to the dark ones in the underworld. But they will revel in drinking her warm blood anyway because she is yours and it will matter to you. Her fate has been ordered by our masters, because in her suffering, both of her flesh being torn from her bones and then the demons of the underworld having her soul to torment for all time, your pain will be intolerable beyond imagining. That is what awaits her, and you."

It was a threat that not only sent a chill through Kahlan, it crossed a line with Richard.

He looked up from the remorseless eyes of the soulless brute, into the eyes of Commander Fister. Richard pulled a finger across his own throat in silent command.

Once he had given that command, he turned away. Jake Fister was a man devoted to putting down those who served evil. Richard did not need to witness the execution to know that it would be swiftly carried out.

On the way past, Richard took Kahlan's arm, walking her back toward the center campfire where she had been healed. She could feel the hard tension of rage in his muscles.

"Any ideas about what we do next?" she asked him, trying to take his mind off the haunting threat they had just heard.

Before he could answer, before he could say anything, Richard lost a step.

He went to a knee beside her. Kahlan circled her arm tightly around his waist, trying to help him down so that he wouldn't fall on his face. He was too big and heavy for her to hold up. All she could do was to help in easing him down.

He reached a hand up. It was a plea for help— gifted help.

Zedd and Nicci were already there, grabbing hold of Richard's arms and lifting him back to his feet as they kept him from falling over. At Kahlan's urgent signal, several men rushed in to put a shoulder under his arms.

Zedd pressed his fingers to Richard's forehead as the soldiers helped move him along. "It's the poison," he said in a grim voice, telling them what Kahlan already knew. "Get him back by the fire where I can see better and then let's lay him down."

Kahlan's heart pounded with worry. She felt worse than helpless. An icy wave of dread washed through her. She knew that the pull of death had grown stronger and he might die.

"Richard," she said, clutching his big hand tightly, "hold on. Zedd and Nicci are going to help you. Hold on. Don't you dare leave me. Don't you dare."

He didn't respond. His hand was cold and limp.

She tried very hard to hold back her tears.

And then, she heard the howls way off in the darkness of the woods as the half people started their charge.

16

As Kahlan held his hand, Richard hooked his other around the back of Nicci's neck and pulled her down close as they lowered him onto a blanket on the ground near the fire. He gripped Zedd's sleeve and pulled him close as well. He had managed to regain consciousness, if barely.

It took a great deal of effort for Richard to draw each labored breath through the obvious pain he was in. Kahlan knew that pain all too well. The intensity of it made her extremities tingle. The terrible weight of the pain felt as if it would crush her skull at the same time as nausea coursed through her body in dizzying waves.

At least until the blackness overcame her. Then it was worse because she was lost in a dark place, lonely beyond anything she had ever experienced. It was a terrifying, hopeless kind of loneliness that crushed her soul the way the pain felt like it would crush her skull.

But until the darkness overcame you, it stole your

desire to speak. It made you not want to open your eyes because when you did the world spun and tilted in a stomach-churning blur. It made every sound feel sharp and stabbing, like knitting needles pushed in your ears. It took maximum effort simply to endure the agony and draw each breath. It was a struggle just to remain conscious.

She knew that the Hedge Maid had felt all of that when she had died, when that terrible, awful, horrifying scream had escaped her. All that lethal agony had been expressed in that one, long, shriek. Richard and Kahlan had been touched by the same call of death, and while not immediately fatal, they had felt much the same pain of what had taken Jit.

Kahlan knew, too, that such a feeling was part of the lure of death making you want to give up, to give in to it, to let it take you. It made you suffer, and in the suffering promised to make the agony stop, if only you would heed the call and step through the veil toward the blessed darkness. It was that beguiling call at the intolerable end of life that made death just beyond life seem so sweet, made it seem like a mere, simple, single step to the other side and then it would all so mercifully end.

Resisting that call was difficult in the extreme, especially when it meant you had to continue to endure the unendurable while telling yourself that you must.

Richard's voice, when he was finally able to force himself to speak, betrayed all of that suffering and more.

"You two," he said to Zedd and Nicci leaning close over him, "have Irena help you and the men fight off the Shun-tuk. They must be held back for a little longer."

Zedd obviously thought Richard was too delirious

to make any decisions. "I need to help you," Zedd told his grandson. "I can't leave you like this. I must help you now before it can take you. You can't fight it on your own. The men can hold off the Shun-tuk. You can't wait."

Richard, his eyes closed, rolled his head from side to side. "The men won't be able to hold them off."

The certainty in his voice caused Kahlan to steal a quick glance around at the men rushing to the defensive lines. She met Nicci's troubled blue eyes.

Nicci gripped Richard's shoulder as she leaned in. "You need our help, Richard. If we don't save you, we will all be lost. We must help you in order to help all the rest of us. Without you, we are lost."

"Samantha can help me," Richard told her. "The trackers can sense my weakness. They know that this is their chance. They will put all their effort into finishing us off quickly while they have the chance, while I can't fight them. If you don't help stop them, then we will be lost."

Zedd's bushy brows drew tight as he, too, stole a quick glance around at the frantic activity of men preparing to do battle. He looked back down at Richard.

"Samantha? Richard, this is too serious. She is little more than a child. Without the right help—"

The breathless young woman rushed in, then, sliding to a halt on her knees. "I'm here, Lord Rahl." She gulped air as she gathered up one of his hands in both of hers and held it tightly to her. "I'm here."

"Listen, Samantha," Richard said, "you helped give me strength to hold it off before—fight off the sickness. Remember?"

In the firelight Kahlan could see the tears welling

up in the young sorceress's eyes. She was on the verge of panic.

"What? You want me to do this? Lord Rahl, there are people here much better able to help you than me."

"After we came across that man in the woods, before we made it to the north wall. I grew weak and you helped me. You gave me strength. Remember?"

Samantha nodded as if her life depended on it. "Sure, I remember."

"I need you to do that again," he told her. He opened his eyes to look up at the others. "While she helps me, the rest of you need to keep the Shun tuk from overrunning the camp and killing us all. You need to buy us a little time."

"It's that unholy half person who did this," Irena said. "I told you that he had occult powers and Richard should not go near him, but you wouldn't listen. Now look what has happened!"

"I know a lot more about healing than Samantha. I should be able to do something to help. Get back and let me see if I can do something to help."

She immediately pushed in beside Zedd and pressed the palm of her hand over Richard's forehead.

Before Kahlan could say anything, or Nicci had a chance to remove the woman's hand from Richard, Irena yelped and jerked her hand back on her own.

"Dear spirits. Richard, I had no idea . . . We can't heal such a thing."

Concerned more with Richard and the erupting battle than wasting time lecturing the woman, Nicci didn't say anything, but she did give Kahlan a look that betrayed her smoldering anger. The look in those blue eyes said it all to Kahlan.

Kahlan thought that Irena would be wise to be more respectful of Nicci. The seductively beautiful sorceress might have looked young and less experienced than Irena, but she was a former Sister of the Dark and as such possessed not only a wizard's power, but the accumulated power of the gift from others she had killed.

Irena had no conception of where life had taken Nicci, or what she was capable of. Considering how far she had been to the dark side of life, and the journey back, to say nothing of all she had done for them, including all the times she had saved Richard when no other living person had the ability or knowledge to succeed at it, they could have no better friend and ally.

"That's not what I need," Richard insisted. His impatience with them was evident. Kahlan was beginning to suspect that he had something in mind, something bigger than the rest of them realized.

She could clearly see that the sickness was keeping him from explaining himself the way he would have liked and that was adding to his frustration. It was taking most of his effort simply to remain conscious, and more yet to speak even the small amount he had spoken. He wanted them to follow orders without having to explain it to them.

Off behind her, Kahlan could hear the sounds of the first of the Shun-tuk slamming into the defensive line. Men of the First File bellowing in rage as they slaughtered the first of the enemy and drove others back. Some of the half people screamed as they fell. Off in the darkness, Kahlan could hear the sounds of swords and axes slashing into people and the cries of pain as maces broke bones.

"Do as he says," Nicci growled as she seized a fistful of Irena's dress at the shoulder and hauled the woman up and out of the way. "Let Samantha deal with it."

Nicci apparently realized that there was some purpose in Richard's insistence. Nicci knew enough not to question Richard when there was no time for it.

"But, but, I know nothing about fighting," Irena said. She looked on the verge of lapsing into a daze at what was happening.

Kahlan felt a pang of sorrow for the woman. She had, after all, seen the Shun-tuk eat her husband alive before she had been taken away to captivity herself to await the same fate. The idea of being overrun by the same bloodthirsty half people had her nearly paralyzed with fright.

"I understand," Nicci said with surprising compassion to the hesitating Irena. "But we have to help keep the half people back. We need everyone helping, including you. Your daughter's life depends on all of us helping in this."

Irena met Samantha's gaze and then nodded. "I understand."

Zedd urgently leaned in and placed his fingers under his grandson's chin. Richard's eyes squeezed closed in pain. "Hold on, my boy. We'll be back to help you just as soon as there is enough of a break."

Richard inexplicably shook his head, but there was no time to try to wait for him to explain what he meant.

Without pause, Zedd turned and cast out a fist of air that knocked back a man who seemed to come out of nowhere to dive in toward them. Kahlan realized that some of the half people had already breached their defensive line and were in the camp. The soldiers fell on the man when Zedd's blow threw him back into their midst.

Nicci paused, then turned back and went to a knee, quickly placing her fingers to Richard's temples, assessing for herself. "I know," she said in a very low voice to comfort him. "I know. I can feel it. Hold on, Richard. Zedd and I will be back as soon as we can. Hold on. Fight it until then. Samantha will help give you strength."

Kahlan swallowed back the lump in her throat as she watched Nicci and Zedd stand and turn to the sounds of the battle erupting at the edge of camp. She wanted them to help Richard, but she knew it would have to wait. For now, their gifted ability was needed to fight off the attack and to try to keep the area around Richard clear of Shun-tuk. She hoped it was enough to help the men of the First File keep the enemy from taking the camp.

CHAPTER

17

S uddenly alone with Samantha and Richard as battle erupted in the night around them, Kahlan put a hand on Richard's chest, unable to do anything more than to offer him silent comfort.

Kahlan had been in enough combat to know that what was raging around them wasn't a conventional battle. This was different. This was fighting off predators possessed by a maniacal drive to devour them. She knew the nature of these soulless people, and their numbers, and she knew that she was soon going to have to join the fight. She didn't have her powers, but she did have a knife and knew how to use it.

What she really needed was a sword. She had learned to use a sword from her father, but she had become truly adept with such a weapon only under Richard's guidance. Richard was in so many ways a master of the blade, any blade, even a knife or chisel he used to carve the most astoundingly beautiful statues.

Behind her, Zedd sent a thundering bolt of fire slamming into a ghostly figure trying to climb up on the back of a big soldier fighting the enemy to the other side. The soldier was trying to elbow the man off his back, teeth snapping at his neck, while he used his other hand to stab his sword at half people rushing him from the front. The flash sent by Zedd ignited the Shun-tuk in a ball of fiercely glowing flame. He twisted in horrific pain as he sloughed from the soldier's back into a heap on the ground. His entire body aflame, his flesh bubbling, the man rose up and stumbled blindly through the camp as he screamed. With a battle raging all around, no one noticed his desperate screams. They didn't last long.

Unfortunately, many more of the ghostly figures seemed immune to the effects of ordinary Additive Magic, such as the fire Zedd was casting. In the tight confines of the camp, Zedd was unable to unleash wizard's fire. Such a conflagration was not selective enough, and would have engulfed their own men in that lethal, sticky fire that burned with fierce intensity. So, Zedd was forced to use lesser, more targeted forms of fire.

Kahlan saw a number of the Shun-tuk emerge unscathed from those rolling balls of flame sent by the wizard, as if they were untouched by it. One of those men gave Zedd a murderous look, and started for him, only to be run through from behind by a lance. The soldier who had speared the man heaved him off to the side, like a carp speared in a pond, letting the body slide from the weapon so it would be free to use against the next intruder.

Kahlan and Richard had been unconscious and hidden in a wagon at the time, but it must have been very much like this before, at the first battle, when they had all been captured. Without Zedd and Nicci being able to bring the power of magic to bear effectively, the sheer numbers of Shun-tuk had been too much and they had overrun the men. The appalling number of casualties taken by the Shun-tuk in that attack didn't seem to discourage them in the least. Nor did it seem to faze them in this battle, either.

After hearing the prisoner, Kahlan now understood why. Without souls, without the higher reasoning ability that having a soul implied, these people had no empathy for their own who were injured or killed. Even though they hunted in packs, they didn't actually care about one another, the way these soldiers did. Men in battle fought to protect their friends as much as they fought to defeat the enemy. They cared about their fellow soldiers.

Each half person that was attacking only cared about getting a soul for themselves. What happened to others of their kind made no real difference to them. If one of their fellow Shun-tuk fell to a blade, it meant that they were more likely to be able to sink their teeth into a person with a soul. It was a "more for me" mentality.

Nicci cast out a crackling bolt of sizzling black lightning, like a whip. It cut a whitewashed figure in two. The suddenly exposed cluster of organs and intestines spilled out across the granite ledge. Another Shun-tuk right behind slipped on them and fell, only to have a soldier drive a sword down through him.

As Nicci sent the same kind of power crackling toward another Shun-tuk, he casually blocked it with a hand, diverting it away from himself as if it were a petty annoyance. It was clear to Kahlan that some of the Shun-tuk had occult powers that could somehow smother or deflect the power of the gift. It was similar to the way the pristinely ungifted were not affected directly by magic. The Shun-tuk used their ability to protect themselves, and occasionally others, only because they could help bring down the big soldiers. It was likely that these were the ones who had the ability to raise the dead.

She realized that what the soldiers, Zedd, and Nicci were doing was in many cases simply culling the weakest. They were unwittingly creating an enemy force of the strongest and most able half people who were mostly immune to the power of the gift. Each Shun-tuk Zedd or Nicci killed with their gift only increased the percentage of Shun-tuk coming after them who couldn't be harmed by magic, making the gifted less and less effective all the time. At some point, they were going to face an enemy nearly invincible to gifted powers.

There was nothing they could do about it, of course, but it added a frightening dimension to the evolving nature of the fight.

The men, as well, fought fiercely to keep the ghostly figures back behind their lines. Wherever the chalky figure of a Shun-tuk made it through and appeared out of the darkness, a soldier of the First File was there, running him through with a sword, cleaving limbs with an axe, or crushing skulls with a mace. Irena shared a look with her daughter and then ran off to help the soldiers.

"Samantha, hurry," Richard said. "We're running out of time. I need you to give me some strength and keep me conscious for a few minutes longer."

Kahlan thought that was more than a puzzling thing to say. He needed to have strength to recover enough to get up and help convince the Shun-tuk that he was back and strong enough to fight them off so that they would withdraw.

She wondered if maybe he was delirious and simply didn't know what he was saying. Maybe he just wanted the pain to stop, if even for a few minutes.

Kahlan hoped the young woman could handle it. She was suspicious, though, that Richard had something more in mind. She especially wondered what he meant about keeping him conscious for a few minutes longer. Why wouldn't he ask her to give him strength so that he could fight?

Samantha bit her lower lip as she hurriedly scooted around so that her knees were touching the top of Richard's head. She hesitated, then put her palms on his temples.

"Lord Rahl, I, I . . ."

Richard put his left hand over hers. "You can do it, Samantha . . . like before . . ."

"Like before," she muttered. "I wish I remembered what I did before."

"You don't know?" Kahlan asked in alarm as she shifted closer to the young woman.

As Samantha looked up, a tear ran down her cheek. "I don't know . . . I'm not sure."

"Strength . . ." Richard whispered.

"Strength—I know—strength." She removed her hands from his head and squeezed them in fists. "But I don't remember what I was thinking at the time, what I was trying to do."

"Ignore the sickness," he said. "Don't try to heal anything. Just support me with your strength so I can fight it myself."

She gasped with realization. "Of course." Her face brightened. She placed her hands back on the sides of his head. "Strength. I remember now. I just gave you some of my strength so that you could endure it on your own."

Richard tried but did a poor job of smiling as he nodded in her hands.

Kahlan could hear the sounds of the battle raging behind them. Half people cried out as they ran up on razor-sharp steel. Men grunted with the unrelenting effort of hacking at the endless horde rushing in at them. Skulls cracked, bones broke, men yelled orders, the wounded cried out in agony. Ghostly bodies with ghastly wounds lay sprawled here and there.

To the other side of the encampment, Kahlan heard another attack beginning. The half people were trying to divide the camp and make it more difficult to defend.

In the firelight, Kahlan saw one of the pale figures leap over the crowded front line of men of the First File. He didn't last long, but he was followed by another, and then another. The camp was being overrun. She saw men dragged to ground under the weight of chalky figures as other soldiers chopped at arms and heads, frantically working to get the Shun-tuk off them.

Suddenly, out of the corner of her eye Kahlan saw one of the Shun-tuk leap over the fire, racing right at them. There was no one close enough to stop him in time.

Out of reflex honed by years of training and combat, Kahlan pulled her knife as she sprang up, spun, and with a powerful backhanded swing slammed the knife square into the center of the man's bare chest. The big Shun-tuk, his face covered in the caked and cracked white paste, stopped dead in his tracks, the knife buried up to the hilt right through the center of his breastbone.

Samantha stared, frozen, her eyes wide.

The blade Kahlan carried had been honed to a razor edge by Richard, and it was easily long enough to go all the way through a man's heart. It clearly had.

Kahlan hadn't even really felt any resistance. A knife of that weight, that sharp, and with that much speed behind it was virtually unstoppable. As the man's eyes rolled back in his head and his legs buckled, Kahlan yanked her blade free. She kept it in her fist where it would be handy if needed again. She was sure that it would be.

"Samantha, help him, please," Kahlan said.

Samantha swallowed and bent back over Richard.

W e don't have much time," Richard whispered.

"I'm trying." Samantha pushed some of her mass of black hair back out of the way as she bent lower over him. "There's just so much noise and distraction. . . ."

Kahlan knew that it had to be hard for a sorceress as young and inexperienced as Samantha to concentrate on finding that calm center in order to use her gift. It took concentrated effort in the best of times. Now there was a battle raging all around her and she was frightened. But it was what it was and if she didn't do something, Richard was going to be lost to them for the fight, and if that happened then they would all soon be dead.

In this, as in so many things, the difficulty didn't really matter, only the results counted.

For just an instant, Kahlan had a flash of the memory of what the prisoner had told them, that Sulachan had dark ones waiting for her and Richard in the underworld to drag them down into eternal darkness and torment.

Banishing the memory, Kahlan leaned close, and whispered in Samantha's ear. "There's no one else but you and Richard. Ignore everything else. None of it matters. You are the one in control of this. You alone command your own quiet center. You command your power. You alone command what you do with your gift. No one can take that from you but you."

Samantha looked up at Kahlan with the oddest expression, as if to say she didn't know that anyone else would understand about using the gift. Kahlan knew a great deal about finding that quiet place inside, even in the middle of a raging battle, even on the brink of death, and still releasing her power.

Except that now they were in the middle of a raging battle and on the brink of death, and she could not reach that power.

Samantha's eyes closed in concentration as her head bowed again over Richard's.

Richard's eyes were closed as well, not in concentration but in pain.

Kahlan took up one of his hands and held it to her heart. "Richard," she whispered, "I love you."

He smiled through the pain. Looking like he wanted to answer, to say he loved her, but he couldn't. She didn't need to hear it though. She knew.

Kahlan could see Samantha's fingers trembling as they held Richard's head. She was afraid. Afraid of failing, afraid of the Shun-tuk coming for them all, afraid of the responsibility resting on her shoulders.

"Use anger," Richard whispered to her before his hand went slack and he once again slipped into unconsciousness.

His words seemed to spark some memory in her. "Anger . . . of course."

Almost immediately, through the hand she held, Kahlan could feel the warmth of Samantha's gift flowing into him, finding its way through the darkness and pain that was overwhelming him. Kahlan hoped that it could give him the strength to force the darkness back.

She could feel a bit of the tension return to his hand. He took a deeper breath as he again came aware.

He said one word to Kahlan.

"Sword."

She stared for a moment, and then she understood. She lifted his right hand and pulled it over, placing it over the hilt of his sword. He was only partially conscious and didn't seem to have enough strength to grip it, so she pressed his fingers around the hilt for him.

When his fingers formed around the hilt, gripping it, she could see that something changed in him. He drew an even deeper breath.

When his eyes opened, they were filled with the magic from the sword, its power feeding strength into him.

Richard was the true Seeker, and the sword was bonded to him in every way. It responded to his touch in a way it responded to no other; it recognized its master.

"There is no time to lose," Richard said. "We have to act quickly. Where's the commander?"

Kahlan frowned and leaned in a little. "No time to lose? What do you mean?"

"Fister. Where's Commander Fister?" The anger of the sword was now clearly powering his voice. "I need him."

Kahlan didn't know what Richard could be thinking, or if he really was thinking. It was possible that in the semiconscious state he was in, drifting in and out of comprehension of what was going on around him, he was having some kind of dream or delusion and it was purely the anger from the sword enabling him to voice those delusions.

Rather than question him, Kahlan turned to the scene of the fighting. She saw the big man not far away.

"Commander! Commander! We need you!"

When he heard Kahlan calling for him, he turned from angrily hacking a Shun-tuk to pieces. Almost immediately another half person rammed a shoulder into the commander's side, attempting to tackle him and take him down. The crusty, chalky figure might as well have tried to topple an oak tree. The big commander casually put a headlock on the man and twisted. Kahlan heard tendons pop and bone crack. Commander Fister let the limp form drop in a heap. On his way toward Kahlan, without pause, he smashed the heavy pommel of his sword into the face of another Shun-tuk racing in toward him.

When there was a heavy clash at the perimeter defenses, the struggle of holding the weight of the enemy back allowed others the opportunity to slip by. It was not a planned, coordinated tactic, but rather individuals seeing an opening created by others and taking advantage of the opportunity.

All of the half people were ultimately out after souls for themselves, not dedicated to winning battles. In a way, that made them easier to fight, because they didn't coordinate their attacks or make skillful, strategic moves, but at the same time it made them as unpredictable as a cloud of blood flies. They randomly came in from every direction, each interested only in biting and getting at your blood.

Kahlan saw the ghostly figures of Shun-tuk stalking through the camp, trying to stay hidden in the shadows as they hunted for an opportunity to catch a soldier unaware. Whenever they were spotted by soldiers of the First File they were swiftly cut to pieces, but the fact that they were getting into the camp at all was a very bad sign. You never wanted to let an enemy flank you and get in behind to attack from the rear while you fought the enemy in front.

Commander Fister raced in close and went to one knee beside Richard, across from Kahlan. With the help of the power from his hand on the sword, Richard sat partway up, propping himself on his other elbow, and seized the edge of the commander's leather armor chest plate to pull him closer.

"Listen to me, this is what they have been waiting for—for the sickness to weaken me and put me down. They have been waiting for this opportunity to attack. Without me helping, they are going to overrun us like they did to you before."

"No, Lord Rahl, I won't let—"

"You weren't able to stop them before, when you were captured, were you?"

The commander grudgingly shook his head.

"You have fewer men this time," Richard said. "A great many were lost in that battle, and more yet while you were being held captive. The numbers you started with have dwindled dangerously low. We couldn't fight them off before with all the men, so how do you expect that we will be able to fight them off this time, using the same tactics, but with even fewer men?

"We will lose such a fight—that's why they are pressing us into it. They are making the rules and we are obliging them. They waited until I was weak and down, and then they attacked the rest of you. That's their way: simple, brutal, and effective.

"We have to change the rules or we are going to lose."

Commander Fister shared a look with Kahlan and then looked back at Richard. "I understand what you're saying, Lord Rahl, and I've had the same worry, but I don't know what we can do about it. We fight or we die. That's the only way for us to survive—fight or die. There is no way to change that rule."

Richard was shaking his head. "They're fixated on me. We need to use that against them."

The commander wiped the sweat from his brow with the back of his hand holding a bloody sword. He stole a worried look over at the battle before once again looking back at Richard.

"I'm sorry, Lord Rahl, but I don't follow."

Kahlan thought that it was more like he didn't want to follow. He wanted to get back to the battle. His blood was up for the fight, and he was thinking with that anger.

"What do they want?" Richard asked through gritted teeth, both from the pain and from the rage of the sword.

Samantha tried her best to keep her hands pressed to the sides of his head, but she was not having a great deal of success. It was the magic of the sword, mostly, added to what she had started, that was powering Richard at the moment.

"What do they want?" The commander glanced back over his shoulder, quickly appraising the battle, then heaved an unhappy sigh. "Lord Rahl, they want to kill us, that's what they want. They want to bloody kill us all."

Richard shook his head insistently. "No—yes, that too—but that's not the point. You heard the prisoner. They sense my spirit. They know when the life force in me weakens, when I start going unconscious. They know when I am drifting closer to that pull of death. That's why they attacked now—because they knew I was down."

"So?"

"So, that's what they want, what they are using, what they are counting on and waiting for. That's their strategy. It's no more complex than that. Wait until the prey is weakest and then attack. We need to use that to lay a trap."

The big commander slicked a hand back over his closely cropped hair as he let out a sigh. "Seems to me, Lord Rahl, that it's us that the mouse caught in the trap—especially you."

"You have it backward. I'm not the mouse; I'm the bait."

CHAPTER

19

Commander Fister's brows drew together as he put an elbow on his bent knee and leaned closer.

"What?"

"I'm the bait."

"Well, yes, we know that they want you. But we're holding most of them back. Our lines will hold."

"I don't want them to hold."

The man was confused, frustrated, but most of all alarmed by what he was hearing. "Lord Rahl, I think you had better let Samantha, here, heal you as best she can, let your head clear, and then we can talk. Right now I need to get back to my men."

As the man started to stand to rejoin the battle, Richard lifted his sword a few inches from the scabbard. Commander Fister could not help but notice. He paused. Richard didn't look to have the strength to pull it the rest of the way. He sank back a little as he looked up at Kahlan.

"Help me draw it."

Kahlan was not liking the sounds of his plan and she hadn't even heard it yet, but she did as he asked of her. She suspected that he was counting on the sword, once it was out of its scabbard, inundating him with the full force of its power to give him strength. Kahlan thought that maybe when he had his sword out and finally had that strength, he would recognize the dire circumstances of the battle. Then maybe he would be able to think straight and see that the commander was doing all he could—the best he could—in a very difficult situation, and Richard was needed in that fight.

As Kahlan glanced around at the furious battle raging mostly at the edge of their camp, she saw that there were also fights going on in some places inside their ranks. She wondered if maybe Richard wanted his sword out in order to join the fight. The men at the lines were hacking furiously at the Shun-tuk rushing in at them. Fresh enemy forces were continually pouring in. Such effort was tiring and couldn't go on much longer before exhaustion caused the men to begin to lose their effectiveness.

Zedd was casting some sort of conjuring but it didn't look to be halting a lot of the enemy. He stopped and knelt at wounded men and helped where he could. Nicci was doing the same. Kahlan could see at least half a dozen of their men down.

She didn't see Irena. There were any number of places she could be where Kahlan wouldn't see her. She hoped that Samantha's mother hadn't been taken by the Shun-tuk. Samantha had endured that once before and now that Irena was back with them, it had drawn Samantha even closer to her mother.

Kahlan closed both of her hands tightly around

Richard's big hand on the hilt as she helped him pull. As the Sword of Truth finally slid all the way out, the blade sent its clear, distinctive ring of steel out across the scene of the battle. The sound of it caused a few men of the First File to pause for just an instant and look over. She knew that seeing Richard with his sword out rallied their spirits.

Kahlan could see that having it fully drawn, his hand now firmly on the hilt, had ignited a storm of rage from the sword. She could see in his gray eyes that the power of that ancient weapon was now providing him needed strength. Still, the power of the sword was the twin to his, and that meant that it might have been providing strength, but it needed Richard's strength to fully complete it, and at the moment Richard didn't have sufficient strength of his own.

When Richard held his other arm out, Commander Fister gripped it and helped pull him to his feet. Samantha tried her best to maintain contact with him, but to her frustration once he was standing she could no longer keep her hands on his head.

With the sword in his fist, Richard didn't need Samantha's help. The sword's power was far stronger than any strength she could give him, but she stayed close just in case.

Once up, Richard quickly scanned the battle scene. "We can't keep fighting by their rules or we are soon going to lose."

"It's not like we have a lot of choice," Commander Fister said, his exasperation barely contained.

"Again, you are thinking of the problem, not the solution," Richard told him, absently, as he carefully looked around, studying everything.

Jake Fister assessed Richard's face for a brief

moment, as if trying to tell if he really was thinking clearly or maybe still suffering from a delusional fog from the sickness.

Kahlan knew better. She knew the way Richard thought. While she didn't know what he had in mind in this instance, she knew that he was not delusional— he was thinking like the Richard she knew so well. In a way, it heartened her. While everyone else was focused on the problem they faced, he was thinking of a solution.

Richard looked off to the side, studying the darkness. Kahlan didn't know what he was looking at, but she knew that he could see better in the dark than she could. Richard could see at night almost as well as a cat.

"Casualties are irrelevant to them," he said, "especially since those with occult powers are soon going to start reviving the dead. The more we kill, the bigger the supply of dead they have at hand to turn into those walking dead. Those unholy monsters are a lot harder to take down than the Shun-tuk. Our men are tiring. Matters can only get worse from this point on."

"These are men of the First File," the commander insisted. "They will fight with all their heart and soul."

"The Shun-tuk don't fight very well, though, or use weapons," Richard added, mostly to himself, not seeming to really notice what the commander had said.

"Our men are the best," the commander again insisted. "You know that, Lord Rahl. They are the best fighters there are. The Shun-tuk aren't quality fighters."

Richard finally refocused his attention on the commander. "Yes, but vast numbers have a quality all their own. They don't care how many people they lose. We do."

The commander scratched an eyebrow, deciding against further argument. "You have something in mind, Lord Rahl?"

Richard gestured with his sword. "This camp, set up the way it is with the cliff blocking the back side, is not the worst place to fight from. But it's not the best, either, especially in this case because it works to their advantage. They can surround us from several directions and keep us pinned down. We can't move easily, so they can keep us here and keep coming at us to wear us down.

"We need to draw them into terrain that is to our advantage, not theirs. We need to flank them and get some men behind them."

Commander Fister scanned the battle, looking around at the open area and the dark forest beyond where Shun-tuk kept running in from every direction.

"But how can we hope to do that? We're out in the open. They're scattered all throughout the woods. We have no idea where all of them are. How are we supposed to flank them?"

"By changing the battle. We need to be able to come at them from both sides at once and crush them."

The commander lifted an eyebrow. "Lord Rahl, what you say makes sense—theoretically—but in this case it would be like trying to flank ants. They're all over the place out there."

"Again, you're telling me the problem. I already know the problem." Richard pointed with his sword to the rock wall backing the encampment. "This cliff face, where it goes around over there, is formed by the side of a gorge coming down from higher ground.

That ravine turns out here, in this cliff face, as the terrain broadens into this lower, flatter ground. Look there. See that brook over to the side, where we've been getting water? That brook comes down through that ravine."

"What of it?" the commander asked.

"We need to draw the Shun-tuk in there. The terrain climbs from here and the sides are steep, so the Shun-tuk wouldn't be able to spread out. If they want to come after us, their only choice will be to follow us up the gorge. There is no practical way to go around and catch us. If they tried that, we'd be able to get away from them."

The commander rubbed his chin as he peered off at the gorge.

"Before we go in there," Richard said, "we need to station men to either side. They can slip in over there at the edge of the camp. We need to have men climb up and hide on the slopes to lie in wait for the enemy to pass by. Meanwhile, with the other half of the men, we will run up the gorge, as if we're panicked and running for our lives to try to escape them."

"What if they don't follow us?"

"They're predators. Predators chase running prey. It's one of a predator's strongest instincts."

Commander Fister was listening with more interest. "Then what? A hammer and anvil?"

Richard nodded. "Once we get them to follow half of us into that narrow gorge, the men hiding up on the sides will descend, close off the back door, and come at them from the rear, closing the trap. At that point, we turn back on them. We move in from both ends and crush them in that narrow pass. They won't be able to escape or hide."

Kahlan and Commander Fister peered off at the

steep hillsides where the brook went around the cliff face to then go back up into the more rugged landscape. Kahlan couldn't see it very well, and couldn't make out much of the lay of the land, but she trusted Richard's word in such things. He had spent his life in the woods and he knew what he was talking about.

The commander rubbed his chin as he looked back at Richard.

"How are we supposed to get them to follow us into a narrow defile like that? They may not fight well, and they may be predators, as you say, but they're not stupid."

"Believe me, they will follow us," Richard assured him.

Kahlan knew that Richard already had some kind of plan in mind, and she knew she wasn't going to like it.

Not one bit.

CHAPTER

20

The commander didn't back down and defer to the Lord Rahl, the way some subordinates would have. Richard expected his men to use their heads and not just blindly agree with what he said. Throughout the long war he had instilled that principle in all the officers.

Tyranny had long reigned in D'Hara. Such men ruled with absolute authority and did not tolerate dissenting views. Richard expected people to use their heads and speak up if they thought it was important enough. He valued the experience and knowledge of others. What they could contribute added to, rather than detracted from, a leader's ability to rule. Because of that, there had been times when Richard had been persuaded by reasoned arguments and changed his mind.

"Lord Rahl," Commander Fister said, "they may be predators and all, and as such they may very well have a strong instinct to chase, but the prisoner told us that these Shun-tuk are spirit trackers. They sense spirits—souls—and can follow them. They will be able to sense the men they are to follow into the gorge well enough, but they are also going to be able to sense the men we have hiding to either side."

"Yes," Richard said, "but the group they are chasing will be bunched together and running from them. The men hiding on the slopes to the side will be scattered and stationary. That bunching together of the group they are chasing, that accumulation of souls, will create a much stronger aura for them to follow than scattered individuals.

"Think of it this way. If you are about to go into battle, and you see a large force of the enemy advancing along a tree line, coming toward your position, are you going to be more focused on that main battle formation or on some individuals you spot randomly located out in the fields?"

"I'd pay attention to both, and wonder what the ones out in the field were up to." Commander Fister tapped the hilt of his sword with a thumb. "But I see your point. In the end, the main group is going to have to be the focus of my attention. Even so, I don't see that they will abandon their caution just because we want to draw them into a trap."

Richard smiled. "They will if we make it irresistible."

The commander shared a look with Kahlan before looking suspiciously at Richard. He had aired his view, and if Richard rejected it, he wasn't sure what else to say. He looked like he was hoping that Kahlan would.

Kahlan thought that Richard's sickness was wearing him down and affecting his judgment. So, she stepped in to support Commander Fister's view.

"Richard, they may be primitive, but they are also skilled predators. They may indeed be eager to chase the main group, but decide instead to pick off those lone individuals, first, choosing to go after the easy souls and at the same time reduce our numbers. After all, that's what they did with Ned. They attacked a lone man so they could get at our horses. They didn't directly attack us first. First they went after softer prey. They may choose to do that this time as well."

"Not if they are going after the one thing they want more than anything else but events are moving rapidly and it may slip away from them. Not if they think they finally have us on the run and vulnerable and they have no time to lose."

"Vulnerable," Fister said, suspiciously.

"Yes."

The big D'Haran officer frowned. "And what is this key to their victory that they will have within their grasp if they move swiftly enough?"

"Me, unconscious."

Commander Fister blinked. "You. Unconscious."

Richard nodded. "That's right."

Kahlan ran the fingers of both hands back into her hair, holding her head in barely contained exasperation. "Richard, that's just plain crazy. I don't even know where to begin with how crazy it is."

She could see the anger—the fighting anger—of the sword in his eyes, as if she were looking into the depths of his soul.

"You heard the prisoner," he said. "They can sense when I'm failing and especially when I'm unconscious. He said that they are waiting for me to falter and that was when they would take us. That is their strategy—to wait until I'm unconscious and then attack us. It's a predator's thinking, stalking and waiting until the prey is vulnerable. With me unconscious that's when we are the most vulnerable. That's what they are waiting for and that's when they will be after us."

"But you're awake now," Kahlan said. "You can keep the sword out."

"That's the tough part of the plan."

Richard slid the sword back into its scabbard.

Kahlan gaped at him. "What are you doing?"

"Without the sword's power, I will be unconscious within a few minutes. I can feel the poison waiting to take me into that darkness. It's stronger this time. It's growing in both of us."

The commander was visibly alarmed. "Lord Rahl, that's too risky. We can't—"

"Listen to me," Richard said, his voice still commanding even though it was swiftly beginning to lose its power now that he'd slid the sword home to extinguish its magic. "There isn't much time. You need to listen to me."

When Kahlan and the commander reluctantly fell silent, Richard went on. "The way it stands right now, we're going to lose this battle fighting it this way. Kahlan and I are getting worse all the time. We are running out of time, and each time the poison overtakes us it is stronger. Death is not far off.

"We must act while we still can."

Richard swept an arm out at the defensive line of the desperate battle. "If we keep fighting them like this, by their rules, we will lose. We have to change the rules."

Commander Fister hooked a thumb behind his belt. "All right, what's your plan, then? What do you propose to do?"

"Get half the men positioned up on the sides of the

gorge. Do it now. It won't be long until I'm unconscious. The Shun-tuk will be able to sense when that happens.

"We have one horse left. Once I'm unconscious, lay me over the horse and secure my body. With the remaining half of the men, run up through the chasm with the horse carrying me. Run like you're trying to get away.

"The Shun-tuk will think our men are panicking. Run up the gorge like you're taking me and fleeing for your lives. Leave the rest of the men behind, hiding up on the hillsides out of sight until the Shun-tuk pass. Even if they sense them, they will likely think they are some of the men breaking ranks and running away to hide and save themselves. They will sense that the main group of souls has me with them and they are running away up the gorge, trying to escape.

"If you do a convincing job of running, like you're trying to get the incapacitated, unconscious Lord Rahl away from mortal danger, they will chase us. They behave like any predator. Once predators start chasing prey, they have tunnel vision centered on their prey. They will be focused on the prey and ignore everything else.

"If I'm unconscious, they will come after me.

"Then, once they come after us up into the ravine and the men on the slopes shut the back door to that narrow space, have Zedd lay down wizard's fire back down the gorge. It will be much more devastating in such a confined space.

"Some of them, though, are immune to such magic, so that's when you have the men turn and come in from both ends. In that narrow gorge you can cut the rest of those with occult power to pieces. They may not be vulnerable to magic, but they bleed and die just like anyone else."

"All right, Lord Rahl, but what if you're wrong and they do sense the men hiding there waiting to spring the trap? Then what?"

Richard was shaking his head. "No. This is the dance with death. You give the enemy the one thing he wants more than anything else, dangle it in front of him, and he will abandon his sense of caution to go after it. I am that one thing, the thing that their spirit king sent them for. Just as importantly, if they think they can eliminate me, that will give them the chance to feed on the rest of you.

"They know that if they can get me when I'm incapacitated then they can also get the rest of you. If they see that chance to have it all running away from them, they must chase it down."

"So you really plan to be unconscious during this battle?" Commander Fister asked, incredulous.

Kahlan was beside herself. "If you're unconscious, you will be defenseless."

"Yes, exactly. I have to be unconscious for them to sense that I am vulnerable. It has to be that way if we want it to work. Samantha and the sword helped give me just enough strength to be able to stay conscious long enough to give you the plan. But I can feel that inner darkness overcoming me as I speak. This time, you have to let it take me.

"You have to let me go for now, then throw me over the horse and get moving. The rest of you will have to carry out the plan without me."

"But—" the commander started.

The power of the sword that had been so evident in his gray eyes was gone. His eyes were becoming glassy. Kahlan recognized the sickness coming over him. She was on the verge of panic. On the one hand she knew that Richard was right and that he was giving them the best chance of survival.

But on the other hand . . . it was Richard who would be unconscious, completely helpless, and most at risk. And that was not even taking into account him flirting with the call of death that would be trying to use this opportunity to finally take him.

"Once we get through the gorge, after you cut them to ribbons, then have Zedd and Nicci do their best to revive me," Richard told them.

Kahlan didn't think he sounded sure that they would be able to, this time. If they survived the battle. If Richard wasn't captured. Even if everything went as he planned, it might by then be too late for Zedd and Nicci to revive him. He could die.

"Lord Rahl, I can give you strength now," Samantha said, clearly on the verge of panic. He had always been her strength and she couldn't stand the thought of losing that rock in her world.

"Not this time," he told her. "This is our only chance."

Kahlan could feel tears welling up in her eyes. "Richard . . ."

He gripped her arm as he sank to one knee. "Don't waste this chance. Do as I say. Do it now. I'm counting on you."

Richard pulled Kahlan closer. "Once they have me secured over the horse, then take my sword. You are going to need it." He managed to give her a wink. "Just don't run me through with it this time."

Commander Fister caught Richard as he fell forward and held him upright on his knees. Richard's head hung. He was already unconscious.

The commander looked over at Kahlan. "Did anyone ever tell you that you married a crazy man?"

Kahlan couldn't manage to smile in order to go along with his grim attempt to lighten the terror of the situation.

"He's not crazy. He has just given us all our only chance."

The commander hoisted Richard's limp body up, pulling one arm around his broad shoulders.

"Samantha," Kahlan said as she gestured, "get one of those men right there to bring the horse immediately. Tell the other two to help the commander with Richard."

As Samantha raced off to get help, Kahlan turned to Commander Fister. "You had better protect him and keep him alive until Zedd and Nicci can heal him. I'm counting on you."

The commander nodded. "You have my oath, Mother Confessor. No one will get near him as long as I'm alive."

Kahlan held back her tears. There was too much to do to give in to emotion.

"One condition in all of this, Mother Confessor," the commander said. "I'm not telling Zedd and Nicci about this plan. You have to tell them. If I tell them, they will fry me up and have me for breakfast."

That time Kahlan finally managed a brief smile as she saw men running toward them. One of them tugged the horse along behind.

21

Two of the soldiers helped Commander Fister lift Richard's limp body over the back of the horse while the other held the reins. Seeing Richard in this condition was sobering for the men. This was the Lord Rahl who had believed in them, liberated them from servitude to Darken Rahl, and then led them through the long and terrible war with the Old World. He had survived countless dangers and done the impossible—brought peace and prosperity they had never imagined possible in their lifetimes. Now, he was unconscious and the situation looked grim.

After getting Richard laid over the back of the mare, the men helped the commander quickly lash him down with ropes. They didn't pause to ask questions. The men of the First File stayed focused and did their job regardless of what was going on.

Commander Fister seized one of the men, Sergeant

Remkin, by the shoulder. "How many men do we have left?"

"Before the battle we had close to a hundred. I know that I've seen some go down, though I don't know how many we've lost, but there has to be something less than that by now."

"All right. Get three dozen men together as fast as you can." The commander pointed with his sword. "We're going to take Lord Rahl and the Mother Confessor around the side of the cliff over there and up the gorge. Divide the men. You take half up on the slope to the far side. Have them spread out and hide on the hillside." He gestured to the other man. "Jenkins, you take the other half onto the left slope and do the same—spread out and hide."

The sergeant glanced back in the darkness to appraise the barely visible pass. "Consider it done, Commander. Then what?"

"Once the two of you have your men in place, the rest of us will head up the gorge with Lord Rahl. We want the Shun-tuk to chase us, thinking this is their chance to finish us off. Once we get far enough in that the Shun-tuk are in the gorge and coming after us, Remkin, you use a mockingbird signal and bring the men on both sides down to shut the back door. Once we have them trapped in the ravine, stay well back at first because Zedd is going to lay down an inferno of wizard's fire to incinerate as many as we can."

"Then hammer them on your anvil?" Sergeant Remkin guessed.

"Right," the commander said with a firm nod. "As you select men along the line, spread the word and let the others know the plan. Don't leave undefended gaps when you pick out your men. Now get going and get your men in place. We're having enough trouble holding them back the way it is. Once you take those men and leave, we won't be able to hold the line for long before the rest of us get overrun, so you won't have much time."

The sergeant tapped a fist to his heart in salute. He turned to Jenkins and the man who had brought the horse. "Let's go. Since we're going to be climbing the slopes in the dark, be sure to pick men you know were raised in rugged country. We need ones who know how to move quickly in mountainous terrain."

"When you pick men from the line," the commander reminded them again, "have the remaining men pull back a little to shrink the front perimeter in order to close the gaps so we don't make a weak spot for the enemy to break through."

Kahlan could hear the worry in his voice. She knew that once the men left, the rest of them wouldn't be able to hold the line for long.

"Jenkins," the sergeant said, "just pick your men and get moving. You can explain the plan on the way up onto the right slope. I'll do the same."

As the two men raced off into the darkness, Kahlan turned to Samantha. "Find your mother. Tell her we're leaving and we need her with us to help protect Richard. Hurry, now."

Samantha nodded and ran off across the camp, dodging around big soldiers, to look for her mother.

Several Shun-tuk suddenly leaped out of the night onto Commander Fister, trying to pin his sword arm to his body. Even as they grappled to get him under control, both opened their mouths, trying to bite into him.

Kahlan spun back toward Richard lying over the horse to get his sword. She turned just in time to see a Shun-tuk racing right toward her out of the darkness. A thick layer of cracked white coating made his face look like an old clay pot about to fall apart.

As his arm stretched out to grab her, she snatched the palm of his hand and used his forward momentum to bend it down as hard as she could. He stumbled, sinking forward, helpless from the excruciatingly painful pressure on his wrist. She felt the joint pop. As he cried out in pain, Kahlan rammed the elbow of her other arm into the center of his face. She could not only hear bones in the center of his face break, she could feel them shatter.

As the man fell, curled into a ball on the ground, using his good hand to cover the blood gushing from his face, Kahlan saw another Shun-tuk racing in. His eyes were wild, his mouth opened wide, teeth bared, intent on taking her down with a bite to her neck.

Without pause, Kahlan yanked Richard's sword out of the scabbard, spun, and drove the blade right through his open mouth as he ran up on her. It came out at the base of his skull, severing his brain stem.

He dropped so fast with a boneless dead weight that she just managed to yank the sword free before it was ripped from her hand. She swung around, ready for any threat from the other side.

As she came around, sword-first, Commander Fister was right there, sword in hand, about to come to her aid. He skidded to a halt just out of reach of her sword's point.

He put both hands up. "Easy. It's me." Just behind him lay the crumpled forms of the two who had tried to tackle him. It was obvious that their attempt to get his sword arm under control had failed. One had taken a deep wound across the middle of his face, the other across his ribs deep enough to almost cut him in two.

Kahlan knew, of course, how holding the sword liberated its rage, but remembering it was entirely different from once again experiencing it. The power of it, the fury of it, the thundering rage of it raced through her unchecked. She could feel herself panting with that rage, feel her jaw clench with her own anger that had been liberated by the weapon.

It was like grabbing hold of a bolt of lightning and having it at her command.

Now that she had given it a taste of blood, it demanded more.

Kahlan spotted Sergeant Remkin and Jenkins, each with a group of men, racing across the encampment toward the gorge. It would take them little time to climb up into position and out of sight. She knew that with many of the men now gone, their defensive lines were dangerously fragile. The rage from the sword wanted her to join the men at the line, cutting down the Shun-tuk trying to break through.

But she knew better than to give in to that need. Protecting Richard was her first priority and that meant following his plan, but they were going to have to move quickly before they were overrun, and then they had to make a coordinated, controlled retreat.

She knew that trying to retreat while under attack was a dangerous maneuver that required discipline in executing the plan, lest it turn into a panicked rout. She had a plan, she just needed to make sure it went right.

Kahlan screamed Zedd's and Nicci's names. When they turned to look, Kahlan waved an arm and used the sword to urge them to rush to her. Before abandoning his ground, Zedd unleashed a wall of fire and choking smoke to cover his retreat. Nicci used a gathering of air to cast a gusting wall of wind off to another side that lifted a torrent of dirt and debris toward the Shun-tuk running in from the darkness of the woods. With the blinding wall of dust and dirt loaded with sticks, branches, dirt, sand, and rocks hurtling at them, to say nothing of a rolling wall of flames, the half people hesitated, cowering and covering their faces with their arms.

Zedd and Nicci used the opening to race toward Kahlan and the commander standing beside the horse with an unconscious Richard laid out over its back.

"Dear spirit!" Zedd cried. "What happened?"

Nicci squatted down to look up at Richard's face. With one hand she held his head and with her other used her thumb to lift an eyelid. "He's in danger of—"

"We all are," Kahlan said, cutting her off. "Leave him for now."

"But—" Zedd started.

"Be quiet, both of you, and listen. There's no time to explain it all."

The commander turned and swiftly beheaded a Shun-tuk as he ran past them intent on jumping a soldier from behind.

"We're listening," Zedd said.

"When Commander Fister gives the command, all the men are going to abandon the line all at once and race to follow behind us." Kahlan pointed with the sword toward the corner of the encampment at the edge of the rock wall where the brook came down through the gorge. "We all need to get up that gorge as fast as we can. All of us. Zedd, hang back and then as our men clear the open area of the encampment and the Shun-tuk pour in behind them, lay down wizard's fire across this entire open area."

"They aren't all touched by ordinary magic," he reminded her.

"I know, but many are, and even for the ones who aren't, it will cause confusion and buy us a head start."

"Head start for what?" Nicci asked.

"They can sense that Richard is unconscious. They will come after him, and us, as we race up the gorge."

Nearly apoplectic, Zedd threw his arms up. "We're using Richard as bait?"

"Yes."

"Whose crazy idea was that!"

"Your grandson's."

Zedd grimaced. "Of course it was."

"As they come across the open area, kill as many as you can with wizard's fire as we head up the gorge, then we need to get the rest of these bloodthirsty half people to chase us. We have men taking up positions along the slopes to either side. Once we get far enough up the gorge, with the Shun-tuk coming after us, those men will close the back door.

"In such a narrow space a small number of men can hold back many times their numbers. While the Shun-tuk are confined, you need to lay wizard's fire down through the narrow chasm and fry every one of them that will burn. Then, our men will come in from both ends at once and cut them to pieces."

"What makes you think—" Zedd began.

"That's the plan Richard laid out. He let himself go unconscious so that they will follow us. What we're doing here is not going to save us. We have to do something else or we are all going to die right here. This is the best chance we have. He put his life at great risk for this to work, for us to have a chance, so I'm not about to listen to any argument. Got it?"

"Got it," Zedd said a little more quietly.

"As soon as we make it up the gorge and after we get things under control," Kahlan said to Nicci, "then you and Zedd can revive Richard."

Kahlan could see that Zedd wanted to say something, but when he saw the look in her eyes, a look filled with the rage of the ancient weapon in her fist, he kept his mouth closed.

Nicci, on the other hand, had to speak. "Some of them have occult powers. We don't even know what they are capable of."

With the sword in her hand and its anger unleashed, the plan no longer felt crazy to her. It felt like a chance to kill the Shun-tuk before the Shun-tuk killed them.

"They can use those powers here as well. Sooner or later, they will. At least when we have them hemmed in up in the gorge they can't scatter. That at least gives us a chance to cut them down. Even those with abilities, gifted or otherwise, will die when we run them through with swords."

"You're right," Nicci said with a sigh. "Let's get to it, then."

Kahlan spotted Samantha running toward them with her mother in tow. She judged that the men would have to be in place on the slopes by now, or soon would be. With her free hand, Kahlan snatched up the reins of the horse near the bit.

"Come on," she said to the people crowded around her, "let's go kill these bastards."

CHAPTER

22

At the far edge of the encampment near the brook, the commander used his thumb and a finger in the corners of his mouth to let out a loud whistle. The rising and falling notes, which all the men recognized, were the signal to begin the retreat.

Without hesitation, the men immediately turned and raced toward the spot where Kahlan and the others waited. Along the way they snatched up what gear they had, slinging packs and supplies over a shoulder.

As the men cleared the open area, the Shun-tuk were caught by surprise at how abruptly the soldiers abandoned the defensive line they had fought so hard to hold. For that brief moment they were confused and didn't know what was happening, what to expect, or exactly how to respond. The swiftness of the surprise gave the men a small head start. It wasn't much, but Kahlan knew that in battle such small win-

dows of opportunity could mean the difference between life and death.

In preparation, Zedd had already formed a liquid
ball of wizard's fire between his outstretched hands.
The sinister flame burned and tumbled and rolled like
a thing alive as it hung in midair between his palms,
hissing and spitting spiraling sparks.

Kahlan could see into the liquid core of the sphere,
as if it were a world unto itself, a transparent, glowing, burning, full moon. This was a relic of ancient
power, most of which had been lost over time. This
was a window into the kind of power that used to
exist in the world—the kind of power that Emperor
Sulachan had once wielded, and now again brought
back to the world of life.

Zedd held the spellbinding sight there between his
palms, a lethal, obedient servant to his wishes, as he
waited for the right moment. The lines and creases
of his weathered face looked calm in the hissing, flickering light of his creation.

He appeared utterly tranquil as he waited to unleash
the contained cataclysm he calmly carried between
his hands.

Kahlan understood that calm. When she was about
to release her power, she, too, went dead calm. All
emotion was alien in that pristine moment where she
alone was in control of such ancient power.

Wizard's fire was legend among most people. It was
so rarely seen, and by so few, that many people dismissed it as an ancient myth, a relic of past times. To
those who believed it was real, especially those few
who had ever actually seen it, wizard's fire was greatly
feared. Most who had seen it saw it in the instant before it killed them.

Kahlan had seen Zedd use wizard's fire a number

of times. It had been a necessity in the war, one of
the few circumstances where there was a purpose for
such violent destruction.

The wizards Kahlan had grown up with had lived
their entire lives without ever once conjuring and unleashing such devastating power. It was likely most
would not even know how.

Zedd knew how.

Kahlan noticed, though, that in the times he had
used it before, Zedd had never seemed this calm. She
had also never seen him hold it so close, like a special, beautiful treasure, for so long. And it was beautiful. It was terrifyingly exquisite.

Usually, he cast it out almost as fast as he could
conjure the rare substance. This time, he was keeping it in place, as if letting it come to know the world
it had just been born into, letting it gather strength.
She noticed, too, that the whorls of colors as it burned
seemed more intense than she remembered.

Zedd used wizard's fire only in the most desperate
of circumstances to save lives. This time, the lives he
was trying to save were not only all of theirs, but that
of the Lord Rahl himself, who just happened to be
his grandson.

Knowing what was coming, Kahlan snatched up
a torn strip of a tunic and covered the horse's eyes
to keep it relatively calm. Warhorses were used to
battle and trained for explosions and fire, but she
suspected that this one was not.

At the far side of the encampment, along what had
formerly been the defensive front line protecting their
encampment, the Shun-tuk rapidly realized that those
defenses were abruptly gone and, much like a dam
bursting, they flooded into the void of the open ledge.

They had clear ground to cover and prey they wanted. Now, there was nothing to stop them.

As the last of the soldiers of the First File finally raced past the old wizard, Zedd flung his arms open. At his command, the tightly contained, turbulent furnace of power expanded in an instant and roared away.

The entire area of the open ledge at the foot of the cliff and the towering spruce and pine trees of the forest around them lit under the blinding intensity of yellow-orange flames. Night seemed to turn to day.

The tumbling, liquid inferno raced across the abandoned encampment, shrieking with terrifying menace. The sound it made was so deafening that it caused the Shun-tuk to hesitate. They hunched down, cringing as they covered their ears. Wizard's fire always howled, but this shrieked with painful intensity.

The tumbling globe of liquid flame remained airborne, passing just above the granite ledge where hundreds of dead Shun-tuk lay sprawled. It lit the entire bloody scene, brightly illuminating the whitewashed dead in such stark relief as it passed above them that it made them look supernatural, like a graveyard of dead spirits.

Kahlan spotted men of the First File lying dead among the Shun-tuk. They were beyond help, now. At least their remains would be turned to ash rather than be eaten by the half people. Dead was dead, and it couldn't matter to them any longer, but it mattered to Kahlan. Being incinerated somehow seemed better than having the unholy half dead feeding on the remains.

The wizard's fire, a tumbling, burning fury, hit the ground with such thundering force it shook the trees.

Pine needles rained down, igniting as they fell, looking like burning rain. As it crashed down, the dense, blazing, molten orb burst apart, splashing the brightly burning liquid fire out across the open ground. Like a towering rogue wave it swamped the advancing horde of Shun-tuk. It actually lifted many of them up into the air, like so much flotsam, and carried them along in the flow as they were incinerated.

Wizard's fire burned with unparalleled intensity. It was sticky, and once it was stuck fast, not only could you not get it off, you couldn't extinguish the flame. It burned until its power was spent. So much as a drop of it stuck to a leg could burn down to the bone. To say that it was excruciatingly painful did not begin to describe the horror of it. Those touched by even a speck of it could think of nothing but getting it off.

Kahlan had seen men in battle splashed with small amounts of it on an arm or hand. They would use their own sword to hack off the limbs to prevent the wizard's fire from climbing up onto the rest of them. Others, in their mad panic to escape it, would accidentally run into pools of it.

In the blindingly intense light of the exploding sea of fire, Kahlan could see silhouetted Shun-tuk reduced momentarily to little more than black skeletons. In the next instant, even that much vaporized to nothing.

For the most part, as they ran they tried not to look back because of the intensity of the light. It was so blindingly bright that, like the rest of them, Kahlan not only had to turn her face from it, she also squinted against the painful illumination. The wave of heat it gave off felt like it might ignite her hair and melt her skin.

The fire made the horse carrying Richard more

than a little skittish. Kahlan kept a firm hold on the reins up near the bit to prevent it from bolting. She was thankful that she had covered the horse's eyes.

She had no idea of how many of the Shun-tuk were consumed in the burning sea of wizard's fire, or how many might not be harmed by it at all. She had trouble imagining anyone who would not be harmed by it. She did know that now that it had been unleashed, there was no time to worry about it.

"Let's go," she said as she took hold of Zedd's sleeve.

His eyes looked vacant. He had put everything he had into the creation of the conflagration. He had been determined to make sure he used every ounce of effort he could muster to protect them, to protect his unconscious grandson.

Zedd blinked. "What?"

"You did good, Zedd. You have given us a chance." Kahlan again tugged his sleeve. "Now come on—we have to go."

The old wizard looked more than exhausted, but he kept up with Kahlan as she started pulling the horse ahead into the gorge. The horse was only too glad to be led away from the burning nightmare behind them. Kahlan knew that the wizard's fire would continue to burn for quite a while and continue to catch victims in its fiery snare. Those with even a little of it on them would be incapacitated and it would be months before they healed, if ever. Many of those burned would die within hours or days. Yet more, those not vaporized by the intensity of the fire, but who had been close enough to inhale the noxious heat, would die in breathless agony within a short time.

As Kahlan pulled the horse up the dark gorge, Nicci

stepped up beside her. "I've never seen him do that before," she whispered to Kahlan. "I think he put everything he had into it to try to stop even those with occult powers."

Kahlan glanced over at the sorceress. "Do you think it worked?"

"No. But it was a noble effort. I know what such things take to create, and that took more than a lot. I hope he saved some for when we get them farther up into the gorge. When we do, I'll help him with some Subtractive Magic."

The sorceress quickly moved out in front of Kahlan and cast her hand out. A flame floated ahead, gently lifting up through the air, among the pine boughs. It was not fire meant to be destructive, but a small flame meant to show them where they were going and light the ground enough that they wouldn't trip over tree roots and rocks.

Nicci turned to the tightly packed group of men following behind them. "Keep your eyes ahead. They need to adjust to the darkness. Try not to look back because once we get farther in Zedd is going to be laying down more wizard's fire behind us. Within the confines of the gorge it will be even brighter. It will help blind the enemy to the darkness of the trail ahead and slow them down. Don't look back and let it blind you too."

The men following behind nodded that they understood.

Nicci led the way, with Kahlan right behind her. They had to pick their way carefully along the side of the brook, frequently over slick, moss-covered rocks. While Kahlan, in her official capacity as a Confessor, had traveled the countryside her whole life,

Nicci had grown up in cities and until she met Richard had rarely set foot on dirt. Being with Richard for as long as she had been, she had learned how to walk in the woods, which was fortunate because there was no trail up the gorge. They were in uncharted wilderness and had to pick their way as best they could.

Sometimes some of the men had to rush out ahead to hack away at fallen limbs or saplings to clear them out of the way for the horse. Kahlan was especially careful to let the horse pick where it wanted to step. They couldn't afford to have it break a leg.

The small lights Nicci released from time to time revealed rock walls rising up in places. The sheer rock faces were wet with water seeping through the tiniest cracks. Slime grew in long strings that hung down, their tips dripping water. Where there were rocky hillsides, cedar trees grew down close to the brook. In places up higher on those steep hillsides, where they could get a good foothold, towering pines grew. Where it was too rocky or steep for the forest monarchs, smaller trees and shrubs with roots fanning out like claws clung to the rugged hillside.

The terrain at the bottom of the gorge would not be easy to traverse in the daytime. At night it was quite difficult, but not entirely impossible. Picking their way up the ever-rising ground was slow going, though. At least it would be no easier for the Shun-tuk.

With the cliffs and perilously steep hillsides, Kahlan was confident that the Shun-tuk would not be able to get out around them, especially since the fastest route was the one they were taking at the bottom of the gorge where the footing was better. The slopes were far trickier to traverse. Traveling that way would be slower and dangerous. That meant that Richard had been right, and by going this way they would be able to funnel the Shun-tuk into a narrow space.

The trees up ahead suddenly lit with bright yellow light as Zedd, bringing up the rear, unleashed more wizard's fire back at the enemy following them. It lit the way for them.

The jolt of another explosion shook the ground. She could feel the thump from the concussion deep in her chest. Kahlan didn't know how many Shun-tuk it was killing, or how many were getting through. She and everyone else were being careful not to look back and be night-blinded by the intensity of the thunderous blasts.

Nicci raced back to help Zedd. When Kahlan heard the ripping sound, like tearing canvas, and saw the white light on the treetops around them, Kahlan knew that the sorceress was using a mix of Additive and Subtractive Magic on the enemy. It was as violently destructive as wizard's fire, but she doubted that it would affect those with occult abilities any more than did wizard's fire. At least it would be deadly to those without such protection and reduce their numbers.

With the sword in her hand and its attendant rage, she was eager to encounter some of the enemy that got through. Richard's life was in great peril because of these half people. All of their lives were. She had to resist the urge to turn back and fight.

The time was not yet right. It would come soon enough, she knew, and when it did then her sword—Richard's sword—would taste their blood.

CHAPTER

23

From time to time Kahlan glanced back over her shoulder at her unconscious husband draped over the back of the horse. He was helpless and depending on her. She intended not to let him down. She was determined to get them through the danger, get them to relative safety, and especially get them back to the People's Palace so that Zedd and Nicci could remove the poison that was slowly killing them both.

She was sick and tired of not being able to live her life with him, of not being able to be alone with him, of not being able to have a normal conversation with him, of not being able to make love to him, of not being able to love him in the most simple and joyful of ways because they were always desperately fighting not only for their lives, but so that everyone else could have those things.

The peace that had begun to settle in after the war had been a wonderful taste of all those things. Cara's

marriage celebration at the People's Palace had been
a brief sample of life the way it should be. But all too
soon that joy had turned to ashes for Cara and Ben,
and for everyone else.

Having the Sword of Truth in her hand inflamed
those feelings and brought them boiling to the surface.

Now they were once again in a fight for their lives.
If they were to survive this time, if they were to live,
they not only needed to escape the Shun-tuk chasing
them, they also needed to get home.

But home back in the heart of D'Hara was a long
way off.

Without horses, it was going to be a long and
difficult journey, especially with her and Richard
so weakened. There was no choice, of course. Her
thought was to try to find some towns or cities along
the way where they could get some horses.

Off in the distance behind them, Kahlan could
hear the thunderous explosions from Zedd's wizard's
fire rolling up the gorge, punctuated by the sharp
thunder of Nicci's dark lightning. Sometimes, she
could hear the screams of the dying. The sounds reverberated off the walls of the gorge, like a war emanat-
ing from the spirit world, as if it were an otherworldly
battle between good and evil.

The gorge narrowed as they climbed higher, with
rock walls soaring up in the darkness to either side.
It felt like they were climbing up through a deep
split in the mountains—a crack in the world itself.
Intermittently the walls to each side, normally hidden in the darkness, were suddenly revealed in the
flashes of light from the explosions in the distance
behind.

Irena remained close to the horse as gifted help to

defend Richard if need be. She watched all around, looking for any sign of trouble. Kahlan didn't know what Irena's capabilities were, or if she could be of any help to Zedd and Nicci in reviving Richard.

Kahlan wanted to get to safety so that they could work on bringing him back to consciousness. She knew what a terrifyingly forsaken experience Richard was enduring. The longer the blackness lasted, the worse it became, and the more dangerous. She was eager for Zedd and Nicci to help him, but at the moment the Shun-tuk were a more urgent threat.

With Nicci using her abilities against the enemy, Irena and Samantha had taken over the duty of casting small flames out ahead to light their way up the ravine. As trickles of water ran down from above, they gathered to cascade over rocks in a number of places, splashing and getting them wet, making traveling with the terror of being chased even more miserable.

Kahlan realized, then, that except for the small lights floating out ahead, the darkness hadn't been interrupted for quite a while by the reflections of wizard's fire off the towering rock walls. Nor had she heard the thumping explosions of Nicci's power. After climbing in the quiet for a time, Samantha dropped back beside Kahlan.

"How is Lord Rahl doing?" the young sorceress asked.

Kahlan laid a hand over Richard's back. "He's still breathing, but other than that I have no way of telling."

"I do," Samantha said as she placed her small hand against the side of his face. "I'm familiar with the feel of the poison in both of you. I should be able to judge any change in it."

It wasn't long before she reluctantly withdrew the hand.

"Well?" Kahlan asked when Samantha didn't say anything.

The young woman's dark eyes looked up. "I'm sorry, Mother Confessor, but it's worse than I've ever felt before."

For the first time, Kahlan had the feeling, the real, fully realized feeling, that Richard was dying. He was slipping away from her and there was nothing she could do about it. Against her best efforts, she imagined Richard dying, and what a dead world it would be without him.

She swallowed and gripped the sword tighter.

When she heard the distant call of a mockingbird, she recognized it as a signal from men of the First File. The wizard's fire had killed all that it was going to kill. That meant that the rest of the Shun-tuk they would face would be the ones with some degree of occult powers—powers that Kahlan and the rest of those with her knew nothing about. There was no telling what they were capable of, except she knew they could raise the dead, and that was certainly trouble enough.

Powers or no powers, though, they would bleed. It was up to the soldiers, now, to be the steel to protect them, to protect their Lord Rahl. Now was the time the threat had to be ended.

Kahlan looked down at Samantha. "Take the reins."

"What?"

"Take the reins. We don't have a lot of men. Every sword counts." She lifted the point of the Sword of Truth, its power thundering through her. "I have to help the men. You need to lead the horse, now."

Despite the fear in her eyes, Samantha nodded. "I understand."

Kahlan spotted Nicci weaving her way up through the soldiers to get Kahlan. The sorceress's beautiful features were set with grim determination.

"Let's go," she said. "It's time to end this."

This time, it was Kahlan who pushed out in front of Nicci, taking the lead.

The time had come at last for her sword to taste all the Shun-tuk blood it could ever want.

Both Kahlan and the sword were eager for the fight.

24

They didn't have to go far before they encountered the soldiers. They had been slowing, hanging back a bit, trying to create a gap in case those with Richard had to take him and run for their lives. The men were trying to create a head start for the others if it ended up being a last-stand fight to the death. As Kahlan and Nicci squeezed between the men, headed back down the gorge, Nicci cast a small spark of flame out in front to provide enough light so they could get their footing, but it was only enough to light up a short distance ahead of them.

She knew that they had outpaced the Shun-tuk and been able to give themselves at least a slight lead, but the soldiers had now given back some of that gap to insulate Richard. Kahlan didn't know how far they would need to go before they encountered the enemy.

When Nicci finally cast out a larger flame to drift higher up and out ahead of them, and it lit the entire scene beyond, Kahlan's blood went cold.

"Dear spirits," she whispered.

Beyond the dark figures of their own men in their chain mail and dark leather armor, all down the gorge was what looked like an endless sea of white figures snaking up the chasm. There were so many that Kahlan couldn't see the far end of the serpent.

After all the Shun-tuk had entered the gorge, Sergeant Remkin was supposed to close them off from behind. Those men were supposed to be the hammer that would smash the Shun-tuk against Commander Fister's anvil. Since she couldn't see the end, she had no way of knowing if Remkin had been able to shut the back door.

Kahlan quickly recognized that there were a great deal more of the enemy than she had expected to see. She had expected vast numbers to have been vaporized by the wizard's fire and Nicci's power. Despite how many had died, there were more than ample Shun-tuk left to do the job they had been sent to do.

When they had been back in the encampment they had no way of knowing the numbers of the Shun-tuk scattered out beyond in the woods. She remembered the way they kept coming, but she now realized that they had been seeing only a limited view. She never realized how many more there were back in those woods.

She didn't think that Commander Fister or any of the rest of them expected that there might be this many. These weren't merely spirit trackers; this was an army. It was apparent that when Sulachan and Hannis Arc sent men to accomplish a task, they sent enough to make sure they could not possibly fail.

She now knew something important about both of them: they were never careless. They planned carefully and then deployed overwhelming, withering, brute force to accomplish what they were after. Neither employed subtlety—they were dedicated to applying overpowering might to crush any opposition.

As disheartening as that knowledge might be, she had just learned something important about their enemy. It would keep Kahlan from ever underestimating them.

It also brought to mind what the prisoner had told them—that Sulachan had dark spirits waiting for her and Richard beyond the veil to the world of the dead. Sulachan was not a man who was satisfied to merely kill those who opposed him.

In a flash of comprehension, Kahlan now realized that they had not captured that prisoner by chance or accident. Sulachan intended the man to be caught. Sulachan had wanted to deliver a message. The spirit king had wanted Richard and Kahlan to know that death would not be an ending of suffering, but the beginning of an eternity of it.

There would be no peace to be found in death for either her or Richard, no eternal rest.

Pushing the worry of such thoughts aside and focusing on the task at hand, Kahlan knew that the one thing they did have working for them was the narrowness of the gorge. In such a narrow space, the Shun-tuk couldn't spread out to apply that overwhelming crushing weight of numbers. They could only present a limited leading edge of forces.

Because the pass was narrow, it allowed the First File to use a limited number of men to span the gap. That meant they could continually rotate fresh men to the front, so that the ones who had been fighting fiercely for a time could take a break to regain their breath while fresh men stepped in to work with maximum effort at hacking the enemy to pieces. By rotating men in that way, they could fight much longer, and with sustained, deadly brutality.

Richard, of course, had known that, and that was why he didn't want to continue to try to fight them at the encampment. Seeing the numbers, now, seeing how many Shun-tuk they faced, Kahlan understood that he had made that call none too soon. Richard had known that their best chance was to fight them in the narrow gorge as opposed to back in the open of the encampment.

The tactic of rotating the men so the ones at the front were always fresh, especially when driven from both ends in a confined space like the narrow gorge, was a killing machine that could grind through a lightly armed enemy such as the Shun-tuk with frightening efficiency. In such a situation, the vast numbers the Shun-tuk had were not as much of an advantage. This kind of battle was more akin to butchery than fighting. But then, that was what war was. The purpose of warriors was to kill the enemy as swiftly and efficiently as possible in order to end the conflict.

The well-disciplined and practiced men of the First File stood in tight ranks, overlapping their shields like links of armor, and mowed down the enemy as they tried to advance. Lances laid over the shoulders of the foremost rank were used to stab at the unprotected enemy. If the enemy saw the danger and stopped advancing, it made no difference because the soldiers would then begin to advance toward them, pushing from both ends at once. The enemy couldn't retreat. They were caught in the teeth of a meat grinder that relentlessly chewed through them.

The only problem in the plan, the thing that nagged

at the back of Kahlan's mind, was that not only were these half people driven by an insane desire to eat living flesh so that they could steal a soul, these were now the ones with occult powers.

That worry kept whispering from the back of her mind.

In the dimly lit, narrow defile, Kahlan could see that some of the sea of figures coming for them had glowing red eyes. Some of them were the dead that had been reanimated. That was going to be another problem with the tactic the First File was using.

Even the Shun-tuk who had no occult powers, and were still sufficiently intact, could be brought back from the dead to be more lethal than they ever had been in life. Even the ones who had been burned to death, as long as they still had arms and legs, could be used. They didn't bleed and die like living people. Since they weren't alive, simply stabbing them through vital organs wouldn't stop them. They had to be hacked to pieces or burned to ash.

Zedd shuffled past Kahlan on his way back up the gorge. He gave her a vacant look. That single look frightened her almost as much as the sight of the Shun-tuk.

Kahlan knew by the way his feet dragged and his arms hung that Zedd was near the end of his ability to use his gift, much less focus the strength needed to create wizard's fire. What he had already done was exhausting work and he had been at it for quite some time. He would need to rest and recover some strength if he was to continue fighting. He had to be rotated back, much as the men fighting at the leading edge needed to catch their breath and recover some of their strength. Zedd would need water and a quick bite to eat to give him strength.

Kahlan cupped her free hand to the side of the old man's face. "Why don't you stay back up behind and watch over Richard for a while."

He nodded, offering her a brief smile as he moved on.

Kahlan spotted Nicci and saw that she was exhausted as well, but the sorceress had no intention of resting just yet.

Below them, the writhing mass of ghostly figures struggled with all their might to climb up the gorge as fast as they could. Only the difficulty of the terrain, the narrowness of the gorge, and their own numbers interfering with each other slowed them. Having to funnel through narrower spots in the walls meant that they had to slow to wait their turn. In their impatience to get a soul, some pushed the ones in front down and stepped on or over them. Despite how they might have been slowed in the tight spots, once through, each of the half people raced ahead with reckless determination.

Richard had been right. They were predators fixated on the bait and they were now in full chase mode.

With a sense of hopeless realization, Kahlan grasped that Richard's plan had worked—the Shun-tuk would follow them up the gorge. The only problem was that despite the effectiveness of that plan, Kahlan instinctively understood that there were too many. The odds were too great. The sheer weight of numbers was going to be more than a problem. It could spell their doom.

But the sword she held didn't care about such odds. If anything, the odds only stimulated the power of rage from the weapon. It demanded their blood, and the confined space still gave them the best chance to stop the Shun-tuk.

The problem for the soldiers was going to be the revived dead.

The sword she carried, though, had been created for just such problems.

Kahlan pushed her way through the men, racing down to the front of their lines, toward the men fighting closest to the enemy.

She descended into madness.

CHAPTER

25

The Shun-tuk, in their insane drive for the souls of these men, were eager for the fight. They reached with clawed hands and snapped their jaws, hoping to get their teeth into flesh. Men cut them down relentlessly. The white figures coming from behind were equally determined. They were undeterred by how many white bodies lay dead at their feet. Those that had died only meant that they would have their chance. They climbed over their own dead to get at the soldiers, only to be run through with lances or laid open with swords and axes.

Kahlan spotted the first of the dead coming toward them. In the dim light, his glowing red eyes were easy to spot. She saw that he had only one arm. His chest had been ripped open, the ribs broken, so that she could see his lungs exposed. His lungs were still, though, as he had no need to breathe, but he was certainly coming for them. It was now occult powers that gave them strength and purpose.

This was the part that Kahlan had the best chance to handle. The dead didn't fall easily to regular steel, but the Sword of Truth was an ancient weapon that existed for eliminating just such evil.

Finally able to unleash the fury of the sword, Kahlan brought it down so hard it split the dead man's head and most of his body. He tried to move, to come after them, but he was far too damaged and only thrashed ineffectively. His right side fell over while the left side tried to drag the rest along. Her second blow ended the effort for good.

Kahlan was already past him, going after the walking dead. She could see their glowing red eyes glaring out from the darkness. The soldiers could fight the Shun-tuk; she needed to eliminate those difficult-to-stop awakened dead and leave the Shun-tuk for the men of the First File.

Kahlan scanned the faces, the gaping mouths, the painted black eye sockets, until she saw another pair of glowing red eyes. An instant after she saw them, her sword arced around and shattered the head. On the backswing she took off the head of another dead woman with glowing eyes, then stabbed the blade through the chest of a living Shun-tuk. His eyes opened wide in surprise before the life went out of them. As she yanked the blade free, she swiftly delivered several more blows to disable the headless dead to prevent them from using their arms against the soldiers.

Through the fury to get at the enemy, Kahlan recognized that half people were starting to come after her, specifically. She remembered, then, that they recognized her soul. She was a prize they wanted. She remembered what the prisoner had said about what they wanted to do to her.

She remembered the promise of the spirit king's dark ones waiting for her in the underworld.

She realized, too, that in going after the reawakened dead, she had waded too far into the regular Shun-tuk.

Surrounded as she was, she still felt euphoric with each one she killed. More Shun-tuk coming closer in around her meant that she didn't have to go after them in order to kill them. She could stand her ground and kill half people all around her as they came to her. The danger of her situation was a distant concern compared to the exhilaration of killing them. Each life the blade took fed the anger, giving glorious satisfaction that in turn only drove the blade's insatiable need for the enemy's blood.

Her sword scythed white-painted men and women down by the dozens. What had been a trap closing around her turned into mounds of bodies clogging the gorge, making it more difficult for others to climb over the dead to get at her. Some slipped on blood and gore and fell, some smacking their heads on rocks, while others were stabbed to death before they could scramble to their feet.

Despite the blade's hunger for enemy blood, Kahlan paid particular care to being sure she cut down any she saw with the red glowing eyes.

Killing the others between finding those with glowing red eyes was just a delicious treat until she could find another walking dead.

As she swung the sword, laying open chests, severing limbs, shattering skulls, she could feel their warm blood splattering across her face. Blood dripped from the stringy wet tips of her hair.

Still, the blood wasn't enough. She wanted more. She went after them with ever-increasing fury. Teeth gritted with rage, she cut them down as fast as they could come at her.

Even as she fought, though, somewhere in the dim recesses of her mind, she knew that there were too many.

Soldiers recognized the danger she was in by wading too far into the enemy to get at the ones with glowing red eyes. Commander Fister hacked his way in close to her, trying to keep the chalky figures from getting to her. His powerful arms looked made for the task of cleaving an enemy apart with his sword.

Other soldiers chopped their way through Shuntuk to get in close to her, and helped her to continually grind the leading edge of the enemy down under their blades.

Kahlan was only dimly aware of such things, though. She was lost in the killing.

With the Sword of Truth in her hands and this many of the enemy around her, it felt as if the purpose of her entire life had come down to this perfect moment of delivering death. Her training, her experiences, her beliefs, everything in her life, had brought her to this moment as the perfect killing machine.

The Sword of Truth fed off the intent of the one holding it. It read what the person considered good or evil. The blade would not harm what the person holding it believed to be good. It was committed to destroying what the holder of the blade considered evil. In the right hands, in the hands of one committed to reason and life, the sword became manifest justice.

Kahlan considered the half people and the ones who had sent them to be pure, unredeemable evil. She had never felt this kind of unleashed wrath. Anything white drew her blade. Severed arms spun through the air. Heads tumbled across the rocks. Bodies and parts of bodies littered the ground. Blood covered everything.

In places, advancing Shun-tuk had to wade through ankle-deep viscera. A head she took off with an angry swing of the sword tumbled and bounced down the rocks of the gorge. Even over the screams and yelling, she could hear the skull crack each time it bounced off a rock. Advancing Shun-tuk stepped aside to avoid it.

The men fighting beside her were just as lethal. The Shun-tuk, after all, were not all that hard to kill. They wore no armor, they carried no shields, and they did not use weapons to block attacks. Shielding their face with an arm cost them the arm before the sword buried itself in their face. She had yet to see one Shun-tuk draw a knife. Their teeth were their weapon of choice. They were animals racing in to slaughter their prey, and they in turn were being slaughtered.

Axes relentlessly chopped them down. Maces crushed skulls and caved in ribs and lungs. Swords of the First File cut apart the figures, and yet they kept coming. There was no sign of the end of the white throng snaking up the gorge. Sergeant Remkin and his men were too distant, and no doubt engaged in the same kind of fight for their lives.

And then one of the Shun-tuk not far in front of her did the oddest thing. He stood still in the center of the chaos, and smiled. It was a smile that, despite the sword's rage, made Kahlan pause and her blood run cold.

As he gazed into her eyes, without ever looking away, he lifted a hand out toward one of the soldiers to her right.

The soldier screamed as the skin on his face immediately started bubbling and melting. The screams gurgled away.

His scalp split open in bloody strings as it sloughed down his head, exposing the top of his skull. His eyes liquefied in their sockets, running down and mixing with the gooey mess of his bloody, bubbling flesh. He was already dead, his joints separating as he crumpled.

The smiling Shun-tuk, his gaze still on Kahlan, almost at the same time lifted his other arm out toward the soldier to her left. The man screamed as his flesh and muscle liquefied and fell away from the bones of his arms in sticky strings. His nose and lips melted away even as he screamed in horrified agony. Flesh parted from cheekbones and skull. Both men had died in hardly more than a heartbeat.

Even as it was still happening, Kahlan's sword was already coming around with lightning speed. Evil was targeted in the center of her vision. The blade flew toward where her eyes were focused. The tip whistled with its incredible speed as she brought it down with all her might. She could hear herself screaming in rage, adding her fury to that of the blade. It caught the smiling man on the side of his neck, just below his left ear, before the smug smile could leave his lips. The blade drove down with such force that it cleaved off his head at an angle along with his right shoulder and still-extended arm. With part of his chest attached, the head, shoulder, and arm tumbled away. As the bottom half fell, organs spilled out across the rocks.

Although she had killed this one, she now realized the danger they were in from those among the Shun-tuk who possessed the same kind of occult ability.

This kind of Shun-tuk might not have armor, or shields, or swords, but the men of the First File had no defense against their occult weapons. The soldiers' chain mail had done them no good; their flesh had melted and dripped right through it. Kahlan didn't think that Zedd or Nicci or Irena would be able to offer any defense against such sorcery. If regular magic worked against such half people, it already would have. Kahlan had seen some of these ghostly figures walk through fire unharmed. The smiling Shun-tuk would not be there in the first place if regular magic could kill them.

Blades obviously worked just fine, but how many would those with such occult sorcery kill before they could be cut down? Worse, there was no telling if the man she had just killed was the only one, the way they had only one wizard, Zedd, among them, or if there were dozens more like the smiling Shun-tuk. For all she knew, there could be hundreds.

In an instant, the equation had changed.

Kahlan spun around and frantically pushed at the men near her, turning them around.

"Run!" she screamed. "Run!"

Commander Fister, having seen the same thing that Kahlan had just witnessed, windmilled his arm in command to his men. "Pull back! Run! Pull back, pull back!"

The men of the First File would have stayed and fought to the death had they been commanded to do so, but at her command and that of their commander they abandoned the hopeless cause and turned to run for their lives.

Nicci caught Kahlan's arm on her way by. "What is it? What's happening?"

Kahlan spun the sorceress and shoved her to get

her moving with the rest of them. "After what I just saw, unless you know how to stop occult sorcery, you had better run for your life."

Nicci didn't argue. Kahlan had no idea what they were going to do. As far as she could tell, without any effective defense at hand, their only hope was to outrun the Shun-tuk.

And trying to outrun a predator was a very bad option.

CHAPTER

26

As they ran up the narrow ravine between the towering walls of dark stone to either side, at least the Shun-tuk also had to funnel through the narrow defile the same as Kahlan and the soldiers, so they couldn't spread out and try to get out around them.

Kahlan knew that if some of the soldiers slipped and fell in the dark, it would be disastrous. Running as fast as they could, if some of them at the front fell, others would be unable to avoid tripping and falling over them. If that happened, they could all be slowed enough to be caught by the river of white figures coming after them.

What Kahlan had just seen terrified her. She had seen men die often enough, and in such agonizing and horrifying ways as to color every aspect of her thinking for the rest of her life, but she'd never before seen anything like what she had just witnessed. She knew that Zedd, Nicci, and Irena had no defense against such deadly occult sorcery. As far as Kahlan knew, the only option they had was to outrun the savages snapping at their heels. She had no idea how they would ever be able to stop men with such powers.

If mere half people had this kind of occult ability, she shuddered to think of what a spirit king returned from the dead might be able to do.

Because they had boots and the Shun-tuk were barefoot, on such rough terrain they were little by little able to begin to outpace the half people. Running over sharp rocks was difficult even for people used to running without shoes. At such a breakneck pace it was all too easy for even tough feet to impact the edge of a sharp rock and split open their flesh. They were better at running over rocks in the dark than Kahlan would have thought possible, but it was still slowing them just enough to allow her and the soldiers to begin to pull out a lead.

It wasn't much of a lead, but it was something and it was growing. It also clearly wasn't enough that it was going to allow them to escape, but at least the distance seemed to keep the Shun-tuk from using their occult sorcery to take them all down from behind.

But if the ground grew any less rugged and rocky, the bloodthirsty half people would soon catch up with them, because the soldiers had to run with heavy gear and armor. Most of them were muscular, brawny men, men good with weapons and hand-to-hand combat, so they were easily able to carry their loads, but in such circumstances carrying any extra weight slowed them down. On top of that, these men weren't especially built for running the way the wiry Shun-tuk were. The soldiers of the First File had to be the best at everything, including running, but the Shun-tuk appeared to be built for the singular purpose of running down prey.

Kahlan glanced back over her shoulder from time to time. As unlikely as it seemed, they had gained more distance on the Shun-tuk chasing them. She could have run a little faster herself, but the men were already exhausted from the long hours of battle back at the encampment before this one in the gorge had even begun. She knew that they were running on pure First File mettle.

The men of the First File did not ever give up. For these men failure was not an option. Failure never entered their minds. Giving up wasn't a part of their way of thinking. They focused only on finding a way to win.

It was maddening the way the battle, despite the odds, had been working so well, and then in an instant everything had changed. But Kahlan knew that in battle you had to be prepared to switch tactics in an instant.

Those who continued to press on with tactics that could not work ended up dead. Facing an enemy who refused to admit the reality of the futility of their strategy became a simple matter of killing them.

Successful warriors always preferred that to a fair fight. Successful warriors were the ones who won wars. That ability came naturally to Richard and for good reason—he was a war wizard. He was always searching for solutions that would work. If he found himself facing an impossible situation, he found a way to change the rules.

But at the moment, the rules were simple: run or die.

With the sword in her hand, Kahlan was not about to run ahead and leave the soldiers without her help at the rear, close to the enemy. If there were revived dead among the Shun-tuk chasing them, then short of Richard wielding it, the Sword of Truth in her hands was the best chance they had of defeating that threat.

As they ran up the steep ground, they came upon Zedd making slower progress up the rocky gully. He was losing ground to the rest of the men. He was wiry and stronger than he looked and ordinarily would have been able to run with the best of the Shun-tuk, but he had used a lot of his strength creating wizard's fire. His endurance was waning.

Kahlan snatched a chain-mail sleeve of a soldier and pulled him close. "Help him. Don't tell him that I told you to do so."

The man nodded and then took one of Zedd's arms. "Let me help, sir. I know you put up a valiant effort. You have to be exhausted. I saw what you did back there. I've never seen the like of it. It was truly magnificent."

"Yes, it was magnificent," Zedd said, momentarily cheered. "Unfortunately, it was not nearly enough . . ." he said, his cheer sinking.

"That's all right," another man said as he took Zedd's other arm, helping to practically carry the wizard up the hill. Both men's arms were nearly as big around as the skinny wizard's waist. Kahlan saw that Zedd's feet touched the ground only every third or fourth step.

It took all of Kahlan's effort to make herself stay with the men rather than turn and fight the enemy. That was what she wanted to do. The sword was in full rage after the fighting had started and it demanded blood. Once it was out and engaged in battle, the magic of it was never satisfied as long as there was an enemy still standing. With the threat still existent, the sword wanted only to take it out. That was its nature. It was pristine purpose, pure power, devoted only to destroying what the one holding it wanted destroyed. It was up to the one holding it to choose what it considered to be the enemy and to place limits on what they did with the weapon. It required a thinking mind to properly apply its power.

It was a challenge just holding it and not letting it tell her what to do. She had a new appreciation for Richard's ability to function calmly with the weapon in his hand.

Water dripping in little rivulets off the cliff faces to each side drenched them as they ran through it. The Dark Lands were a gloomy place where, from what Kahlan had seen so far, it was almost always dark and overcast. There was frequent mist, drizzle, and it rained almost every day.

All that water continually drained down the mountains, seeping through all the hairline cracks and fractures in the granite, soaking it through and through. It caused the granite to decompose over time and those crumbled bits accumulated in the gorge, making for difficult footing in places.

Because of the water, the rocks were covered in wet moss and slime. Having boots helped some, but it was still treacherous to run in such conditions, especially in the dark. Fortunately Nicci was casting flares of light to help the men see well enough to run at full speed.

Kahlan glanced back and saw several Shun-tuk slip

and fall on an especially slimy, broad flat rock. Others tripped and fell over them. Because the ravine was so narrow, it slowed them until they could get the fallen men back up and out of the way. The next time she saw men slip and fall, frustrated half people didn't bother to slow to help them. Rather, they simply trampled their companions to death under hundreds of feet. The tangle of limbs and bodies caused others to trip and fall, breaking arms and legs, only to be in turn trampled. There were spots where the falling figures upended dozens and dozens coming upon them, creating bottlenecks.

It bought Kahlan and the men with her some precious breathing room. The way it kept happening, and the more of the barefoot half people that slipped on blood and slime and fell, the more it allowed her and the men of the First File to put a decent gap on their pursuers.

But the gap wasn't great, and she knew that the Shun-tuk were now fixated on their prey and they would not stop for anything.

Kahlan saw the men ahead going around someone in the center of the gorge. She soon reached the spot and realized that it was Samantha.

The young woman inexplicably stood motionless on a flat rock in the middle of the brook, the water pouring around either side of the rock.

Kahlan came to an abrupt halt, letting the rest of the men run on past. When they saw her stop, they all skidded to a halt and turned back to protect her.

Kahlan motioned frantically. "Keep going! Go, go, go!"

Reluctantly, they followed her orders. She looked up the gorge. Everyone was running as hard as they could. Behind, the Shun-tuk, too, ran up the gorge as hard as they could.

Samantha stood motionless all by herself in no-man's-land.

Her head was bowed. Her bony elbows stuck out to the sides. The first two fingers of each hand were pressed to her temples. Her mass of black hair was as motionless as the rest of her.

Kahlan glanced back down the defile. There was precious little time until the half people caught up with where Kahlan and Samantha stood all alone.

"Samantha, what in the world are you doing?"

When she didn't answer, Kahlan leaned in and yelled her name.

"Samantha!"

Without looking up, the young woman whispered one word.

"Run."

Kahlan leaned closer. "Where's Richard? You were supposed to be with him. I told you to take care of him."

"Run," she repeated in a softly feminine voice.

"What?"

When the young woman didn't answer, in frantic uncertainty, Kahlan ran the bloody fingers of her left hand back into her blood-soaked hair as she stole a quick look up the gorge. She didn't see the horse among the men racing up the steep defile. She realized that if she couldn't see it, that meant that someone else had to be leading the horse carrying Richard, probably Irena, or Kahlan would have seen it left behind. Richard had to still be safe.

Kahlan leaned down farther and saw that Samantha's eyes were closed. The young woman had not moved an inch. Eyes closed, her expression serene, fingers pressed to her temples, she didn't move a muscle.

The Shun-tuk coming for them started howling, eager for blood.

"Samantha—"

"Run."

27

Kahlan straightened.

She felt goose bumps tingling along her arms. She blinked at the mystifyingly motionless Samantha. She had no idea what the problem could be, but there was no time to stand there and work it out.

Kahlan frantically tried to think. For sure they couldn't stay there. They were mere moments from it being too late even to run.

Just as Kahlan looked back down in the darkness, unable to tell for sure exactly how close the Shun-tuk were, the moon, almost directly overhead, broke through a hole in the thick cloud cover for the first time that night, lighting the narrow defile in pale, eerie light. Kahlan could see the wet, slick, nearly vertical stone walls soaring up from the narrow chasm of broken rock with the brook running down through it.

At the base of those towering rock walls the river

of white figures of the Shun-tuk raced up the ravine, predators with their prey almost within reach.

Hundreds of men and women in the lead stretched clawed hands forward in anticipation, each wanting to be the first to have the soul in front of them. Mouths gaped open, teeth bared. They wailed like wolves after prey.

Kahlan had no idea what Samantha was doing or what might be wrong with her. The thought occurred to her that maybe she was frozen in terror. Kahlan had seen that happen in battle. A person would be so panicked, so afraid, that their mind could no longer think and they would give up, just standing there in place waiting for death to take them. Sometimes, death was less frightening than what life had to offer.

Kahlan's first thought was that maybe she could circle an arm around Samantha's skinny waist, hike her up, hold her against a hip, and carry her up the gorge, but as soon as she thought of it she realized that she certainly couldn't outpace the Shun-tuk while carrying the young woman, even if she was small and skinny.

She knew that if she tried, they would both die.

Kahlan knew that she was going to have to fight or run.

Leaving Samantha and running meant abandoning her to the savages to be eaten alive. Kahlan gripped her sword tighter.

Despite the magic from the sword desperately wanting the fight, wanting the blood of the enemy, Kahlan knew that fighting the Shun-tuk alone, even with the Sword of Truth, would be suicide.

There was no time. It was now or never. Run or fight.

The only thing that made any sense at all was to run.

If it was to be running, then it had to be now. They had to run or they were going to die.

"Samantha—there's no time—"

"Run."

That time the young woman said it with such cold power that it ran a chill through Kahlan.

Kahlan straightened and stared for a second at the motionless young sorceress, her fingers pressed to her temples, her head bowed, her eyes closed.

Kahlan glanced back at the black eye sockets, clawed hands, and open mouths of the Shun-tuk running wildly up the defile toward them.

There was no choice. If she stayed, they both died. Kahlan couldn't help anyone else if she died trying to save this one person.

Viewed in that light, there was no choice.

Heartbroken at the choice, Kahlan bolted and took off running up the gorge, racing as if her life depended on it—because it did.

There was a good-size gap ahead to the men. A glance back over her shoulder showed another gap back to the Shun-tuk, but not much of one. Samantha stood motionless on the rock in the middle of the brook, in the center of that gap.

As Kahlan turned once more up the hill, running as fast as her legs would carry her, the ground suddenly shook with such a violent shock that she fell sprawling face-first in the center of the brook.

She twisted as she sat up, coughing out water, looking back when the concussion from the blast flattened her. It was so powerful that it felt as if it had stopped her heart for a beat.

Confused, Kahlan sat up again just in time to see the air of the moonlit defile filled with flying rock. She blinked at what she was seeing. It made no sense. Large jagged pieces of granite spiraled through the air. Huge slabs that had broken along rift lines slid downward with ever-accelerating speed. As they dropped, they trailed shattered bits of stone and smoke from the friction created under such tremendous weight.

To either side of the narrow defile explosions expanded the rock, lifting great chunks up and outward. Inside those expanding, interlocking pieces of rock, Kahlan could see the remnants of the flashes that had ignited deep inside the rock and blasted it apart. The sound of the explosions thundered and boomed, tearing the rock walls apart. More explosions in quick succession raced down the gorge on both sides, dozens of heart-stopping thumps in a rapid series, blowing the mountain to pieces. Flashes ripped in sequence down the faces of bluffs, loosening the bedrock from the mountain.

In the center of the turmoil below her, Samantha hadn't moved an inch.

Below her, the thundering booms that shook the ground took the feet of the Shun-tuk out from under them.

The rock walls to either side below the young woman shook with repeated explosions racing down the length of the defile, blowing the walls apart. In the moonlight Kahlan could see stone spires topple, folding as they dropped. Countless tons of rock came crashing down atop the Shun-tuk trapped in the gorge below.

Through the thundering, echoing booms and the singular ripping sound of granite cracking and breaking, Kahlan could hear men and women screaming. The Shun-tuk were helpless beneath the cataclysm violently ripping rock apart above them. They had no time to escape and had nowhere to run.

Kahlan blinked as she saw a series of thundering booms rip along in an extensive chain down the rock walls. The flashes, like lightning within the stone itself, hammered in quick succession, one following almost atop the boom of the one before, rippling one after another down the gorge.

There could be no doubt whatsoever that whatever was happening was being directed intelligently. It was obvious to Kahlan by the order and placement of the rock-ripping explosions that it was meant to collapse the walls to both sides of the defile into the gorge at the bottom. Every blast that blew stone outward was timed in an ordered sequence that knocked out support to ensure that the colossal weight of the rock would help pull the walls down. By the enormity of the blasts, and their locations, the walls had to fall.

It was the most elegantly composed scene of utter destruction Kahlan had ever witnessed.

As she watched the walls tumbling in, sending clouds of dust and debris rolling up through the trees, it went on and on, as if in a livid tantrum of destruction.

It sounded like the world was being ripped apart by the rapid series of thundering explosions. The sound reverberated through the mountains all around. Stone fragments of every size and shape sailed through the air, tumbling down the collapsing walls of the gorge, lifting above the flashes of explosions, or cascading and bouncing down atop what had already fallen.

All up and down the gorge below Samantha the

world looked like it was coming apart. As a particularly immense cliff toppled, twisting as it fell so that it landed down the length of the defile, dust, like smoke, expelled from under where the cliff landed, billowed out to roll up the gorge. The wall of wind from the explosions and buckling walls nearly knocked Kahlan down again.

For just an instant, Kahlan wondered if this was the end of the world of life, if it was actually being caused by Sulachan, furious that they might escape his Shun-tuk.

Yet more cliffs, thrown forward by internal explosions that lit like lightning rippling along inside the rock, toppled out and then dropped with thundering force. They hit so hard the ground shook. The world rocked and moved as if it was all being caused by an earthquake. But Kahlan saw the explosions and she knew that this was no earthquake. It was directed destruction to a purpose.

The sound of cracking granite continued popping and reverberating through the canyon without abating. Another series of booming explosions farther down the gorge shook the ground with each thumping explosion. Each concussion felt like a fist pounding Kahlan's chest.

Clouds of dusty rock boiled up as yet more rock and debris came crashing down in specific places, ensuring that no part of the gorge escaped the calamity.

In a brief pause, Kahlan scrambled to her feet and raced back down the gorge to Samantha. The young woman still hadn't moved. Her black hair was covered in a layer of dust that made her look gray. The world around her was coming apart and she hadn't moved. Shun-tuk below her were dying by the hundreds, if not thousands, and still she had not moved.

There was no doubt in Kahlan's mind as to the intelligence directing the spectacle still going on.

Impossibly, Kahlan saw a few Shun-tuk, covered in dust, scrambling out from the leading edge of the rubble. There had to be a few dozen. They saw Kahlan and Samantha and started for them. Kahlan hoped they weren't the ones with occult sorcery, and that her sword could stop them.

Just then, Kahlan heard granite cracking in the cliff right above them. She looked up and saw the cliff tremble and shake. She could see huge cracks racing through the wet rock. Sections pulled apart, taking trees with them. A sudden thundering boom to each side over her head made Kahlan gasp.

She scooped the wisp of a young woman up in her arms and started running up the gorge. She ran with all her strength.

Right behind, the towering wall of rock cracked away from the mountain, toppled, and crashed down with thunderous force right where Samantha had been standing only a moment before. Kahlan almost lost her footing as the ground shook violently, but she managed to keep going.

Sections of rock the size of small palaces came to a rocking halt where Samantha had been standing moments before. Had Kahlan not snatched her up, the young woman would have been killed.

The Shun-tuk that had temporarily escaped had been buried under countless tons of the fallen mountain.

Kahlan stopped, turning back, trying to catch her breath. All down the gorge she could see loosened slabs continuing to topple. Enormous blocks, no longer having any support, slid with accelerating speed to sail out past the remaining edges to fall through space and pound down atop the rubble-filled gorge.

As she watched, spellbound, a few remaining sections that were fractured and loose gave way, collapsing down atop the masses of stone already fallen from the mountains. The gorge was filled with hundreds of feet of the stone debris. As far down the mountain as she could see, the sides of the gorge had all fallen in.

Kahlan couldn't be certain, of course, but she could not imagine how a single Shun-tuk could still be alive.

"Dear spirits, girl, what in the world did you just do?"

"What Lord Rahl taught me to do," Samantha said, her voice choked with tears.

Her thin arms clutched Kahlan's neck as she wept into her shoulder.

Kahlan didn't know what Samantha was talking about.

"I was so afraid," she cried, "I was so afraid we were all going to be eaten. I couldn't let that happen. I had to do something. I was so angry that they were going to eat us thinking they could steal our souls for themselves. I was so angry that they would eat my mother, especially after we just got her free, and that they would eat Lord Rahl, and you, and everyone else—all for some stupid belief. I was so angry."

"So you used some kind of magic?" Kahlan asked. She couldn't understand what she had done or how.

"I knew my mother, and Zedd, and Nicci had tried to use regular magic, and it didn't harm the Shun-tuk, so I knew magic wouldn't work against them. But I heard you say that even if they had occult powers, they would still bleed. So then I knew that was the way to stop them—kill them without magic.

"All I could think of was to do what Lord Rahl taught me."

Kahlan held the young sorceress's head of thick black hair to her shoulder. "It's all right, Samantha. You did good. Richard will be proud when I tell him that you just saved us all."

Kahlan could not for the life of her imagine what in the world Richard could have taught Samantha that could bring mountains crashing down.

Kahlan watched carefully in the moonlight for a time.

There was no one chasing them.

28

An impatient Commander Fister stood waiting in front of his men as Kahlan reached them.

"What in the world just happened?" he asked, sounding angry and frightened at the same time.

"The walls fell down," Kahlan said.

He made the oddest face, and opened his mouth to say something, but then decided better of it.

Kahlan didn't think that any of them had ever seen such an extraordinary thing happen before. They had all just witnessed power on a rarefied level.

"Is Richard all right?" Kahlan asked the commander.

Fister nodded. "As all right as he was before, anyway."

Samantha was still clutching Kahlan tightly and still weeping. It seemed she had been frightened, too, frightened by the realization of what she had done.

Samantha had just used her power to kill probably thousands of people. Half people, anyway.

Kahlan suspected, though, that it was as much from the emotional exhaustion of the ordeal and the terror that had driven her to do such a thing as anything else. At the end of a particularly violent and exhausting battle, Kahlan sometimes felt like sitting down and having a good cry.

But she was a Confessor, and her mother had taught her from an early age that she couldn't let people who depended on her see such weakness. Seeing weakness in leaders made people lose confidence in that leader, and in themselves.

"Well, from what I was told," the commander said, "Samantha had stopped in the middle of the brook and was just standing there. So what—"

"Not now, Jake," Kahlan said. She gestured. "Let's get moving. I don't think that any of the Shun-tuk survived what I just saw, but if they did I don't want to have them catch us sitting around celebrating. I want to put some distance between us and them—if any are still alive."

He pointed up to the soaring walls on each side of the gorge. "Besides, it's probably not the best idea to stand around under rocks and cliffs that might have been loosened by all that shaking. I wouldn't want what happened to the Shun-tuk to happen to us."

Kahlan nodded with a worried look back down the gorge. It wasn't that far to the site of the buried Shun-tuk. That much violence could easily have weakened the walls above them.

The commander cocked his head. "Do you think any are still alive? I mean, they have that occult sorcery, after all."

Kahlan considered his question briefly. "I can't be certain, of course, but I can't imagine how they could have survived the mountains to each side falling in on them. I think they were all crushed under hundreds of feet of rock. Doesn't matter how much sorcery you have if a boulder the size of a house falls on you. I'm pretty sure they are all dead."

"Pretty sure." He still sounded hesitant. "Couldn't there be a pocket created by a huge slab that spared some of them? If there are any alive, they might be able to dig out. They can bring the dead back to life, remember? If even one of them with such powers is alive, he could raise an army of dead to come after us."

"After what I witnessed, I don't see how there could be anyone left to dig out and bring the dead back to life. Even if they survived in a pocket, they are still buried by hundreds of feet of rock. I can't imagine they could ever dig out."

Kahlan let out a deep breath. "But just in case, and more importantly, to get out from under these steep walls, it's a good idea to keep moving. At least for a little while so we can put some distance between us and all the Shun-tuk buried down there. I don't like being this close to them, even if it is a graveyard now. I don't especially like sleeping beside a graveyard. Let's keep going, but take it a little slower. I think we're all pretty tired."

"These are men of the First File, Mother Confessor. They can carry you on their shoulders and march double-time all night long."

Kahlan nodded. "I know, but I think it's up to us to decide to give them the rest they may not be aware they need." She arched an eyebrow at him. "Didn't I

always make sure that you and your men were rested
before you went out at night to bring me back strings
of enemy ears?"

Commander Fister snorted a short laugh.

"Let's move a little farther up the mountain," Kahlan said, "and then let the men get some sleep before
morning."

Commander Fister tapped a fist to his heart in
salute.

"Where's Richard?" Kahlan asked.

The commander pointed a thumb up the gorge.
"Nicci is watching over him. Zedd and Irena are
farther up making sure the way ahead is safe."

Kahlan was glad to hear that. If there was one per
son she would want watching over Richard, it was
Nicci.

Samantha hadn't moved. She seemed to be content
where she was in Kahlan's arms. Kahlan thought that
maybe she didn't want the others to see the tearstains
running down her dusty face.

"You okay?" Kahlan whispered.

Samantha nodded. "Just tired . . . so tired."

Kahlan could imagine that well enough.

As Kahlan carried Samantha up the gorge, making her way through the relieved men, she finally
reached the horse. By the time she got there, Samantha
was hanging limp, asleep in Kahlan's arms. Kahlan
was dead tired, and as thin as Samantha was, she was
still heavy. But Kahlan felt good holding the young
woman. It felt good to be needed for comfort and
shelter.

Nicci stood in a rush as Kahlan came close. "What
in the world was that?"

"What are you so angry about?" Kahlan asked

with a frown. The woman looked like she wanted to skin a dragon. "It killed the Shun-tuk, not us."

Nicci cast a suspicious look at Samantha asleep in Kahlan's arms. "Did she do that?"

Kahlan nodded.

Nicci appraised the young woman a moment longer. "How?"

"She said that Richard taught her."

Nicci shot a look back over her shoulder at the unconscious Richard. "Of course he did."

Kahlan spotted Irena in the distance racing toward them. "Look, Nicci, let's not frighten her mother about this right now. We'll talk about it later. I think we need to get away from here just in case. Then we all need to get some rest. You and Zedd—and Samantha—need to rest if you are to recover your abilities. All right?"

Nicci heaved a sigh as in the distance Irena was calling her daughter's name.

"All right," Nicci said. "Let's get moving. I want to find a safe place, then Zedd and I can work on waking Richard."

"It can't be soon enough for me," Kahlan said. "Irena might be able to help with it."

Nicci folded her arms. "Zedd and I can do it. We'll get him back, I swear."

Kahlan nodded. "Thanks, Nicci."

She wondered why Nicci didn't want Irena helping. It was Richard, though, so she supposed that Nicci was not willing to take any chances with letting someone she didn't really know touch him with her power.

Nicci leaned close and shook her finger in Kahlan's face.

"But when I wake that husband of yours, I intend to ask him just what in the world he taught that girl."

Kahlan smiled. "I bet you will."

After a march of nearly two hours, they came to a prominence at the head of the gorge from where a small waterfall fed the brook down where they stood. They needed to get up the steep rise and out of the gorge. While not as difficult as it would be to ascend the steep walls to the sides, Kahlan didn't much like the idea of climbing rugged terrain in the dark. She also didn't want to use torches or lanterns because it would allow anyone hunting them to be able to spot them from miles away. At least the moon was still out.

Commander Fister was eager to be onto higher ground for the defensive protection that it afforded. In much the same way they had used the gorge to trap the Shun-tuk, in the confines of a gorge those same tactics could be used to corner them.

Kahlan didn't think that there could be any Shun-tuk left alive, but she had put the sword back in the scabbard Richard was wearing, which also meant putting away its attendant rage. Without the sword's intoxicating drive to fight, she took seriously the commander's advice for the extra measure of safety. Besides, she had no way to be certain that every one of the Shun-tuk was dead. What if there really had been a pocket under a slab of granite where some of them might have survived? What if even one of those with occult sorcery was still alive and later emerged to sneak up on them?

What if, because she didn't want to climb a hillside in the dark, that remaining Shun-tuk killed Zedd, or Nicci? Or Richard.

Or any of them, for that matter. Each life was precious. That was, after all, ultimately what they were fighting to protect—the sanctity of every life. Kahlan didn't want any of these men dying. She wanted them to be able to live in peace and not have to do the job at which they were so good.

Perhaps worst of all, the thought of being awakened suddenly and trying to scramble up out of the gorge in the dark with bloodthirsty Shun-tuk grabbing their ankles and pulling them back down into waiting arms of flesh-eating half people had her more than willing to do what was necessary to get up and out of the gorge before they stopped for the remainder of the night.

With the sword no longer gripped in her fist, exhaustion was setting in, but she was mostly interested in Zedd and Nicci having a safe place to get the rest and food they needed so they would be able to apply their full gifted ability to strengthen Richard and bring him back from the pull of death.

When Kahlan agreed to the commander's advice to press on and make the difficult climb to find a safer place to set up camp, he sent some men ahead first to scout the best way up.

Kahlan's clothes were stiff and sticky from all the blood of the Shun-tuk she had killed. She had no idea how many she had slaughtered. The memory of it was a blur of relentless fighting interspersed with halting mental visions of particularly desperate, violent moments.

Her hair was stiff and matted with blood. She was glad she didn't have a mirror handy, but by the looks she got, she could imagine well enough what a sight she must be.

In the war, some of the men she had led in battle at the time had called her their warrior queen. They hadn't meant it as the demotion such a title actually was, but it was meant as their highest tribute, so she had always accepted it in the spirit in which it had been intended.

Titles meant more to Kahlan than they did to Richard, but probably because she had been born a Confessor—her title was part of her inherent nature. That power she carried within her couldn't be separated from her by removing the title. It had taken the touch of death from the Hedge Maid to block her from that inner ability.

People had avoided and feared her all her life for the power she carried. That fear set her apart, kept her from so many of the simple pleasures of life that they could enjoy without a thought, even as simple a thing as a benevolent smile or nod in passing. It was not because she wanted to be set apart—she didn't—but because people had always distanced themselves from Confessors.

Most everyone feared Confessors, and in many, that fear had curdled into hatred.

No one smiled or nodded at a Confessor the way they did a normal person. Even those who respected the Confessors still feared them. She had always been able to see the tension in the face of anyone who spotted her. All her life, she could detect the tremble in most people's voices when they spoke to her. She could often see their hands start to shake when she spoke to them. She always did her best to pretend not to notice in order to as gracefully as possible put them at ease. That was usually the best she could do. They feared what they feared.

Most of those who had been close to her for a time grew more used to her as they came to realize that a Confessor was not going to suddenly lose control and unleash her power on them. At times they came to almost forget about her power. Almost.

That inherent nature also drew those who wanted to kill her. For that reason, Confessors had once each been assigned a wizard to protect them. But all those other Confessors were long dead, as were the wizards assigned to them, including Giller, the wizard once assigned to Kahlan. Those who hated a Confessor's ability to uncover truth had finally been able to kill them all. All but her.

Now, Kahlan was married to her wizard, Richard, who was more importantly the man she loved.

In a way, her title, the one she was born with, Confessor, and then Mother Confessor, the title given her by her sister Confessors, represented her armor, the armor she wore to fight for truth. In that way, she was a warrior queen. Those other Confessors had wanted her to be the one who led them in that fight for truth. She was the one.

Born a simple Confessor, she now was and always would be the Mother Confessor, the last of her kind.

Richard was the first man who had not avoided her because of what she was. Of course, he hadn't known at the time that she was the Mother Confessor, or even known what being a Confessor really meant. As she had come to know Richard, though, she came to understand that even had he known, it wouldn't have stopped him from wanting to get closer to her. Nothing would have.

Richard was a very rare person.

He was the one.

He was the one for her, the only one. In so many ways, Richard was the only one. He was a point of singularity.

She had felt a pull to him that they had both felt from the first moment their eyes had met that fateful day in the Hartland woods.

Richard was referred to in prophecy as the pebble in the pond. Ripples from that pebble touched everything. He rippled through so much about prophecy that in that way he had created ripples through time itself.

Sometimes it made her head hurt to think about all the interlocking connections, so she simply loved him and tried not to think about all the wider implications of any of it.

But Richard was always thinking about it, even when he didn't consciously realize it. She could see it in his gray eyes when he was quietly watching the sun set. Even when he looked into her eyes, she could tell that there were always some kind of cosmic calculations going on somewhere in the deep recesses of his mind.

Since he had come into her life, others had come to treat her differently, to accept her. She now got smiles and sincere nods. Especially from soldiers like these. She had fought beside them and they had come to know her for who she was, and that she was more than simply a Confessor.

Richard had done that. He had changed everything.

While she waited for the men to scout the climb, Kahlan joined some of the soldiers under the gentle falls to wash blood out of her hair and off her clothes. They shared a bar of soap with her—soldiers all, passing it around to wash off the blood of their enemy. Fortunately, after the exertion of battle, the cold water felt good on her sore muscles. It wasn't a proper bath with her clothes on, but they needed to be washed as well, and in the wilds of the Dark Lands even this much was a luxury she very much appreciated.

As she wiped the clean water back off her long hair, some of the men told her how proud they were of how much blood she'd had all over her. They had viewed her blood-soaked hair as a mantle she had earned. They seemed especially pleased to see that she was just as committed as they were to killing the enemy, that she was willing to do all that she asked of them, and that she had waded into the task with every ounce of commitment they did.

Kahlan understood their feelings, but she still wanted all the blood off her.

She was looking forward to Richard waking and giving him a kiss. She wanted to look her best for that first kiss welcoming him back to the world of life.

30

Once the scouts had found a good route, the climb was easier than they'd thought it would be. Fortunately, the way up was easy enough that the horse could negotiate the steep climb without too much difficulty, so they were able to save time by leaving Richard lashed in place.

The climb was mercifully short, but Kahlan's legs kept cramping from the effort of the long scramble up through the gorge, much of it at a dead run, to say nothing of what had seemed like an endless battle. The steeper ascent up the prominence and out of the gorge, short as it was, demanded that she dig deep for enough strength to make it.

Her arms felt like lead from swinging the sword. She knew that she was going to be sore for a couple of days. She reminded herself to be thankful for the sore muscles; it was better to be alive to feel sore than to be dead. She tried not to think of how many times she had come close to dying. She thought of Richard and tried not to think of how close both of them still were to dying.

At the top of the climb, in the lap of surrounding mountains, the land flattened out. A small lake collecting mountain runoff fed the falls and the brook down in the gorge. One of the men scouted out ahead beyond swampy ground thick with reeds and then through the woods beyond the far shore while another two scouted to either side. The center scout ran back from the woods and motioned for them with three sparks from his steel and flint. At seeing the three small flashes of sparks, they all hurried around the small moonlit lake, beyond the expanse of reeds, and into the woods beyond.

After following the man a brief distance across ground covered with a soft bed of pine needles beneath a stand of towering pines, they emerged on the far side, where they were brought to a halt at the brink of a chasm. In the moonlight it looked like a black snake stretching off to the left and right as far in each direction as they could see. Nicci cast a sparkling flame down the deep fissure. The light continued sinking far longer than Kahlan would have expected. Seeing how deep it was, they all took a step back from the edge. It was far too steep and too deep to climb down.

As far as she could see, there was no way over the chasm.

"Looks like we're going to have to go either left or right," Zedd offered.

Kahlan scanned the forest on the far side of the chasm. "Not a lot of choice. We're hemmed by the gorge and this rift. If we could get to the other side, this kind of natural barrier would make it a safer place to get the rest we all need."

"I left my wings at home," Zedd grumbled.

Kahlan was at least cheered to hear that his imp-ish nature was returning.

She turned when she heard a commotion coming through the woods. As a group of soldiers approached, getting slaps on the back from other soldiers, Kahlan recognized the men.

It was Sergeant Remkin and the men he had taken to block the rear of the gorge in order to trap the Shun-tuk.

"Remkin! How did you get here?" Commander Fister asked. "I feared we'd lost you. How did you manage to escape the walls falling in?"

"Blocking the rear turned out not to be so simple," he said as he paused to catch his breath for a moment.

"What do you mean?" Kahlan asked.

"We waited and waited for the Shun-tuk to all get into the gorge so we could close it off. But they just kept coming. We were getting pretty nervous that there would be too many to fit the length of the gorge, and then we wouldn't be able to trap them. We knew that would ruin the whole plan.

"Then we saw the wizard's fire far off in the dis-tance ahead. It slowed their advance at times, but rather than turning and running, they kept moving toward it. The whole time more of them coming out of the woods and racing into the gorge."

"Did they all enter, though?" Kahlan asked. "Did all of them get into the gorge?"

The sergeant nodded. "When we saw the wizard's fire begin and felt the ground shake, we knew we needed to get behind the tail end of them in case they decided to try to escape. Finally, we were pretty sure that they had all filed into the gorge. We waited a bit, wanting to make sure there wouldn't be any stragglers to come out of the woods and surprise us from behind. We wanted to close the trap, not get trapped ourselves.

"So when we didn't see more for a time, we knew that was our chance to finally close the gate on them. Despite the fire and lightning we could see off in the distance up ahead, they were so intent on chasing the rest of you they kept going. That's when we came down the slopes to cut them off from behind.

"And then . . . a couple of them appeared, coming back at us. They were smiling." He looked at each of them to make his point. "Smiling! Then they started doing something to our men."

"Doing something? What do you mean?" Fister asked.

The sergeant rubbed a shoulder as he stared off again. "I don't know. It sounds crazy." He looked back at them. "I saw a man just seem to, to, I don't know . . ."

"Melt," Kahlan said.

His brow lifted in surprise. "Yes. Exactly. The skin started melting right off several of my men. Their bones came apart and they went down in a mess that no longer looked human."

"Are you saying that there was more than one of these smiling Shun-tuk?" Kahlan asked.

"At least two that I saw. There might have been more, but I saw two for sure. Two was enough. I realized that if we stayed there trying to hold the back door, we were all going to die. I thought our best chance was to get up here and warn you of what kind of powers they had. Help you fight to get away."

"It's disheartening to know that the one we saw wasn't the only one," Kahlan said. "You did the right thing. There is no way to stand and fight such men."

"You did," Commander Fister reminded her. "You went after him. You killed the one we saw."

Kahlan dismissed the notion with a gesture. "Yes, but I had Richard's sword. Sergeant Remkin and his men would have been slaughtered for no good reason. They did the right thing. I would imagine that men with such dark talents would have been there as rear guards."

Sergeant Remkin nodded. "I thought the same thing because after they killed several of our men and we took off, those smiling Shun-tuk rushed back like they were intent on protecting their rear."

"But how did you get around all the rest of them and catch up with us?" Kahlan asked.

"It wasn't easy," he said. "Those I have with me, the ones still alive, are all mountain men. We grew up in this kind of country and we are used to traveling in mountains. We were able to get up on the higher portions of the hillsides, out of sight of those demons with occult powers.

"We knew by the lay of the land that ridges often run parallel to gorges. The higher ones can make good routes through this kind of country. We were lucky and found a ridge we could follow and quickly cover a lot of distance."

He gestured down into the abyss. "We were following the edge of the ridge and keeping contact with the gorge to make sure we could get to you. From up there we encountered this chasm running in the same direction as some of the ridges, like a rift in the mountains. Far as we could tell, it cuts through a lot of territory. We didn't follow the lower end to see how far it went back that way because we were trying to stay closer to the gorge. That's when we saw you climbing up."

"So then we at least know that this chasm runs back that direction for quite a distance," Kahlan said, trying to think of what they would do to get around it. "So were you able to see if the Shun-tuk stayed in the gorge? Did any of them try to escape the lower end when you went up onto the ridge?"

"When we were still farther back, we reached the top after the wizard's fire ended. We hung back to see if they would turn back, but they kept going, howling, intent on getting to you. They probably felt pretty safe with those smiling bastards bringing up the rear. We never saw any of them turn back.

"Then we started to hear explosions. The entire length of the gorge shook as it started exploding apart. At times up on the ridge, with the way the ground was shaking, we couldn't even maintain our footing and stand up. It was crazy. The cliffs to both sides down the entire gorge all blew apart and collapsed down into the defile and buried the Shun-tuk."

"Do you think it buried them all?" Kahlan asked.

He shrugged. "Hard telling from up as high as we were on the mountain. As far as I could tell, the explosions and the falling walls extended back well past where I'd seen the tail end of the line of Shun-tuk, so I'm pretty sure that with as fast as it all happened, it caught them all in the gorge and buried them. With as much stone as fell in on them, surely none of them could have escaped with their lives. After it ended, we didn't hear them howling anymore. There weren't even any cries or screams of any left alive and injured. It was dead silent."

Commander Fister let out a sigh. "That's good news."

"Still," Kahlan said as she gestured at the dark rift before them. "I'd feel better if we could get across this chasm to the other side."

"So then let's get across," Sergeant Remkin said, as if it were only a skip and a hop. It wasn't. It was discouragingly wide—far too wide by a long shot for any person to jump.

"We don't have a way to get across," Kahlan said.

Remkin shrugged. "Easy."

She frowned at the man. "Easy?"

Zedd leaned a bony shoulder into the conversation. "Nothing is ever easy."

Sergeant Remkin shrugged again. "Sure it is." He flicked a hand up at the trees towering over them as they stood near the edge of the chasm. "Just fell a tree and walk over. Then, when we all get across, push the tree down into the chasm. Even if there were any Shun-tuk left, they won't be able to follow us."

Kahlan shared a look with Commander Fister. She wondered if he felt as stupid as she did.

"That would work," Fister said, trying not to sound too surprised by the idea. "Good thinking, Remkin."

"What about the horse?" Zedd asked. "How are you going to get the horse carrying Richard to walk across a log spanning that chasm? Horses can't walk on a log. Not so easy, now, is it?"

Sergeant Remkin shrugged again. "All we need to do is fell a second tree right next to it. Then cut down another tree and split it into planks. Lay planks between the two tree trunks to make a kind of road-bed, blindfold the horse, and lead him across." He shrugged again. "Easy. After we're done it's a simple enough matter with all the men we have and a few ropes to send the whole thing crashing down into the gorge.

"I haven't seen the Shun-tuk with anything more than a knife, so I don't know that they would be able to fell a tree to follow the same way. They'll have to go around, and from what I've seen on the way up here, it would be a long journey."

Kahlan shared another look with Commander Fister.

"Unless they can fly," the sergeant added with a smile.

"Still not easy," Zedd said. "It's a lot more work than it sounds like." He folded his arms. "But a bit of magic would speed the task."

Sergeant Remkin bowed his head. "It certainly would, sir."

"Well, you sound like the man to handle it, Sergeant," the commander said. "Why don't you take the men you need and get it done as fast as you can. Zedd will help. We need to get across to a safe place to set up camp. It's already the middle of the night and we need to get what rest we can before morning."

The sergeant tapped a fist to his heart. "At once, Commander."

After the man had rushed off to collect his men, Zedd stepped closer. "I'd be a lot happier about the sergeant's plan if he didn't look so blasted young."

Kahlan's worry returned to Richard as she laid an arm over his back.

"We will be able to help him soon," Nicci said.

Kahlan nodded. She had been to that dark place where he was now. She knew the effort from the gifted that it was going to take to bring him back to her.

Zedd put a hand on her shoulder. "Nicci is right, Kahlan. We will get him back. I promise."

Kahlan forced a smile. "Wizards always keep their promises."

He nodded with an earnest look. "Indeed they do."

Kahlan found a private spot to lay out a blanket at the far side of the encampment, right up against a small rock outcropping at the edge of the forest. The rock sheltered her from the occasional night breeze. The moon was still out, so at least they didn't need to worry about building any kind of shelter from rain. It was a rare respite from the foul weather, and it meant they wouldn't need to build shelters. It was already so late into the night that they would get precious little sleep as it was.

Most of the men had had a quick bite of rations and were already asleep. Watches had been posted, but Kahlan felt unusually safe where they were camped. Once they had crossed the chasm they had sent the bridge to its grave in the darkness below. She felt better with a physical barrier between them and any Shun-tuk who could theoretically still be alive.

She had been there right at the edge of the devastation as stone walls of the gorge had fallen in and nearly found herself right under it. She knew better than any of the rest of them the massive violence of what had taken place.

She found it very hard to believe that anyone under those falling cliffs could have lived through it. Even if they had, that didn't mean they could ever claw their way out from under all that rock. They were buried under half a mountain and if any were still alive, they would die a slow death of starvation if nothing else. If the rubble dammed up the brook, it would build up the water level and anyone trapped under there would drown.

Of course, Emperor Sulachan and Hannis Arc would eventually send more half people to track their spirits.

Perhaps even more frightening, that was not their worst problem.

Because she felt safe in their camp for the time being, she hadn't objected too strongly when the commander told her that she wasn't allowed to stand watch. He told her that she had fought as much as ten men and he wanted her to get some sleep so she would be rested in case he needed her to fight for them again. He said she was too valuable with the sword while Richard was still unconscious and he wanted her to be rested and ready to fight.

She had made a show of objecting, but only a small show. By the smile she caught when he turned to walk away, he knew full well that her objections had only been for show.

In truth, she was dead tired and would make a very poor sentry. She thought she would probably fall asleep standing up.

Although she was dead tired, she was also famished. The protracted fighting, from their original encampment and then all the way up the gorge, had taken a lot of energy and she needed to have something before she lay down and went to sleep. It was too late to cook, so everyone had to be satisfied with traveling rations. Zedd had been eating one thing or another since they had found the campsite and finally stopped. He seemed perfectly content with the available fare.

The bridge building had been surprisingly quick. The men with axes had the arms to swing them and they felled the trees in no time. They were experienced at woodcutting and laid the two main trees down right across the chasm, tight beside each other. Zedd helped with the task. Or at least he said he did. She thought the men knew what they were doing.

While some of the men crossed over to scout, others walked along the logs using their axes to clean off any branches that would be in the way. Another two trees were felled along the edge of the chasm, cut into lengths, and then split into planks to lay a roadbed for the horse. It also made crossing safer for all the rest of them as well, rather than balancing on a log over an abyss in the middle of the night.

The horse hadn't been especially eager, but with the blindfold and Zedd trickling calming magic into the animal as he murmured soft words of comfort to it, the crossing had been both swift and uneventful.

For the first time in quite a while, Kahlan felt safe.

Richard had been laid out comfortably. Kahlan would have slept next to him, but Zedd and Nicci wanted to snatch a bit of sleep lying to either side of him until they were rested enough to be able to work on him. Kahlan didn't want to interfere with them doing as they must.

In the moonlight, she looked over at Richard not

far away. Zedd was sitting up beside his grandson, munching on a length of sausage. Nicci lay beside Richard, already fast asleep, an arm draped over his chest, comforted by his slow breathing and knowing that he was still alive.

Not far beyond, Samantha was dead asleep beside her mother. Irena had her knees pulled up, her arms hugging them, as she watched over the camp. Occasionally she took a few bites of dried biscuit to suck on. It had been so late that Kahlan had not had time to discuss with Irena the astonishing things her daughter had done. Irena had seemed strangely incurious about it. Kahlan figured that maybe she feared to know. Some people liked things to go on unchanged and for their children to remain perpetually children.

Kahlan suspected that might be at least part of the reason for Samantha's apparent lack of training as a sorceress. Richard had said that Samantha seemed to have received less instruction in her ability than he had heard was normal with sorceresses.

Some people, like Richard, never received any training about their gift. In Richard's case, he had never been told that he was born gifted, in order to protect and hide him from those bent on destroying him. Kahlan, on the other hand, had been instructed, trained, and disciplined in everything surrounding her powers from as early as she could remember so that she could protect herself from those bent on destroying her. Though completely opposite experiences, they both seemed the right choices for them. After all, Zedd had his reasons for hiding and protecting Richard from any knowledge of his ability, while Kahlan's mother had hers for insisting on rigorous education.

Samantha also seemed to know very little of the

lonely mission of her people, especially the gifted, in the remote village of Stroyza. Perhaps over the millennia her people had lost touch with that mission and the purpose of the barrier.

Once Richard was awake, they were going to have to question Irena to find out if there was anything she knew that could help them. What had been locked away behind that barrier for thousands of years was now again loose in the world and they had precious little knowledge of how to stop it before it was too late.

Kahlan scanned the camp and saw that the men were settled and quiet. She was so relieved that so few of their men had been lost, and that they had escaped, that she felt like breaking down in tears. But she didn't.

Instead, she unwrapped an oiled cloth with dried meat, a chunk of hard sausage, and some salted fish. She guzzled water from a waterskin to wash down the first piece of fish. She wasn't especially fond of dried meat, or salted fish, but right then it was a feast she savored. She was saving the flavorful smoked sausage for last.

When she thought she heard a kind of soft murmuring, purring sound, she looked up. There, on top of the rock she was leaning against, she found herself looking into the big green eyes of a crouched creature. It hunkered silently, staring at her.

Kahlan's chewing paused, her hand holding a piece of dried meat still halfway to her mouth. The animal was at least two or three times the size of a regular cat, with the same kind of almond-shaped eyes. In the moonlight she could see that its tan back was covered in darkly spotted fur becoming darker down toward its haunches and shoulders. It was broader than a typical cat, something like a wolverine or badger, with muscular shoulders, but it didn't have the long nose or short legs of one of those animals. The head was more like that of a cougar, with a heavier brow. The fur was short as well.

Whatever it was, she had never seen anything quite like it.

Since the animal was sitting peacefully and wasn't showing any signs of aggression, her initial alarm relaxed a bit. The fingers of her left hand, though, touched the handle of the knife sheathed at her belt, making sure the weapon was there and easy to get at quickly.

The animal's ears swiveled, tracking the smallest movement of her left hand as she checked that her knife was handy. The long, pointed ears had tufts of fur at the ends. It had whiskers something like a cat's. Its legs looked considerably stockier than those of any cat she had ever seen. Its paws were disproportionately huge. A lot of animals had big feet or paws when they were immature and grew into them, making Kahlan think that the creature was possibly young. But that wasn't always true, so she couldn't be sure.

The creature looked up at her with big green eyes and then looked down at the food she was holding. The eyes beneath a heavy brow had the same kind of vertical slit in the iris as a cat's. It had an expressive face that almost told her what it was thinking, with the calm confidence in its own abilities that gave it a curious but relaxed posture. Its ears perked toward her. It apparently found her interesting and worthy of investigation.

"You have green eyes like me," she said softly.

The creature purred louder at the sound of her voice and squeezed its eyes closed for a second. It looked at her again and then inched forward in a cautious crouch, trying to sniff the dried meat in her hand, judging the distance should it decide to lunge.

Kahlan held up the piece. "Would you like one?"

The animal looked up at her as if it understood her words. It clearly wanted the food, but it was also being cautious.

So as not to frighten the creature, Kahlan stayed where she was as she slowly stretched her arm out to offer the piece of meat.

The animal also stretched, leaning forward on its powerful-looking forelegs, its nose twitching as it smelled her hand all the way around. She could see the muscles rippling under the sleek fur of its shoulders. Satisfied, it then smelled the meat, and finally, carefully lifted the piece of the meat from her fingers. When it took the meat she saw that it had a broad mouth of long, needle-sharp, and quite formidable teeth.

Watching her the whole time, it dragged the prize back a short distance and hunched over, gnawing at it very much the way a cat hunched over food as it ate.

Kahlan used her teeth to tear off a piece of her own and chewed as she watched the animal, letting it know she was hungry, too. As happy as the creature was to take the handout, it certainly looked like it was getting enough to eat. By the looks of it, it was built for hunting. By its robust build, it was clearly successful at it.

The dark spots on its back seemed to grow together the farther down they went along the side of the body and up onto the neck. The fur on the head, legs, and big paws was very dark. In the moonlight it was hard to tell if it was dark brown or black. Since the light-colored area on the back under the spots was tan, she guessed that it was probably dark brown. The one exception was the almost white tufts of hair at the points of its ears.

When it finished, the animal looked up and started purring again, content where it was, not yet ready to leave.

"Still hungry?" Kahlan asked with a smile as she offered it another piece. It took the second piece with equal care and withdrew a short distance to gnaw at the second prize.

Kahlan drank water after another piece of salted fish. The animal watched out of the corner of an eye. Kahlan lifted her waterskin.

"You thirsty, little one?"

The creature just watched her with big green eyes. It seemed interested in everything she did, appraising every movement, its ears perked toward her.

Kahlan poured some water into her cupped hand and held it out. The animal rose up a little and moved forward and crouched down to greedily lap at the water with a rough, catlike tongue. When it finished, Kahlan poured a second handful as it waited and watched. It drank most of the second handful, finally seeming satisfied.

Kahlan offered it a third piece of meat. When it rose up and stepped forward she saw that it favored its front left paw.

This time it stayed close as it gnawed the meat in two before swallowing down half of it. As it picked up the other half to gulp it down, it lifted its weight off its front left paw. It seemed less afraid after having the snack, so Kahlan cautiously reached out and with a single finger stroked the sable-soft fur on the foreleg that it held partially up off the rock.

"Do you have something wrong with your foot, little one?"

It backed away. Moving slowly and deliberately, Kahlan reached out toward the paw.

"Can I take a look? Maybe I can help."

The animal stayed in place, tipping its head down, watching her hand as she gently lifted the paw. With her thumb, she stroked the top of the paw while slipping her fingers under the big, soft pads.

She felt the sharp points of a burr lodged between the toes. The fur was wet where the animal had been licking at it, and probably trying to get it out with its teeth.

"It would feel better if you would let me take that out for you. Would you let me?"

She knew that the creature couldn't understand her, but by the way it continued to purr she thought that maybe it found her soft voice comforting.

Since the animal wasn't going to come closer, she turned a little and got up on her knees so she could lean closer and see. With her one hand, she carefully spread the toes and saw the thorny burr lodged between the two of them.

"That has to hurt to walk on. It's not going to kill you, but why don't you let me see if I can get it out," she cooed. "It would feel better."

The thing watched her without showing any reaction, but she was well aware of how close that wide mouth full of teeth was to her face. Other than its thrumming purr, it was as silent as a cat when it moved.

Not wanting the wicked-looking thorns stuck in her own fingers, Kahlan grabbed a nearby stick and bent it in half with the fingers of one hand to use as pincers. She leaned in on her elbows, holding the toes spread with one hand while she worked her thumb and finger on the stick with her other hand to start to pull the burr out. It was one of those small spheres with thorns all around and it was lodged tightly in place.

The animal's purr changed to a low, gurgling whimper as she rocked the burr, trying to pull it out. She hoped that what she was hearing wasn't a growl. The burr was stuck fast.

Its heavy brow drawing down, ears forward, the

animal started pulling the paw back away from her grip on it.

She looked up into green eyes only inches away from hers. "I need to pull it out, all right? Let me help you."

The animal tugged once but then stopped trying to take the paw back. Kahlan took that as consent. Despite the frowning look, she was pretty sure that it understood she was trying to help. She pulled harder trying to draw the burr out. She could see the skin being tugged outward, stuck on the hooked tips of the thorns.

The creature let out a soft wail of pain, but didn't move, so she yanked. The thorn finally came out. Kahlan pressed a thumb over the bloody spot a moment to soften the sting.

She held the thorn up to show the creature and distract it from the hurt. "See? It's out now. All better."

As she let go of the paw, the animal leaned in and sniffed the offending thorn burr, then stretched out its front legs with its chest against the ground and its haunches high in the air. As it stretched, it flexed its paws against the rock and Kahlan saw that it had claws that were just as formidable as its teeth. Finally finished stretching, it turned and walked off toward the woods with that silent, relaxed, loping gait of a cat. As it left she saw that it had a very short, flat, bobbed tail. She also saw that it was a male.

The animal paused to look back over a shoulder at Kahlan for a moment, then silently hopped down off the rock and into the woods. Without making a sound, it vanished in a heartbeat.

Kahlan smiled as she lay down, happy that she had given the beautiful little mountain cat, or whatever it was, a nice meal and rid it of the thorn burr in its paw.

Despite how warm a night it had been at first, once the clouds had broken up it had started turning colder. Kahlan wrapped the small blanket over herself as best she could. She curled up on her side, holding the blanket over her shoulder trying to keep warm so she could sleep. She was exhausted.

She thought about Richard, thought about so many things about him. Despite her worry for him, she knew that Zedd had promised to bring him awake, so she felt somewhat confident. She felt herself drifting off with fits of images flashing through her mind's eye. She was asleep in moments.

At some point in the night, Kahlan woke up.

33

Kahlan squinted as she glanced up and saw that the moon had moved quite a distance across the sky. Dawn was still several hours off.

Even partially submerged in sleep, Kahlan was awake enough to realize that she felt warm and comfortable. That didn't make a lot of sense.

Concerned for the reason, and at how odd it seemed, she forced herself awake in order to figure it out. It was then that she realized she felt something soft and warm against her middle.

Kahlan was astonished to find the furry creature curled up in a ball, sleeping spooned against her stomach.

Its back was to her, its head tucked under the big paw that was now thorn-free.

Kahlan smiled at the unexpected comfort of her little friend nested up with her as she slept. With it pressed tight against her, she realized that it wasn't all that little. It was actually a pretty good size, with a landscape of firm muscles under the silken fur.

Kahlan gently put her hand over it. The fur was short and as soft as sable. The fur was so soft to the touch that she yearned to work her fingers deep into it, but resisted for fear of scaring the animal off, so instead she gently stroked a shoulder and back before letting her hand come to rest on the warm fur, feeling the rise and fall of its even breathing.

The paw moved a little as the eye opened to peer up at who was stroking its back. When it saw Kahlan, the eye slowly closed. It readjusted itself slightly and put the paw back over its face.

Since it purred a little louder and made no effort to get away from her hand, Kahlan was pretty sure that it was content with her touch. That purr was unusual-sounding. It was a more husky sound than a cat made, almost growly.

But then, she knew that this was no typical cat.

It was then that she noticed something else in the moonlight. Atop the rock, three dead rabbits had been laid out neatly side by side in a row. Although freshly killed, none had been eaten.

The creature had brought her a gift.

Kahlan looked down at the animal curled up against her middle.

"Now I know your name. Hunter," she said softly but with emphasis. "Hunter fits you." She stroked behind a tufted ear. "Hunter sound good to you?"

Hunter's only response was to purr a little louder. She could feel the vibration of that contented purr against her stomach.

Kahlan laid her head back down, her hand resting on little Hunter's back, feeling his even breathing and the soft, steady throbbing of his purr.

She smiled as she recalled Richard once admonishing her not to name wild creatures. He had brought her a jar of little fish one time to entertain her while she was recovering from terrible injuries. He had told her not to name them. It wasn't long before she and Cara had named them all.

"Sleep well, Hunter."

Kahlan couldn't help smiling as she fell back to sleep.

34

Ludwig Dreier's gaze drifted around the cramped, narrow streets of Saavedra as he and Erika rode their horses up through the city toward the citadel. Two-story buildings packed with people in cramped apartments crowded in close to the muddy road. Small shops or work areas filled some of the lower floors while carts and vendor stands stood wedged between buildings or in alleyways. Some were covered with tarps to protect the goods of hopeful merchants from the light drizzle.

Ludwig had been to Saavedra to visit the citadel a number of times over the years, and he rather liked the feel of the city. And, he liked the way it smelled.

It smelled of fear.

The people of Saavedra feared the citadel on the hill looking down on them, watching them. Actually, it had been Hannis Arc watching them, and Hannis Arc they feared. The citadel was merely a symbol that embodied those fears. Hannis Arc believed that fear equaled respect, so most everything he did was aimed at earning their full and complete respect.

The bishop had believed that if people feared him, they respected him, they obeyed him, they bowed down to him. He made sure that people were never without cause to fear him.

Ludwig Dreier leaned over in his saddle and spat to the side. Hannis Arc was nothing but a petty despot, the ruler of the pathetic little land of Fajin Province, proud of himself for the way he could instill fear, and because of that he thought himself respected and worthy of more.

He thought himself worthy of an empire.

Because the Dark Lands were such a dangerous place, people were drawn to Saavedra for protection from those dangers. Those people needed food, clothing, and a myriad of other things, which drew in yet more people to service those needs and every other sort of need, from butchers to bakers to healers to merchants to woodcutters to prostitutes. All those people found shelter and relative safety in Saavedra, but it made the whole city feel like it was hunched inward, cowering in fear of everything out in the dark forests beyond and the citadel watching over them. Such fears, both the external and the internal, were wholly justified.

Hannis Arc, if nothing else, was a man of considerable occult talent, and in return for their "respect," he protected the people of his province in general and Saavedra in particular from things even less forgiving than he was. While they lived in fear of the man, at least they lived.

Out in the wilds of the Dark Lands people died

easily, swiftly, and often. There were claws and fangs always ready to take the careless, or even the properly cautious, but there were also things out there that were far worse than claws and fangs always ready to take them when they least expected it.

The Dark Lands were mostly a deserted, trackless waste for good reason. So, people wanted to live in Saavedra or places like it as salvation from those very real dangers beyond the expanse of dark forests.

Weighed in that light, Hannis Arc was a leader they were more than willing to tolerate—not that they had any real choice in the matter. As Ludwig knew so well, if given a choice people always chose the less painful of their options. It was the task of an intelligent leader to limit and properly frame those options so that people could see those choices in stark terms.

The people walking in every direction on the narrow street scattered out of the way when Ludwig and Erika made no effort to take any care in guiding their horses among them. If people didn't get out of the way that was their problem. He was in no mood to indulge inconsiderate people not paying attention to where they were walking. It was their choice to get stepped on by a huge horse, or pay attention and get out of the way.

His mind was on dark thoughts about the tasks that lay ahead.

People stared at him because they recognized his black coat buttoned to his neck, the straight collar closed at his throat, and his rimless, four-sided hat. Even if they hadn't seen him before, they would have heard of him. They knew by his distinctive clothes that he could be none other than Bishop Arc's abbot. They knew that Ludwig ran the abbey, and the abbey was one of those places out in the vast forests beyond the city that they rightfully feared.

Ludwig Dreier smiled as he suddenly realized that he, too, was "respected."

The men and women on the street also stared because Mistress Erika rode beside him. The stunningly beautiful creature, her posture perfect as she swayed easily in her saddle, was worthy of more than a long look, but most people averted their eyes the first instant they recognized her for what she was and then quickly made themselves scarce. Those who did not look away quickly enough risked finding themselves looking into her cold, blue eyed gaze.

A Mord-Sith in black leather was more than enough on her own to make people scatter without the horses urging them to move. Much like the abbot himself, people didn't want a Mord-Sith taking note of them, especially not a Mord-Sith as intimidating as Erika. They believed such a woman's gaze was capable of weighing their very soul.

Ludwig Dreier smiled to himself because that fear was closer to the truth than people realized.

Erika was a Mord-Sith who was more than merely talented at her craft. Others he had used were bumbling oafs in comparison to Erika. Their clumsy ability could hardly be compared to her talents. Erika was an artist.

She could hold a person at the cusp of death for days on end, suspended between the world of life and the world of the dead, from where, when Ludwig Dreier applied his own occult abilities, those people could look into the dark, timeless depths of the underworld and then draw from that dark well to trade him prophecy in exchange for the favor of finally being allowed to cross over and escape the pain that was all that life, and Erika, had left to offer them.

Demoralized people, once their choices were properly framed for them, begged for death, knowing full well that death was their only escape from Mistress Erika. When Ludwig Dreier added the final occult ingredients, they were more than willing to trade the task he asked of them in exchange for that escape.

In that way, Ludwig considered himself an agent of the Grace. He carried them along that thread of the gift coming from the heart of the Grace, and eventually across the boundary between life and death.

But Ludwig Dreier's days as an abbot were over. That was merely a phase of his past, a period of edification, a stepping-stone to his wider future. He had always been considerably more than a mere abbot. No one recognized that, of course—especially Hannis Arc—but he was. In his modest occupation as the loyal abbot, he had remained inconspicuous and unnoticed from where he observed and learned as he waited. That anonymity was a powerful tool he used to leverage his inborn ability into powers he had kept hidden.

Until now.

Ludwig had been content to spend years in obscurity honing his craft and making his plans. All the while, he helped Hannis Arc toward the man's wider goals. Ludwig helped him because it served Ludwig's own plans, and for no other reason.

Ludwig had been born close to the profound occult powers contained for thousands of years beyond the great barrier to the north. All of that occult power could not be contained forever, and the barrier had failed to prevent it from occasionally escaping, even before the barrier itself had finally failed completely. Ludwig had always known that at least some of his innate ability had been a result of those powers slipping through the barrier, unnoticed, and settling in his spark of life at conception.

That had been the source of much of Hannis Arc's ability, as well as many of the lesser talents of some of the cunning folk out in the wilds of the Dark Lands. But Ludwig had such abilities as well, and in greater abundance, augmenting his gift. For that reason, his abilities, and his powers, were unique even if they had remained unrecognized all this time.

He supposed that he had that in common with Richard Rahl. Lord Rahl had grown up completely unaware of his latent abilities. No one recognized those powers in him, much the same as no one recognized them in Ludwig Dreier, except that in Ludwig's case he had been self-aware of his abilities. On his own, keeping to himself, he had studied, worked on, and developed those abilities.

Hannis Arc wore those ancient abilities he had been born with on his sleeve, literally, in the form of his tattoos. He wanted the world to see him standing out. Ludwig Dreier chose to keep his ability concealed until the time was right. With much of his planning coming to fruition, the time was finally right.

Hannis Arc was an agent of chaos, thinking that creating disorder and turmoil would make him powerful. But Ludwig understood that true power accrued to the one who could step into a world swamped by chaos and galvanize the masses to lift him up as the champion of a new order that they so desperately needed. At such a point, given the choices Ludwig would carefully frame for them, whatever order they were offered by him would be embraced as salvation compared to a world crumbling around them at Hannis Arc's hands.

Hannis Arc believed himself the one who would create a new world order by fundamentally changing the nature of life. In reality, Ludwig had actually been the one who had helped Bishop Arc from the beginning to break the world apart, to start sending it spiraling out of control and into chaos, and Ludwig would be the one who was there to put the pieces back together for people desperate for a savior. But he would put things back together his way.

It had all been going well, according to that plan, until the spirit king brought information to Hannis Arc from the underworld, telling him of the things Ludwig had been doing and what he had been planning all along. The two of them had sent the savages, the half people, to extract vengeance by eliminating Ludwig.

Ludwig Dreier possessed profound powers, but even such powers had their limits. He was still only one man and could be overwhelmed by numbers such as the half people had. Hannis Arc and Sulachan had surprised him. They caught him off guard and they had almost crushed him.

Oddly enough, and fortunately enough, Richard Rahl of all people had shown up to rescue his wife before Ludwig and Erika could begin their work on her. Ludwig imagined that the Mother Confessor could unlock profoundly important prophecy. He had been particularly interested in working with her, but Lord Rahl and his troops had arrived just in time to ruin those plans. They had also been just in time to encounter the rampaging half people sent to assassinate Ludwig. The Lord Rahl had been so kind as to eliminate the savages, saving Ludwig and Erika from the fate Hannis Arc and the spirit Sulachan had intended for them.

Sometimes chaos, once set in motion, worked against its agent.

Ludwig had been the one who had helped Hannis Arc with prophecy in order for him to bring the long-dead Emperor Sulachan back from the world of the dead so he could fundamentally change the nature of the world. Ludwig thought that reviving the dead to again fight a failed war was unwise, but it served his purposes so he had helped the bishop in his single-minded task.

In part with the help of pivotal prophecy that Ludwig had provided, Hannis Arc had been able to bring the long-dead Emperor Sulachan back to the world of life.

Neither trusted the other one bit, but both believed they were getting the better end of the deal by far, so for the time being they were trusting companions—the best of chums. Ludwig imagined that each of them smiled amicably, inwardly believing that in the end he would cut the other's throat and be the last one standing.

For now, Ludwig didn't care about their plans—actually it benefited him for the two of them to focus on each other as they initiated the world's fall into chaos. That chaos was, after all, one of the choices Ludwig needed to offer people—the most undesirable choice, of course. Ludwig was content to leave them to it. It would keep them busy for the time being.

Ludwig had his own work to do. After barely escaping the abbey with his life, he needed to establish

a new place from which to work and set in motion
his own plans.

With the citadel only just recently vacated by
Hannis Arc in his rush to be off after bigger things,
it made the perfect place for Ludwig to establish his
new base and at last begin multiplying his power.

Hannis Arc hated being confined to the distant and
forgotten Fajin Province in the dirty little city of Saavedra. He had no intentions of ever coming back to
the place.

Hannis Arc had his eye on the People's Palace. He
viewed himself as worthy of the seat of power for
the D'Haran Empire. He wanted revenge against the
House of Rahl. His eyes were filled with visions of
vanquishing the House of Rahl and taking rule for
himself. As part of his vision, he wanted to rule in
their place from the grand People's Palace, the an-
cestral home of the House of Rahl.

Ludwig had been to the wedding of one of Lord
Rahl's Mord-Sith. The People's Palace was certainly
grand on a scale unparalleled as far as Ludwig knew.
He supposed it was impressive, if you went in for that
sort of thing. He didn't. He wanted to live in the minds
of his subjects, to rule from the perspective of their
every conscious thought—not from a cold marble
palace.

He would live in people's minds, not their palace.

Hannis Arc was instead fixated on basking in the
glittering glory of the palace.

What made the citadel so undesirable to Hannis
Arc made it the perfect spot for Ludwig Dreier to
establish himself. It was a nearly forgotten place. No
one would think to look for him there, least of all
Hannis Arc. Hannis Arc, after all, thought he had

eliminated his abbot. No one would interfere or bother Ludwig as he went about his work.

One day, though, everyone would come to know him and eagerly take the choice he offered them: order rather than chaos. That was what would make him powerful—people choosing to have him rule over them.

Hannis Arc thought that one ruled through fear. Ludwig understood that, ultimately, one ruled people only with their consent. Through the choices he would shape and offer them, they would embrace his rule.

It mattered not to Ludwig where that process started. Ruling the citadel, Saavedra, and Fajin Province was a perfectly satisfactory place to start. It was too small for the likes of Hannis Arc to bother with, or even to think about.

But one day, people would think about it, and then they would wish they had bothered.

In his position as abbot, Ludwig had extracted prophecies and passed important ones along to Hannis Arc at the citadel—the ones he wanted Hannis Arc to see, anyway. Hannis Arc was a pompous ass. He had no idea that Ludwig Dreier was spoon-feeding him what Dreier wanted him to know.

By the way the people on the streets were staring at him, Ludwig realized that the time had come for a new wardrobe, one more befitting his new importance. He was a careful man and didn't make a move without knowing the outcome before he started. He never started a fight unless he knew he could win.

Now it was time to start. It was time to establish rule over his new foothold.

Hannis Arc had done him a considerable favor by

abandoning the citadel and leaving him the beginnings of an armed force. As powerful as his occult power might be, he was still only one man. He needed protection and men to watch his back while he devoted himself to greater things.

Ludwig Dreier turned his horse up the cobbled main road toward the Fajin garrison headquarters and the citadel beyond that those soldiers protected.

A s Ludwig walked his horse between the gates and into the cobblestone square outside the Fajin garrison he got his first close glimpse of the citadel higher up above them. Erika rode beside him, half a length behind, his ever-present protection. For now, his only protection. He would soon have more.

He was pleased to see that the troops had been alerted to his approach and had already set up massive defensive positions. That was the kind of response he would want to defend himself against non-gifted threats.

Since these men knew him, it was a rather respectful show of arms. The soldiers were all out in the open, standing in formation. The slick, wet cobblestone reflected the neat array of lances held out at a uniform angle, but with their butts resting on the ground. It was a cautious defensive line, but he was at least glad to see that they were trusting of no one, not even the bishop's abbot, probably the highest-ranking person in Fajin Province after the bishop himself.

Of course, Hannis Arc never favored other people holding positions of power. Hannis Arc viewed his talents as sufficient to rule Fajin Province without the need of other high-ranking officials. He thought such powerful people might cause him trouble. He tolerated his abbot because Ludwig was smart enough to make himself seem insignificant.

To either side as they rode in, men in brown tunics lined the way into the square. In the square beyond the men lining the road were formations of men set in ranks at an angle designed to funnel the visitors to a central point of the square.

The men in the front row of those ranks wore chain mail. Their swords remained sheathed but at the ready. The second row of men behind them held the angled lances. On one knee in front of the men in chain mail were the archers, arrows nocked but strings not drawn back.

All of the preparations were protective stances, ready but not openly threatening or aggressive to the visitor. The formations were also designed to place the visitors in the center of the square where they could swiftly be surrounded if necessary, with any route of escape cut off.

It was also meant to be a clear signal that any unwelcome actions—from anyone—would not be tolerated.

Officers blocked the open center of the funnel formation leading to the road beyond that went the rest of the way up to the citadel. Since the officers knew him, they stood openly in the key position to block him. They probably thought it would be better if commanding officers turned him away, rather than a lowly foot soldier. Had it been a threat rather than Bishop Arc's abbot, the opening would be totally closed off and the officers would likely have been somewhere in the rear, directing the men at turning away or eliminating the threat.

Beyond the ranks of soldiers in the square, tiered terraces, each with shaggy olive trees, stepped up the rising hillside toward the grounds around the citadel at the top. It was an attempt at an imposing entrance to the seat of power in the sorry little land of Fajin Province. These men were protecting that pathetic seat of power, as if it were a great prize.

Ludwig smiled. In this case, it just so happened that from now on it was going to be just that.

The four men of rank stood almost shoulder-to-shoulder blocking the opening flanked by men with lances, swords, and bows at the ready. Since Bishop Arc had likely left instructions that no one was to enter the citadel in his absence, these men intended to guard the crown jewel of Saavedra.

Ludwig sighed inwardly.

Bishop Arc had, of course, never considered his abbot to be anything other than his loyal minion. No one, really, other than those from whom he gained prophecy, considered Ludwig to be at all dangerous. It was not until after Hannis Arc had left the citadel that he came to see Ludwig as a threat and sent half people to assassinate him. That had been a mistake, because Hannis Arc had not counted on Richard Rahl showing up.

Hannis Arc expected his loyal abbot to carry out his duties, but he never paid much attention to how he accomplished those duties. Hannis Arc assumed that his abbot brought gifted people and some of the cunning folk to the abbey to investigate any prophecy about which they might have knowledge. The bishop never really knew how his abbot collected such a wealth of prophecy, or the work involved, or the talent it had taken. Hannis Arc never realized the powers that Ludwig Dreier possessed.

No one, really, with the exception of those he worked closely with, such as Erika, had any idea of the abilities Ludwig Dreier kept hidden. Ludwig had never trumpeted his talents. He never thought it was a good idea to be boastful and show off, the way Hannis Arc did.

Ludwig's abilities were his own business. He used them as necessary without drawing attention to himself.

Because of that, few people had ever had any real understanding of the powers he wielded.

He thought that it was about time they started to come to understand.

Ludwig and Erika could, of course, have simply charged their horses through the four officers, but that would have brought an obnoxious hail of arrows at their backs. Ludwig could have dealt with those, but it would not have served to further his goal to shape choices. These men would prove useful once he established the new order of things in Fajin Province.

"Abbot Dreier?" General Dobson asked. "What are you doing here? We weren't told to expect you."

Ludwig Dreier calmly stared at the man, letting the silence grow uncomfortable. The general finally felt compelled to speak up again.

"As trusted an aide as you might be to Bishop Arc, he has left very specific instructions. I'm afraid that in his absence we can't allow you to visit the citadel. So, if you would be so kind, please turn around and go back down into the city. You will find accommodations there. Better yet, you would be well advised to go home to your abbey and stay there until the bishop returns and summons you."

"Or what?" Ludwig asked with a small smile. "You going to have your archers shoot me out of my saddle, are you?"

Unaccustomed to such a confrontation from the bishop's abbot, the big general scowled. "If I have to. My orders are that no one is allowed to visit until further notice."

"Ah, well then . . . problem solved." Ludwig lifted an arm in a grand, sweeping gesture. "Notice is hereby given. Now, step aside, General."

The man's scowl deepened. To each side Ludwig saw all the bowstrings drawn back. He sat calmly, letting his horse paw at the wet cobblestones.

"I'm afraid that you don't have the authority to give any such notice, Abbot."

Ludwig readjusted himself in the saddle. "Well now, there you are simply wrong. You see, I am no longer the abbot serving the citadel. I am now Lord Dreier, and I am in charge at the citadel."

"Lord Dreier?" the general asked with a derisive snort. "Lord Dreier! I don't think so."

Ludwig's smile faded. "I suggest that you rethink it while you still can. You can either serve as my general in charge of my troops, or you will be replaced. Last chance given, General Dobson. Make your choice carefully."

The burly general took a step forward and planted his fists on his hips.

"Or what?" He gestured up at Erika. "You will send your Mord-Sith down here to teach me to respect you?"

"Well, the thing is," Ludwig said, almost apologetically, clearing his throat as he leaned down toward the man a bit, "Mistress Erika has been riding hard all day and I'm afraid that the poor girl is far too exhausted to climb down off her horse just to teach you some respect." He turned to Erika. "Isn't that right, my dear?"

Erika's smooth face showed no reaction as she sat tall in her saddle while her horse danced around a little under her. "No, Lord Dreier, it isn't." She pulled her long blond braid over the front of her shoulder, stroking a hand down the length of it. "I am feeling quite fine and nothing would please me more than to dismount and teach this pig to show you proper respect."

Ludwig held an arm out toward her as he spoke to the general. "There, you see? The poor girl is simply far too exhausted from her long ride to carry out such a chore."

Ludwig smiled. "So I will have to do it myself."

36

The general took another step forward as he flicked a finger in command at the archers. Without looking, Ludwig heard the "whoosh" as all the bows ignited in the hands of the men before they could loose their arrows, and then the sounds of the weapons rattling against the cobblestone as they were thrown to the ground before they could burn the hands of the archers. He never took his gaze from the general's increasingly red face.

But he did lift a finger of his own, pointing.

"What's that, there, General? At the corner of your mouth. It looks like you are bleeding."

The man was so angry that he hadn't even noticed yet.

"What?"

Ludwig gestured again. "There, at the corners of your mouth. Isn't that blood starting to run down your chin?"

The general swiped at his jaw and looked down at his hand to see it covered in blood.

"You seem to have caught a disease, or something. I believe I do recall hearing about some sort of illness that has been befalling people. Quite painful, from the accounts I've heard."

The officers to either side began stepping forward, but Ludwig shot them a glare. "I don't think you want to get close to the man. He looks quite infectious." He lifted a cautionary finger. "It could possibly be the plague. I would hate for anyone else to catch the horrifying sickness your commanding general appears to have contracted."

The officers paused, uncertain about what to do.

The soldiers stared in horror at the man. The general's face was almost as red as the strings of blood that had begun dripping from his chin.

"Dreier!" the general shouted. "How dare you . . ."

His voice trailed off in a choking gurgle.

"I am so sorry to have to tell you, General, but your symptoms appear to match the terrible disease I've been hearing about. When I heard the stories, I had thought it might be nothing more than the rumors of country folk, but those rumors appear to be proving true. From what I have been told, it comes on swiftly, first with sores bursting open in the mouth and throat. Such sores are said to bleed profusely."

The general's hands went to his throat. His eyes looked nearly ready to pop from his head. Blood splattered all over the wet cobblestones at his feet.

"From what I've heard of this disease," Ludwig said as he turned his eyes skyward while tapping his chin as if trying to recall, "the second set of symptoms set in quite rapidly."

"What—" The man coughed out a spray of blood, unable to ask what symptoms.

"I've heard that soon after the sores burst, the bones themselves that have become brittle from the malady start breaking. It is said that the ones holding up the most weight, like the leg bones, go first."

A loud snap echoed around the courtyard. It was quickly followed by a second. As both of his lower legs broke, the general dropped heavily to his knees.

"From what I've heard tell," Ludwig went on, "it quickly becomes a rapid progression from there to the embrittled bones all over the body breaking. Quite a horrifying thought, actually, considering how many bones there are in the human body. I'm afraid that I don't know the number, but I've heard there are a lot of them."

Ludwig turned to the men in ranks to his left. "Any of you know the number of bones in the human body?"

They all shook their heads.

Ludwig shrugged. "Well, don't hold me to it, but I seem to recall that the number might be over a hundred, possibly two."

All the men now hung on his every word. They watched in horror as their general held his throat while vomiting blood.

Intermittently, more loud snaps reverberated through the drizzle of the courtyard. The general collapsed onto his side.

"Quite painful, I heard tell, the way they just keep breaking, one at a time," Ludwig said. He let out a deep sigh. "I think I recall hearing that the next thing that happens is that the mere act of breathing is too much for the now brittle bones of the ribs, and they all break."

With that, there is a rapid, ripping succession of pops, like a fistful of dry twigs snapping.

The general gasped and choked as his feet kicked wildly at the ends of broken legs. His muscles could no longer move his broken limbs properly, so the effort made them flop around.

"Well, now," Ludwig said in feigned concerned observation, "you do seem to exhibit the symptoms I've heard about. You seem to have contracted the plague of fools."

The men, standing in stiff panic, glanced at one another, not knowing what to do, not daring to move as they watched their general going through the terrifying throes of a painful death.

"Enough of this," Ludwig said, his patience spent. He flicked out a hand.

In the gloom of the drizzly afternoon, there was a dull red flash deep within the general's chest that could be seen through his body and heavy uniform. In an instant the man's flesh turned black as coal. In the next instant his blackened body seemed to break apart from great pressure and disintegrate into small black nuggets looking something like fragments of charcoal. In the next heartbeat that body, now nothing but blackened bits, crumbled and poured out of the openings in the man's uniform. Some of the dark, jagged pieces of what had been General Dobson tumbled out, bouncing across the cobblestones.

Everyone stood rigid and still, unsure just what they should do. It was now time for Lord Dreier to offer them the choice he had just so carefully crafted.

Ludwig folded his wrists over the horn of his saddle. "Who is next in command?"

Two of the remaining officers took a step away from the third officer left in the middle. He glanced at the men to either side as they distanced themselves from him.

He finally swallowed and said, "I guess that would be me, Lord Dreier. I am Lieutenant Wolsey."

Ludwig smiled. "It would seem, Lieutenant, that the citadel guard of the Fajin army is in need of a general. I appoint you. Congratulations, General Wolsey."

The man blinked in surprise, but he hesitated only for an instant before clapping a fist to his heart and bowing deeply. He knew his life had been spared—at least for the moment.

He made his choice. "Thank you, Lord Dreier."

"Let us all pray that you and your men do not contract the same fatal disease afflicting your former general. I would hate for any more of you to fall ill. You are feeling healthy, aren't you, General? You are in good shape and prepared to carry out your duties?"

The man nodded furiously. "Yes, of course, Lord Dreier. I am healthy and totally prepared to carry out my duties under your command. How may my men and I be of assistance?"

Ludwig glanced to the side. "Well, it appears my archers will need new bows. Theirs fortunately fell apart before the men could accidentally do something stupid—like getting themselves burned."

"Not a problem, Lord Dreier," Wolsey quickly put it. "We have a stock of bows, as well as bow makers and fletchers. I will take care of it immediately so that they are properly armed and can man their positions defending you and the citadel."

Ludwig looked over at the archers. "Is that acceptable to you men?"

They all jumped to attention and clapped fists to hearts.

"Anything else I can do to be of assistance, Lord Dreier?" the new general asked.

"Yes, as a matter of fact, there is. You see, the bishop has gone off on an adventure of some sort." Ludwig wagged a hand vaguely toward the southwest. His nose wrinkled with distaste. "I'm afraid that he is destined not to return, so I am now in command of the citadel. I realize that all you men here have wisely chosen to be loyal to me, but you need to see to it that the staff and the rest of the soldiers and guards are made aware of the new head of household."

"At once, Lord Dreier," the man said as he bowed.

Ludwig leaned forward in his saddle. "I would hate it if anyone else were to catch the disease that so tragically afflicted the general. With such a miasma in the air, it could cause great harm to the people of Saavedra and Fajin Province. Such an illness could easily wipe out half the people of a city, and drive the rest out into the wilderness. Understand?"

General Wolsey clapped his fist to his heart as he nodded. "Absolutely, Lord Dreier. I will personally see to it at once. I am certain that everyone will take the utmost care not to catch the same foul sickness that the general so carelessly caught. I will see to it that my men do their duty of enforcing the rule of law. Anyone disrespecting the Lord Dreier will be dealt with severely, I can assure you."

Ludwig flicked a hand at the crumpled pile of bloody uniform with mounds of black pieces that had poured out and others that had rolled across the ground. "And see to it that this mess is swept up and thrown in the midden heap where it belongs, will you?"

"At once, Lord Dreier."

The new general snapped his fingers at a man closest to him on the end of the rank of lancers. The man nodded and ran off to get something to clean up the mess.

General Wolsey turned back to Ludwig. "With your permission, Lord Dreier, I will take some men and we will go at once to see that the staff makes preparations and that everything is in order for you. I will see to it that you are well pleased with everything and everyone."

Ludwig nodded with satisfaction.

"Are there any Mord-Sith remaining at the citadel?" Erika asked.

The man immediately bowed. "Yes, Mistress, Lord Dreier. Several."

"Have them assembled inside," she said.

Ludwig nodded his agreement. "We will need to speak with them."

Erika smiled at the prospect as she stroked a hand down the long blond braid lying over the front of her shoulder.

As Ludwig threw open the towering main doors and entered the grand greeting room of the citadel, he could see servants in dark gray dresses and crisp white aprons carrying linens and other supplies as they raced through the galleries beyond the stone columns to each side. An older man down on one knee fed sticks of wood into one of the two fireplaces in order to build up the flames to help take the dampness out of the air. A few women to the sides in the same gray dresses were throwing back heavy draperies to let in streamers of gray light. Other women of the staff were lighting lamps on side tables to brighten the gloomy room and welcome the new master of the house.

At the far end of the grand room, a split staircase led up to balconies running along either side of the room above the galleries supported by the stone columns. Halls and doors up on that level led to different areas of the citadel. Ahead, on the balcony level, a single grand staircase in the center beginning with spiraled, marble newel posts on each side led up to the top floor, where Ludwig had heard on previous visits were to be found Hannis Arc's main work area and recording room.

Soldiers, who had decided to take the choice Lord Dreier had offered them, also rushed through the gallery and into halls both on the lower floor and up on the balcony level to make sure that everyone recognized the new order of things in the citadel. Ludwig could hear orders being called out in the distance down various passageways. Everyone, it seemed, was rushing about, urgently seeing to it that proper preparations were being made to receive the new lord of the house.

Once the draperies had been opened wide, the large windows on the front wall beside the entrance doors let in the gloomy light to show off the rich, deeply colored carpets and tapestries, the tasteful chairs and couches in muted tans, and small, polished mahogany tables near the chairs. A thin haze from the fireplaces hung in the air, adding the pungent aroma of wood smoke to the otherwise musty smell.

Ludwig had seen it before and had never been all that impressed. It wasn't that it lacked elegance, it was that the people were what mattered to him. He had never been preoccupied with belongings.

His belief was that if you focused on people and gave them the proper attention required, then the possessions would naturally follow. It seemed to him that most people had it backward, focusing on the value of mere objects, never getting matters right with the people, first, thinking instead that such trappings would convince others that they had attained great power. They had attained only possessions.

"Rather disappointing," Ludwig commented to Erika.

"What's disappointing?" she asked.

"That they folded so quickly. I expect you were looking forward to . . . corrective measures."

"Only when necessary," she said. She clasped her hands behind her back as they stood overlooking the room, watching the servants rush about. "Besides, I know your talents, so I wasn't all that surprised when you only had to kill one of them before the rest had a change of heart. You do have a way with people."

He smiled. "Well, I have found that beheading a snake does tend to take the fight out of the rest of it, making it more flexible and easy to handle."

Erika nodded as she surveyed the room, taking note of each person she saw. "We still have the Mord-Sith."

Ludwig shrugged. "Even less trouble. Generals are plentiful, but Mord-Sith are valuable so I am reluctant to be quite that 'blunt' when explaining it to them."

Erika gave him a testy side glance. "I know these women, Lord Dreier," she said. "I've served with them since we were with Darken Rahl. While I realize that you value the Mord-Sith, and want to conserve a valuable resource, there is one among these here that I think you should know about."

"Why is that?"

"She is the kind who will smile to the face of power and cross you behind your back."

He cast a dark look her way. "You all did that. You all smiled to your master, Darken Rahl, and served him, but you all left him when his back was turned."

"To go to a better master," Erika pointed out.

When Ludwig let out a small grunt, dismissing the excuse, Erika went on. "I took up your offer and willingly turned my loyalty over to you. In your service, you have given me the chance to use my training to fulfill myself as a Mord-Sith, more so than Darken Rahl ever did. You have shown me trust by giving me wide-ranging responsibilities.

"Since then, in return for that trust in me, have I not proven myself to you, Lord Dreier? Have I not carried out all of your instructions and satisfied all of your desires, no matter how difficult, how easy, how large, or how small? Have I not kept your secrets? Have I not stood my ground at your side even in the face of death?

"When the half people came flooding into the abbey to assassinate you, I could have left you. You would have been ripped apart by that many soulless ones. I could have left you to them, when you died my bond to you would be dissolved, and I would have been free. No one would ever have known but me.

"Instead I stood with you when you didn't know what to do. I protected you until I could get you away from there with your life. In all of that, have I not proven my loyalty to you?"

Ludwig's mouth twisted with a pang of guilt for being so quick with an accusation. There had been so many of those bloodthirsty half people coming for him all at once that he hadn't been able to think clearly. In that bewildering moment, Erika had gotten the two of them out of there and to safety. She had known what to do. She had never before mentioned it or ever asked for any recognition for what she had done.

"You have," he conceded quietly. "You have more than proven yourself, Erika. In every possible way."

She smiled, a rare sight other than when using her Agiel on those who required it. She had the pride of a true Mord-Sith, and the devotion to duty.

He supposed that she had indeed proven that while she had left Darken Rahl and Hannis Arc, there was good reason and in turn she had proven loyal to him.

He considered her words about the others, though, realizing that there might be more to it. He didn't like having to worry about a knife in his back, so to speak.

"So which one?" he asked. "Which one would scheme against me behind my back?"

"The brunette. Alice. She is older than the others and her braid is longer—as if that is supposed to mean something to the rest of us. She is the one who first suggested we could leave Darken Rahl and instead throw our lot in with Bishop Arc. We thought such a thing was impossible. We were bonded to Lord Rahl, after all. You can't so simply break such a bond.

"Darken Rahl sent Mord-Sith to visit any number of lands in his far-flung empire. On one such a mission, Alice had come here to the citadel. That was when she first met Hannis Arc.

"Several of the Mord-Sith with her died during the journey. Darken Rahl shrugged when she returned and reported losing several of her sister Mord-Sith. He said it was a dangerous place and it was to be expected. He considered the Mord-Sith to be an expendable asset. He had plenty of Mord-Sith and more than enough of any other woman he might want.

"Alice told us that it was then that she decided that if she ever had the chance, she would break her bond to the man.

"Then, one spring, he again sent some of us off to check up on the petty ruler here, Bishop Arc. Since she had been here before, Alice led us on that mission.

During the journey she began to suggest that we could make it appear that our lives had been lost on the long mission to a far-off and dangerous place."

As he listened, Ludwig stroked his thumb and first finger along the stiff upright collar to either side of his throat. "What made her think that Hannis Arc could take all of you in? After all, you were still bonded to his ruler."

"I asked her that. I told her that leaving him is one thing, but we would still be linked to him through the power of that bond. He would know we were alive. Just leaving wasn't a solution.

"She said that in this case it was. She said that on her first visit to Fajin Province, she had learned of Hannis Arc's hatred for the House of Rahl. He told Alice that if she and any of her sisters ever wanted to leave Darken Rahl, he would provide refuge and with his power he could break their bond, replacing it with a bond to him instead.

"She told us that this was finally her chance and she wanted us to join her, to stay, and be free of Darken Rahl. We accepted and never returned to the People's Palace. With our bond to Darken Rahl broken, everyone there believed us dead.

"So, we had traded one master for another.

"Only much later did I come to discover that, knowing Bishop Arc wanted anything that belonged to the House of Rahl, it had actually been Alice who suggested the scheme to Hannis Arc in the first place. He wanted a number of Mord-Sith as the price of going along with her scheme. She had cooked up the entire plan and delivered us to Hannis Arc.

"It also turned out that in return for delivering us to him, Alice was given mastery over us. The authority Hannis Arc gave Alice over us outside the bond—a separate link all of her own—was not only improper, but went entirely to her head. We are her sisters, not her subjects. Yet she relished her dominion over us merely for the sake of exerting her petty power to make herself feel important. We still had to serve him first and do his bidding, so Hannis Arc never cared.

"She exploits that link not to serve her master, but purely for herself, to feel superior to her peers.

"When several of us were sent to assist you at the abbey, like Hannis Arc she never knew that you had abilities of your own. The truth is, she sent me to work for you as punishment, to humiliate me by having me help you in what she and Hannis Arc often scoffed at as petty and unimportant work."

Hearing that Alice judged his work to be petty was giving him a whole new perspective on the woman.

"It wasn't until after you made your offer to me that I even knew of your actual abilities," Erika said. "Since then I haven't been back here to the citadel. Alice isn't aware that I have taken your bond and I am no longer her chattel.

"For those reasons and others, I do not consider Alice trustworthy. I believe that, given the chance, she would sell you as cheaply as she sold us."

He glanced over at Erika's brooding look. "Would you like me to eliminate her?"

Erika really was an achingly beautiful woman. One of his weaknesses. No doubt one of the reasons Alice enjoyed having the power to dominate her.

Erika gave him a resolute, meaningful look. "Lord Dreier, things have changed completely since then. I am now bonded to you, not Hannis Arc, and therefore Alice has no power over me. I can now deal with Alice if you would like to have her in your service. I assure you, I can not only deal with her, I in fact would take great pleasure in it.

"But, because I don't trust her, I don't know that having me deal with her is in your best interest. I am telling you what I know about her so that you will be better able to make your own decision. I consider that part of my service to you."

He arched an eyebrow as he nodded. "Indeed it is."

"I don't trust the woman one little bit, but you have ways of making even those kind choose to follow you," Erika said. "I only want to warn you so that should you choose to use her services, you are aware of her nature and don't turn your back on her."

He nodded thoughtfully. "Of course." He glanced her way again. "What about the others?"

"The others are like me. They, too, were traded cheaply to Hannis Arc. I trust them.

"But that's me. They will not be at all inclined to trust you. They are still Mord-Sith, and at this moment they are still bonded to Hannis Arc. He is alive, so that bond is active. They would be only too glad to kill you if they even suspected that you are a threat to their master or his rule. Their job is to see that you or someone like you does not pilfer so much as a teacup from his citadel, much less attempt to pull off what you intend to do. When they hear that you want to rule his land, they will be more than trouble."

He smiled over at her as he started across the room. The carpets muffled their boots on the way. "Not to worry."

38

A cross the room, led by a pair of soldiers with short spears, five Mord-Sith in red leather filed into the room. Another pair of soldiers came in behind them. It was purely for show to set the stage. Just one of the Mord-Sith could easily have killed all four soldiers.

The soldiers took up positions at attention at the sides of the room while the five Mord-Sith stood stiffly at the head of the room, up three steps on the platform between the twin staircases. As he approached, Ludwig didn't think that they looked all that pleased to be summoned by a mere abbot.

By now they surely would have already heard rumors of that abbot taking over the citadel. They might not be happy about being forced into servitude to Alice, but that didn't mean they wanted anything to do with him, or intended to allow him to remain a threat to their master for long. Ludwig knew that it would be only a matter of moments before they decided to take matters into their own hands.

He thought it time they had their attitudes adjusted, and they were given a choice of how they would like things to go for them.

"I am Lord Dreier," he said as soon as he came to a halt.

None of the five showed any reaction other than a glare. They were waiting to see what that meant. More than that, though, these were Mord-Sith, and they feared very little, death least of all. This would require a different set of choices.

The brunette, Alice, stood second from his right. She looked like a coiled viper waiting to strike.

Ludwig stepped directly to her. "You have something to say, Mistress Alice?"

She ran her tongue around the inside of her cheek a moment as she stared back, appraising him the way the Mord-Sith appraised people just before they struck out and killed them.

"Hannis Arc told us nothing of such a change," she finally said. "I can't imagine what delusions would make you believe that you can walk into his home when he is gone and proclaim yourself to be 'Lord Dreier' and the master of the house, and expect to be taken seriously."

"The master of Fajin Province," he corrected. "Not merely the master of the house, but the master of all of Fajin Province."

She arched her eyebrow even higher. "Lord Arc told us that he was going to bring down our common enemy, the House of Rahl." She gestured among the Mord-Sith with her in red leather. "We fled the House of Rahl. Hannis Arc took us in. He is our master. As our master, he powers our Agiel and has our loyalty."

"Hannis Arc does not power Mistress Erika's Agiel."

Her scowl deepened. "What are you talking about? Of course he does."

Ludwig looked over at Erika. "Why don't you show one of them how well your Agiel works." He gestured in their general direction. "You pick."

Without delay, Erika gritted her teeth as she rammed her Agiel into the middle of the big blond Mord-Sith on the far right, beside Alice.

The woman gasped in shock as she doubled over, folding around Erika's Agiel. It hurt too much for her to be able to cry out, or even to draw a breath. Erika withdrew her Agiel and let it drop from her fingers to dangle once again at the end of the fine gold chain on her right wrist.

The blond Mord-Sith, blue eyes wide, toppled on her side, curled into a ball on the floor, shivering in agony, still unable to draw a breath despite how hard she struggled.

Ludwig held a hand out toward Erika in invitation. "Feel free to return the favor. Any of you. Feel free to give as good as Erika gave. Show her you are not weak Mord-Sith to be pushed around and that your master still powers your Agiel."

"Gladly," Alice said through gritted teeth.

She spun her Agiel up into her fist. She froze before taking a step. With an astonished expression, she slowly looked down at the weapon in her fist.

Ludwig leaned in, cocking his head. "Problem?"

"It . . . it's dead," Alice said in a confused whisper. "I feel nothing from it. That's impossible. . . ."

The woman Erika had put down struggled back

on her feet and managed to straighten. They all took their Agiel up into their fingers, rolling them around, holding them in a fist. All of them looked confused and a great deal less confident than they had only moments before.

"Puzzling, isn't it?" he asked the five women standing in a row as he paced before them.

Servants to the sides rushed on their way, making sure not to look over at the Mord-Sith and what was going on with the new master of the house. They were obviously trying to get out of the room as quickly as possible. Soldiers rushing through the halls on their way to deliver new orders also quickened their step. Two guards to either side of the room stood at attention, keeping their eyes strictly ahead as if they were statues that saw nothing.

Ludwig stepped forward and circled an arm around Alice's shoulders. "Well, you see, the thing is, Alice, your Agiel is powered by your bond to your master. You were once bonded to Darken Rahl, and that loyalty to him is what powered your Agiel."

"We know that," Alice snapped, her fire back. "Hannis Arc is now our master. Through his profound ability he freed us from our bond to Darken Rahl to become our master and the one to power our Agiel. We are bonded to him."

Ludwig, gripping her shoulders tightly with his encircling arm, gave her an intimate joggle. "Isn't it pretty obvious what has happened?" He gestured toward Erika and then leaned back in, looking at Alice's face from only inches away. "Erika's Agiel works quite well, as I think the woman next to you could attest, but none of yours do. What do you suppose could explain that?"

Alice moved her arms restlessly as she began to

notice a cramping that made her feel uncomfortable. She lifted a hand, and saw that her skin was wrinkled. Prominent blue veins and brown spots covered the back of her hand. She stared for a long moment, trying to understand how her smooth, clear skin had changed.

She abruptly reached up and touched her hair. She pulled the single braid forward and saw her brunette hair now streaked with gray. Moment by moment, as the other Mord-Sith watched, her hair gradually turned ever more gray and brittle. Her skin continued to thin and wrinkle.

Abruptly, one of her upper front teeth dropped from her open mouth and bounced across the carpet. The other four women stared.

Two more teeth quickly followed. Alice reached into her mouth with trembling, arthritic, deformed fingers and took out several more teeth that had loosened and fallen out within her mouth. She scooped out the handful of teeth and stared at them.

In mere moments she looked to have aged at least an additional sixty years.

"You aren't looking well, Alice," Ludwig said with feigned concern, his arm still around her shoulders. "Not well at all." He looked up at Erika. "I don't think she looks well. Do you?"

"No, Lord Dreier, I don't," Erika said in a calm voice. "Not well at all."

"I . . . I . . . don't understand," Alice stammered.

The confusion on her deeply wrinkled face showed that she was clearly telling the truth. She didn't understand. She touched her face, her sagging jowls, her blotchy wrist. She put a hand over her loose red leather, feeling her shrunken breasts.

"What's happening to me?"

Ludwig, still leaning in, his arm still around her shoulders, frowned with a look of concern as he peered up into her face. "Well, do you know, Alice, what I have heard tell a Mord-Sith fears above all else?"

Her panic-stricken, washed-out eyes suddenly turned up to him. "Dying old and toothless in bed . . ."

He nodded earnestly. "That's right, Alice. Dying old and toothless in bed." He finally removed his arm from around her frail shoulders and gestured toward the hallway. "Now, Alice, I want you to go off to bed."

Without objection, looking confused and addled with advanced age, the stooped old woman in drooping red leather started shuffling off to do as instructed.

Once she had shambled off down a hall, Ludwig resumed his place before the other four, clasping his hands behind his back.

"I'm afraid that Alice's worst fears have come to pass. She is shortly going to die in bed, old and toothless." He shook his head sadly as he sighed. "Such a shame."

One of the others swallowed. "Abbot, I mean, Lord Dreier, what is going on?"

He smiled. "Well, it would seem that you have just taken the first step. You recognized me as Lord Dreier. Does that mean that you accept me as your master?"

He cocked his head with a questioning look. "Fully and completely? The master for whom you would lay down your lives? The master who will now hold your bond and power your Agiel?"

Ludwig did not for one moment underestimate the powers that Hannis Arc wielded, but he didn't think the man could do what Ludwig had just done, and apparently the Mord-Sith didn't think so either.

One by one, all four of them nodded.

"Good," he said, smiling, vigorously rubbing his hands together. "Very good. Now, why don't you try those Agiel again."

They did, flicking the weapons back up into their hands, and by the look of resolve coming back into their eyes, it was clear that their Agiel now worked again. The women had been restored to Mord-Sith. They were bonded to him.

"Each of you has given up your bond to your old master, and taken up a new one. You have made wise choices at the right times. First, you gave up your bond to Darken Rahl and instead willingly gave your loyalty and service to Hannis Arc. But Hannis Arc has proven himself unworthy of you, to say nothing of letting Alice rule you in a way unfitting to Mord-Sith."

They shared looks among themselves.

"Now, each of you has again taken a new master— but this time one worthy of your unwavering loyalty. You are now all bonded to me, Lord Dreier, as is Erika. Like Darken Rahl, Hannis Arc is a fallen, unworthy past master. It is now my ability that powers your Agiel."

"We understand, Lord Dreier," one of them said as her back stiffened and her shoulders squared up. "Thank you for the opportunity to serve you."

The others straightened and swore their service, their loyalty, and their lives to him as well.

Ludwig placed a hand on Erika's shoulder. "Mistress Erika has been with me for quite a while." He offered them a smile. "She will of course be your mistress. She is in charge of you and you will do as she says. But that is merely a chain of command; she does not own you, as Alice did. You are again sisters of the Agiel. Understand?"

All of them, standing up straighter, looking well pleased, nodded without reservation.

"Now," he said, "I know enough about Hannis Arc to be able to tell you that I have different requirements of my Mord-Sith. First of all, you are to wear black leather to indicate that you are in service to me. Is that understood?"

Again, they all nodded.

"That service to me extends to the bedroom."

They blinked at the unexpected command, and how blunt he had been about it. But they were far from shocked. It had been one of the reasons they had left Darken Rahl. Ludwig had heard about the way Darken Rahl used women. Hannis Arc, on the other hand, didn't care about their bodies, just their service to him. Ludwig Dreier cared about both.

But unlike their link to Darken Rahl, their link to Ludwig was forged with occult powers. They might have believed that it was in part a function of their belief in his mastery over them and their sworn loyalty as was their previous bond, but it was not. This time it was a bond forged with powers that they could not break as long as they lived, as long as he lived. This time death was their only escape from their bond, no matter how badly they might come to wish they could leave their service to him, the way they had left their service to Darken Rahl.

But he didn't have the same rather exotic cravings with which Darken Rahl had been obsessed. In fact, he considered the things he had heard about what the man did to women in the bedroom to be repugnant. Hardly a wonder they had wanted to be free of him.

Ludwig's Mord-Sith would not be plagued by the same wish to leave him just because he took them to his bed. He had simple tastes and simply enjoyed being with women the way the Creator intended. Mostly.

"Any questions? Comments?"

"No, Lord Dreier," they all said as one.

He turned to Erika. "You pick for me. Pick which one will spend tonight with me."

Erika pointed at the one she knew he would like best, the blonde she had used her Agiel on.

"You."

The Mord-Sith bowed her head. "Yes, Mistress. I am yours tonight, then, Lord Dreier, and any night you would have me."

Ludwig was pleased that, once again, given the choices that he had shaped for them, they had chosen wisely. Once again, his insistence on focusing on people had advanced his cause. It so happened that it had also gotten him a comfortable new home from where he would prepare to offer choices to Hannis Arc's chaos.

He nodded. "It's still early. First, show me Bishop Arc's study—the recording room where he used the prophecy I sent to him."

Although Ludwig had sometimes personally brought some of his important prophecies to Hannis Arc—the ones he wanted to make sure the bishop saw—the man had always insisted on meeting with him in a small secondary office, or in the grand entrance hall, sitting in the chairs, sharing tea, as they discussed the prophecy. While they sipped tea, Ludwig fed the bishop the prophecies he wanted the man to know.

Hannis Arc had never let him see the recording

room, though, the place where he did most of his work. Ludwig wanted to see it himself and know why not.

The woman that Erika had picked for him held her arm out to the side. "This way, Lord Dreier."

Up on the top floor, an old scribe named Mohler nervously fumbled with the keys with one hand while holding a lantern in his other. Ludwig knew the man. He was the one person Hannis Arc seemed to trust, at least as much as he trusted anyone. He was the only scribe allowed to handle the prophecies that Ludwig sent to the citadel.

As Ludwig Dreier impatiently watched the man groping through all the keys on the ring, flipping them over one at a time with a thumb looking for the right one, he gave consideration to simply using his ability to blow the heavy door off its hinges. With a sigh, he reminded himself that there was no need to rush, or use his ability for trivialities.

That was one of the ways he had managed to remain hidden under Hannis Arc's nose for so long—he didn't use his power when he didn't absolutely need to. No one was going to come chase him away from

Hannis Arc's office door. The whole place belonged to Ludwig, now. So he continued to wait patiently.

Mohler looked up. "Sorry, Master Dreier—"

"Lord Dreier."

"Yes," Mohler said, absently, his head bobbing, "Lord Dreier, I meant to say."

Erika lifted the lantern from the man's hand so that he could use both hands to search through his fat ring of keys. Glancing up from time to time, nervous, fearing to be too slow, he sighed with relief when he at last found the key he was looking for. He tried to poke the trembling key in the lock, but he missed several times. Erika finally took hold of the man's gnarled hand, steadied it, and fed the key into the lock.

He looked up. "Thank you, Mistress. I've been opening this door nearly all my life." He hesitated. "I've just never had to open it for anyone other than . . ."

"Understandable," Ludwig said, peering down at the sparse gray hair that lay over the top of the hunched old scribe's bald head. "But you are still opening it for your master."

Mohler looked up and blinked. "Yes, I suppose I am."

The man smiled at the notion as he started turning the key in the lock, jiggling it in a way that he apparently knew the old lock needed in order to give up the secrets beyond. With the proper touch of the scribe's experienced hand, the bolt finally clanged back, freeing the door. Mohler pushed the door in as he stood aside to admit the new master.

Inside, the scribe took his lantern back from Erika as he plucked a long sliver from an iron holder on the wall near the door. He lit the sliver in the flame of his lantern, dropped the glass cover back down, and then rushed around the room using the flaming sliver of fat wood to light candles and lamps.

The recording room was far more expansive than Ludwig had expected, with a high beamed ceiling but no windows. Even with all the candles and lanterns Mohler was lighting, it was rather dark and gloomy. Ludwig scanned the odd collection of various things standing on display.

Those displays were all placed in an even grid pattern, almost resembling pieces placed on a chessboard, and yet the way the cabinets, cases, statues, and pedestals were mixed together randomly made no logical sense, except perhaps as a representation of chess pieces of a game in play.

Ludwig found the confusing arrangement rather obnoxious. He realized, then, that if he wanted, he might have them lined up together in an orderly manner, or placed against walls. He thought it would make more sense if he grouped like things together. As he walked through the room, he mentally began redecorating the place, placing specific things together and making it more convenient to find particular items.

He didn't know how Hannis Arc had worked in such seeming chaos. He supposed that he had lived here his entire life and was used to it. And, of course, Hannis Arc was an advocate of chaos, so in an odd way it did seem fitting.

But it also told Ludwig something important about the way Hannis Arc thought. He was in certain ways brilliant, and in many ways highly focused, while in other ways incredibly powerful, effective, and dangerous, yet he wasn't necessarily logical. At times, he went about things on whim, or became fixated on one thing to the exclusion of all else, such as his obsession with the House of Rahl.

Ludwig saw that the glassed cabinets he walked past held an odd mixture of rarities such as bones from strange creatures, or small statues, mechanical devices, and even round tubes with carved symbols all over them. The symbols resembled those tattooed all over Hannis Arc. They were called story tubes and they had been written in the language of Creation. Ludwig knew that items with those symbols were ancient and exceedingly rare. Lives had been traded for such rare treasures.

There were a number of stuffed animals in various places around the room. Besides the more common creatures in common poses—deer standing in an oval display of grass; a family of beavers on a mound of sticks; and raptors, wings spread, on bare branches—there was a large bear towering up on its hind legs, jaws spread wide, with its claws raised so that it looked perpetually ready to attack.

The things that really drew Ludwig Dreier's attention, though, were the dozens of pedestals evenly spaced in various places throughout the room, conforming to the grid pattern. Each pedestal held an open book. The books were all enormous, with heavy leather bindings that showed great age and wear all around the edges. They would have been hard to move because of their sheer size, but also because they looked quite frail, so they appeared to have permanent homes on their pedestals, rather than on some of the bookshelves against the back wall.

Tables near the book pedestals were piled with disorderly stacks of scrolls. Ludwig recognized many as scrolls he had sent to the citadel—to Hannis Arc—to be recorded in the books of prophecy.

Some of those scrolls still had unbroken seals as they sat waiting their turn to be opened and recorded. Ludwig found that irritating. He had gone to enormous trouble in both time and effort to collect each and every one of those prophecies, to say nothing of the people who had given their lives in that work.

Mohler held out a hand of gnarled, arthritic fingers. "This is my work, Lord Dreier. These are the books you asked about." He gently laid his hand on one of the open books with a kind of reverent affection. "This is where I write down all the prophecy brought to the citadel."

Ludwig frowned. "You mean the prophecy that I sent to the citadel."

The old scribe stroked the knuckle of his first finger back along his gaunt cheek. "Well, yes, Lord Dreier, those, and others."

Ludwig's frown deepened. "Others. What do you mean, others? I was Bishop Arc's abbot. I am the one who uncovered prophecies on his behalf and sent them here, to the bishop."

Mohler dipped his head. "Yes, but there were others."

"Others? What others?"

The old man shrugged his hunched shoulders, hands opened out to the sides. "I am sorry, Lord Dreier, but I was not privy to such things." He gestured to one of the tables piled high. "Scrolls and books are brought in, and I record what is in them here, in these books."

"And only you record prophecy? You recorded all of what is in these books?"

He again placed a deformed hand on one of the books on a pedestal. "These books are my work, but they predate me, of course. They contain the work of many who came before me. All of it is recorded here. I have entered all the prophecy found in these books since Bishop Arc entrusted me with the task back when I was still young. I have worked at this my entire life."

Ludwig realized that Hannis Arc was not the only one privy to prophecy. Ludwig was sure that in all those many years of working with the books, Mohler would have had to go through the books and read what had come before. This unassuming old man probably knew more prophecy than just about anyone else alive.

That made the man useful. Or dangerous.

Ludwig had a sudden thought. "How do you know which book to write the prophecy in? Do you fill one book and then go on to the next?"

"No, each prophecy must go in its proper book."

"How in the world do you determine that?"

Mohler frowned at the expanse of pedestals throughout the room that held books. He seemed confused by the question. "Well, Lord Dreier, each prophecy must be recorded where it belongs."

"How do you know where a prophecy belongs?" he asked patiently. "Did the bishop tell you?"

"No . . . no, that was my job." He gestured at the scrolls. "As you can see, he did not open them beforehand. He would review them after I had entered them. He said that it was easier for him to read it all once it was in my hand. Some of the writing is sloppy, or rushed, or poorly done so they can sometimes be quite difficult to read, so he always waited until I recorded them. It is my job to figure out what they say and then write it down clearly for the bishop."

"But what makes you decide to enter any given prophecy in a particular book?"

"The subject, of course," the scribe said with simple sincerity. "I put them where they belong. That way, if the bishop wanted to review a particular subject, he could go directly to that book, rather than spend time searching through everything."

He gestured to a particular volume not far away. "For example, all the prophecy in that volume is about the House of Rahl. Of course, it is often difficult to categorize prophecy because it is usually about more than one thing. So, I must use my discretion. I try to determine the thrust of the prophecy, what it pertains to, and then I put it in the proper book."

"That's complete lunacy," Ludwig said half to himself.

"Lord Dreier?"

He frowned at the scribe. "That means they would not be set down according to any chronology. There is nothing—no chronology—to link all of these subjects and events."

Ludwig knew quite well that chronology was what mattered most. What did it matter what prophecy had to say about a particular event meant to happen thousands of years ago?

Unless you wanted to know about that event.

Say, the great war and the fate of Emperor Sulachan.

Mohler shrugged. "I rarely have any way of determining chronology, Lord Dreier, so we use the subject as the category."

Ludwig realized instinctively that all of this work was virtually for nothing. There was no real way of determining what a prophecy was really about simply by reading the words. Prophecy was almost always occulted, the true meaning hidden. The words were largely only a trigger for one properly gifted.

Often the words of the prophecy were meant to disguise the true meaning.

All of this work, Mohler's entire lifetime of work, had in reality been for nothing. The categories would be meaningless unless gifted or occulted talents were used to see into the vision of the prophecy to determine the true, hidden, subject and therefore where it actually belonged.

Ludwig supposed that the bishop didn't really care that he was gradually wasting the scribe's entire life on meaningless work. It gave him a place to go look at prophecy as he wished, all written out in the same hand for easy reading. Hannis Arc would have likely completely ignored Mohler's categories.

Before he went to the books of prophecy to inspect them, to see what prophecy Hannis Arc could have gotten from other sources, something on the large desk caught his attention. He decided that he could look at the books later. They probably contained nothing more than redundant prophecy, prophecy Ludwig already knew about because he was the one who had collected prophecy on the subject if it was important enough. The rest couldn't be as valuable as the ones Ludwig had discovered and sent to the citadel, so they could wait.

At the cluttered desk, he went to the ancient-looking scroll that had caught his attention. Unrolling it partway on the desk, he saw a complex tapestry of lines connecting constellations of elements that constituted the language of Creation. Ludwig frowned as he leaned in, studying the writing on the scroll.

"This is a Cerulean scroll," he whispered in astonishment as he straightened. He looked over at the old man watching him. "This is a Cerulean scroll," he said again, louder.

The old scribe showed no reaction. "If you say so, Lord Dreier. I don't know of such things. I can't read it. I only record the regular prophecy. Hannis Arc was the only one to work with items like this. They were his specialty."

His specialty.

A very dangerous specialty.

"You mean to say there are more of these?"

Mohler licked his lips. "I'm not sure. As I say, that was Hannis Arc's specialty. I believe that this is one of the few, at most, with these symbols. But he had other written oddities, Lord Dreier, that might be similar."

"Show me."

Ludwig followed the hunched man as he headed to a cabinet against the stone wall. On the way, Ludwig stopped abruptly. An icy chill ran through him.

"Spirits . . ." he whispered.

"Lord Dreier?" Mohler asked, turning back.

Ludwig looked up. "Spirits have been in this room. I can feel the essence trail they left behind."

Mohler looked a bit uneasy as he glanced around, as if he expected them to pop out of thin air. The four Mord-Sith back near the door watched but had nothing to offer. Erika, standing nearby, looked around and then shrugged.

"What do you know of the spirits that have been in this room?" Ludwig asked the old man.

"Spirits? Nothing, Lord Dreier." He hesitated, then added a thought. "I can tell you that there have been times when I have had the feeling that this room was haunted."

"I've been in here with the bishop before," one of the Mord-Sith back by the door said, "and I have had that same feeling—the feeling that this room was haunted."

"That's because it has been haunted," Ludwig said.

Mohler looked around again, as if fearing there might be invisible spirits about to alight on his shoulder. "So it really is haunted, then?"

"Has been, I said. Not now. Before. Spirits have been to this room."

Mohler blinked. "If you say so, Lord Dreier. I wouldn't know of such things. The bishop never spoke to me of spirits."

Ludwig knew that Hannis Arc would not have spoken to his humble scribe about such matters as he discussed with beings from another realm.

He nodded as he gestured for the old man to continue with what he had been going to show him. Mohler turned and opened a cabinet door to reveal a wall of cubbyholes, nearly all of them holding scrolls.

Ludwig withdrew one with an age-darkened edge. He opened it carefully so as not to damage it. As he thought, it was another Cerulean scroll. He didn't recognize the azimuth angles. He was familiar with the language of Creation, though, and he was disturbed to see that the scroll spoke of prophecy.

Not prophecy, as in revealing prophecy, but about prophecy itself almost as if it were a living thing.

The scroll spoke of a time when prophecy itself might be ended.

40

Ludwig replaced the scroll and hurried over to one of the huge books lying open on a pedestal. A table nearby held some of the scrolls that he recognized as being ones he had sent to the citadel.

Not all had been opened.

"I was working there last," Mohler said as he lifted a hand toward the book, "entering the most recent prophecies."

Ludwig set aside his thoughts about the death of prophecy spoken of in the ancient scroll and instead turned his attention to the book lying open before him. He saw a prophecy that he recognized. It was a prophecy he had recently sent to the bishop. He was satisfied, to a degree, that the prophecy had at least been entered in a book. He had begun to wonder if it had all been left to sit around unopened.

He began carefully lifting the large pages and turning them back, scanning the prophecies, going back to the older things written in the books. He saw prophecy he didn't recognize. Important prophecy.

Growing more suspicious, Ludwig went to the nearest table with the scrolls. He set unopened ones of his own that he had sent to the bishop aside, and pushed the ones he didn't recognize to the other side. Once the scrolls were separated, he selected one of the latter and broke a seal he didn't recognize, opening the prophecy that had come from another source.

As Ludwig read, his mood darkened.

While he didn't recognize the scroll or the hand that had written it, he knew the prophecy all too well.

It was a prophecy he had withheld from the bishop. It was one of the prophecies that Ludwig had uncovered himself and considered too important to send to Hannis Arc.

He quickly broke a seal and opened another scroll and again it was an important prophecy that Ludwig had withheld from the bishop. Quickly opening several more of the scrolls only added to his alarm. One was a trivial prophecy he had submitted to the bishop, but the rest of the prophecies were ones he had extracted himself and deliberately kept from the bishop's eyes.

Someone else, though, had been providing the bishop with those divinations that Ludwig and Erika had discovered by taking people to the cusp of death. Such foretelling had taken great effort to retrieve. He couldn't imagine how anyone else had managed to discover the same prophecy.

While Ludwig had kept to himself what he had discovered, someone else had turned them over to Hannis Arc.

He knew it couldn't possibly be Erika. What he was reading was beyond her ability to reproduce.

Mord-Sith didn't understand complex magic such as prophecy, and it was far too detailed for her to remember.

Such writings took his occult talents to transcribe.

Besides, she was with him almost all the time. She was his bodyguard, as well as his assistant. In those brief times when she wasn't at his side, she would never have had the time to write out even this one scroll, much less all the others.

More than that, there was no way she could have gotten the scrolls out of the abbey and to the citadel. Ludwig had known every coming and going to the abbey. His occult abilities would have alerted him had anyone been sneaking anything out.

No, it had not been Erika. But if not her, then who? No one else at the abbey could have produced these scrolls; no one else had been present to hear the prophecies. No one could transcribe what they had not been there to hear. He would have known if anyone had been using gifted talent to hear the prophecy given by the ones on the cusp of death.

These scrolls containing such important prophecy had come from somewhere else. Hannis Arc had someone else also providing him with prophecy. But who, and more importantly, how?

Ludwig gritted his teeth in anger.

He went to other books on pedestals and scanned a few of the pages. There were prophecies in them that should not be there, prophecies he had not wanted Hannis Arc to see, prophecies that Ludwig had discovered and withheld.

He cast a dark look at the old scribe as he pointed to the table of scrolls he had examined. "Where did these come from? Who sent them?"

Mohler's face paled at the look Ludwig was giving him. "I'm sorry, Lord Dreier, but I don't know. Sometimes soldiers brought in a scroll for the bishop. Sometimes when I arrived in the morning, the bishop was already here and he told me that there were more prophecies that had arrived in the night for me to record. He never said where they had come from and I knew better than to question the man.

"I knew the scrolls that had come from the abbey because I recognized the messenger who brought them, and sometimes you brought them yourself. Even if I had not been around to see them arrive, I recognize the scrolls written in your hand. But I don't know about the others. I can tell you that they are written by at least half a dozen different people and apparently arrived from different places."

"From different places? More than one place? Are you sure?"

Mohler shrugged nervously. "I don't know for sure, Lord Dreier. It could be that they all came from the same place but were written out by different people. Being in different hands, I assumed they were from different places."

That made the most sense, he supposed. Ludwig always worked alone, but that was because he'd had ulterior motives in the prophecy he collected. Other places wouldn't have had that need to work alone, and might have employed a staff, all collecting prophecy from the same source.

Ludwig paced as he considered. This was not good news. Not good news at all. It was going to take a lot of work to catalog all of the prophecies to see which ones Ludwig had withheld that had somehow been provided to Hannis Arc anyway.

He needed to know how much Hannis Arc knew. He didn't like surprises. He needed to know what he wasn't aware of. Prophecy was a blade that the man used to cut down opposition. Ludwig needed to know how sharp was the edge on that blade.

As he paced, his attention was caught by something in a cabinet.

There, on a glass shelf, was a knife. The knife was speared through a withered hand.

But not just any hand.

It was the hand of a spirit, with a faint glow about it, caught and frozen in corporeal form.

The door of the case squeaked as he opened it and took out the knife. He held it up, showing Erika the skewered, mostly transparent hand.

"I don't know for sure what that is," she said, "but I think you have found some pretty convincing evidence of ghosts having been in this room."

"More importantly," he said with a smile, "I have also found a knife that interacts with them."

He pushed the hand off the blade, and once free it vanished in a twisting wisp of vapor. The blade had apparently trapped it in the world of life.

Satisfied that the knife was what he thought it was, he slipped it under his belt until he could look around to see if he could find the sheath for it. The knife was far too valuable to leave lying around. He wondered what other things of such profound value he would find in the room. He wondered, too, what items Hannis Arc might have taken with him.

Ludwig let his gaze roam across the books of prophecy lying open all throughout the room. Prophecy that he had not wanted Hannis Arc to see. But despite his efforts, the man had seen it.

Ludwig sighed.

"Is it going to be a problem?" Erika asked, seeing his worried look at the prophecy.

"The die has already been cast," he said, looking into her steely blue eyes. "Events have already been set into motion. There is no calling them back, now. Hannis Arc has a demon by its tail. It is no less perilous a problem for the spirit king. They need each other. I need neither of them.

"Chaos has now been loosed on the world, but I will rein it in."

Just then, he felt something giving off the slightest tingle at his waist. He reached inside his coat and ran a thumb under his belt until he found the hidden pocket.

Slipping his finger into the pocket, he scooped out his journey book. He flipped open the black leather cover and turned over the first page. He always erased the previous messages as a precaution.

There, he saw new writing.

"My, my, my. Now isn't this interesting."

"What is it?" Erika asked.

"It would seem . . ." he murmured to her as he read the message again to himself, "that things are suddenly looking up."

41

Richard heard someone screaming at him.

They were screaming at him to breathe.

When he tried, he realized that he couldn't draw a breath. He tried again, pulling harder, but it wouldn't come. His lungs burned and it felt like he had the weight of a mountain pressing down on top of his chest.

He felt a hard shock, like a jolt of lightning slamming into him.

The woman screamed again, louder. "Breathe!"

He sat bolt upright and gasped. His eyes popped open.

He sucked in another desperate breath, as if he had been sinking under dark, black waters and unable to breathe and now he had finally gotten his head back up above the water.

He had seen them there, waiting in the blackness, dark wings opening in anticipation of having him.

Nicci was kneeling on the ground to his left, Zedd

to the right. They both had flinched back at how fast he'd sat up. They pressed their fingers back to his temples. It had been Nicci he'd heard screaming at him to breathe, and he now recognized that it had been Zedd's gift crackling through him like lightning.

Nicci closed her eyes as she bowed her head and put trembling fingers of her other hand to her forehead.

"Dear spirits . . . thank you . . ." she whispered to herself.

Richard panted, still confused, still trying to get enough air, still trying to make sense of where he was and what was happening. It felt so good having air fill his burning lungs that he simply wanted to feel himself breathe. It was such a relief not to see the dark ones coming for him.

As his dazed, murky awareness cleared, he could begin to sense the air of desperation around him.

Irena leaned in with joyful surprise. In her exuberance she knocked Nicci's and Zedd's hands off him in order to grip his shoulders. "Richard!" She gave him a gleeful shake. "You're back! You're at last awake!"

Richard blinked as he looked around, finally starting to catch his breath. Then he saw her.

Kahlan, beaming with a big smile, crowded Irena aside as she leaned in to put her arms around him in a tight hug, almost squeezing all the air back out of his lungs. She finally leaned back only because she needed to gaze into his eyes.

Her green eyes, even though they brimmed with tears, had never looked more beautiful to him.

"Welcome back," she whispered to him in relief.

She bent forward, then, and kissed him.

It took his breath, but this time in a good way.

In that instant, it seemed that all the wonderful moments of being with her flashed across his mind's eyes, everything from the first time he had looked into her eyes in the Hartland woods, to the day they were married, to seeing her again, now.

The world was still spinning as all the sights and sounds rushed in around him, but Kahlan's soft lips on his made it all come gracefully to a halt.

Everything at last settled and seemed right again.

As Kahlan finally backed away to let him catch his breath, he saw men of the First File at a respectful distance back beyond the immediate group, all with serious, concerned expressions. Their postures eased in relief.

Towering pines sheltered them under a late-afternoon, leaden sky that threatened drizzle. The light there in the woods, under those low clouds and with the trees all around, was muted and mellow. Richard spotted a squirrel running across a limb, and heard birds singing and chirping. Leaves of a leaning birch tree shimmered in a breath of breeze. He found the sight of the woods all around them, the life all around them, cozy and comforting. It was like being home. It felt safe.

In a way, he was home, back home to the world of life.

It felt as if he had been in a dark place for a hundred years, unsure if he would ever find his way back.

Seeing Kahlan made him forget even the pain and made the vision of the dark ones recede.

He saw a tear run down Nicci's cheek. Zedd, too, looked shaken.

"We made it, then," Richard said, more a statement to himself than a question, and also meant to reassure them that he was indeed back and all right. "We made it up through the gorge. It worked."

Samantha stuffed her head of frizzy black hair under Zedd's arm to worm her skinny body in closer in order to hug her thin arms around Richard's chest.

"Lord Rahl, you're all right! We were so worried."

"I wasn't," Zedd said to the girl who had snuck in under his arm. "Nothing to be worried about." He paused to swallow. "Just a matter of applying the proper skills to the task at hand."

Richard glanced over at Nicci. She rolled her wet blue eyes. He knew, then, that it had not been at all easy.

Although everyone in the camp looked relatively calm, except with regard to his wellness, he was worried that they might still be in danger from the Shun-tuk.

"Where are we? Did you manage to kill all the Shun-tuk that were after us? Were there any survivors? Did we get away from them? Are all of our men safe? Did we take any casualties?"

"Unfortunately, we lost a few of the men, but the rest of us are safe, now," Kahlan assured him. "We made it up out of the gorge, and then the men built a bridge so we could cross a deep chasm."

"A chasm?"

"A deep one, and it's a long, long way around," Commander Fister said from back behind Samantha and her mother. "On the off chance any survived, they will be a long time going around it to get to us."

"They can track us," Richard reminded them.

"With the bridge now at the bottom of that chasm," Kahlan said, "we think we're pretty safe for now."

"Sulachan could have sent others," he reminded

them. "Maybe even worse, it's not only the ones he sends that we need to worry about. Now that the barrier to the third kingdom has been breached, all the various tribes and nations of half people are now free to come out and hunt for those with souls. They migrate like swarms of locusts. Any of them could show up anywhere, anytime."

"We had to stop so Nicci and Zedd could revive you," Kahlan said in their defense. "We had no choice. They didn't think they dared to wait any longer."

Nicci and Zedd looked grim, as if to say Kahlan wasn't telling him the half of it.

Irena leaned to the side so she could see him around Kahlan. "I helped, too."

"Thank you," Richard said to her. He saw the look Nicci gave the woman, but Irena was smiling at him, so she didn't notice. If she had, she might have kept her mouth shut.

He was suddenly aware of how little any of them were actually saying about the battle with the Shuntuk, or what had become of them.

"The plan worked, then?" he asked.

"We're safe for now," Kahlan assured him when she saw him looking from one person to the next, not quite believing it had been all that easy.

His gaze finally settled on Kahlan. No one else existed in that moment.

"Did you have to use the sword?"

The question visibly rattled her.

Looking into the depths of Kahlan's bewitching green eyes for a long moment, watching the specter of that experience ghost across her face, he knew that she had.

He knew what it was like. He knew all about it.

"It's different," he said softly to her, "than killing those with a soul."

Kahlan gave him a knowing nod. Now she knew as well.

"I don't know how you are even able to think with that sword in your hand," she said to him.

"Different?" Zedd interrupted, lifting a hand, leaning in a little, looking back and forth between the two of them. "What do you two mean, different?"

"When you use the sword to take a life," Richard said, "the sword exacts a price for doing your bidding. It brings pain of taking a life. Righteous anger is your shield against the pain.

"Using the sword to kill separates a soul from its worldly anchor of its body, and thus life from death. But half people have no soul, so the sword is freed from any responsibility of guilt in breaking the Grace, so its rage is unbounded, and in turn it gives you no pain for your rampage."

"Guilt?" he asked. "What do you mean?"

Richard thought for a moment how to explain such an experience.

"Well, there is a kind of pressure, a resistance, pushing back at your determination to kill. The soul of that person is struggling to remain here in this world, and their will to live is resisting crossing the boundaries between life and death.

"At the same time, in the back of your mind, there is always a comprehension of the full meaning of life as something sacred. Although necessarily committed to killing in order to preserve the lives of innocent people, that awareness of the soul you are sending to the underworld, and your own innate reverence for life, gives you a counter pressure to the need to do it. Because it was created by one with a soul, that same innate, inward resistance was inescapably forged into the blade.

"But when you kill half people without a soul—and although it is still killing and they may look human—they aren't really human, so there is no resistance to the sword's fury, or yours. You are not sending a soul to the underworld. Battling half people is like being plunged in a world of madness, where you feel boundless ecstasy at the bloodshed the magic can bring to them.

"Both you and the sword are free to kill without that innate resistance. You wade into the slaughter with a kind of immunity to guilt. As a result, your anger, the sword's anger, are liberated on a whole new level.

"It's as frightening as it is glorious."

He was still gazing into Kahlan's eyes. "You used the sword in that way, so you know what I mean."

When she slowly nodded, he knew what she had been through.

"Commander Fister," Nicci said into the sudden silence, "would you please take Irena and Samantha back to get them some of that stew you have had cooking. They have both been standing by for quite a while in case they were needed. Now that Richard is awake they finally have a chance to get a bite to eat. They should do it now, in case we need them later."

By her tone of voice, Commander Fister understood that it was a command she expected to be carried out. He put a big hand under Irena's arm and lifted the woman back with him.

"Come on, ladies, let me get you some of the boar stew," he said, cheerfully eager for her to try it. "I helped make it myself. We added rabbit, spices, mushrooms we collected from stumps, marsh spinach, and some fat snails from along the stream. I'd really like a woman's opinion of how I did."

"Well, I, I would really rather—" Irena stammered, looking back toward Richard, hoping for him to intervene. He only smiled his assurance that the commander was right and she should eat.

"It has to be done by now," Commander Fister said as he dragged her along with him. "Before we serve it to anyone else, I would be honored if you would be the first to taste it and tell me what you think. Samantha, come along and taste it with your mother."

Samantha stood, torn between staying close to Richard and going with her mother. After a moment's hesitation, she ran to catch up with her mother.

"I guess that I could give it a taste," Irena said, looking back over her shoulder as she was being hauled away. Her face brightened then. "I'll give it a taste to make sure it's finished and then bring Richard a bowl. He needs to eat more than any of us."

"Good idea," Commander Fister said. "Let's go have a bowl and see what you think, first."

42

As soon as the two women were dragged far enough away, Nicci, looking particularly displeased, leaned toward Richard, her blue eyes ablaze. Some of her long blond hair fell forward over her shoulder as she peered intently at him.

"What did you teach that girl about using magic?"

He could see Kahlan's small smile as she sat back out of the way, not wanting to get in the middle of it.

"What are you talking about?"

Nicci gritted her teeth. "That girl has a temper. A very bad temper."

"And you don't?" Richard asked.

"Not like hers."

Richard frowned suspiciously as he looked at Zedd's guarded expression and then back at Nicci. "Why? What did she do?"

"That's what I want to know. I asked her where she learned such things"—Nicci jabbed a finger into his shoulder—"and she said that you taught her."

Richard tipped his head back as he realized what she had to be talking about. "Ah. That."

"Yes, that," Nicci growled as she punctuated each word with another poke of her finger. "What did you teach her, Mister 'I don't know how to use my gift'?"

"Actually," Richard said, "I only taught her what you taught me."

Her frown faltered. "What are you talking about?"

"Remember when you explained to me how you made trees explode?"

Nicci's gaze wandered as she tried to recall what she might have said. "All I ever told you was that by using my gift I concentrated heat inside one spot in a tree trunk so that the heat rapidly turned the sap to steam and with nowhere to go it expanded and blew the tree apart."

"That's it. That's the explanation I gave her." Richard tilted his head in toward her. "But, let me tell you, Samantha is really good at it. *Really* good."

"What I told you about how I explode a tree trunk was a superficial explanation." Nicci fixed him with a cynical scowl. "I never gave you any of the important details about how to do such a thing because I was never able to teach you about your gift. That means you have no knowledge of underlying principles or causative factors that you could pass along to her.

"So, you are trying to tell me that you simply gave her that superficial explanation and she was able to do it, like telling her to flap her arms and she could fly like a bird?"

"Well," he admitted, "it wasn't exactly that simple."

"Really," she mocked. "Then how did she manage to do such powerful conjuring from what you told her?"

"Sometimes, in a desperate situation, people can instinctively apply their knowledge to a new problem. We were being chased by a lot of desperate half people. They were like swarms of locusts coming at us. It seemed like there were thousands of them. I didn't stop to count, but I probably cut down hundreds and it made little difference. They just kept coming. There were far too many for me to fight off with the sword.

"Samantha tried everything she knew, but regular magic doesn't work very well on half people. I knew we were in a lot of trouble and needed something more or we were going to die.

"So, since half people are still harmed by things like swords, or even hitting them with a rock, I told her about making trees explode. I told her that she needed to focus her power inside tree trunks to make them explode to try to help stop the half people who were after us.

"She was afraid. She had never done anything like that before. But she couldn't do it, so at that point all we could do was run.

"Then they managed to get around us and trap us. There were so many half people we couldn't fight them off and we were trapped. We both thought we were going to die. I pushed her into a crevice in the rock and then I squeezed in after her.

"In that moment, hiding down in that dark, narrow crack in the rock, just before they pulled us out and we were eaten, she said that she thought about everything that they were taking away from us, all the friends and loved ones these half people were going to kill, how they killed her father and how they would kill her mother, and she got so angry thinking about it that her ability suddenly broke through that mental block and she started blowing the trees apart in order to stop them.

"But it was nothing like I ever saw the gifted do in the war. It's hard to describe. I mean, this was on a scale you can't imagine."

"Oh I think I can," Nicci said with an even look.

"She blew the forest apart," Richard said. "I don't mean she blew some of the trees apart, or even a bunch of trees. I mean she completely leveled everything in sight all around us. Everything. That storm of shattered splinters blasting out in every direction shredded every last one of the half people thousands of them. Nothing was left standing other than a few splintered stumps."

"Thousands," Zedd repeated.

Richard nodded to his grandfather. "That's right. I've never seen anything like it.

"So, that's what I taught her—that she had to superheat the sap in a tree to make it blow apart."

Nicci looked skeptical. "And that's all you told her?"

His mouth twisted as he remembered the rest of it. "I guess that I also told her that getting angry was how I was able to power my gift. I told her that focusing that anger was both an effective way to fight and to use magic."

He looked around at the three faces watching him. "Why, what did she do this time?"

"She stood there all by herself," Kahlan said, "and brought the cliff walls to the sides of the gorge down on the Shun-tuk. They were trapped in the bottom of the narrow pass. For a time, it looked like the whole mountain was coming down."

"Really?" Richard looked around at the grim faces. "You mean she actually brought the cliffs down? But the soldiers were going to handle it." He frowned at Kahlan. "What happened?"

Kahlan sighed. "Zedd and Nicci used magic to eliminate all the ones they could. They killed a great many. But there were many more that were not touched by regular magic. The soldiers needed to take care of the rest of them.

"That battle was going well, and, despite their numbers, your plan was working—it was ruthlessly effective, as a matter of fact. We had them trapped and we were cutting them down.

"But then some of the Shun-tuk with occult powers appeared and started to melt our men."

Richard leaned forward. "Melt them? What do you mean, melt them?"

Kahlan lifted a hand in an uncomfortable gesture at the memory. "It was horrifying. The Shun-tuk used some kind of occult sorcery. In an instant the flesh on the men standing to either side of me seemed to boil as it melted right off them. At the same time their bones came apart. They were killed in a heartbeat. I knew that there was no way we could stop such half people. We had no defense against such occult sorcery."

"The sword could stop them," Richard said.

"I know," Kahlan said. "I killed that one before he could kill any more of us. But I didn't know how many more there were like him. One more? A hundred? A thousand? Later, the sergeant sent to close off the rear reported the same thing.

"The Shun-tuk didn't care how many casualties they were taking. Once they had that bloodlust driving them, they kept coming no matter what, and those with that occult power were going to kill all our men to get at you and me.

"I had to make a split-second decision before we lost everything. I did the only thing I could do. I ordered a retreat. I turned the men back and we ran for our lives. The Shun-tuk were coming after us. We knew that we stood no chance against those Shun-tuk sorcerers."

"So what happened?" Richard asked.

"Your little student happened," Nicci said. "She stood there all by herself in the middle of the gorge with her eyes closed and blew the towering cliffs to either side of the defile completely apart. It looked like the end of the world. It seemed like the entire mountain caved in on the Shun-tuk. It buried the lot of them." Nicci leaned back. "Now I know how she did it."

Zedd's bushy brow drew down. "You think she did with rock what you do with trees?"

"She used what Richard taught her," Nicci told him. "She basically did the same thing as blowing apart a tree. The principle is the same. She concentrated heat into the water seeping through all the cracks in the rock. As wet as it is, the rock is soaked through. With nowhere for the superheated water to escape, much like in the trunk of a tree, the force of it as it was turned to steam blew the rock apart. Actually, since rock is so much harder than wood, it creates a more powerful explosion."

"Can you do such a thing?" Kahlan asked.

Nicci looked at her a long moment. "Maybe, on a small scale. But I couldn't do what she did, I know that much. I can't even imagine how much ability that girl has."

"She said that her mother taught her how to heat

a rock to keep warm at night," Richard said. "She must have used the same technique, but on a larger scale. She's quite talented."

Nicci shot him an angry glare. "She has a dangerous temper."

He shrugged. "Sure, if you're one of the half people her temper is pretty dangerous. But she would never hurt us. She only wants to help."

"That kind of temper—"

"That temper saved all of our lives," Richard said. "She also saved my life along with hers that day in the woods. She also helped me get into the third kingdom, find all of you, and then I was able to get all of you out of there. If not for that temper of hers, we'd all be dead."

"I suppose." Nicci folded her arms. "We don't know nearly enough about her, though, or about her mother. We haven't been together long enough for you to tell me much about what you learned or what happened in the third kingdom, and we've been almost continually on the run so I haven't been able to ask any questions of Irena. I want to know what Samantha and her mother are capable of, what kind of abilities they have."

"As far as I know," Richard said, "they're sorceresses."

"There are sorceresses, and then there are sorceresses."

Richard nodded. "I guess I have a few questions of my own."

"There is still a lot about their village of Stroyza, and their purpose there, that I'd like to know about," Zedd put in. "I would like to have some of the gaps filled in and get some details about them and the people where they live."

"Richard, I brought you some stew!" Irena called out as she rushed toward them, holding it out in both hands.

"Now's your chance," Richard said.

Y ou need to eat," Irena said as she leaned in with a tin bowl filled to the brim with stew. "It's good—lots of wild boar meat. It will help you to get your strength back." She lifted it out toward him again. "Go on, eat."

Richard thanked her as he took the bowl. He was starving.

He held out a hand. "Sit with us, Irena. We'd like to know more about you and your home of Stroyza. We wonder what you can tell us about the north wall, as your village called it."

Her face, an older version of Samantha's, brightened at the invitation. As she was sitting, soldiers brought bowls of stew for everyone else. Kahlan smiled up at the soldier who handed her a bowl. Nicci took one but set it down on the ground beside her. Zedd started eating as soon as he had a bowl in his hands.

Richard was famished, so he had to take a bite, first.

"Mmm. Commander Fister, you make a great stew."

He smiled, happy that the Lord Rahl liked it.

"That's what I told him," Irena said. "I told him you would like it."

Now that the soldiers had brought over more, she and Samantha each had a bowl as well. Their likeness was uncanny. Sitting there beside each other on a small blanket, both skinny, both with the same thick thatch of frizzy black hair, dark eyes, and narrow faces, they looked like an older and younger version of the same person.

The immature femininity of Samantha's smooth features gave her a sweet look. Those same features had hardened on Irena's face into a calculating countenance. Richard could see that behind Irena's smile and dark eyes was a woman who had led a hard life. Where Samantha still possessed the treasure of youthful optimism, Irena had traded that optimism for pragmatism, and it looked like it had been an eager trade.

After swallowing another bite, Richard gestured with his spoon toward Irena. "Tell me about Stroyza. I'd like to hear what you know about the third kingdom and the evil hidden behind that barrier. Tell me what you know of it."

Irena shrugged. "We were given an ancient duty, passed down from one generation to the next, to watch over that barrier. Samantha told me that she showed you the viewing port, where we watched the north wall, as we called it. Our duty was to check that the gates still held."

When she fell silent and went back to eating stew, Richard asked something more specific. "Have there always been gifted living at Stroyza?"

"Yes," she said after swallowing a mouthful. "My husband had an older sister, Clarice. She was the sorceress who led the rest of us gifted in Stroyza, and the rest of the village, for that matter. She had been the matriarch for, my, I can't even remember how many years. Since well before Samantha was born. She was a hard woman, with an iron will, but fair."

"And I take it she passed away?" Zedd asked.

"Yes, a little over a year and a half ago. The men who found her dead in the woods said that she was just sitting there, leaned up against a tree, looking like she had taken a nap and in the middle of it never woke back up."

"Then my mother took her place," Samantha said with obvious pride.

"So, there were no other gifted in Stroyza?" Zedd asked.

"Yes, I have—had—two sisters, both gifted, as were their husbands, although to a lesser extent. I never actually took Clarice's place, though. Stroyza is a small village. It wasn't like it needed a queen to rule over it."

"So this Clarice thought of herself as the queen of the people of Stroyza?" Zedd asked.

Irena shrugged one shoulder. "At times. After her death, the six of us discussed matters when there was need. We didn't include Samantha in those discussions because she is still too young." She thought better of it and smiled over at her daughter. "Well, she was too young. No longer, it seems. She is growing into a fine sorceress."

Zedd reached out, patted Samantha's knee, and gave her a wink. "Yes she is." Samantha beamed.

"So the six of you discussed things, like when you started hearing rumors about the Hedge Maid?" Richard asked, having heard all this before, when Samantha had originally told him. He wanted to hear Irena's version, though.

"That's right. Millicent's husband felt he had a gift of prophecy, and he had long warned of wicked forces loose in the Dark Lands. He considered the rumors to be proof of his ability, but I thought otherwise."

"What do you mean, you thought otherwise?" Zedd asked, looking up from shoveling stew into his mouth.

Irena again shrugged the one shoulder. "The Dark Lands are a vast and dangerous place. In such a place there are always dark forces at work, always evil about. To state the obvious, that they will cause trouble, hardly seems prophecy to me."

"And you believe that's because the evil behind the barrier has long been leaking out," Richard said.

She blinked at him. "That's right. How did you know that?"

"It has been my experience," he said, glancing at his grandfather out of the corner of his eye, "that barriers holding back evil do not fail all at once. Over time, they begin to degrade so that small bits of what is beyond can begin to slip through that barrier. It tends to go unnoticed because the barrier still stands and people have long since forgotten what to look for. They get complacent. As time passes, what slips through grows stronger, until there are precursor events."

Samantha waggled a finger at him. "I bet you're right. I never thought of that, but I bet that's the reason for some in the Dark Lands to have strange powers."

"Like the cunning folk?" Richard asked before taking a spoonful of stew.

"That's right," Irena said, giving him a funny look, as if wondering what else he might already know. "The occult powers locked away behind the barrier thousands of years ago were incredibly powerful. After all, some of those half people have occult powers that can bring the dead back to life again."

"Well, make them move about, anyway," Richard said. "Those powers can animate them and so they can be sent to attack people, but I don't think they are actually alive."

"We read that in the writing on the walls in the tunnels back in Stroyza," Samantha told her mother. "The tunnel outside the viewing port."

Irena frowned at her daughter. "What in the world are you talking about? What writing? What do you mean you read about it in the writing on the walls?"

"All those designs carved into the walls are writing."

"Writing?" She stared in surprise. "Are you sure?"

Samantha nodded that it was so. "The language of Creation."

Irena gave her daughter an admonishing look. "You mean that Richard read the writing."

"Well, yes, it was Lord Rahl who told me it was writing, and what it said."

Zedd was frowning at Richard again. "What was this writing? Who put it there?"

Richard gestured with a spoonful of stew. "It was in the language of Creation, like we found at the People's Palace."

He didn't want to mention out loud about the ancient omen machine associated with the writing they had found back at the People's Palace. He wanted to know things, not reveal them.

Zedd caught his drift and nodded with an "ah."

"So, do you know who put it there? Or when?" Irena asked.

"It was put there by a sorceress named Naja Moon," Richard said. "She intended it to explain to the people of Stroyza, and all the rest of us, the evil that Emperor Sulachan had created in the great war. Her people had not been able to extinguish that evil, but they were able to build a barrier with magic to seal it off and contain it. They warned that it wouldn't hold forever, so the people of Stroyza were to keep watch. It said that was all they could do until the right person came along to put an end to the threat of what was behind those walls."

Zedd was frowning again. Richard realized he had already said too much.

"Did this sorceress from back so long ago say if they knew who would be able to put an end to this evil?" Zedd asked.

When Richard hesitated in answering, Samantha spoke up, eager to tell the story. She drifted her spoon before them, as if pulling back the curtain of time, and then leaned in with the secret sent across time itself.

"Naja Moon said that only the bringer of death could do it, and even then, only by ending prophecy."

Zedd almost dropped his bowl of stew. "The bringer of—"

"So you were saying . . ." Richard interrupted, rolling his spoon toward Irena to get her to go on, "about the evil behind the barrier leaking out?"

Richard ignored his grandfather, turning the conversation back to what he really wanted to know, not what he already knew.

Irena's attention was again riveted on Richard.

"Yes, that's right. My sisters and I always suspected that a little bit of that occult power has been seeping out through the barrier for, for, well, the Creator only knows how long. But I think it explains a lot of things about the Dark Lands."

"That certainly makes a lot of sense," Zedd said as he thought it over. He seemed to have gotten the message that this was not the time or place to discuss the bringer of death. Zedd knew all too well that the bringer of death referred to Richard.

"Power like that is not easy to contain," he explained. "While that barrier may have held for thousands of years, it would have begun to deteriorate long before it finally suffered a total catastrophic failure. That's the way such things work."

"My suspicion as well," Irena said. "When we started hearing rumors about this Hedge Maid, Jit, as the country people called her, and the strange healing powers she was said to have, my sisters and I began to suspect that power leaking out through the barrier had something to do with it. We thought that it might even foretell that the barrier was getting close to failing.

"So, in the fall, when the water level was at its lowest, Martha and her gifted husband went into Kharga Trace to look into the rumors about the Hedge Maid. Martha was experienced and powerfully gifted, so she thought it best if she were the one to go investigate.

"We never heard from them again. Half the village searched for them for weeks. We didn't know where in Kharga Trace to look for this Hedge Maid, and besides how vast it is, that foul swamp is dangerous. We feared more of our people might be hurt or killed, so we had to give up the search.

"Eventually, the spring rains came and the swamp overflowed, washing out remains in the overflow. The remains belonged to my sister and her husband."

Nicci looked up from her bowl of stew. "What kind of remains?" she asked, obviously incredulous that much of anything could be left after all that time in a swamp.

"Bones." Irena tapped her thigh with her spoon. "Just some of the larger, heavier bones, like these."

Nicci frowned. "If Kharga Trace is so dangerous, and people went into the place to see the Hedge Maid for her healing powers, then a lot of people may have died in that swamp. The bones could have belonged to anyone. How did the people in your village know that they were your sister's bones?"

Irena rested her hand with the spoon on her knee, looking off into the distant memories for a moment.

"I'm the one who identified my sister's bones. They carried the telltale trace of the gift. I recognized those traces of the gift as belonging to my sister Martha."

"I see," Nicci said as she put her head down over her bowl and went back to eating her stew.

"Then, not long after that, soldiers came and took my other sister, Millicent, and her husband, Gyles, away to the abbey. I suspect that it was probably because Gyles was always boasting to people that he had the gift for prophecy. The abbey was where Abbot Dreier collected prophecy for Hannis Arc. The soldiers said that prophecy belonged to all the people."

Irena stirred her stew as she stared down into it. "They never returned."

"I know all about Ludwig Dreier," Kahlan said, her

expression darkening. "I have sworn that I will kill him."

By the condition Kahlan had been in when Richard had shown up, just before Dreier and his Mord-Sith, Erika, had started torturing her in earnest, he knew that Kahlan was bound and determined to keep that vow. If Richard didn't get to Dreier first.

"Anyway," Irena said, "when I saw that the gates in the north wall were open, that the barrier had been breached, my husband and I left at once to inform the wizards' council at the Keep."

Zedd looked up from his bowl to share a look with Richard.

"There is no longer a wizards' council at the Keep," Zedd told Irena.

Her expression had turned grim. "I know that now. But at the time I didn't. We didn't make it far before the half people captured us." She swallowed back the anguish. "Well, they captured me. They . . ."

"I'm terribly sorry about your husband," Richard said. "And your father, Samantha."

Samantha, looking dispirited, nodded her thanks.

"Lord Rahl says that in High D'Haran, '*stroyza*' means 'sentinel,'" Samantha told her mother.

"I guess that makes perfect sense. We were there to warn people if the north wall was ever breached."

"And you never knew the meaning of all that writing in the passageway?" Richard asked. "That writing was left there to tell your people the whole story, to explain everything."

Irena looked up into his eyes. "Richard, what difference does it make, now? All of that past history? The barrier is breached. We can't afford to bother with history, supposition, and speculation right now.

"What matters now is healing you. We have to get that taint of death out of you or you will die."

"And Kahlan," Richard said.

Irena glanced over at Kahlan. "Yes, of course, and Kahlan."

44

B elieve me," Richard said, "I know how badly we need to be rid of this deadly poison, but in the meantime there are still—"

"I don't think you do." Irena was finished with being patient. Her expression turned serious in the way sorceresses had of turning serious. "That poison is deadly. We need to get it out of you. That is what matters above all else. Everything else can wait."

"We know that," Richard said, "and we will be able to take care of it just as soon as we get back to the People's Palace. I assure you, I want this out of us more than you do, and I'm going to push to get us back to the People's Palace as fast as we can. Besides needing to get there simply to heal us, we need to get there ahead of Hannis Arc.

"I'm pretty sure that's where he's headed. We have to push hard and get there first. I need to help them prepare for what is coming and set up defenses. The army needs to protect cities in the way of Hannis Arc and his half people."

Irena seemed confused as she looked from one face to another. Her frown turned back to him. "Richard, it can't wait until then. It needs to be done now. Right now."

Zedd paused from scraping the rest of his stew over to the edge of his tin bowl where he could scoop it all up. "We are all concerned about healing them. Although you may not believe it, as his grandfather, I am even more concerned than you, Irena. That is above all else in all our minds at all times."

"Good. So then we should—" she began again.

"But we have to get to the palace in order to do that healing," Zedd continued with the solemn weight of authority as First Wizard.

Irena threw her arms up. "Dear Creator! Aren't any of you people listening? It can't wait that long!"

"It has to," Zedd told her. "We need a containment field in order to do it."

"A containment field? Why?" She gestured toward Zedd, then at Nicci. "We have a wizard and—well three—sorceresses, actually, right here, right now. We can all link our gift to multiply our power. Our linked ability will be strong enough to draw that deadly poison out of them.

"We need to get it out, now. That's all there is to it. We need to get it done at once!"

"We agree with you that it needs to be removed and believe me, we share that urgency." Zedd set down his bowl without taking the last bite. "But I'm telling you, it must be done in a containment field."

As well as Richard knew his grandfather, he knew

that something was wrong and Zedd was trying to avoid saying that something aloud.

"Are you crazy, old man?" Irena said as she scowled at Zedd. "It can't wait for the luxury of being at a palace to take care of it."

"It will have to," Zedd told her with a kind of quiet insistence that covered some deeper worry. "It's not a matter of the luxury of being at a palace, but of having the proper tools to do the job. The taint they have in them is the call of death itself. If we try to extract it outside of a containment field, it would do the same thing to them as it did to Jit—it would call death to them. The only way to get it out without killing them and us along with them is to do it in a containment field. If we were to try to do it now, here, even if we link our gift, it won't matter. The attempt would kill them."

Everyone fell silent. When he listened carefully enough, Richard was able to hear the faint sound of screams deep inside his mind. It was the open void within him between the world of life and the world of the dead. That gateway to the world of the dead was always there inside him—and inside Kahlan—waiting to pull them through.

Right then, he and Kahlan existed in both worlds.

"But with all the gifted talent we have here, we must try to do it now," Irena insisted.

"I'm telling you this for the last time, Irena, and you need to listen to me. It can only be removed in a containment field in order to safely trap and drain that poison," Zedd said with quiet authority that was on the verge of outright anger, "otherwise, that poison will not only kill them, it will also kill any of us trying to draw it out of them."

Richard and Kahlan shared a look. They both knew

that it was getting worse. They could both feel that darkness trying to pull them in. They both knew that Zedd was right.

"But, but," Irena stammered, "they won't live that long."

The surprise of her words sent an icy chill through Richard. "What?"

"I admit," she said, "I am not as experienced at healing as a wizard, but even I can tell from sensing with my gift what was in you that you don't have that long to live. Richard, you will never make it that far. You won't live long enough to make it even halfway back to the People's Palace. You have no chance of making it the whole way. None."

Richard and Kahlan both looked at Zedd. He didn't look back at them.

Richard turned to Nicci, expecting an answer. Nicci stared back into his eyes for a long time before she finally gave him that answer.

"I'm afraid she's right, Richard. We intend to try, of course, to use our ability to give you both strength for as long as we can, but we know that the reality is you won't live long enough to make it to the People's Palace."

"But . . ." Richard searched for words. "There must be something . . ."

Nicci looked away from him as she answered. "Richard, we worked on you ever since the moment we got across the chasm. You were . . . you were close to death that whole time. Kahlan's infection was worse, before, but the poison in you has caught up with hers and you are both slipping away.

"This morning, we lost you to that poison."

Richard frowned at her. "What are you talking about?"

"You stopped breathing. Death was taking you. You were at the cusp of death and crossing over. We were losing you. Zedd did something that pulled you back. Another few heartbeats would have been your last had he not done what he did."

Richard looked over at Zedd. His grandfather's hazel eyes finally turned up to meet his gaze. "I know what I'm doing." A sly smile creased his weathered face. "I still have a few tricks left in me."

It made Richard smile. Despite the gravity of the situation, it made him smile. "Yes, you do."

"All we can do," Nicci said, "is try to keep you alive as long as possible. But the truth is, you don't have long enough to live to make it back to the containment field at the palace."

Irena looked around at everyone else. "Well, all right, if it really needs to be done in a containment field, and the People's Palace is too far, then we simply need to use another one, somewhere closer, that's all."

"Containment fields are quite rare," Zedd said with a heavy sigh. "I hardly think we'll find one in the Dark Lands, of all places."

"Yes, you will," she said.

Zedd's brow drew down, hooding his eyes as he looked intently at her. "Where?"

"Ah, so now you want to listen to me?"

"This is a matter of life and death, Irena. There is no time for games. If you know of any closer containment fields, then tell us where they are."

"I only know of one, actually," she said. "It's at the citadel."

Everyone stared at her.

"A real, functioning containment field?" Zedd

asked. "From a time when our ancestors still possessed such powers that could create such wonders?"

Irena nodded, looking a bit confused at their skepticism.

"A real containment field?" he pressed, again. "A real, working containment field. At the citadel. In Saavedra. In the heart of the Dark Lands."

Again, Irena nodded.

"I have been to important palaces, built back in those ancient times," Nicci said, "that weren't important enough to possess a containment field. I find it more than a little difficult to believe that there would be one out here in the Dark Lands, at a petty citadel in Saavedra. How can you be so sure that you're right?"

"I've been there," she said. "I've seen it."

Nicci still looked more than a little skeptical. "What would a containment field be doing out here in the Dark Lands?"

"Well," she said, "I imagine that it was placed there because of the barrier being so close. My suspicion is that the people who built the barrier thought it would be a good idea to have one handy, if need be, when the barrier finally failed, or maybe for when the occult forces started seeping out before it failed."

"That actually makes a lot of sense," Richard said. "Naja said that they knew the barrier would fail. They knew what we would face when it did. They might have left it there as a precaution to help us, for just such a problem as Jit created."

Zedd rubbed his chin. "That's true. . . ."

Richard had an even more disturbing thought. "Those people back then knew a lot more about

prophecy than we do. They knew a great deal about
the events happening now. They may even have
known that the Mother Confessor and I would
need it."

Zedd arched a bushy eyebrow. "That doesn't seem
entirely outside the realm of possibility."

"They might have known it would be needed," Samantha said, silent up until then, "because you are
the one."

Zedd's frown was back. "The one? What one?"

"The one to stop what is happening now."

Zedd could only let out a deep sigh before looking back at Irena with the more important matter at
hand. "Do you know how to get to Saavedra?"

She pointed to the southeast. "It's off in that direction. It's certainly a lot closer than the palace."

Richard frowned. "You live in the remote village
of Stroyza. What were you doing at the citadel in Saavedra?"

The woman looked flustered to be questioned
about her reasons. "Well, after my sister Millicent
and her husband had been at the abbey for a time, I
feared for them. I had heard that people taken to the
abbey were usually never seen again. We don't get
much news in Stroyza, so I don't know what goes
on there. But I had heard of relatives going to the
abbey to plead for their loved ones to be released
from service to the abbot.

"Knowing that such pleas never worked, and since
I am a sorceress, I went instead to the citadel in Saavedra to plead directly to the bishop to try to get my
gifted sister and her husband released because they
were needed for our important duty at Stroyza. I
thought that perhaps I could appeal to him as one

of the gifted in his service and get him to order their release."

"What did Hannis Arc have to say?" Richard asked.

Irena rubbed the palms of her hands on her knees. "I met with the bishop's scribe every morning, asking for an audience. One was never granted. The scribe told me the bishop was a busy man. I asked him to relay the request, but I never got an audience so I never was able to petition directly to the bishop for the release of my sister.

"But while I was there, waiting every day in hopes of an audience being granted, pacing or sitting around the citadel's grand entrance, the guards got used to me being around. They had heard me speak with the scribe every morning and so they knew what I wanted, but they could do nothing to help me.

"One day the captain of the guards who felt sorry for me asked, since I was a sorceress in service, if I would like to have a tour of the citadel to help pass the time while I awaited word on my petition. Being from a very tiny village, it was a rare opportunity. Even though I was distraught, I accepted the offer. During that tour, he showed me the containment field. It was deep down underground."

"Why would he show you a containment field?" Nicci asked. "They are usually heavily guarded and often shielded."

Irena's gaze roamed as she tried to recall the event. "Well, the guard told me that the area around it gave people gooseflesh, so they stayed well away from the place. He said that being a sorceress, he thought I would appreciate seeing it.

"Since I'm from Stroyza, I don't know what is commonly done elsewhere to protect such places. While he stood outside I briefly went into the stone room. It was pretty plain, old, and covered with dust. There were shackles on one wall. I was more concerned about speaking with the bishop than inspecting the room. There really wasn't anything to see, anyway, so I left.

"But the point is, it was a containment field—I could feel the power of the shields as I walked through the doorway—and it's a lot closer than the People's Palace. We can make it there in time. We can heal Richard and Kahlan there. It's their only chance."

Zedd and Nicci stared at each other. They both smiled.

"We're fortunate that Hannis Arc is no longer at the citadel to interfere," Richard said. "Unfortunately, he is headed to the People's Palace. I had planned to push and get around them so we could reach the palace first. We need to alert the people there. But at least Hannis Arc will not be at the citadel."

Irena leaned in. "If as you say, Hannis Arc has deserted the citadel, then that makes it all that much easier to borrow the containment field so that we can heal the two of you."

In the back of his mind, Richard remembered Zedd's frequent admonition, *Nothing is ever easy*.

He looked over at his grandfather. "What do you think?"

Zedd's hazel eyes turned to look from under his brow at Irena, and then back at Richard. "Desperate times call for desperate measures."

Richard wasn't surprised that Zedd was thinking the same thing he was: the palace was a known quantity; the citadel wasn't. He looked over at Nicci. He noticed that she had not eaten much of her stew.

"Well?"

"Well," she said, "if there really is a functioning containment field there, it's your only chance to live.

I just hope Zedd and I can keep you and Kahlan alive until we can get there."

Richard nodded before looking to Kahlan's green eyes. "What do you think?"

"I want to live, and I want you to live. I don't really see that we have any alternative."

Richard didn't see one, either, but that didn't mean he had to be happy about it. A lot of other lives were at stake. He needed to get to the palace.

He let out a deep sigh as he gazed up at the darkening sky. All the leaves had stilled as the light breeze had died out. Night was closing in around them. Their time was running out. Kahlan's time was running out. The palace was too far.

More than anything else, he could not bear the thought of Kahlan dying. He would do anything he had to do—anything—to keep her alive and out of the clutches of what Sulachan had waiting for her in the underworld. While he feared his own fate there, he feared any harm coming to Kahlan far more.

"All right," he said with finality to all the people watching him, "we go to the citadel. That means a change of other plans, though."

"What do you mean?" Zedd asked.

"No one at the People's Palace has any idea what is coming their way. Hannis Arc and Emperor Sulachan have an army of half people and all the dead they could possibly need. The palace is built to withstand a siege from an army, but this is something different. Everyone at that palace needs to understand the nature of what is headed there so they can prepare."

"Prepare?" Irena exclaimed. "The people there have no chance. If they stay they will be trapped there and slaughtered. Hannis Arc and his forces will kill anyone who resists.

"The situation is hopeless. The palace has to be evacuated. It's the only chance those people have."

Richard regarded her alarm calmly. "Accepting that a situation is hopeless ensures that it is. Defeat is not an option I accept. We need to figure out a way to win."

Zedd cleared his throat. "While I don't agree with Irena that the situation is hopeless, I don't see how we can fight this threat. A number of painful lessons have shown us that magic doesn't work against many of the half people. Hannis Arc and Emperor Sulachan have powerful occult abilities. Perhaps even more frightening, they and many of the half people can raise the dead to send against us. I don't need to remind you that it's pretty hard to kill someone who is already dead."

"You're right," Richard said. "Magic doesn't work all that well against most of the half people, and weapons don't work well against the dead they send at us. But our small force here has proven that we can fight against great numbers of the half people. We also know that, as difficult as it is, we can defeat their dead warriors. They can be stopped with any kind of fire, for one thing, and they can be hacked to pieces.

"The spirit king, risen from the dead, is from that ancient time when people wielded powers that no longer exist. In the world the way it is now, I doubt he has any equal. Hannis Arc, too, is able to wield powerful occult sorcery. After all, Hannis Arc did bring Sulachan back from the world of the dead. I can't even imagine the two of them working together."

"That's what I mean," Irena insisted. "Trying to fight such occult powers is hopeless!"

"If you accept that it's hopeless, then you are doomed to that fate."

Irena spread her arms in frustration. "How do you propose we fight such powers? Magic doesn't work against them!"

"Really? Well, despite their frightening occult powers, and their numbers, little Samantha, here, proved all by herself that they are vulnerable in some ways to what can be done with magic if you are not willing to accept failure."

Samantha silently beamed with pride.

"I'm not saying it will be easy," Richard told them. "I'm saying that it must be done. We can't let them take the world into the nightmare they envision."

Everyone looked grim.

"The people at the palace don't stand a chance unless they understand the true nature of what's coming and are prepared," Kahlan said with quiet resignation. "We need to warn them."

Richard nodded. "Exactly."

"But warn them to do what?" Zedd asked. "I certainly don't think we should give up hope, or abandon the palace as Irena suggested, but how can the people there fight what's headed their way? Out on the Azrith Plain there are no cliffs we can bring down on top of them."

"There are gifted there," Richard said. "There are Sisters of the Light there. Nathan is there. Most of his life has been spent studying prophecy, history, and all sorts of forgotten matters having to do with magic. He often knows about things we've never even heard of before. He may be able to provide valuable information on what we can do. If nothing else, he can lay down wizard's fire on the legions of walking dead.

"Also, the palace has natural defenses. As long as they know what is coming, they can shut the great inner door, and they can seal off the tombs so that Sulachan can't raise the dead within the palace. The First File is there and they have special weapons, remember?"

Nicci frowned. "Special weapons?"

"Nathan found red-fletched bolts for the crossbows. They were relics from the great war left hidden in the palace. They have some kind of ancient power that can penetrate shields and magic. Since they were from back in that time, maybe they can take down those with occult powers the way they can the gifted."

Zedd nodded in thought. "Richard is right. The palace must be defended. There are incredibly valuable and dangerous things there—books of magic and items of great power. It would be disastrous if Hannis Arc got his hands on them."

Richard rubbed his forehead as he considered. "The First File will never surrender. It's not in their nature. We need to warn them what is coming so they can prepare as best they can. They will hold off Hannis Arc and Sulachan's army."

"For a time," Kahlan said.

"For a time," Richard agreed. "If Hannis Arc and that unholy spirit king aren't stopped . . . The First File must hold the palace. At least until we can be cured at the citadel and get there.

"Until then, they need to send the army out to help protect the cities in the way of the advancing horde. They need to do what they can to keep Hannis Arc from capturing cities and laying waste to the places on the way to the palace."

"Do you seriously think any of that is going to work, or do any good at all?" Irena asked.

"Yes," Richard said. "I will make it work. I will not allow the world to be lost to this madness. I am the Lord Rahl. The people of D'Hara are depending on me to be the magic against magic. I will not abandon them to such a threat. I will find a way. There is no other option.

"If I have to come back from the dead to fight for our people, I will."

No one said a word against the grim finality of his vow.

Darkness was settling down around them. There was no time to waste. Richard reached an arm up and called out to get Commander Fister's attention. When he trotted over to them, Richard gestured to a rock and invited the man to have a seat.

"What is it, Lord Rahl?"

"Who is our best rider?" Richard asked him.

Surprised by the question, the commander made a face. "Lord Rahl, these men are all First File. They are all the best. You don't get to be one of the First File unless you are the best of the best at everything. Few men make the cut. Just pick one, Lord Rahl, and he can do whatever job you ask of him."

"We need to get word to the palace," Richard told him. "We only have one horse. We can't afford to have him be too slow, or get caught, and yet he must take care not to kill his horse by driving it too hard. He must reach the palace as soon as possible with my orders."

"What orders, if you don't mind me asking? What does he need to tell them?"

"We must warn the palace that Hannis Arc is coming with an army of half people and likely legions of the dead.

"There is a lot of the Dark Lands the rider will have to get through before he ever makes it back to the palace, and he will also have to somehow get around Sulachan and his forces. It is absolutely essential that our man make it there with instructions. He cannot fail."

"Then we should send Ned," Commander Fister said after a moment's thought. "He was born in the Dark Lands. He grew up in this vile place, a ways southwest from here, I think he said. Southwest is the direction he needs to go to get back to the palace from here. He would best know the lay of the land."

Nicci looked up. "Ned. He is the one who was attacked right after Richard saw those people who vanished, when the Shun-tuk first attacked us."

"That's the man," the commander confirmed. "He would have the best chance to get through. He's tough, he knows the countryside, and he's a good rider. Like the rest of the men, he doesn't know the meaning of giving up."

"Lucky," Nicci said.

Richard looked over at her. Her knees were drawn up with her arms locked around them. Her chin rested on her knees.

"Lucky?" he asked.

She looked into his eyes. "Lucky that he didn't get eaten. Lucky the Lord Rahl would not abandon his people."

She pointedly didn't look at Irena, who had wanted to leave the man to his fate during that first attack.

Not wanting to get into it, Richard merely nodded before looking back at the commander. "Good. Ned it is, then. It's getting dark fast. I want to talk to him before he goes off to get some sleep. There is a lot he needs to know. I have a number of orders for those at the palace. I want him to get a good rest, then in the morning at first light, before he leaves, I want to talk to him again to make sure he remembers it all."

Commander Fister nodded. "Anything else, Lord Rahl?"

"I hear that it was an exhausting, hard-fought battle with those Shun-tuk for most of last night. Everyone needs a good rest. In the morning we all leave for Saavedra."

"And there is no time to waste on that journey," Irena chimed in as she shook a finger at the man. "We need to get there as quickly as possible."

Commander Fister smoothed a hand back over his hair. "Saavedra . . ." he said as he thought about it. He finally looked up. "I'm sorry to admit it, Lord Rahl, but I don't know for certain where, exactly, Saavedra is located."

"Irena says that it's to the southeast. She will lead us."

Irena looked surprised. "Richard, I don't know the land well enough. I set out from Stroyza by trail and then road when I went to Saavedra that one time. Other than that, I rarely left Stroyza. Since you rescued us from beyond the north wall, we've been running all over Creation. I don't really know for sure exactly where we are, now, at least not well enough to lead us to Saavedra."

"It's a big enough city that there will be roads going there," Richard said. "We know the general direction, so sooner or later we will run into a road that leads to Saavedra."

"I'll ask Ned as well," the commander offered. "I imagine he has a pretty good idea of the direction and how to get there."

Richard nodded. "I also want double watches tonight."

Commander Fister clapped a fist to his heart. "Already done, Lord Rahl."

"And Commander," Richard said, making the man turn back, "I want everyone to stay alert. There is a creature out there in the woods that has been watching us."

Commander Fister frowned as he scanned the woods briefly. "A creature? What sort of creature?"

Richard gestured in the direction he had last seen the thing, in the woods behind Kahlan.

"It's back that way. Some kind of mountain cat. Dark spots on its back. It's been watching us, but I don't think it means us any harm or it would have already caused it. Just be aware."

"What color are its eyes?" Kahlan asked.

Richard thought it an odd question. "Green."

"Leave him be," she said. "He won't hurt us. He's just curious."

Richard arched an eyebrow at Kahlan. "He?"

"His name is Hunter." Kahlan smiled at him as she dismissed it with a coy shrug. "Just a little friend I met while you were off visiting the underworld."

"Hunter. You named him." It was not a question, but a reminder of what he had told her once before.

She shrugged again. "He brought me three rabbits. Seemed a pretty obvious name."

"That's where you got the rabbits for the stew?" the commander asked in astonishment. "I had been wondering. . . ."

"He slept with me last night," Kahlan told Richard. "I was upset and afraid for you. The little thing kept me warm and kept me company."

"You named him," Richard said again in admonishment.

Kahlan smiled at him. Her own green eyes sparkled.

"He needed a name."

"Of course he did," Richard said as he shook his head.

W hat are you doing up?" Zedd asked as Richard stepped closer in the darkness.

The flickering light from the low fire in the distance made Zedd's wavy white hair look a little like it was made of flames.

"I was asleep all day," Richard reminded him. "I'm not really tired. I want to check on the men standing watch."

"Ah," Zedd said with a nod.

"What are you doing up?" Richard asked his grandfather.

Zedd stroked a finger along his lower lip. "I confess that I saw you go by, and I wanted to talk to you. Alone."

"Ah," Richard said with a nod. "Maybe something about the bringer of death?"

Zedd smiled in a way Richard knew well. Ever since he had been a boy, when Richard caught on before his grandfather had finished explaining, Zedd would give him that particular smile.

"Well, yes, that was one of the things I wanted to talk to you about. Would you like to tell me about it, or am I going to have to drag it out of you one question at a time?"

Richard held up a hand in surrender. "No, I've been wanting to tell you what I've learned in the hopes that maybe you could shed some light on it."

"So what was written in the language of Creation on those walls you found in Stroyza?"

"I found an account written by Naja Moon. She was a sorceress who worked with Magda Searus and Merritt."

Zedd arched an eyebrow in wonder. "Remarkable. I've never read anything from anyone so close to them."

"It was remarkable to read her account of that time," Richard said. "She explained how Emperor Sulachan had conjured weapons out of people during the great war, and in the process learned how to animate the dead—in part by drawing their souls back out from the world of the dead."

Zedd shook his head with a troubled look. "Crossing the boundary between the worlds of life and death in such a way requires powers I can't begin to fathom. Had I not seen the dead reanimated with my own eyes I would not believe it true."

"Naja said that when the half people were originally created, he instilled occult ability in some to enable them to revive the dead, the same as Sulachan and his wizards were able to do. In the process of creating them, the spirits of those original half people were discarded and left to wander forever between worlds."

Zedd lifted a finger with a sudden thought. "Those people that you said snuck up on you when you were on watch, and then vanished. Do you think . . ."

Richard was nodding. "I think they very well might have been some of those lost souls who wandered back into this world, looking for where they belong."

Zedd shook his head. "The poor souls."

"Indeed. Naja mentioned that some of them show up in this plane of existence and cause trouble. Sometimes they even harm people here."

"Much like the half people."

Richard nodded. "The half people want a soul and think that they can get one by devouring the living to get one, and the lost souls want to be able to find the place they belong. Sulachan doomed both to never being at peace."

The wrinkles in Zedd's face deepened with a troubled frown. He idly rubbed a hand back and forth across his mouth as he considered it. His hazel eyes finally turned to Richard.

"And what does the bringer of death have to do with all that?"

Richard rested the palm of his left hand on the hilt of his sword. "According to Naja, despite everything they tried in order to stop Sulachan's creations, in the end all they could do to keep from being annihilated was to build the barrier to lock that evil away."

Richard smiled. "I guess they did much the same as you did long ago when you created the boundaries to lock D'Hara and the House of Rahl away so that the Midlands and Westland could live in peace."

Zedd nodded in thought. "Yes, except that, by comparison, I built a little fence out of sticks while those people back in the great war built a fortress wall out of stone. Mine lasted decades, while theirs lasted thousands of years."

Richard nodded. "But both were still fated to eventually fail. Naja knew that the barrier, much like the boundaries you put up, wouldn't last forever and then the people of the New World would once again have to face the evil they had locked away. She said that they could do no more than leave people to stand watch."

"I know the feeling," Zedd said, deep in thought. "That's all I had been able to do—lock evil away for a time. Sometimes, you can't eliminate evil; you can only keep it contained."

"Naja also explained, much the same as that Shuntuk prisoner told us, that Sulachan's plan is to dissolve the boundary between life and death in order to rule a united world where life and death exist together. It wouldn't be the world of life anymore, or the world of death, but a third kingdom."

Zedd looked up from his thoughts. "That's crazy."

"Yes, but because of the forces he is using—occult powers that can not only bend but break the elements of the Grace—the mere attempt, no matter how crazy, could very well destroy the world of life."

Zedd peered at Richard. "Do you think him more powerful than the Keeper of the underworld? That's like saying that one man is more powerful than all of Creation and he can take over and dictate everything in life, from how fast grass grows to how high birds can fly to how people must serve him. Thinking he can rule life and death is the very definition of delusional."

"Look, Zedd, I'm not arguing that the man can do what he wants, and neither was Naja. The point is that by the things he has done—creating the half

people, animating the dead, and pulling spirits out of
the world of the dead into this world—Naja's people were sure that he has the wherewithal to rip the
veil. That's all that really matters."

"I still say it's delusional."

"It may be delusional to think you can steal a man's
thoughts by breaking his head open with a rock to
have a look at them, but the man with the head full
of thoughts is dead either way."

Zedd grunted unhappily. "I suppose you're right.
Did she offer any solution, any answers?"

"She said that Sulachan's scheme could only be
stopped by the bringer of death."

Zedd shot Richard a sharp look. "What is the
bringer of death supposed to do to stop such powers?"

Richard's gaze wandered across the dark woods.
The low clouds had drifted silently back overhead
and blanketed the heat of the day, so that it wasn't
as cold as Kahlan said it had been the night before,
when he had been at death's door.

"Have you ever heard of something called 'the Twilight Count'?" he finally asked his waiting grandfather.

"No, I can't say that I have. What is it?"

"I don't know. The way Naja talked about it makes
me think it might have something to do with the chronology of prophecy, like a calendar of prophecy, or
something. It involved some kind of formal calcula-
tion, but she didn't explain it—I guess because people
in her time knew all about it. She did say that they
were able to determine from this Twilight Count that
prophecy holds the key to stopping the threat."

"Prophecy." Zedd's face twisted with a sour expression. "It would have to be prophecy."

"Actually, you may be surprised to hear that she said the threat can only be ended by ending prophecy."

Zedd's frown deepened. "Ending prophecy? How in the world are we supposed to end prophecy?"

Richard looked over at his grandfather. "We? Naja said that according to the Twilight Count, prophecy can only be ended by the bringer of death. That means it can only be ended by me."

"Samantha called you 'the one.' What's that about?"

Richard shrugged. "In many different ways, books of prophecy have all identified me as the bringer of death. In the same way they say I'm the one who is supposed to stop Sulachan by ending prophecy. I think that's why Samantha and the sorceresses of Stroyza have always expected 'the one' to come along and solve the problem they are there to watch over. It could be that they have been taught that the right person would come along at the right time."

"Or it could be something as simple as them knowing that the barrier would eventually fail, and they assume that when it did someone would come along and set things right."

"That makes sense, too," Richard said. "People are always looking for a simple answer, looking for 'the one' who will solve their problems."

Zedd clasped his hands behind his back. "Sounds simple enough."

It was Richard's turn to frown. "Simple?"

"Certainly. The barrier comes down, as Naja's people knew it would. The people of Stroyza were meant to watch for that event. Even if over the centuries they lost the ability to read Naja's message, they probably continued to pass the general concept down from generation to generation, teaching their children that when the barrier failed they had to report it and someone would stop the threat. Over time, the gifted of Stroyza might have simply come to think of that person as 'the one.'"

Richard shot his grandfather an unhappy look. "It may sound simple, but the problem is I'm the one named in prophecy and I don't have any idea how to end prophecy."

Zedd's sour expression returned. "Yes, that part does sound tricky."

"That isn't all," Richard said as he showed Zedd his ring with the Grace on it. "Magda Searus and Merritt left it for me."

Zedd frowned, "The first Confessor herself?"

"That would be the one."

"How do you know it's for you? Was there a message with it?"

Richard nodded. "There were three emblems written in the language of Creation hidden in a shielded door along with this ring. They have been hidden there, undisturbed and undiscovered, for three thousand years.

"The first of the three emblems said, *If you are reading this it is because you are the bringer of death and the barrier has been breached. What we could not stop you now face. War is upon you.*"

"Well, that certainly seems to confirm the business with you being 'the one.' What about the other two emblems?"

Richard squinted in thought, making sure he got the words right. "The second said, *Know that you are the only chance life has, now. Know, too, that you are balanced between life and death. You have the potential to be the one to save the world of life or end it. You are not destined for anything. You make your own destiny.*"

"That sounds like it's referring to the poison in you," Zedd said. "That touch of death you carry means you are balanced between the world of life and the world of the dead."

"That's what I thought," Richard said. "But the problem is that the combinations of cause and effect that result in me being the one to save life, or to end it, are so complex, and there are so many variables, that I don't know how what she said is supposed to do me any good."

Zedd made a sound of agreement deep in his throat. "What about the third part? Did that shed any light on it?"

"Not really. The third emblem said, *Know that you have within you what you need to survive. Use it. Seek the truth. Know that our hearts are with you. Make your own destiny and make it true, for life hangs in the balance. We leave you a reminder to keep with you, of all that is important.*

"Magda Searus and Wizard Merritt wanted me to have this ring as a reminder of what we all fight for."

Zedd considered the words in silence.

"Do you have any idea what I should do?" Richard finally asked.

Zedd's face turned away to stare off into the darkness. "As a matter of fact, my boy, I do."

CHAPTER

47

Richard frowned over at his grandfather, his face shadowed by the light of the campfire. "Really? You know what I need to do?"

Zedd grunted with a nod. "I do. As a matter of fact, that is what I wanted to talk to you about. It's why I came out here to speak with you alone. The message from Magda and Merritt only confirms my thoughts."

Richard rubbed the creases in his forehead. He stopped when he realized that he was trying to rub away the distant sounds of screams deep in his own mind. He focused instead on the buzz and chirp of night insects. Silhouetted against the faint light of the sky, he could see bats from time to time as they silently swooped by on erratic courses to catch flying bugs.

"I could use some advice about now, Zedd," Richard said in a quiet voice. "I'm about at my wits' end. Everyone is depending on me."

Zedd looked over at him. In the hard angles of the old man's face, Richard could see that it was one of those troubled looks that told him this was as serious as Zedd got.

"My boy, after we get to the citadel and remove that poison from you, I think that you should quit."

Richard stared for a moment, not sure he had heard correctly. "What are you talking about, quit? What do you mean?"

"Just what I said. Quit. Give it all up."

Richard frowned, trying to understand. "Give what up?"

"Everything and everyone. It's time you and Kahlan lived your lives for each other. You've both sacrificed your lives together and given up everything you could have with each other in order to fight on behalf of everyone else. I think the time has come for you both to give up everything else and go live for yourselves, for your own happiness. You have done enough, Richard. You have done more than enough."

Richard was stunned. Richard knew by his grandfather's tone of voice that he was deadly serious.

"I don't understand, Zedd. How can I possibly do such a thing when everyone is depending on me?"

Zedd let out a sigh. "Richard, the world was getting by for a very long time before you ever came along. How many times throughout history has disaster been right around the corner? How many times has the world of life been threatened and on the brink? Such things have been going on since long before you ever came along to save the day."

"Yes, but this is one of those threats that even the people back in the great war warned about, and they identified me as the only one who would have a chance to stop it. This is the time when I'm the one meant to step in and act."

Zedd thought about his answer for a moment. "Since the dawn of man, there have always been people bent on harming others. There have been periods of peace and enlightenment, and there have been dark times, but through it all, mankind survived. That cycle has repeated itself over and over. It wasn't always easy, and despite those who would have it otherwise, life went on."

Richard let out a sigh of his own. "It seems like people would learn from that, and let others live their lives."

Zedd shrugged. "I personally believe that it's a basic flaw in mankind's makeup."

"What do you mean? What sort of flaw?"

"Hate. I believe it is a fundamental defect in mankind. While other creatures live to nurture and live their lives, only some of mankind lives that way."

"Sure, there are both good and bad people. I don't understand what you mean by a flaw, though."

"Well, revulsion—hate—is a fundamental function of nature. Hate is a judgment, and judgment is necessary to life. Mice hate owls, so they hide. Rabbits hate wolves. That judgment makes them always ready to run.

"It's necessary and natural to be repelled by things that are harmful to life. It's a built-in natural protective mechanism. We don't have to think it through each time because the judgment is automatic.

"We hate the smell of corpses, for example. We hate it when thieves steal what belongs to us. We hate murderers. It's natural to hate those things, the same way it is natural for birds to hate cats and make a racket in protest whenever one roams by."

Some of Richard's earliest memories were of Zedd speaking in this role, passing along lessons, so he simply listened as his grandfather went on.

"Hatred of the smell of corpses make us bury or burn the dead, which keeps us from getting diseases. Hatred of thieves prompts us to guard against those who would sneak in and steal the food from our children's mouths. We hate murderers because they steal our lives. That kind of hatred breeds caution and causes us to take measures to protect ourselves. We lock doors, we carry weapons, we take a variety of measures to protect our loved ones from those who would cause them harm.

"In animals that hatred stops there. A rabbit does not hate sheep, for example. You will see rabbits and sheep eating grass side by side. Animals will protect their own territory so that they can provide for themselves and their young, but they don't take more territory simply to possess it.

"In humans, we communicate, enabling us to pass our judgment on to others. We might say 'I hated traveling that route because it's so steep that I almost fell and broke my neck.' That judgment, framed in the emotion of hate, is so basic to our nature that it is easily transferred to others.

"But in many people that capacity for hatred loses its natural, rational motive. The emotion runs wild and becomes their dominant trait. They are no longer able to appreciate the good in anything. Having lost the link to rational purpose, they react purely on the emotion. Because of the power of that emotion, their minds become set in that single direction. It becomes so all-consuming that many of those people lose even their capacity to love life. They can only hate.

"The good in life is what quenches hatred in normal people, the way a smile can calm a quarrel. But in those people who carry this flaw, their hatred burns so hot they come to hate what is good in life specifically because they don't want to stop hating. Hatred becomes the driving purpose of their lives. They live to hate.

"That flaw twists nature in on itself. In order to preserve their state of hatred, they must attack the good, wipe away that smile, so to speak.

"That single-minded emotion of hate has been a fundamental, inherent flaw in mankind's nature since the dawn of time. It drives people to fight, to conquer, to dominate, to destroy. Hatred has such powerful emotions attached to it that others take it up out of fear. In that way, hate spreads like a panic in a crowd.

"Expanded beyond its rational bounds, hate exists entirely in the realm of raw emotion, where it ceases to serve a useful purpose, and instead becomes a powerful corrosive that eats away at the fabric of civilization itself, at the very ability of people to interact peacefully. It spawns fights among children and among neighbors, it spawns wars, it spawns genocide and slaughter. It's present in every great land and every tiny village. It creates bullies and tyrants. That unquenchable, passionate, rampant flaw is universal throughout mankind.

"One of the wizard's rules, actually: There have always been those who hate, and there always will be.

"You can't change it. You can only try to keep such people from harming you, for if they can they will. In many ways, fighting them only reinforces that emotion of hate. Even protecting yourself from them only makes them more determined to cause you harm.

"People born with that inherent, tragic defect are like an animal born without eyes. They can only perceive things through the prism of hate. Since they have in a way lost their ability to see, lost that compassionate, tolerant connection to the rest of humanity, they have in a way lost their souls.

"The half people are driven by their nature of being born without a soul, so that trait drives them to behave the way they do. It is a fundamental flaw in their nature that they cannot change. Everything they do is driven by that flaw.

"In much the same way, those driven by hate are like the half people, and in a fundamental way they, too, are alive but without a soul. Both are driven by their inherent defect to destroy life that is complete and wholesome.

"That hatred is so all-consuming in some that they would even deliberately destroy themselves if it enabled them to destroy others along with them. Hatred provides them with the justification for every sort of evil.

"People who carry this inherent trait have been around long before you ever came along, Richard, and they will be around long after you are gone. It's a constant struggle for balance in mankind itself—those who create and those who want only to destroy."

"But we can't let them win," Richard insisted.

Zedd smiled sadly. "Even if you win this battle, the next day someone else will rise up. This is the basic struggle for mankind's destiny—the struggle between civilized reason and savage emotion. It is endless and will go on until it eventually destroys the human race.

"In a perverse way, such evil is encouraged by the mere act of trying to do right by others. That good inflames their hate, drives them on, so in a way trying to do good only feeds evil.

"Maybe the meaning of ending prophecy to stop Sulachan is that you must end life itself. Perhaps it is nature's intent for mankind to die out because the defect disqualifies us as a viable species. Perhaps our species does not deserve to survive.

"In the end, it's a self-canceling flaw in mankind. After all, if those who hate win, then mankind itself is destroyed. Who are you to decide what the outcome of nature should be? That our species deserves to survive?

"In a way, your thinking that you can decide the course of nature is just as deluded as Sulachan's. Who are you, in the scheme of things?

"If it is nature's way to correct its mistakes, then mankind will die out. If that is the case, it matters little what you do. If the die is cast, then if not this time, if not now, then perhaps right after you have left this life, having squandered your entire existence on an ultimately hopeless struggle, the world of man will end anyway.

"Perhaps on the day you die and are no longer in the world of life, after fighting to save the good and decent people of the world, the final man will be born who will tip the scales and have what in his hatred of life he wants most, and finally succeed in throwing mankind into the oblivion of extinction.

"That is why I think you should choose to live your own life, Richard. Take what life you have left and live it for yourself. Leave this fight for mankind to mankind. Ease the world down off your shoulders. Take the weight off Kahlan's shoulders. She carries that weight in part because you choose to do so. Let her live, Richard. Let yourself live."

"But I am the Lord Rahl—"

"Are you doing any of this in order to rule? No. You are not fighting so that others will lift you up as an emperor. You instead want to lift others by letting them live up to their own potential. You are not struggling to rule, but to give others a chance at ruling their own lives. So stop ruling and let them live those lives.

"It should not be up to you alone to fight on behalf of life, it should be up to everyone. That is how nature balances itself.

"If enough people are strong enough in their love of life, then mankind will survive. If there are too many who do not value their lives, but instead hate life and those who love it, then mankind will not survive. You alone can't tip the balance.

"Perhaps mankind does not deserve to survive. If that is the case, then nothing you do can really change the course.

"You have saved the day for everyone enough times, Richard, given them all another day to live. When is it time for your life, for you and Kahlan to live?

"I think the time has come for you to go off and save yourself. Leave the world of life to work it out on its own, the way all of nature in the end must do."

CHAPTER

48

Richard couldn't believe what he was hearing, especially from Zedd. It made him feel very lonely, and very lost.

It made the world seem too big, too overwhelming.

"After all you've taught me, Zedd, how can you give me such advice?"

"I am First Wizard Zeddicus Zu'l Zorander, that's how. I, too, have lived—and live now again—for duty, as you do now. Perhaps I can see better from the perspective of my age what matters in life, what slips away from us when we aren't paying attention, when we're fighting all the time for others."

"Zedd, I'm sorry, but I just don't know how you can suggest such a thing. Would you advise me to let everyone die? I can understand you telling me that I need to remember to live life along the way, but how can you suggest that I let Hannis Arc and Emperor Sulachan go on unchecked? They will kill countless people and very possibly destroy all of mankind in their crazy scheme to rule everything."

Zedd smiled sadly. "There is always someone who wants to rule the world, my boy, someone who wants power, someone who is willing to kill everyone they need to kill in order to get what they want. Wizard's rule, remember? There have always been those who hate, and there always will be.

"Is it your responsibility to save everyone from them?"

Richard searched for words. "It kind of is, Zedd. I'm Lord Rahl. I'm the head of the D'Haran Empire. I took on that responsibility because I want people to be able to live in peace and safety. I am the Lord Rahl who is the magic against magic, the holder of the bond, the one who is duty-bound to protect those people."

"Your duty." Zedd sadly shook his head. "Duty is overrated. And as for your bond, that sickness in you has taken that away."

Richard ran his fingers back through his hair. "I know, but if I don't—"

"What did Magda Searus tell you?" He rolled a finger. "In that second emblem, what did she tell you?"

Richard thought a moment and then repeated the words. "*Know that you are the only chance life has, now. Know, too, that you are balanced between life and death. You have the potential to be the one to save the world of life or end it. You are not destined for anything. You make your own destiny.*"

Zedd arched an eyebrow at Richard. "It seems to me she is giving you the same advice I'm giving you. *You have the potential to be the one to save the world of life or end it. You are not destined for anything. You make your own destiny.* That means that by interfering, trying to help, since you have the touch of death in you, you might inadvertently be the one who causes the world of life to be ended. When she said that you are the only chance life has now, maybe she meant that you must walk away in order to give the world of life that chance."

"I had that same thought," Richard admitted. "But I could also be the one to save it. What if it means that by giving up, and not trying, then life will be destroyed? That would make it my fault."

Richard recognized the mistake before he'd finished saying it.

Zedd didn't miss it either. "Don't blame the victim for the crime. It is not your fault for what others choose to do. Don't let people hang guilt on you if you decide, after all you have done for everyone, after all the sacrifices you have made, to finally live your own life."

Richard nodded. "I know. But if I have the ability to help and I don't, then I don't know how I could live with myself."

"Look, Richard," his grandfather said with a sigh, "it's not like I don't understand. I've been in your place, where half the world depended on me to save them while the other half was trying to kill me and those I loved. I carried the weight of the world on my shoulders, much as you do now."

Richard shared a long look with his grandfather. "So what did you do?"

"After the world had knocked some sense into me, I did the same as I'm advising you to do. I left—quit everything—and went off to live my own life."

"You mean when you fled to Westland and let everyone think you were dead?"

Zedd nodded as he stared off into the memories.

"I gave it all up and took your mother to Westland where we lived our lives in peace and happiness. We had a good life until she died. Then, after that, I mostly had the joy of raising you, away from that call of duty and those who would harm you, away from those who needed me.

"We had a good life, didn't we? Didn't we have the best time?"

Richard couldn't help smiling at the memory. "We did. The best life ever. At least until the boundary failed and Darken Rahl came after me. I miss it, that time when it was you and me. I miss Hartland."

With his bony fingers, Zedd gripped Richard's shoulder. "My advice is that you do the same, now, Richard, as I did. Take your precious wife and go off somewhere all alone with her. Find a safe place where you can be lost to everyone else. Leave the world to work out its own problems while you love Kahlan, maybe raise a family of your own. Leave mankind to work it out, to either survive or drive itself into oblivion.

"Maybe your destiny, your way of saving everyone, is to have children and teach them as I have taught you."

Richard felt a tear rolling down his cheek at such a thought. He remembered when Kahlan had been hurt so badly that he didn't know if she would live. She had lost her child to those brutes. She had almost lost her life. How could he live without her? Life would not be worth living without her.

When she had been hurt so terribly, he had quit everything and taken her back deep into Westland, where no one lived, and built a small home where they could live in peace as she recovered. It was one of the happiest times of his life. It had been life as Zedd was telling him to live it now.

He wondered if Zedd could be right, if he was not only throwing away his own life on a hopeless quest to save mankind from itself, but was also throwing away Kahlan's life. After all, Cara had eventually found happiness, and while she and her husband had been doing their duty, fighting those who lusted to destroy life, she had lost him and lost her chance at happiness. And for what? Was the world any better off?

He felt sick and dizzy at the implications. He felt lost and confused.

"Zedd, with so many good people depending on you, how could you make such a decision? I mean, how were you able to do it?"

Zedd thought for a time. "It was one of the hardest things I've ever done. At the same time, it was easy because I was doing it out of love for your mother, and for you, even though you hadn't been born, yet. I wanted you both to have a life away from any duty but to live for the joy of living. In that time and place, while I had quit and was lost to the rest of the world, you learned what made you the man you are today.

"After all is said and done, Richard, perhaps Magda Searus was telling you the exact same thing, that you can't really save the world of life, and in fact your attempt to do so may be what ends it. Maybe she also saw in the Twilight Count that you needed to take your own beloved Confessor, and go make your own destiny.

"Maybe ending prophecy meant to quit being a slave to it."

With his left hand Richard gripped the hilt of the Sword of Truth sheathed at his hip. He spoke softly, but firmly.

"I'm fighting for the kind of world I want to live in, Zedd, the kind of world where people can live their lives for themselves, where they can work, create, trade, and live without the threat of others taking everything from them—much like the world you fled to and where you raised me."

"That's the kind of world I would wish to live in, too, Richard, but it is nothing more than a wish.

"For those reasons and more, I know that I have grown tired of life. I am weary of struggling against such endless depravity. It seems to me that there is less and less to live for all the time. The two people I love most in the world, you and Kahlan, seem condemned to lives of endless fighting and war that is gradually destroying everything good in the world.

"I ask myself all the time, what is there to live for anymore? I can't live in peace. My whole life, until I quit and fled to Westland, was spent in a life-and-death struggle with that evil. It never ends. I am tired of it, tired of the struggle, tired of the withering plague of hatred, tired of everything.

"That is why I say you need to quit and enjoy what you can of your life while you have it, while you still can.

"Give it up, Richard. Go and live for yourself. Forget the rest of the world. Let the inevitable happen as it will. In the meantime, turn your back to all the hate, take the joy you can, and live for yourselves. Just as I did, you will find that after a time the savage streak in mankind becomes a distant memory and unimportant. Let it become unimportant to you and Kahlan."

Richard fell back on what was most important to him. "But fighting this struggle has also won me Kahlan."

Zedd shot him a look. "Then take what you have won and walk away before you end up losing it.

"When we get that poison out of you, just walk away, Richard. That's my advice. Walk away before you lose it all.

"I will miss you, and may die of a broken heart not to have you close to me, but I will be able to die happy knowing that you are happy and at peace somewhere with Kahlan. I will fight on, knowing that you two are safe and living life.

"I love you both and want you to have that life together.

"That's what love really is, you know, wanting the best for those you love, no matter how much it may hurt you to let them go."

Richard smiled, then. "Zedd, how in the world could I ever be happy without you in my life?"

"Ah, well, my boy, there is that problem."

K ahlan, are you awake?"

Kahlan looked back over her shoulder and saw that it was Nicci leaning down close.

She turned and sat up. "What is it?"

Nicci glanced at the empty bedroll. "Where's Richard?"

Kahlan gestured across the encampment. "He said that he wasn't tired after being unconscious for so long so he wanted to go check on the sentries. He told me to get some rest and he would be back soon. Why, what is it? Is something wrong?"

Nicci drew her lower lip between her teeth as she briefly glanced to each side. "Can I talk to you? Privately?"

Kahlan was exhausted and in no mood to talk, but she knew that Nicci had to be just as tired. She also knew that the woman never engaged in idle chitchat.

If she wanted to talk, it was because it was important or there was something wrong.

Kahlan looked around. There were other people not too far away. They had wanted to keep the encampment tight in case there was an attack. Now that everyone was bedded down and quiet they could easily be within earshot. Nicci had said "privately." Kahlan pointed off to the side of camp.

"Sure. Let's go over there. We can sit on that low boulder under the ash trees."

Nicci glanced back at the place Kahlan had pointed to. "That works."

As it turned out, Kahlan was the one who sat on the rock and covered her yawn with a hand as Nicci paced before her. Kahlan waited, watching Nicci walk back and forth for a while, before she finally decided that the sorceress wasn't going to talk unless encouraged.

"Nicci, what is it? What's wrong?"

It occurred to Kahlan that it was a pretty open-ended question. There were whole constellations of things that were wrong.

"I don't trust Irena."

That was not one of the stars that had been twinkling for attention among the constellations of problems in Kahlan's mind. She would have picked something like her and Richard being on death's doorway.

"All right," Kahlan said in an even tone.

Nicci stopped pacing and faced her. "Didn't you hear me? I'm telling you, I don't trust the woman."

Kahlan shrugged. "All right. Why not?"

Nicci scowled. "Do I need to have a reason?"

Kahlan thought about it a moment as Nicci stared

at her. People usually found such a glare from the be-witching sorceress uncomfortable in the extreme, but Kahlan was not one of those people. She was in no mood for cryptic personal reports in the dead of night. If there was a point, she wanted to hear it.

"Well, if you're asking me to cross her off the guest list for the next palace ball, I suppose I don't need to have your reasons. You've got it. Consider it done.

"But on the other hand, if you are asking me for permission to kill the woman, then I guess I ought to hear your reasons."

Nicci folded her arms as she went back to pacing. She huffed a sigh. "Irena said that when the bones washed out of the swamp, she identified them as the remains of her sister."

"That's right. She said that she detected the residue of the gift in them and she recognized it as her sister's gift."

Nicci came to a halt and leaned toward Kahlan, arms still folded. "Kahlan, I'm pretty experienced—I've been a Sister of the Light, a Sister of the Dark, and Death's Mistress—and I've never heard of the gift being detectable in bones."

That gave Kahlan pause. "You can't recognize traces of the gift in the bones of a person?"

"No."

Kahlan was surprised, but she was tired and didn't feel like working out what seemed like a trivial puzzle.

"Well, just because you never heard of it and you can't do it, that doesn't mean it can't be done."

"In this case I'm pretty sure it does." By her tone of voice, Nicci was in no mood for games, either. She expected her word in this to be taken seriously. "I know a lot about the gift. I used to teach its use. I've worked and studied at the Palace of the Prophets for more than four of your lifetimes, plus the lifetimes of Irena and her daughter added in.

"I'm telling you, I know about these things and you can't detect the gift in human remains, much less identify the person they came from. Maybe occult conjuring can do such things, but the gift cannot. She also said that she knew the captive had occult powers. Zedd and I couldn't detect anything."

"Well, I admit that is kind of odd, but maybe, as she explained, living this close to the barrier some people may have begun to accumulate some of those occult abilities."

"Maybe," Nicci admitted under her breath.

"Is that it? That's the reason you don't trust her?"

Nicci started pacing again. "How did you get to Jit's lair in Kharga Trace?"

Realizing that this was far from over, Kahlan pushed some of her hair back away from her face and turned more serious. "I followed the road toward Kharga Trace until it eventually diminished down into a small trail that led out across the swamp. The trail was hard to miss. It was built out of branches and saplings and such to keep you up out of the water. In some places it was like a bridge, spanning long stretches of open water on its way to Jit's place."

"So it was all up above water, where you could see it."

"Of course. You must know that, though. You would have had to come in the same way to get Richard and me out."

Nicci confirmed with a nod that she did indeed know it.

"Irena said that none of her people knew where the Hedge Maid's lair was located in the swamp, so she didn't know where to look for her sister."

Kahlan scratched an eyebrow. "What of it?"

"You found the way into Jit's. That boy, Henrik, found his way in. People hoping to be healed found their way in. We found the trail made of branches and vines. It's the only way into the Hedge Maid's lair. None of us has ever been in the Dark Lands before and we found it. Stroyza is the nearest village to Kharga Trace. How could Irena not know where Jit's lair was, or about the trail across the swamp?"

Kahlan frowned. "I don't know, Nicci. That does seem a bit strange, but then her people very well might stay close to their cave. The Dark Lands are dangerous. Samantha said that she had never really been anywhere until she went with Richard.

"Do you really think it's all that important? Is that reason enough not to trust her?"

Nicci stopped and gave Kahlan a cold glare. "The woman is in love with Richard."

"So are you."

Had it been any more light than just the moon through the cloud cover and the distant campfire, Kahlan was sure that she would have seen Nicci's face go scarlet.

She went back to pacing for a bit before she spoke again.

"I don't know how to answer to that, Kahlan. You know the entire situation better than anyone, except, I guess, for Richard. A lot of people love Richard, and in a lot of different ways. No one loves him the way you do. Richard loves no woman but you—in that way. You know what I mean."

Kahlan didn't answer.

Nicci flicked her hand in annoyance. "Samantha is in love with Richard as well."

"I know that," Kahlan said.

Nicci stopped her pacing again and faced Kahlan. "But Samantha is an innocent young woman, and she is merely infatuated with a handsome, strong, wise, older man. It's innocent enough. Still, I don't trust her temper."

"It may be much the same with Irena, then," Kahlan offered. "Just an innocent infatuation."

"Really?" Nicci paused in her pacing to give Kahlan a look. "The woman's husband was murdered not that long ago—eaten alive before her eyes. She seems to have gotten over it pretty quickly."

"We can't know that, Nicci. We don't know if she cries herself to sleep."

"I suppose," Nicci grumbled. She shook her head. "But there is something about Irena that seems off. She tries to get close to Richard in a way I don't like. She is always putting her hands on him, touching him, fawning over him, keeping herself in his focus, trying to monopolize his attention." She growled in frustration. "I don't know how to explain it."

"It gives you a knot in your stomach when you see her touching Richard," Kahlan said.

Nicci stopped and pointed a finger at Kahlan. "Yes! That's it."

"Me too," Kahlan said.

50

Nicci was caught off guard. "You don't trust Irena, either?"

Kahlan showed the woman a small smile. "Nicci, I don't trust most people where Richard is concerned. I want him all to myself. But I know that he belongs to everyone, in a way, and I have to tolerate certain things."

"Like me?"

Kahlan was a long time answering. "Nicci, at one time I wanted nothing more desperately than to kill you—over and over in every imaginable horrible manner. I wanted to scream at you as I killed you a hundred times over.

"After all, you had been a Sister of the Dark. You were also a devoted, dedicated believer in the ways of the Imperial Order and Emperor Jagang, whose forces were slaughtering my people and trying to destroy our way of life.

"But worse, you took Richard captive and took

him away from me, away from everyone who needed him . . . for a very long time.

"I hated you.

"But Richard understood how the Imperial Order had controlled and conditioned you from a very young age. Despite that indoctrination, Richard saw something worthwhile deep down inside you. He saw that you were different, and that while you were disciplined in their ways, you were not blind. He only needed a way to encourage you to see again.

"Richard believed in you, believed in your intellect, believed that you had the spark of spirit that could see things for yourself, that you had the capacity to see the truth. Over time, as you came to know him and understand him, you finally began to think through the reasons behind your loyalties. You used your head to try to reason out the why of things and in so doing you discovered the truth for yourself.

"In that instant, when reason won out over the blind faith you had been taught, you changed. You came to embrace life instead of death. You had the courage to see your own failings. You had the courage to see the harm you had done and the inner character to want to set it right.

"You have fought on our side since then and you've proven yourself to me a thousand times over. You have saved both our lives on any number of occasions. You have helped bring truth to others.

"I came to understand how you were in fact also a victim of the same depraved ideology we were fighting. In a way, the Imperial Order had crushed you the same way it wanted to crush us. Because of what you did to lift yourself out of the darkness you were in, I was able to come to appreciate you for the woman you really were, underneath the things you did because of the corrupt doctrine you had been taught. I came to see your inner strength and the courage it took to face reality and step out of your darkness and into the light.

"Once that happened, I no longer had any reason to hate you. That hatred no longer served a purpose, so I was able to set it aside. That also means I have no reason to harbor bitterness or resentment against you.

"You've changed, and as a result, I've changed. We're both better for it.

"I know that you are still in love with Richard, but I also know that because you love him, you want him to be happy. You understand him now, and know that the reality is you can't force someone to love you.

"But you still love him. You can't help how you feel and I understand that. Sometimes a person can't talk their heart out of how it feels, despite how hard you try. But now you have placed that in perspective with what he wants for himself."

Nicci swallowed. "You're right about that. I can't help how I feel. I wish it were otherwise—I truly do— but I can't change my heart.

"I would do anything Richard asked of me. I would lay down my life if he asked it of me. I would do anything for him.

"But I would never again try to steal him from you because I know that would be treason against him. Because I love him, truly love him, I could never do that to him."

Kahlan stared into Nicci's blue eyes. "I know."

She felt profound sorrow for Nicci. She couldn't imagine being as in love with Richard as she was and having him not love her back. That would be a living death. She hoped that one day Nicci could find a man worthy of her, the way Cara had, even if Cara's joy had been all too short.

Nicci's gaze stayed on Kahlan's. "I had Richard down in the Old World a long time. I came to know what is in that man's heart. It matters not who loves him. All that matters is who he loves. And he loves you, Kahlan."

Kahlan nodded. "I know that, too, Nicci."

Nicci let out a relieved sigh. "Good."

"So," Kahlan said after a moment's silence, "you don't think Irena can really tell a person's gift from bones, unless, of course, she has powers you don't know about, perhaps from living her whole life out here close to the power leaking out of that barrier to the third kingdom. And you think she should have known where the Hedge Maid lived. And, she loves Richard."

"I don't know that she actually loves him, now that I think about it, so much as she seems obsessed with him."

"Even so, she has also fought beside us, fought to protect our lives. So, what do you expect me to do about her?"

"I don't know," Nicci grumbled. "Maybe tell me I'm crazy."

"I don't think you're crazy. I don't trust the woman either."

Nicci halted her pacing and looked over at Kahlan. "You alluded to that before. Mind telling me why not?"

"Well, I know it sounds a bit intolerant, but I don't trust her because she calls him Richard, instead of Lord Rahl."

Nicci looked puzzled. "Richard doesn't care about titles."

"That's beside the point. Titles imply things. Respect, for one. Country people from remote places like this are usually terrified of people with power. I've grown up seeing people pale when they heard my title announced. People fear what they don't know, and they fear power.

"A woman, even a sorceress, from a little place like Stroyza, should be more respectful—if nothing else—of the leader of the D'Haran Empire, the Lord Rahl himself."

"And the Mother Confessor," Nicci added.

"And the Mother Confessor," Kahlan agreed. "It's a little thing, but little things have reasons behind them. Little things can be a crack in a person's carefully constructed façade that allows you to look deeper inside them.

"Richard wouldn't care that she doesn't call him Lord Rahl, but I do—because it tells me that something deeper is going on, that there is something there that is not what it seems.

"Samantha is infatuated with him, as you say, but she still calls him Lord Rahl. That is consistent with how people typically behave."

Nicci was frowning with concern. "What do you think we should do about it?"

"Be aware. Be vigilant."

"Always." Nicci looked off toward the camp. "Richard is coming back. You had best go be with him and get some sleep." She smiled as she watched him walking silently among the sleeping men. "Give him a hug. I think you could both use one. And I don't want you to worry. We should soon be to the citadel and that containment field and then we will finally rid you of Jit's poison."

Kahlan stood and gave Nicci a hug. "I think you could use one as well."

Nicci hugged her back. "You do know, don't you, that I also love you?"

Kahlan smiled. "I know."

Kahlan knew that loving someone and being in love with someone were two very different things. Still, she trusted Nicci. After Nicci had taken Richard away, she had learned that she couldn't win his heart, and she eventually came around and did the most loving thing she could do. She brought him back to where his heart lay, brought him back to Kahlan.

No one had hurt Kahlan more than Nicci. But she had set things right.

Now, there was probably no one in camp Kahlan trusted more.

Now, because she trusted her, she had to ask her a difficult question.

Nicci, can I ask you a hard question and get an honest answer?"

"Of course."

Kahlan stared off at the encampment for a moment without seeing it, trying to think of how to put such a thing into words, how to say it out loud. Saying it out loud somehow made it irrevocable. Finally she asked as plainly as she could.

"How long do Richard and I have to live if we aren't cured?"

"Well," Nicci said, thinking it over for a moment, "that is a hard question to answer."

"And I don't want to hear things like we have 'a while yet,' before we die, or 'not a terribly long time,' or other wiggle words like that. I want the truth. I want to know. If we don't get this poison out of us, how much time do Richard and I have before we die?"

When Kahlan turned and looked back at her, Nicci was staring at her. Her blue eyes seemed filled with

grim awareness of the death sentence she would pro-
nounce.

"The call of death in both of you is growing ex-
ponentially. I can't give you an exact number, but the
simple truth is that for both of you it's at most only
a matter of a handful of days."

Kahlan swallowed. "Days." It sounded too final.
"That's all?"

"It's difficult to gauge your remaining time exactly.
I must confess to you that when I was working to
bring Richard back to consciousness, I could tell that
you've both passed a critical point and while you
still may have days, death could now come at any
moment."

"But there is a limit," Kahlan guessed. "Even if we
manage to avoid it for a time. Even if we're lucky,
even if we fight it, there is still a limit."

Nicci nodded. "I was a Sister of the Dark, and I
dealt in such wicked things as have touched you both,
so I know more about this than even Zedd. He had
an understanding of the seriousness of it, but feared
to ask me anything more specific because he knew
that I recognize such forces and their full meaning in
a way that he could not. Because of my unique knowledge and experience, I can tell you that the way this
poisonous call of death works, the way it kills, is unlike anything else."

"What do you mean? What is it doing that is different?"

"It's severing your souls."

Kahlan hadn't thought it could be any worse. She
was wrong.

"You mean like the half people? You mean we will
become like them? Soulless bodies, living on in a kind
of meaningless, dead existence?"

Nicci shook her head. "No. You're thinking of it in the wrong way. This is entirely different. In you and Richard, the call of death is slowly severing your link to your souls, much as if you were hanging by a thread over a deep abyss. What Jit unleashed is progressively severing the lifeline to your souls.

"It is the line of the gift that you were born with that in the Grace flows from Creation, through life, and then continues on with you into the world of the dead. Jit's poisonous call crossed the boundary between worlds. It is severing that line connecting your souls to who you are."

"So, you mean," Kahlan asked, repressing her panic, "that when our souls are severed, that's it? That's the end of us? We die?"

Nicci searched for words. "It's kind of difficult to explain, but it's more than being the end of you, more all-encompassing than merely dying. If we don't put a stop to it, pull it out of you, then you both will die, which is bad enough, but also your souls will be severed from everything, meaning not simply from the world of life, but from their connection to the gift that flows through our souls into the world beyond the veil. Once severed, your souls can never find their way to the good spirits beyond.

"So, in a way, by severing your souls in this way, this poison is not only killing your bodies, it is extinguishing your souls' existence.

"At this point, how long you last, I think, is only a matter of your will to hold on to life, how hard your spirits—your souls—fight. Even so, you won't be able to hold on for more than a few days longer, and then the struggle will end. Your souls will be severed from you. Your bodies will die, and your souls themselves will wink out of existence like a dying ember."

Kahlan realized that she had been holding her breath. She could feel tears welling up in her eyes.

"Will we even be remembered?" She thought it was a rather meaningless question as soon as she asked it, but it seemed important to her.

Nicci slowly shook her head. "Once your souls are severed, existence itself is dissolved. It will be as if you never existed."

Somehow, that made it even worse. She looked up at Nicci, resisting the pronouncement. "But that didn't happen to Jit. Her existence wasn't dissolved away by the sound of that scream, that call of death. We remember her."

"Jit was a different kind of creature. The poison she carried inside was intrinsic to her kind. That sound was never meant to be heard by humans. She had no soul to sever."

Nicci wiped a tear from Kahlan's cheek. "You do."

Kahlan could hear the whispers and the screams in the back of her mind, the sound of death hungering to have her. She could feel those whispers getting closer. She knew, from Richard's experience the night before, that if either of them went unconscious again, they most likely would never wake.

In the end, she didn't know which fate was worse, eventually falling into the clutches of what Sulachan had waiting for them in the underworld, or the haunting dread of soulless oblivion.

"Then I guess we had best get an early start so we can get to Saavedra as soon as possible," Kahlan said.

Nicci nodded. "I agree. But try to not lose sight of the fact that I'm not going to let that happen to either of you." She took Kahlan's arm and started back. "I will get it out of you."

CHAPTER

52

The next day took them over a high pass with towering peaks soaring high all around and then, from among the tall pines, lower through the mountains, down into more heavily wooded terrain. The lower forest was wetter, with frequent brooks draining the higher ground. They sometimes had to make their way through muddy areas to get around standing water. Some of the men scouted the way out ahead of the main group to make sure of the quickest route, while yet others protected them from a rear attack.

Any Shun-tuk who might still be alive were a constant worry. After what she had seen, Kahlan was sure they were all dead, but there was no way to be absolutely positive. Worse, though, there was always the possibility that Sulachan could have sent others, or that other tribes of half people who had escaped through the gates of the third kingdom could be hunting the forests. After all, they weren't all that far from that dreaded, broken barrier.

Ned had left at first light, taking their only horse and Richard's orders on the hard ride back to the People's Palace. It was somewhat disconcerting being without a horse because it was their fastest means of travel, but having only one did them little good. It was more important to get word to the palace and all the people there, letting them know what was coming so they could prepare.

Kahlan shuddered to think of Hannis Arc, Emperor Sulachan, and all the Shun-tuk having free run of the palace and all the artifacts kept there. In a way, that palace was the heart of hope for civilization. To have it fall to such evil made her blood run cold. They had to hold it until Richard was healed and could get back there.

While a horse wouldn't get them to Saavedra any faster, should Richard or Kahlan begin to lose strength, the horse could carry them easier than any other method. As much as Kahlan worried about not having the horse with them any longer, the farther they went it was becoming apparent that the mountains they were crossing were too rugged in places for a horse. They could have gone around in certain areas so a horse could make it, but that would have meant more travel time and they didn't have the time to spare.

Every moment of delay meant that she and Richard were a moment closer to dying. Kahlan's thoughts kept drifting back to the dark ones Sulachan had waiting for them on the other side of that veil. There would be no peaceful eternity for the two of them. The spirit king had seen to that.

As they made their way down the mountain the terrain was so difficult in places that the men had to fell small trees and stake them along the steep walls of crumbling rock to give them some kind of sure footing that wouldn't give way. It was a quick, flimsy, very temporary way to make it across otherwise impassable areas, but it was enough for them to keep moving forward without losing their footing or much time. Some of the places they had to traverse were quite steep, slippery, and had loose rock that slid and tumbled down when disturbed. In those places a rope tied to trees gave them a useful handhold.

There was no easy way through the uncharted wilderness. They knew the direction of Saavedra, and if they wanted to get there, the quickest way was a direct route across the mountains. Fortunately, there were passes. Going around would add many days of travel and they had no extra days to waste.

After they had made their way down narrow, rocky trails, the terrain leveled out somewhat. Irena and Samantha used the opportunity to move in close to each side of Richard to protect him as they went through more open birch groves. Nicci stayed behind them where she could keep an eye on Irena. Irena, for her part, always managed to be right there near Richard, sometimes even stepping in front of Kahlan and Nicci to do so.

Kahlan wasn't in the mood to start an argument with the woman. The wise thing to do was to ignore it and get to Saavedra. Besides, for all she knew they might need Irena's extra abilities to cure them.

When the trail narrowed again as they had to go down a narrow pass between steep, gray, rocky slopes to each side, and she had the chance, Kahlan took up Richard's hand and made it clear to the others, in a gentle manner, that she wanted to be with her husband. Irena, surprisingly enough, got the message. Kahlan wondered if perhaps the woman wasn't as inconsiderate as she had believed.

At first, Samantha didn't get the idea, instead staying close to Richard as the way through began to widen so she could pepper him with trivial questions about how the trees could ever come to cling to such stony slopes overhead and how it compared to places he had been to and things he had seen before. She seemed to have an endless supply of questions and looked genuinely interested in every word of his answers. Richard seemed distracted and wasn't in a chatty mood, but he was nice enough as he answered her questions, if briefly.

As they walked along an animal trail through knee-high grass, Zedd finally slipped in close and put an arm around the young woman's shoulders. He told her that he wanted to show her some of the herbs that a young sorceress needed to know about. He steered her off through tall grasses and shrubs to point out plants with red berries growing up the soil bank below the steeper rock above. He launched into a lecture about the many uses of the berries, the leaves, and the roots of the plants he was showing her.

"Everything all right?" Kahlan asked Richard once they were relatively alone.

He gave her a puzzled look. "No, not really."

"Why, what's wrong?"

"Well," he said as if trying to think of something, "there was a man who has been dead for three thousand years and when Hannis Arc poured my blood over his mummified corpse, he came back to life. And now he wants to rule the world of life, with Lord Arc as the ruler of the D'Haran Empire, I suppose. Oh, and you and I are near death from a poison we both carry, but we may all be eaten alive by half people before we ever die from the poison."

"Sorry," she said, "I didn't mean to get you upset."

He waved a hand. "No, it's not that."

"Then what is it?"

He let out a deep sigh. "It's just everything."

"Everything? Anything in particular getting you down? I mean more than the things you mentioned."

For a time he looked off to the sparse woods off through the grass to the side before answering.

"I'd just like to be alone with you, that's all."

"Ah," she said with a knowing smile. "That." It was rather difficult being intimate in the middle of a camp of soldiers.

"That's not what I mean—well, that too—but that's not what I mean."

"Then what do you mean?"

"I mean like when I built that cabin for us way back to the west, in Westland. I've just been thinking about the time when we were alone and far from all the troubles of the world."

Kahlan briefly pressed her head against the side of his shoulder. "It will happen, Richard. Things will get better. We'll get rid of this awful poison and then you will do whatever it is that you need to do to stop the unruly twins and then we will be able to live in peace."

He smiled at her description of Emperor Sulachan and Hannis Arc as if they were little more than mischievous boys.

"But I don't want to live in a tiny cabin," she said. "I mean, I would, if we had to, but I would rather we live at the People's Palace."

"Ah," he said with a smile, "so I've married a girl with her eye on the finer things in life."

Kahlan circled an arm around his waist. "Finer than traipsing through a damp and gloomy wilderness with a bunch of soldiers? You bet. For one thing, I want a real bed. In a room with a door. With a lock on the door."

Richard couldn't help smiling. "I would like that very much."

"I bet you would," she teased with a gentle shove of her hip.

He smiled again. She was happy that she had been able to lighten his mood. She didn't know what was bothering him, but she was at least happy that she had been able to make him smile.

53

B y the end of a long day of making their way down dangerously steep slopes, along narrow cuts between rock walls, and through areas of dense woods, they finally reached flatter ground. There, they were able to follow a brook among moss-covered rocks as it meandered through a forest of young, wispy hardwoods. The rocky brook left the forest canopy more open, helping them to see in the fading light.

Richard watched for a place where they could set up camp.

He had finally managed to put a few people between Kahlan and him, and Irena and Samantha. Kahlan was happy to be left alone with him as well. He didn't know what it was about Samantha's mother, but Richard found her tiresome. She tried to be perpetually cheerful and friendly.

Richard wasn't in the mood for either. He had bigger things on his mind.

He supposed that Irena was simply trying to make the best of a bad situation. After all, she had been in charge of Stroyza when the barrier had failed. On the way to warn others of what had happened, her husband had been eaten alive by half people right before her eyes and she had been taken captive by the savages who did it. People in her village, surely people she knew well, had been murdered by walking corpses sent to kill her daughter. Now she was on a mission to save Richard's and Kahlan's lives. He didn't see that she had a lot to be happy about.

He supposed that she had to be happy that her daughter was alive and well and so was trying to remain optimistic. He still thought, though, that she should be a bit more worried about the situation they were all in—out in the middle of the trackless forests of the Dark Lands, making their way through dangerous and mysterious woods. They had all nearly been killed by the attack of the Shun-tuk, and there was no telling if legions more of the flesh eaters would show up at any moment.

In Samantha's case, though, he knew her exuberance was the innocence of youth. She was worried about their situation, wanted to be helpful, and she was clearly afraid at times, but she was also excited be on an "adventure." She was rightly proud of herself for being able to help them when they had been in an impossible spot. Richard was proud of her, too. It was the second time she had done such a thing.

Nicci thought Samantha had a dangerous temper. Richard, for one, was happy that she had gotten angry enough to do what she'd done, or they would all be dead. There were times when anger was a useful tool, and he was glad that Samantha had been able to call on it.

As Richard carefully picked his way over the spongy ground among the moss-covered rocks, he kept an eye to the woods all around. Kahlan, following close behind, held his hand to help balance herself as she crossed the brook with him. They used rocks as stepping-stones to get over to the other side where the ground was more open, less rocky, and made for easier walking. The light mist made for slick footing, though.

Occasionally Richard checked behind to make sure everyone was keeping up. In the gathering darkness, Zedd smiled and leaned close to Samantha from time to time, pointing out different useful plants. She soaked it all up.

It reminded Richard of when he had been young and Zedd had taken him on walks in the woods to show him where particular things grew and told him of their use. Richard missed that so much. He missed those times he'd had with his grandfather.

He couldn't stop thinking about Zedd's advice to quit, to give everything up, and take Kahlan away to some distant place where they could enjoy a life together. He tried to think of other things, but Zedd's words kept echoing around in his mind.

If there was one person in the world whose advice he took seriously, it was Zedd. And yet, this time . . .

Richard stepped on exposed roots to stay out of the marshy spots where there could be hidden holes. He kept a continuous watch on the shadows to see if they moved. He watched spots of light to see if they vanished beneath shadows. Sometimes both things happened. It was usually a bird, flitting from branch to branch. Once, it had been a squirrel. Both sometimes moved a branch in the still air and made the leaves drop their load of collected mist in a shower of fat drops.

Richard had been watching, but he hadn't seen Kahlan's little friend, Hunter. Whatever the animal with the big green eyes was, it didn't act aggressive. It seemed interested only in watching Kahlan. He shared the feeling, but he didn't necessarily appreciate it in a wild animal. Just because it hadn't acted aggressively yet, that didn't mean it wouldn't at some point.

Still, something about the creature put him at ease. He just didn't think it was dangerous. Whatever it was, he hadn't seen it all day, so it had probably stayed in its home area once they had moved on.

From time to time ravens let out raucous calls to warn others of approaching people. The harsh, echoing cries were grating in the quiet woods. Richard could see some of the soldiers out ahead look up into the trees when a raven made a racket. The men behind kept a careful watch all around as well.

Something about the area they were in made Richard uneasy. The openness by the brook left the forest canopy a little too open for his liking. Through gaps in the leaves he could see the stepped stone of cliffs rising up to the sides. The scouts had said that the pass they were going through was the only practical way to make good progress.

There were hundreds of places from up high where anyone could easily mark their progress along the brook. He felt like a mouse being watched by an owl.

Making good time was always foremost in Richard's mind, though, and this was the only real choice for a route that would get them to Saavedra and the containment field at the citadel.

Richard noticed all the little birds abruptly take to wing, darting away through the branches. Almost at the same time, three ravens lifted silently into the air and raced off together through the trees.

Richard froze an instant before he heard a clipped cry from one of the men behind.

He spun around and looked up just in time to see legs pulled upward through the trees. Something big and dark was carrying the man away. Richard saw the man's legs kicking as he fought whatever it was that had him, and then for just an instant before it vanished beyond the trees overhead, he saw the body go slack and limp.

In the next instant he had his sword out of its scabbard. The distinctive ring of steel being drawn echoed off the stone walls. In the hush of the silent woods, that sound was terrifyingly angry.

All the men swiftly had weapons to hand. Everyone looked up, ducking as they turned, trying to see the threat.

Richard instead watched the shadows down in the darkening woods.

Something dark swooped in at them out of that darkness of the trees to the side and snatched up a man not far ahead, breaking his neck as it yanked him from his feet and up into the air. His sword clattered down on the rocks. The man never even had time to cry out.

Whatever it was, it was not half people, or any kind of occult sorcery. Richard recognized the way it had happened. It was some kind of big predator taking prey.

"Close ranks!" Commander Fister shouted back at everyone.

Men ran in from both directions, collecting Zedd,

Nicci, Irena, and Samantha as they came forward. Richard pulled Kahlan close with his left arm, protecting her and himself with his sword. Zedd frowned as he looked around for an intruder he could strike down with his gift. Nicci turned slowly, searching the canopy. Irena hunched over, sheltering her daughter. Samantha's eyes were wide in terror.

They were all vulnerable targets if they stood still.

"Move," Richard called out to everyone. "Keep going!"

There was no saving the two men who had been taken. All they could do now was keep anyone else from being taken.

"What do you think that was?" Kahlan whispered from close beside him as they raced ahead.

"I have no idea," he told her as he ran along the side of the brook, jumping from rock to root to rock, "but we need to get out of the open of this streambed."

"Some kind of small woods dragon?" she asked as she worked to keep up with him.

"I didn't get a good enough look. There isn't enough light and they were too dark to tell much."

"Keep moving!" Commander Fister called out to his men as he urged them on, waving his sword. "Watch your backs, boys!"

"Commander!" Richard called out as they raced down the open area beside the brook.

When the man paused to look back, Richard pointed with his sword. "Make for that split in the rocks on the side. There are heavy woods beyond. We need to get out of this more open area. Whatever those things are, we're in the middle of their game trail."

Commander Fister nodded and turned the rush of

men toward the place that Richard had pointed to. As he ran through the opening in the huge boulders, Richard could see that the forest beyond was dense and thick. The heavy cover would make it more difficult for any airborne predators.

The only problem was that it was getting dark. They needed to set up camp, not run through the woods in the dark.

He knew they didn't have any choice. Before they dared stop for the night, they first needed to get out of the area.

The woods they entered were populated by spruce and pine crowded in close. Growing that close left the lower trunks free of branches for quite a ways up. That meant that the ground was more open, but in among the maze of trunks was not the kind of place a big, winged creature could easily navigate.

It also meant the forest floor, shaded by the dense growth overhead, was more barren, making it easier for them to run.

And run they did, eager to get out of the area.

everyplace they found had only been so far back up the mountain through the woods. The height of the plateau with the bee-men made it much worse than the valley. Far off in the distance the . . .

CHAPTER

54

I t was late in the night and quite dark by the time they found a place lower on the mountain where Richard thought it might be safe to stop for the night. At least, it was about as safe a place as they were going to find in the dark of an endless forest he didn't know. The area was heavily wooded with dense, tightly spaced young hardwoods all around that made it difficult to move through, at least without making a lot of noise. A few large trees left them a bit of a more open spot where they could lay out bedrolls and get some sleep for the remainder of the night.

It would be difficult to travel through such woods, but it would also make it virtually impossible for any creature to swoop in and pick them off as had happened back near the brook. The dense growth would make it hard for any predator of any size to rush in at them. Since they needed to stop so they could all get a little sleep, it didn't matter how difficult it would be to travel through such an area as long as it made for good protection.

Of course, an attacker, including half people, could still make their way in, but they would face a wall of First File soldiers with weapons. They were all angry that they had not been able to stop the predator, whatever it was, from taking two of their fellow soldiers.

"What do you think?" Commander Fister asked as he peered around in the light of little flames Nicci, Zedd, and Irena each held aloft in a hand.

Richard carefully scanned the area. "This looks about as good a spot as we're going to be able to find, short of finding a stone fortress."

"We've come quite a distance since we saw those things," the commander said. "Maybe we left them behind. Maybe they haven't followed us."

"Or maybe they're full," Irena said. "I told you, the Dark Lands are dangerous and filled with things no one has ever seen—or at least lived to tell about. Most of us have only heard vague stories and rumors."

"It looks like some of those rumors are proving to be true," the commander said.

Richard didn't see what choice they had in it, but he didn't feel like discussing the matter. After a hard day of traveling through difficult terrain, they all needed to get some sleep, not debate the dangers of the Dark Lands.

Richard saw shadows appear as the moon emerged from the broken cloud cover. At least when the clouds began to break up it had stopped drizzling. It was going to be a damp, chilly night, though.

"Have the men find places wherever they can to lay out their bedrolls," Richard said. "We all need to stay in close together."

Jake Fister looked around in the mix of moonlight and conjured flames. "At least it's not so open in here. It will be difficult for anything to pick us off."

"After we get settled, no fires tonight," Richard said.

It meant cold, preserved food, rather than cooking anything, but it was too late to cook, anyway. They needed to have a bite to eat to keep up their strength and then get some sleep so they could be on their way at first light.

Commander Fister quietly gave orders as he moved off among his men, seeing to it that some settled in while he pointed out others and quietly called out names for watches.

"No standing watch for you," Zedd told Richard. "You need to rest."

"You're right," Richard told his grandfather.

There wasn't much room in among the thick growth, so all of them were packed in close. Zedd selected a spot close to Richard and Kahlan. Nicci, Irena, and Samantha started setting up places to sleep nearby. Richard thought that the wizard might have picked his spot deliberately to block Irena and Samantha from being able to get in any closer to him and Kahlan. Whether done deliberately or not, Richard was thankful. He just wanted to get some sleep.

Richard and Kahlan set out a small bedroll and blanket beside a slope of rock. Without building a shelter, there was no real protection from the weather if the rains returned. As Kahlan was settling in, Richard went to where his grandfather was carefully laying out a blanket.

"You going to be comfortable there?" Richard asked.

Zedd smiled. "Perfectly. I can sleep on the point of a thorn."

That made Richard smile because he knew that it was close to the truth. The old wizard always slept with his eyes open, but he usually slept well.

"Zedd," Richard asked in a quiet voice the others couldn't hear, "did you really mean what you said before?"

Zedd puzzled at him. "About what?"

Richard hesitated for a moment, afraid of the answer. "About being tired of living."

"Ah," Zedd said with a knowing nod. "Well, my boy, at times yes, at other times no." Zedd smiled, looking a little less serious. "I think old age is nature's way of preparing us for death, making us more willing to take our leave of this world. It gets tiring after so many years of seeing people continue to do such cruel and awful things. One just gets tired of the stupidity of it all. After a time, it saps the joy out of life.

"But on the other hand, being around for you and Kahlan makes it all worthwhile."

Richard felt a little better. "That's good to hear."

Zedd put a hand on Richard's shoulder as he leaned closer in the moonlight. "You make life worthwhile for me, Richard. You always have. In a way, I no longer live for myself, but instead for you and Kahlan. I think that maybe that's a wonderful way to live—to have something meaningful to live for." He cocked his head. "Isn't it Kahlan who makes you fight for life? Think of life without her, and you will see what I mean, and see what you are really living for."

Richard nodded. "That's certainly true." He looked down at Kahlan not far away as she pulled the blanket up, ready for him to crawl in beside her and keep her warm. "I can't imagine life without her. I wouldn't want to live without her."

Zedd gave a firm nod. "That's what I mean, Richard. That, and I'm perfectly happy to stick around to help you keep from falling on your face. Someone has to."

Richard let out a deep breath as he nodded. "Good. I love you, you know."

"I know. I love you too, my boy." He gestured to Kahlan. "Now go get some sleep. I'll be right here nearby if either of you needs anything—and I'll be with you for a good long time to come. I'm not too old to be of use, you know.

"Soon we will free you of that sickness and then you can decide what you want to do. Either way— quit and go off to live your own lives, or continue to fight—I will still love you and support you in whatever you do. I know you will make the right choice, your own choice. As Magda Searus said, you make your own destiny."

"Thanks, Zedd. I guess we've had quite the adventure since we left Hartland."

"Quite the adventure, indeed. And it hasn't been all bad. There have been a lot of good times along the way."

"I'm all for the adventure being over, though," Richard told his grandfather.

Zedd smiled. "That's my wish, too. Now, get some rest. I don't want to have you going unconscious on me again before I can heal you. The last time was a bother."

"You can really heal us, though, right?"

Zedd stood up straight and looked Richard in the eye. "In a containment field, yes, of course. You have no need to doubt that, Richard. Now let me go so I can get some rest."

"Sure. Rest well, then."

The wizard looked around at the woods. "This really is a beautiful place. It's important to take in beauty whenever you can, my boy. This is a good place for a rest. And then tomorrow we need to be on our way to get to where we can heal you."

Richard smiled and gave his grandfather a nod before he went back and crawled into the blanket beside Kahlan. As he turned on his side, she spooned up against him.

"Everything all right?" she asked. "With Zedd, I mean."

"He wants us to get some sleep."

Kahlan squeezed her arm around his middle. "I'm all for that."

As she snuggled close for warmth and simply to be close, Richard watched out over the camp. Nicci, Irena, and Samantha were already wrapped in their blankets, breathing evenly and slowly, as were most of the men.

Richard watched them all, worrying about them all, afraid to go to sleep lest he never wake.

Richard woke sometime in the night when Zedd rose up. He had been sleeping fitfully because he was worried about a whole variety of things. There were a lot of problems but not very many solutions, other than getting to the citadel. He had also been sleeping lightly because he was on alert, so Zedd standing up was enough to wake him.

In the moonlight he could see his grandfather take the blanket off from around his shoulders, lay it down, and then stretch to one side. He yawned and after stretching to the other side he carefully tiptoed among a sleeping Nicci, Irena, Samantha, and some of the soldiers. Richard knew that while Zedd usually slept well, he sometimes said that his bones ached, and it was not uncommon for him to get up in the night for a while to "walk the kinks out," as he put it.

Something about the night felt strange to Richard. Even the perfectly still woods they were camped in felt somehow peculiar, somehow unnatural. He saw

that the moon had moved across the sky, so he knew
that it was not long until dawn. As soon as there was
enough light, they could all be on their way.

Once Zedd had disappeared beyond a screen of
young spruce and Richard couldn't see him anymore,
he rolled over onto his back and gazed down at Kahlan. In her sleep, she rearranged herself and snuggled
up under his arm. It made him smile to watch her
sleep. It was a picture of perfect innocence. Richard
gently ran a hand down the side of her face, thinking about how much he loved her, how he would do
anything for her. It made him angry to think of anyone harming her.

Once he started to worry about her safety, he
couldn't go back to sleep. Something was wrong and
he could not for the life of him put his finger on it.

As long as he was awake and couldn't sleep, he
pushed himself back to sit up a little so he could scan
the woods, looking for anything out of place. Not a
leaf stirred in the dead air. He didn't hear any night
birds, or even any bugs. It was perfectly quiet in the
woods all around them. He watched everyone sleeping, his gaze going from one soldier to another, checking. No one stirred as they slept. He was at least glad
that the rest of them were able to get some sleep. Zedd
was the only one out of his bedroll besides men on
watch somewhere out among the trees.

At one point, as he dozed off into a light sleep,
Richard heard an odd, muted thump, but the woods
otherwise remained still. Waking instantly, he cocked
his head, listening, waiting for it to happen again so
he could better tell what it was, but the woods remained silent. He thought that it might have been a
big pinecone dropping to the soft mat of the forest

floor. Those sometimes made a thump that jarred him awake on really quiet nights.

Richard slid back down to lie beside Kahlan for a time. He knew he should get some sleep, but he seemed too on edge to sleep. Every time he closed his eyes, they kept coming open. He took every opportunity, when they did, to watch out over the camp, visually checking on Nicci, Irena, Samantha, and the men. None of them had stirred, and no one in camp besides him appeared to have been awakened by the soft thump.

In the moonlight, Richard spotted a dark form in the distance moving through the encampment. He soon realized that it was Commander Fister making his way among the sleeping men. By the way the man was walking, Richard recognized that he had an urgent purpose.

Richard sat up, frowning, as the commander came close and dropped to a knee beside him. Even in the moonlight, Richard could see that the man's face was white.

Richard checked and noticed that Zedd was not back, yet.

He looked back at Commander Fister. "What is it?"

Kahlan woke up and sat up in a rush beside Richard. "What's wrong?" she asked in a whisper.

The commander couldn't seem to find his voice.

"What's wrong?" Richard asked again, more forcefully.

"It's . . . it's Zedd."

Richard frowned as he looked over at his grandfather's empty bedroll. "What about Zedd?" He looked around, checking the camp. "Where is he?"

Commander Fister swallowed. He stood and gestured weakly off in the direction Richard had last seen his grandfather.

Richard shot to his feet. In a heartbeat, Kahlan was up beside him.

Richard could see that the man still couldn't find words. "Show me."

Men were already starting to stir, to sit up, as the commander nodded. He turned to the camp and shouted.

"Everyone up! Weapons!"

Men rushed to scramble out of bedrolls as they snatched up swords, axes, and bows.

Commander Fister stared urgently across the camp as men with their weapons to hand went into defensive positions. The commander, Kahlan, and Richard stepped between Nicci, Irena, and Samantha as they rolled over, rubbing sleep from their eyes while rushing to get to their feet.

Samantha looked up at the men all around standing with weapons drawn. "What is it?" she asked.

No one answered as they all hurried to follow the commander.

Predawn mist drifted close to the ground. Richard and Kahlan followed the hulking form of the commander as he rushed across the small camp and then through the screen of young spruce. He continued on a short distance through the woods beyond to a small, moonlit spot that was open, with trees standing like sentinels all around.

Lit by a small patch of moonlight, under a fine shroud of mist, Zedd lay on his back in the bed of moss.

Richard blinked. Kahlan, right beside him, gasped.

His grandfather's head rested a half dozen feet away among the ferns.

The whole scene looked so peaceful, so restful, so calm.

Richard blinked again, at first not really understanding what he was seeing—or not wanting to.

The reality of what he was seeing filled his mind in a hot rush.

56

The next instant, Richard pulled his sword free from its scabbard, its fury already fully alive the instant his hand had reached the hilt.
It only took a couple of heartbeats after the sound of steel filled the quiet night before the entire force of the First File had rushed in through the woods around them.

Richard stood panting, trying to find a direction for his rage. He scanned the moonlit scene, hunting for a cause, a threat, an explanation. He saw nothing out of the ordinary other than his grandfather lying beheaded in the middle of a soft, moonlit bed of moss surrounded by small, wispy ferns.

In the next heartbeat, Samantha cried out in horror. Her mother stared in disbelief, both hands covering her open mouth.

Nicci, standing beside him, briefly looked at Richard's face before rushing to kneel beside Zedd's body.

"How could this happen?" Richard asked no one

in particular. "Who could have done this? We had watches posted!"

His own booming voice echoed back to him out of the silent woods. He could see nothing out of the ordinary. The only blood he could see was on Zedd.

Men were already racing off in every direction, searching for the killer, shamed that someone had gotten through their defenses. The men of the First File did not make these kinds of mistakes.

One by one, the men returned, each giving the commander a shake of his head, none of them wanting to look at Richard.

"Tracks?" the commander asked his men, looking from one to another.

One of them gestured off toward the woods. "Some of us came through here earlier to check the area and we saw those tracks, but no one other than us has been through here. There aren't any tracks out beyond, either. We can't find any evidence of anyone coming into this area from outside. They had to have snuck in through the camp. That's the only way."

"Unless they were hiding here the whole time we set up camp," Commander Fister said, "waiting for someone important to pass by. Maybe they slipped away after they did this."

Richard didn't know that such an explanation made any sense—unless they were being followed. Other than the animal Kahlan had named Hunter, he hadn't seen anyone or anything watching them. He supposed they could have used occult powers to mask themselves as they shadowed the group. Other than that, he was having trouble understanding how it could have happened. With a thousand thoughts tumbling through his mind all at once, he couldn't think clearly.

No matter how they did it, there was no doubt that the camp had been penetrated by a killer.

The way Richard's heart pounded with rage also made it difficult to think. He needed a direction for that bottled fury, but couldn't find one.

He watched, tears running down his face, as Nicci gently lifted Zedd's head and brought it back, placing it by his body so that the old wizard almost looked right again.

Richard dropped to his knees beside Nicci, staring down at his grandfather. Zedd's dead hazel eyes stared up at the dark sky. Kahlan knelt beside him, one hand on Richard's shoulder as she cried, holding her other trembling hand over her mouth, holding back the scream.

Richard, noting men return and whisper reports to Commander Fister, finally looked up at the man. "Anything? Did the men find anything at all?" His own voice sounded distant and wooden to him, as if it belonged to someone else.

"I'm sorry, Lord Rahl. Other than this," he said with a nod toward Zedd's corpse, "nothing looks wrong or out of the ordinary."

"How could this happen right here, right under our noses? How could we not know, not see anything, not hear anything?"

Richard remembered, then, the soft thump he'd heard. He realized then what he had heard hitting the mossy ground.

"I wish I had an answer for you, Lord Rahl," Commander Fister said in little more than a sorrowful whisper.

"I told you," Irena said in a quiet voice, "things like this are common in the Dark Lands. There are dangers here that no one knows about."

Richard wasn't in the mood to talk about the dangers of the Dark Lands. He stood up, then, his mind racing, his heart hammering, his fist clenched around the hilt of his sword. He forced himself to cap off his emotion. He couldn't let those emotions free. None of them could afford for him to lose control right then.

He could hear his own voice inside his head, telling himself to think. It felt like he was somewhere above, watching himself standing there in the little clearing lit by moonlight, looking down on Zedd's body.

No one knew what to do, what Richard would do. They were afraid to move, afraid to do anything. They all waited for him to give everyone direction.

Richard swallowed and cleared his throat, making sure his voice would not fail him. "We can't carry his remains with us to Saavedra," he said, his own voice sounding surprisingly calm. "There would be no point to it. Zedd didn't know the place. It would have meant nothing to him."

Kahlan still knelt, bent over Zedd's chest, her face buried in her hands as she wept. Zedd had been the wizard she had come through the boundary to find. He had been "the one." Everyone had needed him. She had come to pull him away from his peaceful life in Westland and back into a world ablaze with war. They had all needed the First Wizard so he could name a Seeker. They needed the First Wizard to set things right.

Richard knew what else was going through her mind at that moment—the same memory that was going through his thoughts—Zedd marrying the two of them.

Nicci, standing close to his left shoulder, looked up

at him. "What do you want us to do, Richard?" she asked in a broken voice.

He knew that hesitation, failure to make a decision, was deadly. They were already in enough trouble, and there was obviously yet more they hadn't been aware of lurking in the night. It was most likely something to do with occult sorcery, otherwise Zedd and Nicci would have detected it.

He needed to make a decision, he needed to make it quickly, and he needed it to be the right decision.

He tried to think of what Zedd would want him to do, what he would advise. Richard looked around. No one knew Zedd's wishes better than Richard. He knew that Zedd would tell him that he must push on, that he had to get to the citadel or everything, all their efforts and hopes, would be in vain.

His grandfather would tell him that the living couldn't sacrifice their chance at life to mourn the dead.

"Zedd told me that he thought this was a beautiful place. His soul is in the hands of the good spirits, now. He is safe, there, with them, and finally at peace. He no longer has need of this vessel in which he has for so long sailed the world of life. He would want us to purify his remains in a funeral pyre. We need to build up a platform of wood and place him on it.

"We need to be quick about it. We don't know what danger is here among us. We can't stay here. We need to take care of Zedd, and then we must be gone."

"I will see to it at once, Lord Rahl," the commander said.

Richard turned to Nicci. "If we get to a containment field can you cure Kahlan and me by yourself—without Zedd?"

"Yes."

"Are you sure?"

Nicci did not hesitate. "Absolutely."

"Could you tell how he was beheaded? By what method?"

Nicci swallowed. "No. It looks like a blade, but it could have been something else."

"You mean like the gift?"

"Yes. I've seen it done often enough. It looks much the same. But I can detect no gifted people anywhere near—other than myself, Irena, and Samantha right here with us."

"They could have been lying in wait, and then when they saw an opportunity killed the first person of rank that they could, and then run off," Commander Fister said.

Richard nodded. "Possibly. Send your best trackers out and have them search while we take care of Zedd. But if they do find any evidence of an intruder, they could be gifted so I don't want them following or trying to take them on. Just come get me instead."

He turned back to Nicci. "Could it have been someone using occult sorcery?"

Nicci's eyes brimmed with tears. "Yes, I suppose, but I have no way of knowing, and if it was, I can't sense such people. They could be standing right next to me and I wouldn't be able to detect such powers. Occult powers are like the dark side of the moon. They remain out of sight and a mystery."

Richard turned to a stricken-looking Irena. "Can you?"

She wiped her nose on her sleeve as she shook her head.

Richard gritted his teeth for a moment, fighting to keep control of the rage thundering through him. He was on the razor edge of losing control, but there was no target for his fury. He told himself yet again to think of what his grandfather would advise him to do.

"All right then, we need to see to taking care of Zedd's remains as swiftly as possible. He is with the good spirits now. We can weep for his soul but we have to move while we weep. Though his body is only an empty vessel, now, I don't want animals getting at it. With our gifted, we can have a fire hot enough to purify his remains in short order.

"It's going to be light soon. We can't afford to delay one moment longer than absolutely necessary. We need to see to this and then be on our way to Saavedra. If the trackers haven't found anything by first light, then we must put our efforts toward what matters most right now—getting to the citadel."

All around the small clearing, Richard saw fists go to hearts. Even Samantha, Irena, and Nicci silently bowed their heads as they touched fists to hearts.

"And then," Richard said, "I am going to find out who did this and I am going to kill them with my bare hands."

CHAPTER

57

By first light, when the sky was just beginning to take on a faint blush, the trackers had not found anything meaningful. There were some suspicious indications that Richard would have investigated himself, but it could easily take most of the day to see if those indications led to anything significant. While it was critically important to know who had killed Zedd—after all, that killer could strike again—they couldn't afford the time. Richard and Kahlan's only chance to live was to get to the citadel before the poison overwhelmed them.

In the back of his mind, as he stood staring at the smoking ashes that were his grandfather's worldly remains, Richard was having trouble putting the pieces together. He couldn't make sense of things or understand how it had happened.

He felt numb.

He knelt beside the remains of the funeral pyre and

pushed his hand into the still-warm ashes, wishing he could touch his grandfather one last time.

"I'm sorry, Zedd, but I can't quit just yet."

"What do you mean?" Kahlan asked from above, over his shoulder.

Richard stood. He held his hand up before his face and stared at the glove of gray ashes.

"Nothing." He looked over at Kahlan. "Are you ready?"

She nodded, her chin trembling as she fought back the tears. She fell into his arms, then, as she started crying all over again.

"I'm usually stronger than this," she said between sobs.

Richard held her tightly for a moment, burying his face in her hair at the side of her neck.

"I know," he whispered. "I love you."

After a moment, he straightened and held her by her shoulders as he looked into her green eyes. "I can't lose you, too, Kahlan. We need to get going. Zedd would want us to hurry. He would understand the need. He would not want us standing around staring at his ashes."

Kahlan nodded as she sniffled back her tears. "I know. I understand. He may be gone, but he will live in our hearts as long as they beat."

Richard nodded, unable to smile. He saw Nicci and the others waiting quietly in the background, back among the trees at the edge of the little clearing.

He looked around one last time. "It's a beautiful spot. He told me to take the time to appreciate the beauty of things."

The shadowy shapes of pine and spruce stood around the edge of the clearing like mourners in black silently watching.

Richard took Kahlan's hand, then, and walked quickly to where the others stood waiting. "There is enough light. We need to get moving."

Heads all around nodded.

"There are those dark, flying predators that took two men yesterday, and someone obviously murdered Zedd. The ones yesterday were flying beasts. This here was a two-legged beast. I don't think I need to tell any of you to stay alert." When they all shook their heads, he said, "Let's get moving, then."

"The scouts are back, Lord Rahl," the resolute Commander Fister said. "They have a route for us—but they've only had time to pick a route for the first hour or so."

"That will get us started. Let's go."

Without further word, and with Kahlan at his side, Richard marched away from the ashes. He didn't look back.

Nicci fell in close behind him. Behind her, Irena and Samantha rushed to stay close on her heels as they all wove their way through the thick growth of young hardwoods. As Richard and the women moved through the waiting men, some went on out ahead while others fell in behind.

With sunrise still a ways off, the forest was not only dark and foreboding, it was hiding a killer. In the dim, early blush of light before the approaching dawn, it was hard to make out much of anything in detail other than those in close enough.

As they went over the edge of the rise, Richard could see the black shapes of men out ahead along with the soaring trunks of pines silhouetted against the sky. He took the opportunity of a bit of open sky to check for anything flying that could snatch them up. He didn't see anything close other than a flock of small birds. Higher up in the sky he saw ravens circling, looking for a meal, looking for anything to scavenge.

He turned his eyes back to the ground to watch his footing, glad that he had made the decision to dispose of Zedd's remains in the way he had.

He was still having trouble believing it was real. He had been with Zedd his entire life. He couldn't imagine his grandfather being gone. He didn't want to leave even his ashes. He felt like he was abandoning Zedd. Despite all the people around him he felt lonely and lost.

It felt like he was watching himself walk along through the thick forest, after having gone through the motions of saying words over his grandfather before Nicci had ignited it all. The flames had been hot, burning with a kind of rage at the terrible task they had been called upon to perform. Nicci had seen to it that those flames made quick work of it.

He kept thinking of things he wanted to ask Zedd, things he wanted to say, things he wanted to remember to talk to him about. None of it seemed real. He wanted to recall it all, to pull the river of time back and somehow change its course.

He knew how Zedd thought and what he believed. He knew Zedd's reasoning on just about every subject. He thought about the advice Zedd would give him at that moment. When he realized what Zedd would say, he turned and took Nicci's arm. With Kahlan on his right, he pulled Nicci close on his left as they walked among the forest monarchs. The ground was flat enough that the three of them could walk side by side.

"Only you and Zedd could heal us, as long as you had the containment field," he said, "right?"

"And possibly Irena," Nicci said. "I don't know her ability. It's an incredibly complex task, but it's possible she may be able to do it."

"I don't think it's wise to count on her," Kahlan said, glancing back to make sure the woman was out of earshot before looking past him to Nicci. "We don't know enough about her ability. She could make a mistake at a critical juncture in the conjuring. I wouldn't want to put Richard's life in the hands of someone untested in such things."

"Nor would I," Nicci said. "At least, not as long as we don't have to."

Still holding her by her upper arm, Richard helped Nicci step over a split in the rock and then checked the woods around them before he went on.

"Then for the sake of argument, let's say that you and Zedd are the only two that we were positive could heal us. Let's say we assume that Irena wouldn't know enough, or wouldn't have the experience or ability that would be necessary. Let's just say we have to count her out. While Samantha is obviously quite gifted, I'm sure she doesn't have the knowledge or training to do such a thing, so we have to count her out as well."

"That leaves me," Nicci said. "I told you I could do it."

"Right. The three of us—you, Kahlan, and me—have to get there, though, in order to do it. There were two of you, and now Zedd is dead. I find that more than suspicious. But in any event, that means that we now have only you to count on."

"I'm not letting you out of my sight, if that's what you're worried about."

"It is. But it also means that we have to assume that, because you are one of the two who can heal us, you are a target in much the way Zedd was. I want you in our shadow every step the rest of the way there. Not just so that you can watch over us, but so that I can watch over you."

"Richard, I can take pretty good care of myself."

"So could Zedd."

She met his gaze and then conceded with a nod. "You've got it. You and Kahlan are going to get very tired of turning around, though, and bumping into me."

Richard couldn't make himself smile. "Thanks, Nicci. Kahlan and I are counting on you."

"I wish that my power worked," Kahlan said. "Then I'd be able to protect her as well. But you can believe I know how to use my knife and I intend to have it at the ready every moment. I hope you don't get tired of turning around and bumping into me."

"Never," Nicci said with a smile meant to reassure them.

58

By midmorning they reached the edge of a prominence where Richard was able to get a partial view out over the landscape of smaller mountains ahead and the lower reaches of the forest spread out far below. Saavedra was nowhere in sight, yet, but he only had a partial view and there were a lot of rugged walls of rock that he couldn't see beyond, so it was possible that when they were able to get farther down and beyond some of the difficult terrain they might be able to spot it.

From where they stood, they could easily see that there was higher ground ahead in places. Once they got down into the lower forest, though, they would be blind to what lay ahead. They needed to be aware of the nuances of the lay of the land in order to know how to avoid going off in certain directions or they would end up having to backtrack. They couldn't afford that.

He could see that they were still going to have a

lot of ground to cover before they had any hope of reaching Saavedra. He could also see that they had some tricky country to get through as they made their way lower down through the mountains. It all looked pretty easy when viewed from up high, but experience had taught him what to look for when picking a route.

Since they were moving so swiftly, the scouts hadn't been able to push beyond this point, but Richard had grown up in the woods, scouting trackless woods and picking passages through rugged country. He studied the lay of the land ahead, looking for possible routes and making mental notes of what to avoid.

"What do you think?" Kahlan asked. "It doesn't look promising to me. Do you see a way?"

"It may not look promising, but we have to go in this direction. We don't have a choice." Richard pointed to where two mountains met, creating folds and rugged canyons. "We need to get down there. I can't see what's down in between all those twisting chasms, but that's the way we need to go."

"What about that way?" Nicci asked as she pointed a little more to the left. "It looks easier without all those bends and turns in the chasms. It looks sketchy down in there. Going more to the left avoids that."

"It only looks easy from this distance." Richard leaned close to her and pointed, letting her sight down his arm. "See that there? If we go that way the ground drops away in sheer cliffs. They don't look that bad from here, but I can tell you they are impassable. Trying to climb down is harder than climbing up, and that's a nasty descent. I wouldn't try it, and I know what I'm doing."

Nicci let out a frustrated sigh. "Looks like the chasms, then."

"What about that spot?" Kahlan asked, pointing. "The land is gentler off that way."

"It is," Richard said, gesturing, "until you get to that scree slide. We'd never be able to climb that. It's so eroded that it wouldn't take much for it all to come down on us, or take us down with it. Follow the skirt of it with your eye and see what happens when you try to go around."

"Oh," Kahlan said as she squinted into the distance. "That's nasty."

"It is. Worse, if we got down that far we'd find ourselves in a dead end and then we would have to backtrack and go around on a different route. We would lose half a day, at least, maybe more. We can't afford to make mistakes. We have to get it right the first time."

Kahlan sighed. "So, do you see a way?"

Richard nodded. "There is a way, but it isn't going to be easy. It's easier than wasting extra days going around, though. Our best route is to push on and get through the area down in those chasms."

He was worried about making it to the citadel in time. He couldn't afford to make a mistake in finding a way through the wilderness ahead. In a way, he didn't care. The world seemed empty. He was in the mood to give up and wait for the blackness to take him.

But that same blackness would come for Kahlan. In his numb pain at the loss of his grandfather, the one thing that really mattered to him was Kahlan. He wanted more than anything for her to be safe. He couldn't stand the thought of losing her, too. He would do whatever it took to keep her safe and make sure she was healed.

Zedd had told him that living for those you love

was the best part of living. Richard clung to that idea. He cared that Kahlan lived, and he would do whatever it took to protect her.

Richard's gaze followed a few streams down lower, mentally testing the lay of the land, looking at where they led.

"I can't believe it's this hard to get to the place," Commander Fister said.

"Nothing is ever easy," Richard said, Zedd's frequent words coming to mind.

"We're coming in from the wrong direction," one of the men said. "This is the back door, you might say."

Richard nodded his agreement. "From what Irena knows and what Ned was able to tell us before he left for the palace, there are roads and trails that are well used by traders and merchants coming and going between other cities and towns in Fajin Province and then beyond to the rest of D'Hara. The problem is, none of those roads and trails head off in this direction because there is no real civilization back where we came from—that's why the barrier was placed there in ancient times. The people back in the great war wanted to put evil in the most remote, deserted place they could find."

Saavedra was located in a hook of a river, and Richard knew that they were headed in the right direction, so he knew that the easiest way to get to the city would be to get through the wilderness to the streams and then follow those tributaries downstream to the river. When they got close enough they would finally encounter roads and trails. Either the river or a road would lead them to Saavedra and the citadel. He knew where to go; it was getting there that was going to be the problem.

"So, do you see the way we need to go?" the commander asked.

"I do," Richard said.

As Commander Fister and a number of the men leaned close, Richard pointed out the route, explaining the crossovers, the walls of rock they needed to follow, and the impractical, dangerous climbs and descents they needed to avoid. The scouts all nodded their agreement as Richard explained the plan.

"There are some things down there we still can't see," one of the men said. "We might get down there and find out we can't make it through."

Richard heaved a sigh. "I know. But I don't see any other way. Sometimes there is only one pass through mountains without going a long distance to find another. As far as I can see, that area down there is the best chance to make it through. Even so, the difficulty is likely the reason there are no trails." He looked back at all the men studying the lay of the land. "If anyone has a better suggestion, speak up."

All the men, eyes scanning the land below, shook their heads. They all saw the same problems he did with going any other way.

"Far as I can see," one of the scouts said, frowning as he studied the chasms, "you're right that this is the only pass. We either get through this way or we have to spend extra days getting around those peaks over there."

"I've scouted that direction," another man said. "You hit the skirt of those mountains and have to keep pushing in the wrong direction, hoping to finally be able to make the turn. It would likely take an extra half a dozen days."

"We don't have any extra days," Nicci told the

men, wanting to bring a halt to them even considering it. "We don't have any extra hours."

Her words were sobering to everyone.

The men all knew the consequences of not making it to the citadel in time. Commander Fister had given all the men a talk, explaining exactly what was at stake. These were men devoted to protecting the Lord Rahl. They had competed all their lives to be members of the First File. They were not about to entertain the possibility of failure.

Richard was even more committed, though, because it meant Kahlan's life, and nothing meant more to him than that. But they needed to get through a lot of rugged territory, first. They weren't going to make it that day, but Richard thought it might be possible, if they were able to cover enough ground, that they would reach Saavedra the next day.

Having the cure that close, yet so far, was tormenting.

Richard checked the sky for any sign of a threat. He saw birds, but none of them looked panicked. He didn't see anything more threatening than a red-tailed hawk.

"That's it, then," one of the scouts said. "We will have to come in through the back door to Saavedra."

"Have you heard the old adage advising to always grow oleanders at your back door?" Nicci asked.

The man frowned. "No. Why would you want oleanders at your back door?"

"For protection," she said. "Oleanders are poisonous. Saavedra was probably in part established where it was for a very good reason—because this place guards its back."

The men all shared looks.

"Let's get moving," Richard told everyone.

Some of the scouts who had discussed the best route took the lead. Richard, Kahlan, Nicci, Irena, and Samantha, along with the rest of the men, followed behind as they plunged back into the woods.

B y late in the afternoon, as they worked their way ever downward through the dense, forested landscape, the ground became more rugged as fractures and rifts widened and deepened into wooded chasms. It wasn't long before they found themselves descending between soaring walls of gray granite. Low, heavy, wet clouds scudded by between the mountains soaring up overhead, conspiring with the close walls to make for a confining, gloomy journey. Drizzle dampened the walls and their faces.

Some of the horizontal sections of slick stone in the walls to the sides overhung the stacked slabs of rock below, so there was no hope of climbing out. They were going to have to follow the twisting course of the chasms if they were going to find a pass through the mountains. Richard knew from having seen the crooked canyons from above that it was going to be a confusing, difficult maze to traverse.

If there was ever a natural barrier guarding the back door of a city, this was it. He just hoped it wasn't also poisonous.

As they descended deeper into the main chasm leading them into the only possibility of passage through the mountains, they found it to be surprisingly broad. From up high on the distant prominence behind them it had been hard to tell precisely how big it really was down in the canyons. Now, Richard could see that in places the walls were hundreds, and in places thousands, of feet high. In some spots the floor of the twisting gorges broadened out, with the walls closed in closer overhead, almost touching, to create a murky, sometimes subterranean landscape of thick growth down below. In spots the rock bridged the walls high overhead.

Richard spotted flocks of small birds darting under the stone bridges. The walls probably provided relatively safe nesting spots for a variety of birds. The canyons were alive with small wildlife, everything from gnats and birds in the air, to centipedes and voles on the ground. He knew that where there was such wildlife, there would be predators.

The growth at the bottom of the chasms, while similar to the forests above, was denser. The daylight down in the bottom was limited by the towering walls, so the trees grew more slowly. Ancient, monarch spruce created brief areas where the forest floor at the bottom of the chasm was open among the massive trunks, so that they could see the walls off to either side. The thick beds of brown needles made for a spongy mat to walk on.

In other places, the space between the walls narrowed and smaller hardwoods and brush held sway. The maples made for a denser forest, with tangles of

young saplings crowding the ground where older
trees had fallen, providing some precious light. Soldiers pushed small, slender trunks over with their
boots to make it easier for those following behind.
The ground was deep in places with drifted leaves and
debris that had accumulated between boulders and
rocks, and because of how wet it was, it smelled of
rot. In a few flat areas, the water standing in long,
stagnant stretches was alive with bugs atop and
under the water, and snails around the edges.

The walls above them seemed to continually weep
water. Long green streaks of slime grew down the
walls where it looked like water almost continually
seeped down the rock face, staining it black. In other
spots, where the rock walls higher up tilted inward,
water dripped in thin rivulets from hundreds of feet
overhead, splashing on the ground, creating either
bare spots on the rock floor or in other places thick
wonderlands of mosses growing in shapes like fuzzy,
miniature cities. In a few spots the water fell from
such towering height that it mostly turned to mist before reaching the bottom.

All of that water running and falling down the
walls meant that travel along the bottom of the
chasms was a wet, miserable trek either through a
jungle of wet undergrowth or over stretches of sloping granite ledge with sheets of water running over
a surface of slime that made it extremely slippery. At
times the fall of water echoed, and at other times it
roared.

Richard didn't like having to travel through the
chasms. He knew that it was dangerous to be in such
a confined space. They could usually deviate a little
if need be, but in this case, down in the canyons, they

had no choice but to get through or turn back and spend days going around.

Richard knew that he and Kahlan would not live long enough to go the long way around. He knew they were running out of time.

The thing he didn't like about having to go through such a place, though, was that if they needed to escape any kind of predator that hunted the canyons, they had nowhere to run and rarely anywhere to hide or seek cover. If they were killed by a predator they would be just as dead as dying from the poison. At least the thick growth in most places would prevent the flying predators they had encountered before from easily getting in at them.

Richard shielded his eyes from the falling drizzle of water to look ahead into the various fractured slivers of passageways, divided by thin walls of rock. Some of those slim walls had collapsed, leaving jumbles of boulders and debris filling the narrow canyons. As they made their way farther in, they saw that in places the thin rock walls had disintegrated, leaving holes going back and forth between adjoining canyons.

The farther in they went, the more immense those holes became. In some areas they formed shallow caves. In other places they led a short distance through darkness to mossy rocks at the bottoms of towering cliffs in adjacent chasms on the other side.

To be able to continue on, they had to make their way up and over stacks of granite slabs littering some of the canyon floors. Some of the huge pieces of stone had been worn down and rounded over by the continual fall of water. As the granite eroded over time, it crumbled away to create gravel beds. Mosses, ferns, and small shrubs grew thick and green in the maze of passageways and tunnels. Vines clung to rocks and climbed the walls, making some look more leaf than rock.

Richard snatched Kahlan's arm just before she stepped on a green snake stretched out along folds in the moss. She let out a sigh of relief as she went around the snake. The men passed word back to be careful of it. Richard didn't know if it was poisonous or not, but he and Kahlan already had enough poison in them and Richard wasn't about to test his luck.

The way ahead offered a choice of winding, forested chasms and enormous caverns. Many of those caverns were passageways interconnecting the chasms. Looking through as they passed, they were offered views through the short stretch of darkness at light and lush growth at the other side.

As they climbed the stacked slabs to enter a cavern leading to a chasm on the other side going in the direction they needed to go, he saw something swoop low in the darkness. It wasn't a bat—it was far too big—but the way it flew reminded him of a bat.

Richard's blood ran cold when he peered farther into the dark passageway, over the heads of the men, and saw something dark moving on the surface of the rock above their heads. The whole ceiling of the cavern seemed to come alive, the way a cave full of bats was alive. As the things moved, it stirred the air just enough that the gagging stench of guano wafted out of the cavern.

Richard crossed a finger over his lips, signaling the men behind to be as quiet as possible, then urgently gestured for them to go back the way they had come. The men out front, though, turned back and started running out of the cavern, suddenly yelling for everyone to run. Richard didn't know what they had seen, but by the way these fearless soldiers were running, he was not about to stop them to ask questions. He turned Kahlan around and started back with her.

60

As the men ran back out of the huge, dark maw of the cavern, something with wings, but at least twice the size of a man, dropped from a high ledge up inside the shadows and swooped down toward a running soldier. The man saw it coming and was able to dive to the ground in time to keep from being ripped open by talons. Richard didn't know what the thing was, but even in the gloom he was able to see the size of the claws and knew they didn't want to tangle with it.

As they all ran for a different opening, hoping to find protection and cover, masses of the dark creatures came screaming out of the cavern Richard and the others had only just started to enter. The men all had swords or axes out and took a swing to try to ward the things off whenever they came close enough. A few of the men fired arrows into the billowing dark cloud of creatures streaming out of the cavern. The arrows all found their marks, but it didn't stop any of the animals.

As dark as it was in the confusing maze of chasms with the walls overhead almost closing all the way together, it was difficult to see individual creatures as they raced by overhead, or tell what they were, other than that they were big and aggressive. As fast as they were moving, they mostly melted together into a long black blur of flapping wings. Richard was sure, though, that once the wary creatures got over their initial caution, they would go into a feeding frenzy.

Yet more of them suddenly appeared, pouring out of dark cracks and openings in the walls the way big black bugs emerged from under rocks and logs.

Richard saw one of the winged creatures over his shoulder drop out of the flowing black cloud to swoop down toward him and Kahlan. He spun at the last moment as it plunged in, aiming for Kahlan with its talons extended, streaking right over the top of Richard's head. Richard made contact with a powerful swing of his sword as it swept past. The blade slit the length of its belly open, so that it left a trail of guts and blood on the way down. The matte-black creature crashed to the ground just beyond Kahlan. Teeth snapping, legs flailing, its long neck twisting, it writhed in the throes of death.

Yet more of the winged creatures continued to pour out of the cave, like bats appearing at dusk. As the dark, undulating ribbon of flying beasts curved downward, Nicci, between Richard and Kahlan, lifted her hands, as if pushing back at the creatures. Eight or ten of them folded in midair and plummeted, hitting with ground-shaking thuds.

Richard could see dark flesh between the bones of the wings, much like the skin that formed the wings of bats. But the bodies were covered in sooty black scales, rather than fur. Although they shared characteristics with other creatures, they were unlike any animal he had seen before.

"What did you do?" Richard asked as he urged Nicci and Kahlan back, trying to keep them under cover of trees and out of the way.

"I stopped their hearts," Nicci said. "But I can only do it to a few. There are too many for me to handle. I'm hoping that it will keep the rest of them afraid to come any closer."

As they ran between the trunks of ash and birch trees, toward the safety of another opening in the wall, some kind of creature yowled. It reminded Richard of the sound made by a big cat, like a mountain lion or cougar. The animal screamed again as they continued to run toward the cover of a cavern.

Kahlan snatched Richard's sleeve. "Look!" she said as she pointed into another chasm splitting off to their right. Whatever it was, it was back in a narrow canyon, with sections of bridging stone closing it off overhead. Vines and exposed roots hung down the walls. Green bands of small plants and shrubs had taken root in the horizontal joints of layered stone.

"What is it?" Richard asked, turning as he ran, focused on watching for any of the creatures that might break from the flock and come at them out of the sky and down through the forest canopy. He was not eager to be exposed out in the open just to have a look.

"It's Hunter!" Kahlan pointed urgently. "Look. It's Hunter. Up there."

Richard wasn't all that surprised. He had seen the

animal shadowing them from time to time. He wondered if it had been hoping Kahlan would give it another snack.

He was more concerned about their safety than the green-eyed animal, though. "Come on, we need to get in shelter before these things snatch us up out here in the open."

When they turned and started out of the trees and up into the mouth of the cavern, Hunter cried out again, louder, this time adding an angry snarl that echoed up and down the narrow canyon. It was a menacing sound that got their attention.

This time, nearly everyone turned to look. Once the creature saw that it had their attention, he turned and ran off. A moment later, Hunter was back at the edge of a high rock, watching them. It did the same thing again, running off, then it came back to sit on its haunches.

"Hunter doesn't want us to go this way. He wants us to follow him instead," Kahlan said in astonishment.

Richard hesitated, wondering why. He peered off into the cavern they were about to enter, searching for any threat. Deep inside, he saw them, then. It was like a thousand bats taking to wing all at once, headed their way.

Except these things were twice the size of a man. The air erupted with the roar of all their wings.

Hunter yowled again, more urgently this time.

"Come on!" Richard yelled at everyone. "Follow it!"

They all abandoned the cavern entrance and instead ran for the canyon opening where they had seen Hunter vanish. Behind them, Richard could hear the drone of thousands of wings beating. Looking over his shoulder, it looked like a sinister, churning cloud coming for them. One of the men vanished as the black mass swarmed down on him. Even as he saw it about to happen, Richard knew that it was already too late to do anything to save the man. A mist of blood rained down as he was torn apart high up in the air.

As the twisting black ribbon of creatures came lower over their heads, Richard saw Irena and Samantha hunching over as they ran. Irena had an arm over Samantha's head to protect her. From what Richard had seen, these beasts would only too eagerly rip off any arm they got hold of.

Richard, with his sword out, pushed the two women past him, urging them on faster.

"I've heard rumors of these things," Irena said as she paused to cast a spell of her own, then another, then another, each time causing a few of the beasts to lose their way and slam headlong into the stone walls. "Rumors of places in the Dark Lands infested with what people think might be cave dragons."

"Whatever they are, there are too many to stop," Richard told her. "If you stand here doing that, you'll die. We have to get to safety. Come on—hurry."

As Irena and Samantha took off running for their lives, Nicci kept a hand on Richard's back, pushing him along, making sure he didn't stop. She turned and, as she ran, cast out a boiling cloud of turbulent flame that caught up and incinerated dozens of the black forms, diverting the course of the main mass for a moment.

Wings aflame, trailing oily smoke, some of them bellowed in anger and pain as they spiraled out of the air, hitting the ground with bone-breaking violence. Flaming scales tumbled across the ground. One of them, engulfed in a hot, roaring fire that swiftly consumed the flesh between the bones of its wings, crashed into a pine tree, bending it partway over. The needles went up in a whoosh of flame. Fortunately, the forest was wet enough that the fire didn't spread to other trees.

Nicci turned to push her hands out again, this time stopping the hearts of a dozen in the lead as they headed in toward them. With their hearts stopped, they folded in midair. Others behind, still flying at full speed, crashed into them, tangling their wings together, snapping bones and ripping the membranes of flesh between them. The midair collision caused the rest of them to divert their course, giving the people on the ground precious seconds to make their escape.

As Richard pushed the last man past him and toward the narrow canyon, he grabbed Nicci's arm and pulled her along with him. Kahlan, standing close by, urgently snatched up Nicci's other hand.

The three of them raced after the rest of the men, all chasing after the small, spotted animal as he bounded off over rocks into the distance ahead.

Richard hoped that following Hunter was a good idea. As he looked over his shoulder he knew that the animal had called out just in time before they had gotten too far into that cavern full of the cave dragons. It had probably saved their lives.

Following Hunter, wherever he was leading them, made the most sense.

61

The rock roof of the cavern into which they ran formed a peak along the top. Mosses and other plants hung from the stone roof, giving it a lush, living green softness. Pools of perfectly still water suddenly frothed as all the men ran right through them. The sound of all their boots and the splashing water echoed around the chamber in a deafening clamor. While some of the soldiers took the lead to make sure that the way ahead was clear, most of the men slowed and fell in behind to protect Richard and Kahlan from what was chasing them. Nicci, too, stayed close behind to protect them. Irena and Samantha ran close to him on the opposite side of Kahlan.

Richard looked back over his shoulder and saw in the dim light out through the opening behind them that the winged predators turned aside rather than enter the cavern opening with them. For some reason, they circled just outside like a dark tornado. They roared in anger, none of them daring to enter the cavern. Most rotated in the massive vortex of creatures, while some flapped their enormous wings to hold themselves in place in midair just outside the opening to the cavern. They lowered their long heads, peering in at where their prey had gone.

As eager as they had been before, Richard couldn't imagine why they wouldn't come in after all of them, but he was more than glad not to have to try to fight them off. At the same time, he worried about why they wouldn't enter. They had to be afraid of something. The cavern they were racing into was certainly large enough. It was larger, in fact, than the caves and cracks the creatures had been nesting in.

Up ahead, the short, peaked cavern opened out into a brighter area at the bottom of dark, sheer stone walls. Rock piled in the bottom of the chasm over the millennia had eroded away until it had become rounded. Now it was all covered under thick layers of vibrant green mosses. Vines climbed the walls to the sides. Trees had taken root in the mosses on the mounds of decaying rock, engulfing them in tangled masses of roots.

Water, lit from above, wafted down in streamers and mist. Ahead, thin chutes of waterfalls cascaded down to pools, creating clouds of mist. From there, the water looked like it drained into narrow cracks that carried it underground.

"Do you see where that little furry friend of yours went?" Richard asked Kahlan.

She pointed. "I saw him run up ahead—that way. I saw him stop up higher, on the rocks up there, making sure we followed him."

"I wish I knew why he wanted us to follow him," Richard said.

"Maybe he wants to help," Kahlan said. "Maybe he knows this place and he wants to get us to safety."

Richard didn't think it could be that simple, but he didn't say so. There was more to it. What more there could be, he didn't know, but for the time being the small cat had gotten most of them away from what would surely have been a gruesome death.

The rocky ground ascended on stepped layers of fallen slabs and boulders. A tangled growth of shrubs with large leaves and small, lacy trees had taken root over and among the rock. The ascending floor of the chasm took them up ever higher over the stepped ledges. Ahead, Richard could see that the walls closed off overhead again, with showers of water falling on the far side like a wet curtain.

The whole place looked like a passageway to the good spirits.

Richard recalled what Zedd had told him about always appreciating the beauty of things. It was certainly beautiful down at the bottom of the chasm. The temperatures down deep in the gorges were likely moderated to an extent from the heat and cold up above. Protected as the place was from harsh elements, it allowed everything to grow green and lush in the temperate, wet climate.

The rock at the bottom continued its ascent up the floor of the chasm, making the canyon ever more shallow the farther they went. The more he was able to see of the landmarks off to the sides above them, the more he recognized where they were. Richard realized that they were finally coming out the far end of the maze.

An hour more of hard climbing at last brought them out of the deep canyons to the forest above. All around mountains ascended into low, dark, ragged clouds. The woods, though, were anything but a normal forest.

As the ground flattened out, they found themselves entering a woodland of the trees that were all some kind of gnarled hardwood. They looked something like oaks, but were not oak. Richard had never seen the trees before. The canopy of leaves created a kind of ceiling overhead, leaving it dark and somber at ground level.

The craggy, bare trunks all looked black in the dim light. Higher up on the trunks the wood became increasingly knobby and knotted. Twisted, misshapen branches rose from there up into the thick canopy of blackish green leaves. It almost appeared that they were entering a vast chamber with black pillars holding up the dark green roof. The only light that made it down to the mostly barren forest floor was a hazy gray-green color. As far as Richard could see off into the murky distance there were hundreds of the black trunks supporting the ceiling of leaves.

Ravens somewhere up in the limbs let out calls that echoed through the crooked wood. He could see some of the big birds in the distance to the sides drop down out of the leaves to fly off among the trunks, cawing as they departed.

Kahlan pointed. "Look, there's Hunter."

He saw the animal off in the distance, sitting on its haunches waiting for them. Richard rested the palm of his left hand on the hilt of his sword as he kept watch on everything else around them. The place was creepy. That was the only way to describe it.

He saw that the men of the First File, spread out through the strange woods, ever on guard for any threat, were also looking warily around. Nicci looked as grim as the men. Irena and Samantha were clearly afraid of the place.

As they cautiously made their way ahead through the endless expanse of the half-dead-looking woods, Richard spotted something dark off in the hazy distance that was not trees.

He realized that it looked like people standing still and silent, except that it looked like they had horns.

He saw then more of them emerge from behind trees to the sides. All of the figures carried long, straight staffs that were a little taller than they were. It wasn't long before they were surrounded by the silhouettes of what looked like nothing so much as horned people.

Irena slowly dry-washed her hands as she peered suspiciously from one of the still, silent figures to another.

Richard could see the shadowed form of Hunter off in the distance, watching them from far beyond the figures that had loosely closed in around them.

"What are they?" Samantha whispered to her mother.

Irena's gaze darted among the silent, dark, horned figures.

"Cunning folk."

Richard didn't have to ask if she thought they were dangerous. By how pale Irena's face had gotten, it was clear she thought they were.

62

Cunning folk?" Commander Fister asked in a quiet voice when he overheard what Irena had said.

She nodded to the commander as he leaned down close to her. "I think so. I've never met any of them myself. From things I'd always heard, I never wanted to."

The commander appraised the situation and how many of the strange figures stood scattered throughout the dark wood. There were not enough for the men of the First File to be concerned, if it was only a matter of numbers. No one, though, thought that numbers were the problem.

"Tell the men to stand down," Richard told the commander. "We don't know that they mean us any harm and we don't want to give them cause. This is still part of the D'Haran Empire. We are not invaders, but we are still coming into their home, so we owe them respect. I don't want them to see us as a threat."

"Got it," Commander Fister said as he hiked up his trousers. "Be polite to the nice people with horns."

He moved off, casually passing the word among the waiting men.

Richard saw one of the closer figures thump his staff on the ground three times. Small arcing sparks crackled at the top end of the staff.

Richard looked over at Nicci out of the corner of his eye. "Gifted magic?"

"No," she said. "Some other kind of power, most likely occult abilities."

"All the more reason to be cautious and show them a calm face," Kahlan said.

Richard nodded his agreement. "Wait here."

Nicci immediately seized his shirt at his shoulder. "No you don't. You stay right where you are, protected by all of us. Let him come to us."

Richard let out a deep sigh. "All right."

He lifted an arm, waving, so that the man who had thumped the staff would see him. The dark figure watched Richard for a time, waiting to see what the soldiers off to the sides would do, before finally coming forward to meet them.

As the figure who had thumped his staff approached, he was joined by half a dozen other figures. They followed close behind him, off to the sides a little. All of them looked the same. All had staffs. All were coal black, much like the tree trunks all around them. All of them had long horns.

Once they were close enough, Richard was surprised to see that they were all covered head to toe in what appeared to be thick, black mud heavily loaded with straw. They all had steer skulls over their heads. The steer skulls were covered in the same black, muddy straw.

The idea of people wearing steer skulls over their heads struck him as rather silly, but standing there covered in the thick layer of black straw, eyes staring out from inside those skulls, they didn't look at all silly. They looked intimidating. He knew, though, that intimidation was obviously the purpose. Intimidation often provided safety.

Richard could see nothing of them other than the thick layer of muddy straw and the skulls covering their heads. It was not even possible to tell if they were men or women.

"My name is Richard," he said when the one who had thumped his staff came to a halt.

The man waited without saying anything.

"It is urgent that we get to Saavedra," Richard told them.

"Not to us," the man said in a voice muffled by the skull he was wearing over his head.

Richard noticed that more figures covered in the same pitch-black straw and wearing the same kind of steer skulls had emerged from behind trees. They gathered, closing in around the interlopers. He knew that the soldiers could easily handle the numbers, but he didn't think they could handle the occult powers that he feared these people could wield.

"We mean you and your people no harm," Richard said. "We only wish to pass through here and we will be on our way."

The straw man looked among several of those beside Richard. "There is evil among you."

Richard wasn't sure what he meant. "Evil?"

"You," the man said, tipping his staff toward Richard. "You have it in you." He tipped his staff toward Kahlan. "She does as well."

Richard nodded. "We're sick. That is why we need to get to Saavedra. We need to get there so we can be cured of this sickness. But you needn't worry, you cannot catch it from us."

"We know that."

Richard wondered if that was true, and if so, how the man could know. Of course, he was able to recognize the poison in him and Kahlan, and it certainly was evil. Richard suspected it was an indication of the abilities of their occult powers. Jit had occult abilities, and this poison had come from her, so in a way, it made sense that they would recognize it.

"We mean you no harm," Richard said. "We only wish to pass peacefully through your land. We will hurry and pass through quickly and be swiftly on our way."

"You may only pass if the oracle says that you may pass."

Richard shrugged. "That sounds fair. I would be happy to speak with your oracle."

The head with horns swiveled as the man apparently looked through the eye holes in the skull at the people to each side of Richard.

"You do not choose who will speak to the oracle," he said. "The oracle chooses who will speak to her."

Richard deliberately didn't react to the man's hostile tone, but instead tried to appear calm and agreeable. Even so, he was only a twitch away from drawing his sword if matters took a turn for the worse.

"All right. Will you take us to your oracle, then?"

The man appraised them for a moment longer. He thumped his staff, causing the top end to flicker with little flashes.

"We are the people of the straw. Come with us."

He and the other straw figures turned and started weaving their way among the dark trunks of trees, through the eerie misty haze, toward where Richard had last seen Hunter.

Richard glanced over at Nicci before taking up Kahlan's hand and starting out after the people of the straw.

63

The walk through the strange forest of gnarled trees was longer than Richard had thought it might be. The ground, never getting much light below the thick canopy, was dead-looking, with very little growing in the crusty black ground. There was a bit of weedy growth that spiderwebbed across the ground, but what wasn't dead was brown and sickly-looking. Richard knew of trees with roots that were poisonous to other plants. It kept other things from growing up and crowding out the trees.

Richard wished that Zedd were with them. Richard's grandfather would surely have something to say about this place and the people of the straw. Richard wished that he had his grandfather's advice. And his company. Even though he was gone, Zedd was always in Richard's thoughts. Even those times when they had been far apart, Richard had always been comforted by the knowledge that he was somewhere. Now he was gone.

The world felt like a dead and lonely place without the old wizard, his grandfather, his friend, his most trusted advisor. It seemed impossible that Zedd wasn't alive and well, somewhere. For Richard's entire life Zedd had always been alive, always been there for him.

Richard wanted his grandfather back. He knew that would never happen, but he would one day have his hands around the throat of the person responsible for Zedd's murder.

After a time they arrived at a more open area with a tight cluster of buildings set in the expanse in the dark forest. All the buildings were square, all of them one-story. They appeared to be made of the same muddy straw as that covering the people. Even though the forest had opened up to the sky, the sky was so dark with threatening, leaden clouds that it didn't do much to brighten the scene. Everything, from the trees to the straw men to the black straw buildings, was dark and dead and dismal-looking.

Richard realized that the muddy straw covering the men and the buildings had to be something more stable than mud, or the frequent rains of the Dark Lands would dissolve their straw garb as well as their homes. It also had to be something more flexible than mud, or it would dry, crack, and crumble off when the men walked. From what he saw, none of the thick, muddy straw looked anything but entirely intact.

Richard saw faces in windows that were nothing more than square openings in the plastered straw walls. The faces were not wearing skulls, but looked like normal people.

Back behind some of the buildings he saw frames drying skins of what looked like deer. He also saw smokehouses. There were wooden tubs and other community property for the small village.

When people began emerging from buildings, he was surprised to see that they were all dressed more or less normally. Their clothes were rather drab, but none would have looked out of place just about anywhere. He saw men and women of every age, as well as a few children. The children stayed inside or behind the buildings, too shy to come out, but too curious about the strangers to stay hidden. The people all looked cautious but inquisitive. They didn't show any indications of being hostile. From what Richard had seen of the Dark Lands, caution was more than warranted.

There were fewer than maybe a hundred people in the small village. By the number of buildings, he doubted that there were more that he wasn't seeing. They all hung back as the straw man who had spoken to Richard went to speak with them.

The people had what looked like a heated discussion, arms waving as they talked to the straw man. It went on for a time before the straw man finally thumped his staff. When he did, the conversation ended. Everyone fell silent. The people all vanished back into the simple buildings.

Richard and all those with him had no idea what was going on, and could only wait until the man returned.

"Come with me," the straw man wearing a steer skull told them.

They all followed him into the tiny village, trying to look nonthreatening as they walked among the buildings to an open square in the center. The straw men they had seen at first surrounded the square after

Richard, Kahlan, Nicci, Irena, Samantha, and the soldiers were all packed together.

As they waited for what would happen next, Richard looked over at Samantha. She had told him before how she longed to travel to different places and see new things. She had said that Stroyza was boring and she hoped to one day leave her little village and go on adventures.

"Enough adventure for you yet?" he asked her with a smile.

She looked up at him with big, dark eyes and nodded, finally returning his smile. It looked a little forced.

"Do you think they will let us pass?" she asked.

"They will," Nicci said in Richard's place while she kept her gaze fixed on the straw men, "or they will meet Death's Mistress."

Samantha eased back in the shadow of her mother. Richard didn't feel the need to warn Nicci to take it easy and not do anything rash. She was experienced and he knew that she wouldn't be the one to start something. But if trouble started, she might be the one to swiftly end it.

He could hear some kind of commotion in one of the more distant buildings. Muffled voices were having a spirited conversation. At last the voices fell silent.

In short order, a crowd emerged. They all walked close together, pushing and pulling one another along. They seemed gripped by a sense of occasion, and by fear.

In their midst was a woman, looking like any of the other villagers. She was dressed the same as the rest of them, except that in her case her blouse was dyed a dark henna. Her straight, dark hair was pulled back into a loose ponytail tied with a strip of leather.

She had been blindfolded with a piece of cloth dyed with henna, like her blouse, but much brighter.

It was not hard to tell by the way she walked with her hands held out, feeling blindly for anything in her way, that she was clearly uncomfortable being blindfolded. Richard wondered if she had come willingly. He supposed that as long as she was only blinded with a piece of cloth over her eyes, he wasn't going to make an issue of it.

Many of the people in the crowd around her pressed hands to her, helping guide her, reassuring her, encouraging her. One of the younger men took one of her hands and put it on his shoulder to help show her the way. She looked bewildered, confused, and at the same time, the way she held her chin up, maybe a bit honored to be the one blindfolded. She had certainly become an instant luminary among the people of straw. She also looked like she didn't know for sure what to expect.

The crowd around her shuffled to a stop before Richard and those standing close to either side beside him. Whatever the ceremony was they were involved in appeared to be a rare event. Richard imagined that they didn't often receive strangers out in the wilderness where they lived.

At the same time, if they had an oracle, he was sure that there would occasionally be people come from great distances to see her.

The straw man turned to Richard. "Through this blind woman, the oracle will pick the one who will be allowed to speak to her."

As the woman groped blindly with a hand, the straw man reached out, took hold of her hand, and placed it on his staff. He molded her fingers around the shaft.

When she nodded that she was ready, he stepped aside.

The blindfolded woman shuffled forward, using the staff to help her feel her way. When she got close to the line of strangers, she stopped, her chin held up, trying to sense who stood before her, but she couldn't. She began shuffling ahead again, this time walking down the line of strangers. She kept going until she reached the last soldier, and then she returned, holding her chin up as she blindly made progress back, trying to sense something of each one of those waiting before her.

Finally, she returned to a stop not far away. She turned toward them as she placed her second hand on the staff. Richard knew that they didn't have any time to waste. If this ceremony didn't end pretty soon he was going to have to put an end to it himself. The palm of his left hand rested on the hilt of his sword. They needed to get to the containment field in Saavedra. These people were either going to help or he would have to sweep them aside and get through the pass.

Finally, the blindfolded woman tipped the staff forward to tap Kahlan once on each shoulder.

"You," she said. "The oracle will see you, and no one else."

Richard was about to say he wouldn't allow it when Kahlan stepped forward and spoke before he had a chance.

"Thank you. Please take me to the oracle at once. We have no time to spare."

Two of the straw men crossed their staffs before Richard when he started to take a step forward.

"You will wait while the oracle speaks with her," the straw man said.

Kahlan held a hand back toward Richard, urging him to stay put. "It's all right, Richard. Just wait here."

"I don't like—"

"I am the Mother Confessor. I have been doing this sort of thing my whole life. We don't have any time to waste. Let me get this over with so we can be on our way. That's what matters."

He wanted to say that when she had done this sort of thing in the past, she had always had access to her power. Now, she didn't. But she was right that this would be the fastest way to get past, and less risky than a fight.

As long as it went well.

Richard heaved a sigh. "You're right. We will wait here."

"Call out if you need help," Nicci said. "I will hear you."

Kahlan nodded and then followed after the blindfolded woman with the staff.

Richard didn't know exactly what was going on, but he did know that he didn't like it one bit.

64

Kahlan followed the blindfolded woman as she walked through the center of their village. The woman in the henna-colored blouse seemed to be better able to navigate now that she was holding the staff one of the straw men had given her, almost as if it were showing her the way as she walked down the center of the opening between buildings. The people of the village stood to the sides, silently watching her pass. Children, holding the frames of window openings, rested their chins on their hands. None of them spoke.

Kahlan didn't like how somber they appeared to be over what they were witnessing.

It reminded her of people watching a funeral procession.

"What is your name?" Kahlan asked the woman she was following.

The woman, walking with her chin lifted, turned an ear back toward Kahlan. "I am the one the oracle has chosen to use. I am the one who is in service to her this day."

"I see," Kahlan said half to herself.

At the far edge of the village they plunged back into the somber woods made up entirely of the strange trees. The ground, still barren, dead, and dark, started to incline under the obscuring canopy of leaves. After a time Kahlan noticed rock bluffs to the sides funneling them ahead.

When they came to a place where the passage narrowed somewhat, more normal-looking trees began to take over from the strange forest. Shrubs and other plants dotted the ground among white birch and linden thick with fragrant, fluffy yellowish blossoms.

The blindfolded woman stopped at the fringes of where the dark trees grew.

"This is as far as I am allowed to go," she said.

"And what am I to do?" Kahlan asked.

The woman tilted the staff ahead. "You are to go on alone. I cannot go beyond here. You must go the rest of the way alone."

"How will I know the way?"

The woman tilted the staff again. "The oracle is that way. You will find her if you go that way." When she sensed Kahlan hesitating, she tilted her head in gesture back toward the village. "This is your last chance to turn back. Think carefully on what you are about to do. Not many are pleased to hear what the oracle would tell them."

"People are rarely satisfied by hearing such things," Kahlan said. "But I don't have a choice."

The woman nodded. "I can feel the sickness in you."

Kahlan took a deep breath as she looked off into the woods ahead. "Thank you for bringing me."

"Do not thank me before you see the oracle. Afterwards, for bringing you here, you may yet curse the day I was born."

"I choose to thank you. Neither of us has a choice in what we do today."

The woman smiled. "In that you are right. While you speak with the oracle, I will wait back in our village with those you travel with. If the oracle decides that you may pass, I will know and I will bring them."

Once the blindfolded woman turned back toward the way they had come, Kahlan started off in the other direction. She was glad at least to once again be in a more normal-looking forest rather than the spooky black wood. She found a small brook, where gloomy light filtered down to the lacy leaves of some of the young trees growing along the mossy rocks along the bank. Kahlan fanned her hand in front of her face as she passed through little clouds of gnats hovering above the brook.

Up on the banks to the sides grew thickets of brush and larger trees. Even with the gnats and other buzzing bugs, it was easier to walk along the brook than to make her way through the congested forest to the sides. She could occasionally see through gaps in the trees that the rock walls that had narrowed the passage had receded back to become the lower reaches of forested mountains rising up to either side.

The brook eventually led her through a stand of birches. The dark spots on the white bark looked like a thousand eyes watching her. The birches eventually thinned out as she moved along the brook into a more open grassland. The dark wall of forest receded into the distance to the sides, leaving a flat, grassy plain. The brook broadened out in a series of shallow pools as crystal-clear water moved quietly over gravel beds.

Out in the open at last, Kahlan was finally able to better see the true enormity of the mountains. They stood like hazy, pale gray-blue walls rising up to either side. She couldn't see any other way through the towering, snow-covered peaks. As far as she could tell, they had indeed found the pass through the mountains that would lead them to Saavedra.

Now, all she had to do was get the oracle to give her blessing for them to travel through the pass.

In among small, grassy, rolling rises she found the source of the brook. The water, looking to be fed from a spring below, flowed up through a split in a knee-high boulder and down the sides. Through the clear water in the pool around the boulder, she spotted minnows above the gravelly bottom swimming into the gentle current. The place vaguely reminded Kahlan of something she had seen before, but she couldn't bring it to mind.

Beyond the spring, over a grassy rise, she saw a broad valley forested with huge oaks and maples. The massive trunks of the spreading oaks created a beautiful, natural cathedral below the crowns. Had her mission not been so vital, and her worry for Richard so great, Kahlan would have marveled at the size and beauty of the trees set among the lush expanse of grass.

As she walked through the waist-high grass, something began crunching under her feet. Sometimes the grasses collapsed inward when her foot broke through. She paused and looked down. Among the tussocks, she saw something slightly round just under the brown thatch of dead grass. She noticed that the ground all around looked lumpy. With the side of her boot, she scraped at the thick layer of dead grass down at the base of the new green shoots. Her foot exposed something that looked like bone.

Kahlan scanned the entire area all around her, and saw that all of it was cluttered with the smallish round humps. Those round bulges were what had been crunching and collapsing inward as she had stepped on them. With the side of her boot, she worked to expose more of the round mound.

It was a skull. She squatted and pulled it out so she could turn it over. Empty eye sockets stared blindly up at her.

The skull was human.

Kahlan stood in a rush. She peered out over the grassy area and saw that there were small round mounds everywhere, as far as she could see. Even in the distance she could detect the telltale rounded spots down beneath the grass. They were all so close together that it would be impossible not to tread on a skull with every step.

There had to be hundreds of human skulls littering just the area close in around her. By the way the ground in all directions was mounded, Kahlan suspected that the skulls were not merely lying on the surface of the ground, but heaped up in deep piles. She had no idea how many human skulls she was standing on, but she quickly changed her estimate from hundreds to thousands.

She had no idea what had happened in this place, but she told herself that if she didn't get permission for her and everyone with her to pass, and they tried to pass without that permission, they very well might end up here, with grass growing up out of their bones.

But if she didn't get permission to pass, she and Richard would be dead within days. Nicci had told her how short their remaining lives would be if the poison was not removed.

With no time to waste, she couldn't worry about the dead she was walking over. Her only concern now had to be for the living, not only her and Richard, but everyone else who depended on them.

Making her way through the monarch oaks, eyeing songbirds flitting about up in the branches, she saw that the trees gave way to a central area that looked like it should have been sunlit, but the murky day would not cooperate. She could see someone— no doubt the oracle—sitting on a stone bench near the center of that open area.

Kahlan wasted no time contemplating what she had to do, or what she might say. She marched straight toward the woman.

When she finally reached her, Kahlan came to a stop, waiting behind the woman sitting sideways on the gray granite bench, facing away. Her hair was a thick mass of dozens and dozens of matted ropy locks of hair hanging loosely down on all sides. Her hair was bright red.

"Good afternoon, Mother Confessor," the woman said in a silken voice without turning. "Thank you for coming."

It was then that Kahlan noticed Hunter sitting quietly off to the side, watching with big green eyes.

Kahlan knew in that instant that there was a lot more going on than she had at first realized.

65

The woman on the bench finally turned, gazing up at Kahlan for a moment before standing. Her gray dress looked far too elegant for the woods. Kahlan saw no home, or building of any sort.

The woman's piercing sky-blue eyes made her tight thatch of ropy red locks by contrast look all the more red. They were the sort of eyes that could easily be cruel. They were the kind of eyes that had witnessed many terrible things.

Kahlan thought that the oracle might have been rather attractive, had she not painted her lips black.

"Thank you for seeing me," Kahlan said.

The woman gracefully bowed her head. "Of course. I am honored to have the Mother Confessor herself come to see me. My name is Red."

"Red," Kahlan repeated, glancing to the woman's strange hair, thinking that the name was pretty obvious.

The woman's black lips widened in a slightly amused smile. "You think I am called Red because of my hair."

"It had crossed my mind," Kahlan said.

"Of course it did. But you would be wrong." The tolerant smile stayed on her face, not touching any other of her smooth features. "I am called Red because there have been times when this pass through the mountains"—she swept an arm out first in the direction Kahlan needed to go and then in the direction from which they had come—"has run red with blood. There have been times when I have turned this pass to a river of blood." She shrugged. "So, that was how I came to be called Red. The hair came after." The smile widened. "Because I liked the name."

"I see," Kahlan said.

"You needn't sound so reproachful, Mother Confessor. After all, there have been times when you, too, have turned the countryside red with blood."

"That's true," Kahlan admitted. She sought to clarify the idea with a bit of context. "Sometimes people need killing."

Red laughed. "Yes, indeed they do." The laughter died out as she leaned a bit closer, looking hard into Kahlan's eyes. "I'm glad that you feel that way."

Kahlan glanced over at Hunter sitting quietly, watching.

She gestured at him. "Do you know that small creature?"

Red didn't bother looking. "So cute, isn't he? His mother is a . . . protector of mine. I would not describe her as cute, though. You would never guess from looking at the little fellow just how big she is, or how ferocious. He is quite the good little boy. I sent him to you."

Kahlan frowned. "Why?"

"To make sure that you made it here. I put the thorn in his paw so that you two would become friends. Though he is still small, like his mother, he is quite the fierce protector."

Kahlan was still frowning. "How did you know that he would find me, or that I would find the thorn and take it out? For that matter, how did you know that we would come this way?"

"Oh come now, Mother Confessor, what kind of oracle would I be if I did not see such important events in the flow of time?"

The flow of time . . . It suddenly came to Kahlan why the clear spring coming up from the boulder and the cathedral of trees looked familiar.

"You're a witch woman."

Red smiled indulgently. "Yes. The simple people here have never imagined such a thing. I don't think they would understand. I give them little bits from the flow of time, such as I did when I told them that all of you would come through their home place. So, they think I am an oracle."

Kahlan cocked her head. "I've had dealings with a witch woman in the past. Do you know Shota?"

Red flicked her hand dismissively. "Never heard of the witch."

Kahlan glanced around. "So, where are all your snakes?"

Red made a show of visibly shuddering. "Snakes. Horrid creatures. I hate them."

"Me too," Kahlan said, feeling just the slightest bit better. Maybe Red was not the trouble Shota had proven herself to be. "Shota is rather fond of snakes."

"Disgusting," Red said, shuddering again. "I much prefer worms."

Kahlan blinked. "Worms?"

Red nodded earnestly. "Much more agreeable creatures than snakes. More obedient and much more useful as well."

"What good are worms?"

Amused, Red leaned closer. "You're joking."

"No, really."

Red gestured vaguely behind Kahlan, back toward the mounds of skulls. "Well, for one thing, the little ones are good at cleaning up messes."

Kahlan cocked her head. "The little ones?"

Red straightened. She looked back over her shoulder.

"Worm! Come to me!"

Kahlan had never heard of worms that would come when called. She wondered briefly if Red had all her senses. In a moment, though, she began to feel the ground beneath her feet trembling. And then it shook as if from an earthquake.

Abruptly, not far behind Red, the ground broke open. Dirt flew up and away as something big erupted from under the sod.

Kahlan stared in disbelief. A worm as big around as the trunk of a midsize oak lifted part of itself up and out of the dirt. It stretched its wet head up over Red's shoulder. There was no face, no eyes, only an enormous round mouth ringed with teeth. The opening of the mouth undulated along with the rest of the distended, banded sections of the never-still, rippling body. The teeth clacked together when the mouth snapped closed and open again.

"Worm eats snakes for the fun of it," Red said, amused by the startled look on Kahlan's face.

With that, she bent and snatched a snake up from under the bench. Smiling at Kahlan, she flipped the writhing snake back over her shoulder. The enormous worm snapped it out of midair like a dog snapping up a table scrap tossed its way.

Red waved a hand without looking back, dismissing the thing. The worm's massive body ripped in muscular waves as it pulled itself back down into the ground. The dirt and sod collapsed in around the hole as it vanished beneath the ground.

"Your little furry friend's mother is even more formidable," the witch woman said.

"I can only imagine," Kahlan said as she glanced over at Hunter. "Red, you obviously went to a lot of trouble getting me to come here."

"Not a lot of trouble," Red said with a shrug. "I saw in the flow of time that you would come this way. I didn't want you to be ripped apart and eaten back there in the chasms, so I sent your little friend to show you the way and keep you alive."

"Thank you" was all Kahlan could think to say. "But what am I doing here? We need permission to go through here. We need to be on our way. What is it you want from me?"

"Ah," Red said, "direct and to the point. Well, with the condition you and Lord Rahl are in, I suppose that you have no time to waste, so we had best get right to our business."

"My business is getting to Saavedra," Kahlan told the woman. "We're in a hurry. We don't want any trouble. We simply need you to give us your permission to go through this pass."

"Yes," Red drawled, "but first we have important business."

Kahlan frowned again. "What business?"

Red's piercing blue eyes fixed on her. "I need you to kill someone for me."

CHAPTER

66

"You need me to kill someone?" Kahlan asked. She didn't see why a witch woman with this much ability and reach couldn't do her own killing if it was so important. "I'm not an assassin. Not for anyone, including you."

"Yes, that's all well and good, but you need to do this killing, so I need to make you understand how important it is so that you will not fail."

Kahlan took a deep breath. She knew the woman wasn't going to let them pass until Kahlan at least heard her out. "Fine, let's hear it, then, but be quick about it. I don't have long to live unless I get this sickness out of me."

"Yes," Red drawled again. "The call of death from that vile creature, Jit."

Kahlan cast a suspicious look at the woman. "You know of Jit, and the poison in us?"

Red rolled her eyes. "I am a witch woman. Of course I know of important matters that involve central figures such as you and Lord Rahl. It is all part of the larger issue. It's part of why you must perform the task I have for you."

"You mean killing someone for you."

"That's right." She took a deep breath of her own as she considered how to begin. "Well, since you are rapidly running out of time, I will try to make this as short as I can."

"I would appreciate that," Kahlan said, not really wanting to hear it. She thought about the field of skulls and realized that at least listening to what Red had to say was probably wise. They needed to be on their way. Fighting their way through was not a risk they needed. Listening would take less time.

"You see, Mother Confessor, I have seen the demon. He is here, in the world of life."

"The demon?"

"The one called Sulachan. He has long been dead. He belongs in the world of the dead and—"

"You expect me to kill Sulachan?" Kahlan was incredulous.

"No, not exactly. Not directly, anyway. What I expect is for you to make it possible for him to be sent back to the underworld, where he belongs."

Kahlan certainly wanted Sulachan and his scheme stopped. Since Red seemed to have the same objective, Kahlan suddenly became more interested. "Make it possible. . . . How am I supposed to do that?"

"I am trying to explain the larger picture, if you would allow me. You said you were in a hurry."

Kahlan nodded. "Sorry. Go on."

"Sulachan is an ancient evil that blighted the world. He died long ago and belongs in the world of the dead. By all that is right, he should not be a problem for us today, but he is.

"In life, he was a sickly man. He was also a man of vision. Evil vision, deranged vision, but vision nonetheless. Knowing he was slowly dying, he began making preparations long before he ever passed over into the world of the dead. Despite being sickly, he was a powerful wizard, possessing both the gift and occult powers."

"I don't understand this business with occult powers," Kahlan said. "I've never encountered them before. Why do they suddenly seem to be springing up all over?"

Red swept an arm around. "Everything requires balance. That balance runs the gamut from the minuscule to the most central elements. Conflict seeks balance, balance is often achieved by conflict. Heat and cold; darkness and light; bad balanced by good; hate by love—that sort of thing. Smaller parts, such as the good spirits versus demons, are part of a larger balance of life versus death. All elements are built from smaller, balanced elements.

"The gift itself is balanced between Additive Magic and Subtractive Magic. Yet on a larger scale, the totality of that internal balance within the gift—the gift itself—is balanced by occult powers.

"Back in the great war, those like Sulachan were defeating the gifted. That threatened to throw the worlds of life and death out of balance. The gifted prevailed, though, sealing those with occult powers behind the barrier. The gift thus gained dominance. But because everything always seeks balance, they knew the seals on the barrier could not last forever, and indeed they haven't. Occult powers have been leaking out for some time, and now they are once again fully free and among us."

"I see," Kahlan said, considering the repercussions. "So, you were saying about Sulachan dying?"

"With his own abilities and the help of many others whom he commanded, he manipulated powers in the underworld before he died—occult powers—to prepare his place there.

"His spirit has been working for the three thousand years since his death to reconnect with the forces he had put into place here in this world when he had been alive."

"Forces—you mean like the half people?"

"Yes. He knew that they could not be contained forever. He knew that one day they would be freed from their exile, and then be able to work to call his spirit back from the world of the dead into his body in the world of life.

"He also used the spirits of the dead he reanimated, drawing their spirits out of their eternal rest in the underworld to do his bidding. Once he pulled them away from their link to the gift that had taken them beyond the veil, they lost that connection and no longer knew where they belonged. He used them as his ethereal messengers between worlds.

"Lastly, Sulachan managed to enlist the essential help of the man who used to live a couple of days in that direction," she said, flicking a hand in the direction of Saavedra off through the pass.

"Hannis Arc," Kahlan said. "He ruled Fajin Province from the citadel in Saavedra."

"He ruled much of Fajin Province, but not all," she said, looking abruptly venomous. "I hold sway here.

"But that is the man," she said, retracting her fangs a bit. "Hannis Arc benefited profoundly from the occult powers leaking out from behind the barrier. As a result, he has been able to tamper with the very nature of the Grace—the very way the world of life exists—bending those laws in order to bring Sulachan's spirit back into this world."

"And your abilities are powered by what the Grace represents," Kahlan said, "so your very existence is at stake."

"That's right. As are your abilities, and Lord Rahl's, were you not sick with Jit's touch.

"Sulachan wants to bend those forces until they break. Hannis Arc wants to rule the world of life. He helped Sulachan fulfill his ambitions in return for Sulachan's help.

"Both men also know that there are always those who are all too eager to help them. Those minions serve to provide an audience of sycophants for evil such as Sulachan and Hannis Arc bring into the world. In return, they earn the table scraps of praise from the depraved.

"While powerfully gifted and possessing occult powers able to mine prophecy and bring Sulachan's spirit back through the veil, Hannis Arc didn't have the army necessary to accomplish his more ambitious goals of rule. For that, he needed help. So, he brought Sulachan back to provide that help."

"One hand washes the other," Kahlan said.

"Yes. They formed an alliance. Hannis Arc would do what was needed in this world to bring Sulachan back from the dead. Among other things, that meant using the invaluable blood of the bringer of death—your husband—to call Sulachan back from the dead. One of those matters of balance I spoke of.

"In return, Sulachan provided the army of half people and all the revived corpses Hannis Arc could ever need for conquest. Hannis Arc in turn continues to provide the worldly occult powers necessary to sustain Sulachan here in this world. And so on, round and round it goes, both locked together helping each other, but each with motives of his own, each using the other because he has to.

"Each man also thinks he controls the other. For now they both work together toward the same ends. For now, they share the same goals and need each other.

"But they are like two vipers, each with the tail of the other in his mouth. Unfortunately, we will all be long dead and in the merciless hands of the Keeper before that alliance ever comes to be inconvenient for either.

"By then, if they are not stopped first, it will be too late for this world because Sulachan ultimately wishes to destroy the boundary between the world of life and the world of the dead. The balance of Creation itself would be broken.

"That would be a bad thing. A very bad thing.

"Thus, we must act or we all die."

67

L ook, Red," Kahlan said, "you don't need to explain the consequences to me. I am quite aware of what it would mean."

"Are you, really?" Red asked. "It would mean not only the end of the natural order of life as we know it, but the Keeper would have me. Do you have any idea of how much the Keeper of the underworld lusts to get witch women into his clutches—outside the natural order of the Grace?"

"Yes, as a matter of fact, I do. Shota told me all about it. But you are hardly the only one. All of us would be in an eternity of agony should Sulachan and Hannis Arc succeed. It's not only about you, Red, it's about everyone." Kahlan leaned closer. "Everyone."

Red showed a cunning smile, as if that had been her point all along. "And don't you ever forget it, Mother Confessor. I may have my own self-interest, but that self-interest just happens to be the same as everyone else's. My fate would be everyone's fate. The

Keeper would be loosed on the world, on all of us. The dead would feed on the living."

Red straightened a bit and smoothed her gray dress at her hips. "I'm not sure that you truly comprehend the horror of what that would mean, or that you actually grasp the true enormity of it. Once Sulachan and Hannis Arc destroy the boundary between life and death, there is no putting it back together. All of Creation would be forever out of balance. In such a chaotic, unbalanced state, it would mean the end of all of existence. Creation itself would eventually wink out of existence, like an ember dying.

"But in the grand scale of time, that could still mean a thousand years, or ten thousand years, of ceaseless agony for all of us on the wrong side of that doomed struggle.

"Sulachan, in his arrogant delusions, believes he can control such forces and bend them to his will. Hannis Arc, in his lust for power, sees a thousand years of reign as an eternity. They make the perfect lethal pair: delusion and lust, both possessing great power individually, multiplied by their alliance and driven by their objectives, both cheered on by those who hate, gleeful at the obscenity of lost hope.

"Once such forces of chaos are loosed, there would be no one capable of putting them back. Once everything has spun out of control, it is only a matter of time before it is all over. Life—existence—would be extinguished.

"Therefore, Sulachan and Hannis Arc must be stopped before they can ever bring such insanity to pass."

Kahlan let out an impatient sigh. "Red, I know all of this. You aren't really telling me anything new. I already know how vital it is that they are stopped.

"That is precisely what we are trying to do, and you are wasting my time in that effort. We need to get through the pass and, after we are healed, we are going to try to stop the threat. Get to the point or send us on our way."

Red folded her arms and leaned one shoulder in toward Kahlan. "I am trying to put the nature of what you must do into context so that you will understand how vital it is."

Kahlan pressed a hand to her forehead. She could feel the evil inside her clawing to be freed. It was going to be that way for everyone. She took a breath, trying to be patient.

"Red, I'm dying. Believe me, I get the context. I don't have a lot of time left to do anything to help you. We need to be on our way. I get it that they must be stopped or they will do something irreversible. Would you please just tell me what it is that you think you need me to do?"

Red leveled a sharp look at her. "It is not what I think, it is what I know. I see events in the flow of time. And what I see is that there is only one person who has the potential to stop all of these horrors I have described from coming to pass."

"And who would that be?" Kahlan asked as patiently as possible.

"You know very well, Mother Confessor, who that would be," Red said with a scowl. "It is the pebble in the pond, the bringer of death, the Lord Rahl, the one, your husband."

Kahlan let out a deep sigh. "Again, we know that. Does the flow of time you witch women like to swim around in tell you if he will succeed?"

"It doesn't work that way. I do not choose what I wish to see in the flow of time."

"Great, so all you can do is tell me what I already know, and that you don't know if we will succeed. That's great. Thank you. Now may we pass?"

Red's scowl was back. "I don't get to pick out the answers I need or would like. I don't get to ask questions and have them answered. The flow of time reveals to me what it will reveal. Nothing more, nothing less. I have no say in it. I am but a messenger."

"That's because it's prophecy," Kahlan said.

"In a way. In this case, it reveals to me only that your husband has the potential to succeed. It does not reveal if he will."

Kahlan threw her arms up. "What good, then, is all this flow of time prophecy business if it only tells you potential? I could easily have told you that Richard has the potential to stop all this from happening without you needing to bother to peer into the flow of time!"

Rather than getting angry at Kahlan's tone, Red became more calm, even sorrowful. "That much of it is muddy, but many other events in the flow of time are crystal clear. I can see those things with absolute certainty."

"But not in this case," Kahlan said, contemplating leaving the witch woman and going back to get Richard and the rest of them. Since Red knew that Richard was important, Kahlan figured that she wasn't likely to put up a fight if they simply barged right through the middle of her little lair.

"No, not in this case." It was Red, this time, who let out a patient sigh. "You see, Mother Confessor, in the unique case of that husband of yours, his free will mucks up events in the flow of time."

Kahlan frowned. "Why is that?"

"Because he is a pebble in the pond. He causes

ripples in events. Because he acts on free will, and he is gifted, it can't be foreseen how those ripples will interact with other people and other events. Prophecy does not work so well with that man of yours."

"If it's any consolation, we've always had that problem with prophecy," Kahlan said. "That's why we don't pay it much heed."

Red leaned closer. "Well, in this case, you had better."

"Why?"

"Because while I may not know if he will succeed, I know that if he is dead he will not have a chance to try. If he dies, our fate is sealed and we all die.

"I'm trying to help you keep him alive so that he can do what he needs to do in order to give us a chance. If you don't listen to me, he is going to die. That is not a potential, but a hard, cold certainty.

"I know how to read events in the flow of time. I know those things that are only a potential, and I know those that will happen with an absolute certainty. In this particular case, it is not a maybe, or a potential. It is a dead certain event. . . .

"He is going to die before he has a chance to fulfill his potential unless you do what you need to do to prevent it. Only you can prevent his death. Only you can stop it.

"Now, do you want him to live or not?

"It's all up to you, Mother Confessor."

68

Kahlan stared back into Red's fierce blue eyes. "All right, I'm listening. What is it you see in the flow of time that is so certain?"

"Nicci is going to kill Richard."

"Kill him?" Kahlan blinked in disbelief. "Why would she kill Richard? Dear spirits, the woman loves him!"

"That is why she will kill him . . . because she loves him."

Kahlan shook her head, as if trying to shake it clear of lunacy.

"You really ought to meet Shota," Kahlan said. "You'd like her. You both see events in the flow of time and think you understand their true meaning when you don't. You're both crazy."

"I'm not crazy. I would wager that this Shota has given you information that has been vital, as this is. I'm telling you what will happen in the flow of time if that flow is allowed to run its course. I'm trying to make you see what is at stake."

"I haven't got time for this nonsense."

As Kahlan started to leave, Red grabbed her arm and turned her back. "Nicci knows that Richard's heart belongs to you. She loves him, but she cannot have him. The flow of time says that because of that, she will kill him."

Kahlan pressed her hands to the sides of her head, exasperated with the pointless, circular conversation, wishing she could shut it out. "You said yourself that this flow of time you look into only holds potential, not certainty."

Red shook her head emphatically. "No, that is not what I said. I said that because he is the pebble in the pond, Richard's free will muddies my ability to see how the events he is central to will unfold. It is only undefined potential in his case. But I see other things with absolute clarity."

Kahlan glared, no longer even able to remain polite.

"So you say."

Red gestured angrily toward Hunter. "I sent him because I saw that you would all come this way and would have been killed back there in the chasms had I not acted. It was important that none of you die back there. I could see in that same flow that you would befriend Hunter, as you call him, and follow him when you most needed his help—but only if I sent him to save you.

"It wasn't potential; it was a certainty. I saw the different tributaries, branches, and backwaters in the flow of time and I worked to keep you on the course that would save your lives. Here you stand as a result. I would say that shows I understand the meaning of what I see in the flow of time quite well, wouldn't you?

"While it doesn't work that way with Richard, it does with the people around him. It worked that way with you. It wasn't chance or potential, it was only the deliberate choices I made to effect the outcome that kept you all alive.

"Perhaps, as you say, this witch woman, Shota, only thinks she understands the true meaning of the things she sees in the flow of time, but don't judge me by her inadequacies. I know what I'm talking about, and I know what I'm doing."

Red leaned closer and pointed a finger at Kahlan's face. "I'm telling you, Mother Confessor, and you had better listen to me—Nicci is going to kill Richard unless you kill her first.

"Richard is the only chance we all have. He is the only one with the potential to save the world of life. Even the first Confessor, Magda Searus, saw that three thousand years ago and did what she could to help him. Now, you are the last Confessor. It has come full circle. It is up to you to make sure he has that chance to fulfill his potential.

"You must kill Nicci before she can kill Richard."

Kahlan folded her arms and stared back at the witch woman's piercing blue eyes with a look of her own. "If you think she needs killing, then why don't you just kill her yourself?"

Red straightened. "Wise is the witch woman who knows when not to interfere with events in the flow of time."

"That's an easy excuse. You are already interfering with events in the flow of time. You brought me here and now you are asking me to do your killing for you. It's the same thing."

"No, it's not. This is different. This is a matter between you and Richard and Nicci, between the three of you and fate. You three are caught up in that tangled flow of time. I can't interfere. That fate is yours and in your hands alone.

"The hard reality is that I know for certain that if she is still alive when the time comes, Nicci is going to kill Richard Rahl. I also know for certain that she will do so because she loves him.

"That is why you must kill her first."

In frustration, Kahlan ran her fingers back through her hair, gripping it in her fists. "Red, I'm telling you, I know the woman. I know that she is in love with Richard. But I also know that Nicci wouldn't do that to him. She wouldn't do that to me."

"To you?" The witch woman gave Kahlan a somber look as she slowly shook her head. "I am sorry, Mother Confessor, but I can see in the flow of time that she will. If she is not killed first, she will kill him."

Kahlan couldn't make any sense of it. She could tell that Red was absolutely convinced of it, but Kahlan couldn't make it make any sense in her own mind. She got the feeling that there was something the witch woman was holding back.

"When?" she finally asked. "When do you see Nicci doing such a thing?"

For a long moment the woman regarded Kahlan with the kind of chilling look that could only be summoned by a witch woman.

"That is a question you really should not ask, Mother Confessor. Please take my word for it, and do not ask that question. You will not like the answer."

Kahlan's blood ran cold at the look in Red's eyes.

"I'm in the middle of this. I don't like any of this, but you told me that the context is vital. I need the complete context.

"So I'm asking. When will Nicci kill Richard?"

Red was silent for a long time as she stared into Kahlan's eyes. She finally spoke in a soft, but unwavering voice.

"I can't say when, for certain. I can only tell you that it will be after you have already been murdered."

Kahlan blinked, then frowned, not certain that she had heard correctly. "What?"

"When Nicci kills Richard, it will be sometime after you have been murdered."

"After I've been murdered? As in dead?"

"Yes. You have very little time left before that happens. That is why you must kill the sorceress as soon as possible. You cannot afford to delay. It must be done today, or tomorrow when you arrive at the citadel, or the following day at the very latest. I don't see you having any more time than that before you are murdered."

"And who is it that is going to murder me?"

"Please believe me, if I knew, I would tell you. I have sought that answer, but the flow of time hides it from me. There must be some reason.

"It is the same with the old wizard. I tried to find out who murdered him so that I could tell you, because his murder and yours are connected, but I wasn't able to pull an answer from that river of time."

"His murder is connected to . . . to what will happen to me? How? How are the two connected?"

Red folded her arms in frustration as she looked away. "I wish I knew, but I don't. I can only see that there is a connection of some kind. It could be that the same person who murdered Zedd will murder you, or it could be some form of interconnected cause and effect. I only know that the two are connected."

Red's gaze returned to meet Kahlan's. "What I do know is that you must kill Nicci, now, before you are murdered, or it will be too late and the rest will come to pass. Nicci will kill Richard Rahl, and with him the only hope for the world of life."

Kahlan could feel a tear running down her cheek as she stared at the witch woman. The thought of Richard being killed was too much for her. The thought of her being murdered was crushing, terrifying. It was all too overwhelming to take in.

"There must be a chance that you could be wrong."

"I am sorry, Mother Confessor," she said softly as she reached up, gently cupped her hand under Kahlan's chin, and brushed the tear away with a thumb. "The truth is, either way, whether you kill Nicci or not, every possible branch in the flow of time shows that you are soon going to be murdered.

"I have seen you pass through on occasion as I have looked into the river of time. I saw your integrity, your virtue, your commitment to truth. I saw in the choices you made that you were brave, courageous, compassionate, and cared about others. I have admired you.

"It is a tradition of my kind to paint our lips black in mourning when we see the death of someone we care about. My lips are painted black today for you, Mother Confessor.

"I understand what this means for you, but you need to put your precious life into the context of what is going to happen to everyone else. This is bigger than you alone. You will never have another life, but neither will any of the other innocent people everywhere whose lives will be snuffed out. You need to put all that into perspective.

"Without Richard, they all die. Without you saving his life by killing Nicci, they all die. You have killed before to save the lives of those you care about. This is one of those times. The fate of everyone is in your hands, Mother Confessor.

"There is still a chance for Richard to live, but there is no chance to change what is going to happen to you.

"Only you can save the life of the man you love. If you care about him, about how precious his life is to you, if you care about the lives of everyone else, then you must kill Nicci."

Kahlan felt as if the world was collapsing in on her. All her hopes and dreams were ashes.

All she had wanted was to ask if they could go on through the mountain pass.

She remembered what Zedd had told her once, that a witch woman never told you what you wanted to know without also telling you something that you did not want to know.

69

Richard was at a loss. He had been following a good dozen paces behind Kahlan for over an hour after they had cleared the pass, and there was no improvement in her mood.

After they had been summoned by the blindfolded woman who said that the oracle had granted them safe passage, she led them through the pass without ever seeing the oracle. Richard had stopped the blindfolded woman back in the pass and asked to see the oracle. The oracle, the blindfolded woman had told them, had seen one of their party and she would see no more. She also said that the oracle had warned that if they wished to pass, they had to go right then or not at all.

Kahlan had not said a word the entire time about her meeting with the oracle. In fact, she hadn't spoken to Richard about anything, not one word, since meeting up with them as they came through the pass. She had, however, taken up a lead position ahead of

Richard, Nicci, Irena, and Samantha in their march and it was clear that she wished to be alone. Richard wasn't used to that attitude from her, and it alarmed him in the extreme, but it seemed clear enough, so he hadn't violated that wish.

What made it worse, though, was that she wouldn't even look at him.

The entire time tears had slowly run down her face, despite how deeply her brow furrowed as she tried not to let them escape.

Richard didn't know if he had done something wrong, although he couldn't imagine what, but even if he had, he would never have thought that Kahlan would not want to speak to him. Even on those occasions when he had done something to upset her, she had at least been willing to talk to him about it, to tell him what was upsetting her. Whatever was troubling her this time, he would have thought that she would want to talk to him about it.

He was beside himself with worry for her. Although he couldn't entirely shake the worry that he had done something wrong, he assumed that it had to be that the oracle had given Kahlan a prophecy that upset her. For some reason, that prophecy had gotten to her.

Kahlan knew better than to believe prophecy.

But that didn't mean that this oracle couldn't have said something that had been a dagger through her heart, and for some reason Kahlan was taking it seriously.

"What do you think?" he whispered to Nicci. "Should we try to talk to her?"

Nicci glanced over at him. "I think I know enough not to poke a hornet's nest. My advice is to leave her be for now. Whatever it is, she will get over it or tell you when she is good and ready to tell you. Until then, leave her be."

Samantha stuck her head between Richard and Nicci. "What do you think could be wrong?" she whispered.

"We don't know," Nicci told the young woman. "But a wise sorceress, or wizard, knows when to stay away from a person who wants room to think things through." Nicci glanced down at Samantha. "It's a lesson you need to learn."

"Sorry," Samantha whispered as she pulled her head back.

"She probably just doesn't feel well," Richard told Samantha, wanting to soften the sting of Nicci's words. "The poison we both carry in us is as exhausting as it is frightening. It gets me down at times, too."

Samantha nodded. "I know, Lord Rahl. I've felt it in you both. I know how frightening it is."

He remembered how terrified Samantha had been when she had first encountered that touch of death in them. "I guess you do."

She thought a moment. "If there is anything my mother or I can do to help, just ask. All right?"

Richard smiled briefly over his shoulder. "Thanks, Samantha."

She nodded as she dropped back to walk with her mother.

"You're too nice to her," Nicci whispered.

"Nasty habit of mine," he said, "trying to be nice to nice people. I'll have to try to be more like you and hurt their feelings instead. That always seems to work."

Nicci smiled a little. "Point taken."

"Maybe you should talk to her," he said.

"Who?"

"Kahlan."

"I told you, I know better than to poke at a hornet's nest." Nicci shook her head. "You didn't see the look she gave me."

"What kind of look?"

"Well, if looks could kill . . ."

"What did you do to her to make her give you a look like that?"

"I didn't do anything," Nicci said, opening her hands in a gesture of bewildered innocence. "What did you do? She isn't talking to you either."

Richard sighed. "I wish I knew."

Nicci rested a hand on his shoulder briefly as they walked close together. "She'll be all right, Richard. I'm sure she just needs to work out some things the oracle told her and she doesn't want us bothering her while she thinks it all through."

"That makes sense," Richard said. "I only wished I believed it."

Nicci sighed, then. "Me too."

Richard glanced off through gaps in the trees toward the mountains in the distance. They were growing a deeper shade of steel blue. After the sun dropped behind the towering mountains to the west, darkness descended quickly. The thick clouds would only hasten the approaching darkness.

Richard dropped back, waiting for Commander Fister to pick up his pace and catch up with him.

"Is the Mother Confessor all right?" the commander asked. The commander, like all of the men, could tell that something was wrong and was concerned about what it could be. Kahlan was in many ways their strength. Her spirit always seemed to buoy their spirits. Now, all of them wore somber expressions.

Richard forced a smile for the man. "Kahlan? Oh, she's fine. It's just that this sickness is really exhausting, both physically and mentally."

"Oh," he said, brightened by the solution to the puzzle.

The sickness was bad enough, but the worry of something more being the issue after speaking with the oracle had the commander concerned.

It had Richard even more concerned.

Richard gestured to the silhouette of the mountains to the west. "With the sun behind the mountains, it's going to be dark soon. We're going to need to set up camp."

Commander Fister nodded. "Like the scouts told us, up ahead we'll run into a road leading to Saavedra, but that won't be until sometime tomorrow morning. We can't make it that far tonight."

"The good news, though," Richard said, "is that the road will make for easier traveling and we should be able to reach Saavedra tomorrow. But for today, we're going to need a place to set up camp before we get caught trying to do it in darkness."

"Already ahead of you, Lord Rahl. I've had a report of a suitable spot not far up ahead."

"Good," Richard said. "Give the word for some men to go on then, and clear the area."

The commander clapped a fist to his heart and trotted off to see to it.

As he watched Kahlan's familiar, beautiful shape and fall of long hair as she walked all alone, Richard's heart ached for her. He wished he knew what was wrong. He wanted more than anything to set it right for her and see her special smile, the one she gave only to him.

He hated to see her cry more than just about anything in the world.

After Zedd's murder, Richard had seen her cry enough to last him a lifetime.

The thought of what had happened to Zedd again brought a fresh flash of anger mixed with the ache of grief. Richard forced the anger aside. At the moment it was more important for him to be there for Kahlan.

CHAPTER

70

Commander Fister spotted Richard and hurried over to speak with him. "All clear, Lord Rahl. The men who scouted the area report that there isn't anyone anywhere. Not even any evidence of anyone having been in the area."

"Likely because this place comes directly down from the pass," Nicci said, "and you know what kind of trouble the chasms were, to say nothing of getting permission from the oracle. Not really any reason for anyone to want to head up in that direction, either."

"That makes sense," Richard said. "This is a pretty deserted back door into Saavedra. If it wasn't, the people of straw would be used to seeing travelers, and they aren't."

The commander nodded his agreement. "And I don't see any half people being able to follow us the way we came."

Richard watched men spread out on the leafy forest floor among the thin growth of young hardwoods, laying out bedrolls, and gear, collecting firewood for the dozen small fires. The wood smoke drifting slowly through the camp offered a comfortingly familiar aroma to the quiet woods.

They could all see everyone in the light of those low campfires, and they could see a goodly distance off through the lightly wooded area. The ground wasn't entirely level, with slight rises here and there, but it made for a good campsite. Most of the ground to the right began to rise as it went off to meet hills and mountains in the distance. The men would be able to get a good rest this night, for a change.

Richard had no idea what kind of defenses or orders Hannis Arc might have given at the citadel before he left, but they needed to be ready for anything. He didn't think, though, that the home guard at the citadel would present a credible threat to these battle-hardened men of the First File. They needed to get in to the containment field, and none of them were in the mood to put up with any foolishness. Anyone who had any notion of resistance would be wise to change their mind before they lost their head.

Richard wondered why he was feeling so edgy. The citadel was part of Fajin Province, and Fajin Province was part of the D'Haran Empire. Everyone at the citadel was under his command.

Some of the men were already roasting rabbit, deer meat, and fish trapped in a nearby brook. They were all hungry and needed a good meal to keep up their strength. The next day was going to be critically important.

He supposed that the same went for him, but he wasn't hungry. The roasting meats all smelled delicious, but Richard was too concerned about Kahlan to have much of an appetite. Besides that, the poison inside him was making his head pound, which made his stomach queasy. He had to struggle simply to remain conscious. Eating wasn't high on his priorities.

Unexpectedly, Kahlan walked up on them. She pointed to an outcropping of rocks Richard could just see in the distance.

"Some of the men found a secure, private place where you and I can sleep. I laid out our bedrolls."

"Sounds good to me," Richard said, trying not to act surprised that this was the first time she had spoken to him since going off to see the oracle. "Would you like something to eat, first?"

"No," she said before turning and making her way toward the spot she had pointed out.

Richard and Nicci shared a look.

"I think you had best go keep her warm and make sure she is comfortable," Nicci said. "Just be nice and don't try to be like me and hurt her feelings. I hear that doesn't seem to work."

Richard smiled at the sorceress. "You aren't going to let me forget that, are you?"

"No," she said, returning the smile. "Go tell her you love her, Richard."

Richard nodded. "Thanks, Nicci. I will."

He drew a deep breath, both eager to be with Kahlan and reluctant to find out what was troubling her. Mostly he wanted her to be back to being herself.

He supposed that until they were healed, neither of them was going to be back to themselves.

"Have a good rest," Richard said to the commander and Nicci. "And Commander, keep the men away from us. I think Kahlan needs some privacy tonight."

The big D'Haran officer tapped a fist to his heart. "No problem, Lord Rahl. I will see to it."

As he turned to go, he saw Irena and Samantha sitting side by side on a blanket, eating some sausage.

Irena waved. "Please tell her that I hope she feels better soon. If she needs any gifted help, I would be only too glad to offer my services."

Richard nodded his thanks before starting out across the camp. He walked a crooked course in order to pass by a number of the campfires on his way to check on the men, offer smiles, and wish them a good sleep. Many offered food. Richard thanked them but declined.

When he reached the spot Kahlan had pointed out, he saw that it was indeed some distance away from the rest of the camp, screened by part of the rock outcropping. Larger sections of granite ledge rose up from the forest floor behind, with trees on the far side. It was a cozy, private sanctuary.

Kahlan flipped the blanket back and looked up at him. Her eyes were wet.

Richard got the message and lay down on his back beside her, sitting up just a little with his head propped against the rock so that he could look down at Kahlan.

"Kahlan, please, tell me what's wrong."

That made the tears flow. She fell on him, putting one shoulder under his and her other arm over his chest. She rested her head on his shoulder.

"Please, Richard, just hold me?"

He pulled the blanket up over her partway and closed his arms around her, holding her without a word.

He listened to a mockingbird in the distance repeating a monotonous call, the buzz and chirping of bugs, and the soft, distant murmur of the men. He also listened to her cry quietly for a while, until he could stand it no more.

"Kahlan, you are going to be the death of me if you don't tell me what's wrong."

She didn't answer. She sniffled for a time, trying to get herself under control.

"I don't know what's wrong with me," she said. "My whole life I've been taught to be strong. I've been taught to wear a Confessor face to hide how I feel. But I can't right now."

"Why?"

She shrugged against him as she wiped her nose on a handkerchief.

"What did the oracle say that got you so upset?" he asked.

She shrugged again. "She just made me think about my life. Your life. Our lives together."

"Well, that's a pleasant enough thing to think about."

She didn't answer, so he asked, "Isn't it?"

"Richard, after Nicci heals us tomorrow of this horrid call of death—if we are healed—can we . . . I don't know, go away?"

He frowned in the near darkness as he watched the small campfires in the distance flickering and popping sparks.

"What do you mean?"

"I mean, ever since I first met you, what have we done?"

"Done? I don't know, we've done a lot of things."

"For others. We are always fighting to give everyone else a life. When do we get to have our life?"

"I know what you mean, I really do, but it isn't exactly like we had a lot of choice. There have been people trying to cause great harm to the people we care about—and to us."

"There is aways a choice."

"What do you mean?"

"I mean, there will always be someone trying to cause harm. There will always be those who hate those who prevent them from stealing rule, treasure, and lives. There will always be a threat. There will always be something. The world has never been without threats from those kinds of savages.

"This time the threat is bigger than us. This is bigger than everything. This is beyond our reach or control. This reaches beyond the world of life and into the underworld. We can't fight that. We can't fight this anymore.

"And why should we have to? When is it our time? When do we get to live our lives together?"

"Our time will come, Kahlan," he said softly.

She shook her head against his shoulder. "No it won't, unless we make it our time. Richard, it's time to let go and live what we can of what's left for us, of what's left for everyone."

"Someday," Richard said. "But I can't now. I can't live with myself, live for you, if I don't do this."

"I understand how you feel and I know what's in your heart—I feel no different.

"But this time it's too much. You can't stop this, Richard. True wisdom is accepting your limits, accepting that it's time to admit those limits, and let go of what you can't change.

"It's time for you to quit that fight and live. Live your life with me. Live for me."

Richard swallowed at the lump in his throat. Zedd had told him the same thing. It hurt his heart to hear

Kahlan pleading for him to give them a life of their own. Zedd was right that Richard was not just committing himself to the struggle, he was committing Kahlan to it as well. He couldn't think of anything to say that didn't sound cruel.

"It's time for us to spend what time we have, while we can, being together. Please, Richard, don't deny me what there is to what life I have left. Don't abandon me to a mission.

"Our entire time together has been devoted to serving the cause we have never had the chance to enjoy. We have served the cause of life and haven't had any time for us to live it. Let us live it while we can.

"Please, Richard. It's the only thing I want, the only thing I'm asking of you."

Although he didn't know what the oracle had said that had started it, Richard was beginning to comprehend what she was so upset about.

As he felt a tear run down his cheek, he thought that maybe he felt the same way.

"A very wise woman I know, who I happen to love," he said in a broken voice, "once told me that we all can only be who we are, no more, and no less."

Kahlan reached up and wiped the tear from his jaw.

"I'm sorry, Richard. I'm sorry to show such weakness. I'm sure I'll feel better tomorrow."

"You're not weak," he whispered. "You are the one I love, and you are anything but weak. You are the strongest person I know."

"You think too much of me, Richard. I'm weaker than you think."

He had to ask. "What did the oracle say to you?"

Kahlan laid a finger across his lips. "Hush. We need to get some rest. The poison is giving me a terrible headache."

"My head is killing me, too," he admitted.

"Tomorrow we will get that fixed. Rest now. Tomorrow Nicci will heal us. Tonight I am weak, so please, my love, just hold me and let me be weak for tonight.

"But tomorrow, after I am healed, I need to be strong."

71

As Richard and the main force made their way through the gloomy city of Saavedra, a contingent of soldiers fanned out through the streets and alleyways to make sure that there were no threats lurking around a corner somewhere. Richard didn't really think that Hannis Arc cared about the small, remote city of Saavedra any longer, and couldn't see him bothering to have the place locked down. What would be the point? The man had bigger ambitions. He wanted to rule the world, not Fajin Province.

Jake Fister, in the lead, looked grim and formidable as he strode up the main cobblestone road, presenting the strong, intimidating face of the First File. He understood that strength did not invite trouble, but rather was a deterrent.

The chain mail that some of the men wore sparkled in the drizzle. Soldiers flanked Richard and the women, ready to protect them if need be. Although the soldiers

kept their weapons sheathed, Richard knew just
how fast they could have them out if needed. Those
weapons were not meant for show. They were serious
tools of their profession and the men were experts
with each of them.

Some people stood to the sides and stared, while
many others seemed to be rushing everywhere, both
along the main cobblestone road through the city
and splashing through the mud of the streets and
lanes to the sides. The tightly spaced buildings created
a warren of passageways, alleys, lanes, and narrow
streets. The closeness of everything and everyone
made Richard uneasy after being out in the sprawl of
the endless, trackless Dark Lands. It felt like the whole
city was pulled inward, hiding from that wilderness
out beyond.

Richard and those with him slowed from time to
time to let frightened women in drab dresses get out
of the way. The people off to the sides tried not to
be obvious as they watched the strangers in their
midst, but everyone, from Richard to the soldiers,
noticed every eye following them as they moved up
the street.

Vendors lined up along the sides of the street had
laid tarps over their wares, trying to protect them
from the weather. Shoppers lifted the tarps, selecting
vegetables or meat, trying to look like they didn't notice the troops passing by. People back in shadows
watched the passing visitors from doorways and windows of the dingy, tightly packed, small buildings.

Kahlan walked at Richard's left, looking like herself again. She had been so exhausted the night before
that she had fallen asleep in his arms. Richard had
lain awake half the night, unable to close his eyes.
She had never before voiced such a wish for him to

quit the struggle and leave it to others. In the past, if anything, she had argued against such a notion.

Now she wanted him to quit it all. It had been the same thing Zedd had advised. He hadn't known how much her heart ached to go off somewhere and live their own lives.

He remembered feeling much the same after she had lost their unborn child when she had been so seriously hurt. He had quit everything and taken Kahlan far back in the uncharted wilderness to the west of Hartland. After she recovered it came to be one of the happiest times of his life, being away from everyone and everything.

He wondered if he was crazy for not jumping at Zedd's advice and Kahlan's longings for sanctuary. He wondered if they weren't right, if he shouldn't let the world fend for itself.

Maybe if Cara and her husband had cared more for themselves and done that, Ben would be alive and they would be living happily somewhere. Instead, Cara had lost her chance at such happiness. Richard missed her, and his heart ached for her and for all she had lost. He grieved for Zedd as well.

Who did he think he was, anyway? Where did he ever get the idea that the world couldn't get along without him? He was a woods guide who had taken up the challenge to stop a tyrant and because of that everyone thought he was their savior. He never wanted to be the leader. He had only been doing what was right in protecting himself and people he cared about.

In the end, he thought that was the central issue. He didn't want to be a leader.

But there were others driven by a desire to dominate and dictate. They lusted to tell everyone else how they must live and what they must think. They were willing to torture and slaughter untold numbers to enforce their arrogant visions.

He understood Zedd's advice, and Kahlan's feelings. He just didn't see how he could do anything but what he was doing. If he didn't act, he would end up being slaughtered as well. While he hadn't sought leadership, leadership had fallen to him.

Up ahead, between the dingy two-story buildings crowded in close to the street, he got his first glimpse of the stone citadel high up above the city.

Samantha, walking not far behind him with her mother, leaned closer. "Lord Rahl, I'm so excited that you and the Mother Confessor are finally going to be well. And I can't wait to see the containment chamber and how such a thing is done."

Richard looked back and showed her a smile. She had done a lot to help get them this far. Without her help, they could have lost their lives any number of times.

Besides the people who watched from a corner of their eye, Richard saw others along the roads staring with vacant expressions. None of them looked happy, or expectant, or excited, or even curious about the people accompanied by so many soldiers.

Richard leaned toward Nicci. "What does this place remind you of?"

Nicci glanced over. "The cities of the Old World— cities without hope—where people lived their whole lives under the thumb of the Imperial Order."

"Exactly," he said. "I had no idea that this part of D'Hara was like this. I had no idea that we had a petty tyrant right under our noses all this time. Makes me wonder what other parts of D'Hara are like, parts I've never even heard of."

"Hannis Arc is no longer so petty," Kahlan said without looking over. "He wants to kill everything good, and he has a good chance to accomplish it."

Even here, in the wilds of the Dark Lands, a nest of evil had taken root until eventually it had begun to spread.

Richard was tempted to ask her how, while such a threat existed, he could quit, but he thought better of it.

Kahlan, as the Mother Confessor, had originally come to his home in Hartland in Westland to find the old wizard so that he could name a Seeker. Unbeknownst to Richard, the old wizard had turned out to be Zedd.

It didn't matter, though. Richard knew who Zedd really was. He was his grandfather, his teacher, his friend.

He was also the one who had named Richard the Seeker of Truth and given him the long-hidden sword that went with that duty. Zedd had told them that it was his responsibility as First Wizard to pick the right person, and Richard was the right person to carry that sword. While at first it hadn't seemed so, Richard now understood that Zedd had picked the right man.

As he looked into the eyes of the frightened people silently watching, he wondered how he could now turn his back on the responsibility with which Zedd had entrusted him. How could he turn his back on those who had made this sword? Or any of those who had left him clues to help him along the way in his struggle to see justice prevail? How could he fool himself into thinking that he could go off somewhere safe and be left alone to live his life while turning his back on a firestorm and pretend it didn't exist? How could he live a lie?

The happiest time of his life had been living with Kahlan back in the wilderness. He had tried turning his back on the world. He had tried to give it up to live his life with Kahlan.

When she had recovered, Kahlan had become ever more restless and uneasy, continually trying to convince him that they needed to return to the world and their place in it.

Nicci had shown up and captured him. She had taken him away to a long ordeal of captivity. Richard knew that he had only been fooling himself to think that they could quit the world and find a place to hide, to think they could live in peace without someone coming for him. Someone would always come.

Whether or not he wanted to admit it, the reality was that too many things were connected to him. His only chance at life was to face reality, not hide from it. You either had to fight evil as you encountered it, or evil would come to control your life. Even these people here, way out in the wilds of the Dark Lands, could not escape it.

Nests of depravity always grew stronger and spread if not fought.

What really bothered him, though, was that Kahlan was his rock. He was stronger, physically, than she was, but she was his emotional stability, always steadfast in what was right. There had been times when he had felt too weak to go on. In those times Kahlan had always been his strength. He had always gotten to his feet for her.

It rattled him to see her strength falter.

He knew, though, that she was too strong, too committed, to feel this way for long. He supposed it was unreasonable to expect her to be strong every moment. She was only human.

As much as he wished he could do what Zedd had advised, what she had begged him to do in a moment of human weakness, he knew that in the end she couldn't really live that way. Sooner or later, and likely sooner, she would start to get uneasy and need to return to life's struggle.

He was the Seeker, but she was the Mother Confessor. She was born to it, and for better or worse she couldn't escape it any more than he could escape who he was. In the end, she wore the white dress of office because it belonged on her the same way the Sword of Truth belonged on his hip. Neither was ceremonial. Both were made for battle. Both were weapons meant to be used to fight for truth.

He told himself not to be too discouraged by her weakness the night before. There were times when he had been weak, too. He always picked himself up and so would Kahlan. In fact, when they had started out that morning, he had already begun to see her strength coming back. She had looked determined once again.

He still wished he knew what the oracle had told her.

"Look sharp, boys," Commander Fister said in a low voice as they passed some of the citadel guard in brown tunics standing to either side of the cobblestone road leading up the hill. The dozen men on each side of the road stood at attention, chins up, fists to hearts. They certainly didn't look like they entertained any thoughts of a fight.

But that had been by design. The commander had

sent men ahead to announce the arrival of the Lord Rahl and tell the guards to prepare to receive him and his escort. The scouts reported that the men defending the citadel had been surprised, but friendly and eager to welcome the Lord Rahl and his party. Even though he was from far away, Richard wouldn't be entirely a mystery to the people here. There had been a number of men from distant parts of D'Hara who had fought in the long war, and they would have returned with stories about the Lord Rahl and the Mother Confessor leading them to victory.

Richard tried not to see these men, these people of Saavedra, as a threat, but as people much like any others with the same hopes and dreams. Maybe now that he had come to their part of the world, and Hannis Arc was gone, they would feel more a part of a free D'Hara.

At the top of the road, up the hill beyond the city proper, they finally reached massive iron gates in a high stone wall. In another good sign, the gates stood open. More men lined the road at the top, standing in neat ranks to either side.

Despite every indication, he couldn't help feeling like a bug approaching a spiderweb.

Richard leaned closer to Commander Fister. "Don't forget what I told you."

"Every man's life before any threat gets to Nicci." He cast Richard a look. "And of course you and the Mother Confessor."

It would do them no good to get to the containment field at the citadel if a foolish, jumpy soldier put an arrow through Nicci's heart. Even the most gifted could be felled with a simple blade or arrow. Without Nicci, the containment field wouldn't do them any good.

From what he had learned, to stop the threat Emperor Sulachan and Hannis Arc had unleashed on the world, Richard had to end prophecy. He wished he could have ended prophecy before Kahlan had spoken with the oracle.

"Looks peaceful," Commander Fister said as he scanned the citadel guard, "but every man is ready if that changes."

The men all knew the importance of being the steel against steel so that Richard could be the magic against magic.

Richard just wished that he had some clue as to how he was supposed to end prophecy.

72

The main force of the Fajin garrison stood at attention in a cobblestone square beyond the main gates. Beyond rows of soldiers in chain mail, their swords sheathed, stood a row of archers in brown tunics, all their bows shouldered beside their quivers. Lancers stood in a neat line to the other side of the square, their lances pointing straight up toward the leaden sky with the butts resting on the cobbles left wet and slick by the steady, light drizzle.

All of the men were arranged in such a way as to funnel Richard and those with him down to a man waiting in the center of the road that led up to the citadel.

Richard didn't like being funneled. By his scowl, neither did Commander Fister.

Beyond all the guards, terraces with shaggy olive trees lined the road the rest of the way up to the stone citadel at the top of the hill. Although it would be nothing too special in most cities of any size, in a place like Saavedra the citadel was a magnificent structure that sat like a jewel overlooking the dingy city below. Richard imagined that with Hannis Arc living there, it stood as a symbol of repression, much the way the People's Palace had when Darken Rahl had ruled.

To Richard, a building was just a building, and didn't carry the passions and personality of its occupants. All he cared about with this particular building was the containment field it held down under ground. That was Kahlan's salvation. He could see in her green eyes the weight of the poison within. He felt the same dead weight dragging him down.

When Richard, flanked by a number of heavily armed men carrying battle-axes in addition to knives and swords, some wearing dark, molded leather chest plates and some wearing chain mail over leather tunics, all came to a halt, the man at the center of the square, fist to his heart, bent deeply from his waist.

"I'm General Wolsey," he said when he straightened. "Welcome to the citadel . . . Lord Rahl, I presume?"

"That's right," Richard said with a nod.

"The advance party of your men informed us of your arrival. I can't tell you how honored we are to have you come to our humble city. We are at your disposal. Anything you want—anything at all—you have but to ask, and if it is within our power to provide it, we will."

"Thank you, General, I will keep that in mind," Richard said.

The man glanced around. "You all look, well, like you could use a bit of rest. There are rooms, if you would like, and—"

"Thank you," Richard said, cutting the man off before he was finished trying to ingratiate himself. "As you noted, we have been traveling hard, coming over the pass from up north."

"The pass!" The general blinked. "No one comes over the pass. It's not . . . safe."

"The people there are part of D'Hara, as are you. They were polite and gracious and showed us the way through."

His mouth opened a little as he stared. "That's . . . remarkable."

Richard thought the man seemed a little too tense to be a general, but then again, this was a pretty small place, so a general here wasn't necessarily what Richard would expect elsewhere. This man was probably adequate for the responsibility in the remote city of Saavedra. Besides, people were sometimes more than they appeared to be.

Before General Wolsey could begin talking again, Richard started giving instructions.

"While we are sure that you are prepared to protect the citadel, there are threats that I'm afraid none of you here are prepared to deal with." He held his hand out to the side. "Therefore, Commander Fister, here, will be in charge. You will be taking orders from him."

The man frowned. "But I'm a general. He is just a commander."

"No," Richard said, "you are the general of the citadel guard in Saavedra. He is a commander of the First File from the People's Palace."

"The First File!" The man quickly looked around again at the men with Richard, all dressed in dark armor. "I had no idea, Lord Rahl. I've never met any of the First File before. Of course, we will cooperate in every way."

"Good. That means that any of these men, who are my personal guards, in order to do what they must to protect me, have authority over everyone here should it be necessary. You will all follow their instructions. We have no intention of usurping your authority in your protecting the citadel or the city, and will return command to you once we are rested and can be on our way. It shouldn't be more than a day or two."

"Of course, Lord Rahl."

Richard deliberately looked over at the knot of officers standing to the side. They got the message and clapped fists to hearts. He then looked at the soldiers standing in ranks, watching, and they did the same. There didn't appear to be any dissent or grumbling.

"Thank you all for understanding the importance of our safety," Richard said. "There are threats about that we need to be ready for."

The general lifted a hand. "What sort of threats?" He cleared his throat. "I mean, if I may be so bold as to ask."

Richard met the man's gaze. "Have you ever seen the dead rise up out of graves and attack the living, ripping them limb from limb?"

The man's eyes widened. "The dead . . . ?"

"That's right. Being already dead, they can't be killed in the ordinary sense. My men know how to deal with the threat, so I suggest that you stay out of their way and let them handle any trouble."

The man nodded furiously. "Of course, Lord Rahl."

"Now, we've been traveling for a long time through some very hostile land. We need to get in out of this wet weather for a bit and get some needed rest."

The young General Wolsey held an arm out in invitation. "Then please, Lord Rahl, allow me to show you the way."

Without further word, Richard and all those with him followed the man up the curving cobblestone road toward the citadel at the top. He looked back over his shoulder from time to time to make sure they weren't getting lost along the way.

Richard deliberately hadn't introduced Kahlan, or anyone else. He didn't want them to know exactly who they were. He supposed it was possible he was being overly cautious, but if an assassin had been told to hide and then put an arrow in the Mother Confessor, or Nicci, or Irena, Richard didn't want them identified as targets. Since they all knew his reasoning, they stayed quiet and let him do the talking.

The general opened one of the big double doors and stood to the side to let Richard and everyone with him pass into the grand greeting hall.

Once inside, he gestured to some of the women in uniforms to the side and more across the room. "The staff can show you all to your rooms and get you anything you might need. With the bishop gone for an extended time, we have plenty of room for you and you can have free use of the citadel. We have some lovely guest rooms where I am sure you will be comfortable. Perhaps not as comfortable as you are used to, Lord Rahl, but I trust you will find the accommodations adequate."

The more the general talked, the more nervous he was making Richard. He supposed that in this outpost of civilization the general simply didn't get the chance to meet many important people. Richard saw men and women of the staff lined up at the far end of the room, looking equally nervous, awaiting orders.

"Thank you," Richard said to the general. "We can take care of it from here. Please go back down with your men, close the gates, and see to it that no one comes to visit while we are here."

The general glanced around at the towering, dirty, grimy, armored, battle-hardened D'Haran soldiers of the First File, all bristling with weapons and smelling of sweat, standing in the pristine grand greeting room.

Before the general could object, Commander Fister gave the man the kind of look that tended to render most people speechless. The implication was clear.

The general clapped his fist to his heart. "Of course, Lord Rahl."

The general, reluctantly but with increasing speed, made his way back out the door. One of the men closed it behind him.

None of the men of the First File were anything less than intimidating-looking, and the commander more so. Of course, Richard knew many of them on a more personal level, and some of them were actually quite shy—except when they were in a fight.

"Thank you all," Richard called out to the staff waiting across the room by the grand stairway, "but we have some matters to see to so you aren't needed just yet. Please go about your duties, and one of my men will summon you when we're ready."

The staff, a little confused not to be called upon and given orders, made their way off through the hallways to the sides.

After they had gone, there was one bent, older man who purposefully remained behind.

"May I help you?" Richard asked the man.

The man bowed a little. The way his back was hunched, he didn't have far to go to complete a bow.

When he straightened up as best he could, Richard thought that he detected a ghost of hostility in the man's drooping eyes.

"I am Mohler, Lord Rahl. I am the scribe here at the citadel. I have worked here my whole life." The challenge seeped back into the steady look in his eyes. "I knew your father."

Richard focused his attention more intently on the man. He now understood the shadow of hostility in the old man's eyes.

"I'm sorry to hear that."

Richard's words had not been what the man had expected to hear and it confused him. The creases in his forehead deepened as he frowned. "Excuse me, Lord Rahl?"

Richard needed to get to their business and wasn't in the mood to soften it for him. "Darken Rahl, like his father before him, was a tyrant who tortured and murdered people in order to maintain his grasp on power. He was an evil man. Everyone suffered under his rule. He hurt people I cared about."

The hunched scribe still looked suspicious. "So you knew the man, then."

"I'm the one who killed him."

For the first time, Mohler's eyes seemed to brighten and he showed the hint of a smile. "I had heard the rumor, Lord Rahl. I did not know if it was true. It seems I may have heard wrong."

It was Richard's turn to be confused. "What did you hear?"

"That you killed him in order to seize rule for yourself."

"I was a woods guide, and would be happy to be one today. I only fill the role of Lord Rahl to give people the chance to live their own lives as they choose. Nothing would make me happier than to be able to go back to my life and do the same.

"But sometimes, when the choice presents itself, we all have to decide if we will stand up for what's right. If not, evil people will be the ones to dictate how we live our lives."

The old scribe tipped his head in a nod of appreciation. "Thank you for setting the record straight."

"What does a scribe at the citadel do, exactly?" Richard asked.

"I have worked here my whole life, recording prophecy brought in to Bishop Arc. He has an extensive collection."

Richard couldn't help himself. "Another evil man with the same hate in his heart that Darken Rahl harbored."

The man bowed his nearly bald head covered over with wisps of gray hair. "If you say so, Lord Rahl. I am but a humble scribe and such things are above my station in life."

"No, they aren't," Richard said, holding up an admonishing finger. "You are entitled to live your life for your own ends, just as everyone else is. Your former master, Hannis Arc, will likely not be coming back here. He has gone off to bring misery and suffering, like he has inflicted here, to the rest of the world. Unless I can stop him.

"The prophecy you have recorded here might be of help to me in finding a way to stop Hannis Arc from hurting a great many people, the way Darken Rahl did."

Mohler smiled the slightest bit. Richard thought it looked genuine, like a small ray of sunlight coming from within.

His voice lowered. "I will be here to assist you, Lord Rahl, should you wish my help."

Richard nodded. "Thank you, Mohler. I would like it very much if you would show me the prophecy you are in charge of maintaining, but maybe later, after we've rested."

"Of course, Lord Rahl. I will leave you, then, until I am needed."

Richard watched the old scribe shuffle off toward the grand stairs at the far end of the room, wondering if the prophecy Hannis Arc had used might be of help in finding out exactly what he planned, or even a way to stop him and the dead spirit king.

73

Once the scribe had disappeared up the stairs, Richard turned back to those waiting with him.

"We're in luck. They have horses here. Once we're healed and I take a quick look at the prophecies that Hannis Arc used, and if we hurry, we might still be able to beat him and Sulachan back to the People's Palace. First, though, it's time we finally got rid of Jit's poison."

He pulled Irena forward by her arm. "Where is the containment field? Show us the way."

Irena nodded. "Gladly, Richard. At last! This way," she said, pointing to the right, off between columns holding up a balcony above a dark gallery below it.

She looked thrilled to finally be the center of importance, to finally be able to fulfill her role. She hurried on ahead of them, leading the way, with a gleeful Samantha right on her heels. Samantha, proud of her mother's part in saving their lives, flashed a wide grin back over her shoulder.

Richard couldn't help feeling cheered himself. He acknowledged the smile with a brief one of his own.

He couldn't wait for Kahlan to be healed. He could tell by the dull look in her green eyes that the darkness within was growing ever stronger. He wanted her healed first.

He was also pretty sure that after the poison was out of her, Kahlan would be herself again and realize the need to stop the threat from Hannis Arc and Emperor Sulachan. It aggravated him, every time he thought about it, how his blood had been used to bring the spirit of Sulachan back from the dead. Richard needed to set that right. Once well again, Kahlan would feel the same.

In the corridor beyond the gallery, when Irena headed down the first set of stairs she came to, Richard signaled to the men. Several of them took up stations, guarding the stairwell at the top. He didn't know what was below, but while they went to find out, he wanted men watching their backs.

The rest of the group—Richard, Kahlan, Nicci, Commander Fister, and all the men with them— funneled down a wide stairwell after Irena and Samantha. Kahlan's hand found his. She gave it a silent squeeze that he returned.

At the bottom of the stairs, Nicci used her gift to send sparks of flame into lamps hung at intervals along the wall so they could see as they followed a series of utilitarian passageways toward a door at the end. It was a simple oak door but looked heavily built. With a silent signal from Commander Fister, one of the men drew his axe and rushed out in front of everyone else to get to the door first.

"Is that really necessary?" Irena asked, puzzling back at the commander as they all hurried down the hall toward the door.

"It is," he said without apology or bothering to tell her why. To the commander, the need seemed not only obvious, but routine and hardly worthy of explanation.

Irena shrugged. "I guess it can't hurt to be on the safe side."

They all slowed and waited as the man with the axe took a lamp from the wall and then slipped behind the door to check the hall beyond. When he returned and gave them the all-clear, everyone swiftly followed Irena into the darkness beyond.

She stopped not far ahead where light spheres brightened in her presence. She lifted one of the glass spheres resting in a row of iron brackets and handed it to Nicci, then gave one to Samantha, and finally she took one for herself. The light spheres were powered by the gift, and started glowing brighter with greenish light as each woman took one. Since Richard was cut off from his gift, it wouldn't do him any good to take one, so, like some of the men, he took a cold torch from the assortment standing on end in a woven wicker basket to the side.

He held the torch out and let Samantha light it for him. She ignited a flame over her palm and sent fire into the torches of several men, who hurried off down the hall, in turn lighting torches for others. The flames sent yellow-orange light flickering ahead into the darkness. Acrid smoke from the hissing, popping torches rolled along the sooty ceiling.

Irena's face looked greenish in the strange light of

the sphere she was holding. "Down this way," she said before turning and heading for another, smaller stairway.

The stairs were roughly cut stone, as were the walls, and not as wide as the previous steps. In pairs, they all followed the stairs down around several landings as they descended to the foundation level of the building. Richard supposed that it made sense for the containment field to be in as secluded and secure a place as possible.

At the bottom of the stairs, they held out the light spheres and the torches Richard and several other men carried to peer off into the darkness of the stone corridor. The air was musty and damp, but at least there was no standing water.

"Down there," Irena said, "near the end. I believe it is rarely used anymore so the place is in a mostly forgotten corner."

Leading them onward, she hurried off down the hall, the crunch and pop of crumbled granite littering the floor under their boots echoing back from the distance as they passed rooms off to the sides. Some of the rooms had no doors, but most did. From what Richard could see when he thrust his hissing torch through a few open doorways, the pitch-black rooms beyond looked to be storage rooms for rarely needed supplies and building materials for making repairs—roof slates, beams, and planks in a variety of sizes. Everything was covered in a thick layer of dust.

The commander used hand signals to send men off in various directions to check the rooms and branching passageways. Richard knew that it would take time to conduct a thorough search of what was turning out to be an extensive maze under the citadel, but at least they could clear the immediate area.

The stone hallway, built of granite blocks, looked eerie in the greenish luminescence of the light spheres. It reminded him, in a way, of the veil to the underworld that had infected them. He was relieved that the open passageway to the underworld infecting them would soon be withdrawn and kept by the containment field from escaping out into the world of life.

"Here," Irena said, gesturing to an iron door to the right side of the hallway. "It's through here." She tugged on the door. "Through this place in here."

One of the soldiers stepped up and pulled the heavy iron door open for her. Irena, not waiting for a soldier to check what was beyond, rushed inside with her light sphere.

"This is an entryway of some kind leading to the containment field," she said, her voice echoing in the darkness.

Her sphere dimmed considerably once inside. Their torches gave off somewhat better light, but even they dimmed.

In weak glimmers of light, Richard saw that it was a dusty, dirty room. It was a lot longer than it was wide. The faint rays of light cut through the pitch blackness to reveal abandoned items—a broken loom, some scaffolding, and other worn-out implements—stacked in a careless jumble in one of the far corners. Planks and old tools in the other corner were blanketed with old sheets in an effort to keep the dirt off them. A thick layer of brownish-gray dust covered everything in the room, including the sheets.

Holding out his torch as he passed through the doorway into the dark room, Richard could feel the power of a shield tingle across his flesh. He held Kahlan's hand as she followed him in. Commander Fister and the men took up positions outside in the hall, guarding the doorway.

Irena's light sphere had dimmed to nearly being dark.

"Oh, I forgot," Irena said, sounding disgusted with herself. "We have to go in through here, and these light spheres don't work at all as we get closer to the containment field itself. They have special light spheres made for this area that they keep in a nearby room. I'll run and get them—I'll only be a minute." She rushed back out the doorway before Nicci had a chance to enter. "Samantha, come help me carry them."

Samantha instead ducked under her mother's arm and into the room ahead of Nicci, eager to see the place. "I want to stay with Lord Rahl," she said, her voice echoing as she peered around in the dim light. She held her light sphere up, trying to see, but it was fading fast.

"Oh, all right," Irena said, "I'll do it myself. I can get some of the men to help me carry them. I'll just be a minute—I know right where they are."

"I'll help you," one of the men offered, following after her as she rushed back down the hall.

Richard noticed that for some reason, there were sheets hung on the opposite, long wall, covering something.

"This feels too easy," Kahlan said as she peered around in the dim, flickering light of the torches.

Zedd's frequent admonishment came to mind.

"Nothing is ever easy," Richard said.

He lifted his sword a few inches to check that it was clear before letting it drop back into its scabbard.

"Where's the entrance to the containment field?" Samantha asked as she looked around. "I don't see it."

When Nicci stepped into the room, her light sphere went nearly dark. Richard saw a trace of a frown just beginning to grow on the sorceress's face.

As soon as she was inside, her frown became more troubled. "This isn't a containment field," she said, sounding, now, more than a little suspicious.

"This wouldn't be it," Samantha told her. "My mother said that it was through this room."

"I felt the shields," Kahlan said.

"Me too," Samantha added, "so it has to be through here. There must be a doorway, but it's so dark in here with just one torch, I can't see much."

"They were shields," Nicci agreed, "but I don't recognize them."

"Being close to the barrier to the third kingdom, maybe they used occult powers in building this place," Richard suggested.

Nicci shook her head as she looked around. "There is something about this room . . ."

"Maybe the opening into the containment field is behind one of these sheets," Samantha said.

Too eager to wait for her mother to bring more light, and dying of curiosity, she yanked down on one of the filthy, dusty sheets hanging along the far wall. As the sheet fell away in a choking cloud of dust, Richard saw that the sheets had been hung over four sets of shackles spaced evenly along the wall. Each of the four sets of three metal bands on short chains was pinned into the stone wall.

"This isn't a containment field," Nicci said in sudden alarm. "This is a dungeon. Those are shields to keep the gifted from using their ability. That's why the light spheres don't work in here."

She spun Kahlan and shoved her toward the door. "Get out! Everyone out!"

That was the last thing Richard heard.

His whole body went numb. He didn't feel pain, but rather a heavy, thick, tingling sensation spreading through his body to the tips of his fingers and toes.

He realized that he was on his knees but didn't remember falling. He couldn't hear anything.

His vision dimmed as he felt intense pressure, as if thumbs were being pressed against his eyeballs. It was the only pain he felt. Everything else was numb.

In his fading vision, Richard thought that the room had tilted sideways. He realized, then, that he was lying on his side, curled up in a ball. Kahlan, Nicci, and Samantha were all on the ground, curled into fetal positions, shaking violently from head to toe.

Richard was barely able to discern through shadowy, blurred vision that the dust on the sheet at the end of the room billowed up as it was thrown back.

He tried to pull his sword, but he couldn't feel his fingers. Worse, his arms didn't work. Despite his best effort, he couldn't move them. His whole body was going completely numb and unresponsive. He couldn't even tell if he still had a body, or if he was being pulled into the world of the dead.

He heard the faintest sound, and realized that he was hearing himself screaming.

He thought he could just see someone at the end of the room.

Then, even the screaming sound ceased to exist as a heavy blackness settled through him. All awareness went dark as he lost consciousness.

74

When Richard opened his eyes, he couldn't see anything. He was in total blackness. His eyes hurt from what felt like intense pressure that had been pushing against them. He felt a rising sense of panic, fearing that he had been blinded.

He tried to move, but found that he could only move a little. He was restrained. He looked to the right, but what seemed to be a tall, rough iron collar cut into his flesh under his jaw if he turned his head too far.

His vision gradually began to return. Looking to the side as best he could, he was just able to see Kahlan out of the corner of his eye. Like Richard, she, too, hung by an iron band around her neck and manacles on her wrists. She appeared unconscious. The chains attached to the collars and the manacles were pinned into the stone wall and so short that they only allowed the captive to slump a little, but not sit.

Richard was beside himself with worry at the way Kahlan hung by the collar and manacles. She looked lifeless.

He turned his head the other way, to the left, blinking, trying to clear his vision, and saw that Nicci was similarly restrained. Beyond her, Richard could just make out some black hair and knew that Samantha also hung in the iron restraints.

Nicci's wrists were bleeding. Despite her powers, she looked entirely helpless. She started to stir, then. As she groaned she put some weight on her legs to take the pressure off the collar and manacles. She coughed and blinked, trying to clear her vision.

Richard scanned the room, as best he could in the restrictive iron collar. Two torches in brackets on the opposite side of the room hissed as they burned. He didn't see anyone other than the four of them chained to the wall.

He checked Kahlan again and saw that she was still hanging lifeless. He turned back to Nicci.

"Nicci," he called out. His voice sounded gravelly and his throat felt raw. "Nicci, can you hear me?"

She nodded, swallowing against the pain in her throat. She blinked and squinted as she turned her head as far as the collar would allow.

"Richard, are you all right?"

A flip answer popped to mind but he was too worried to be flip. "I think so. I ache all over."

"Me too," she said. She looked the other way, toward Samantha, then turned back to him. "Where is Kahlan?"

"On the other side of me. She isn't awake yet."

"Do you have any idea how long we've been out?" she asked.

Richard shook his head just a little. "No. But it

would have to be at least a while for someone to get us all chained up in these things. They must have the men, and Irena, too, or we wouldn't be stuck here like this."

He had a sudden flash of worry that the others had been killed because they weren't as valuable.

Another part of him wished that he had been killed as well. He didn't want to have to face whatever was in store for them. He remembered Zedd saying that he was tired of living.

At that moment, with the enormity of everything weighing down on him, Richard felt the same way. It was only Kahlan that kept him from giving into the tempting call of death inside him. It would be so easy to give in and slip into that dark forever.

Except that Kahlan needed him.

He tested his wrists, cuffed with iron manacles and connected to a heavy chain, and saw that they hardly had any slack. As he tried to move forward, he was only able to move inches before the iron collar around his neck brought him up short. He could barely move away from the damp stone wall. He could stand, but had no chance to sit or lie down.

He recognized the method of restraining prisoners. It was a simple but very effective form of torture. Once the prisoners could no longer stay awake and fell asleep or lapsed into unconsciousness, they slumped, basically hanging in the collar and manacles. The pain of the rough iron bands cutting in flesh kept a person awake, but they couldn't remain awake forever, so there were brief periods of sleep or blacking out, when they would hang in the iron. The longer it went on, the worse the wounds would get, eventually festering and becoming infected. Gangrene would set in and turn arms black. As the flesh decomposed it would begin sloughing off and falling away. Death would inevitably follow, but it was a very long and agonizing way to die, all alone and helpless.

"We need to get out of here," Nicci said in an angry voice.

"I'm with you. How do you suggest we go about it?"

Nicci was silent a moment before she spoke. "My gift doesn't work in this room. It's shielded to keep gifted prisoners from using their ability to escape."

"What about Subtractive Magic? Cut the iron with Subtractive Magic."

"Don't you think I tried that?" she asked in frustration. "Subtractive is still part of the gift. It was probably a lot more common when this dungeon was built. The shields are equally as effective against both sides."

Richard sighed in disappointment. "I guess that makes sense." He glanced down. "I still have my sword, but I can't reach it."

"Irena is an idiot," Nicci growled. "She is an inexperienced idiot from an isolated little village in the middle of nowhere and she mistook a containment cell for a containment field."

"Are they similar?" Richard asked.

"In some ways," she admitted. "They both are designed to contain power."

"What's going on?" It was Samantha's groggy voice as she was beginning to wake up. "Where are we? What's going on?"

"We're having an adventure," Richard said.

"I don't think I like it," she said.

"I've never been very fond of adventure, myself," Richard said.

"Is my mother all right? Where is she?"

"We don't know about any of the others," Nicci

told her. "All we know is that the four of us are chained up in here. They must be holding everyone else in other cells."

"What about the Mother Confessor?" Samantha asked. "I can't see her."

"On the other side of me," Richard told her.

He bent his knees, sagging a little, but that was the limit of how much he could move. He was exhausted. He felt like he had been beaten with a club. He hurt everywhere.

"Lord Rahl, what are we going to do?" The young woman sounded desperate and on the verge of panic.

"I don't know yet, Samantha."

"Well, who did this to us? Everyone seemed like they were cooperating."

"I don't know, Samantha. Try to save your strength."

He looked over at Kahlan again. She was still hanging unconscious by the iron bands at the ends of taut chains. Her head hung forward, her arms spread wide and stretched back a little toward the wall. Blood from where the iron collar cut her neck dripped off her chin.

The sight ignited Richard's anger. He tried to talk his anger back down. It could do him no good at the moment, and only wasted what little strength he had left. He needed to save that strength in case he had a chance to use it.

He heard Samantha crying softly over on the other side of Nicci. He couldn't think of anything to say to comfort her.

At that moment, his only hope was that they would be killed quickly, rather than endure a long, agonizing path toward the inevitable end.

CHAPTER

75

Richard's head jerked up. He realized that he must have nodded off briefly. Blood had puddled on the floor in front of him from the iron collar cutting into his neck. The way the rough iron ring dug into the fresh wound stung.

He was exhausted from the grueling effort of trekking through trackless wilderness to reach the citadel, from whatever sort of power had been used to render them unconscious, and also from the relentless weight of darkness within trying to pull him into the forever of death.

Trying to think clearly, trying to come up with some solution, was also sapping his strength. He could barely form a thought, and what thoughts he could form weren't helping.

He looked over and saw that Kahlan hadn't moved. She still hung unconscious. He remembered Nicci telling him that if either of them lost consciousness again from the poison inside them, it would be the last time and they wouldn't wake again. He didn't know why she was unconscious, but if it was from the sickness she carried, then it was possible she had already slipped away and would never wake again. He couldn't bear the thought of losing her, but he would rather she died that way than from a long ordeal of torture.

The thought of her dying made him want to scream. He couldn't endure to contemplate Kahlan being dead. He couldn't stand the thought of life without her. He would do anything to save her life. Anything.

But it didn't seem likely that either of them had any life to look forward to.

He had been so confident that they had been close to the resolution to their sickness, that Nicci would be able to heal them, and that they would then be able to collect the horses they needed to make it back to the palace in time. Not only that, but he had been positive that once Kahlan was herself again, she would also recover her strength of spirit and the commitment to what they were fighting for. That dedication to truth and the well-being of good people was so much a part of her, a part of her that he loved. It was her.

Now, those hopes had been crushed.

It had seemed within their grasp. They had worked so hard to get there, only to discover that there was no containment field. He felt cheated. It seemed so unfair.

Richard's head came up when he heard something out beyond the door. Nicci's head rose as well. They shared a look.

"Be strong, Richard. Be strong."

"You too," he told her.

"Always. We've both faced worse than this and survived."

She actually gave him a smile, then. He actually found himself returning it. She was a rare woman.

He felt a great sadness, then, at the thought of Nicci dying in this miserable dungeon out in the middle of the Dark Lands. Samantha, too, was going to have her life snuffed out before she could live it. It didn't seem fair.

He knew, though, that there was no such thing as fair in life. Existence had no agenda. Life simply existed. It was up to them to fight for life to be worthwhile and good if that was what they wanted. If they didn't, evil would flourish unopposed and have its way. And now, that evil was going to win.

The door squealed in protest when it was pulled open.

Richard stared in disbelief when Ludwig Dreier strolled in. The man wore a smirk that widened as his gaze met Richard's. Rather than the black clothes Richard was used to seeing the man wear, he now had on rather royal-looking purple-and-gold robes that swished around his legs as he walked.

Behind him was a Mord-Sith wearing black leather. Even through his pain, Richard found himself astonished to see the woman. Kahlan had told him about her, but it was puzzling as to why there were Mord-Sith other than the ones he knew at the People's Palace. The Mord-Sith, after all, were a creation of Richard's more ruthless ancestors.

"Well, well, Lord Rahl, how nice to see you again."

Again, a flip answer sprang to mind, but instead of giving voice to it, Richard didn't say anything. This was all part of Ludwig Dreier's elaborate scheme and nothing Richard could do or say was going to change the man's plans.

The abbot walked to Samantha first, leaning down

a little in order to look up into her face. "A sorceress, I see. How lovely. In the past I have been able to get useful prophecy from the gifted." He tweaked her nose. "I believe you might come in handy, little one."

"Let us go," Samantha said, nearly in tears, "we've done nothing to you."

"That's a matter open to debate, but perhaps another time. It's the middle of the night and I'm not in the mood for it."

The Mord-Sith gave Samantha a cold, meaningful look as Ludwig Dreier moved on to Nicci.

"Another sorceress, I see," he said. "But not merely a sorceress. A woman with skills and talents beyond those she was born with."

Nicci glared at the man, and like Richard didn't waste any effort in answering him. Nicci had grown up and spent most of her life in the clutches of sadistic men. She knew not to waste her time trying to talk reason to madness.

"Again, a gifted woman who I believe will be able to provide remarkable prophecy once properly prepared. I am sure her living entrails will reveal great secrets." He looked back over his shoulder. "Don't you think?"

The Mord-Sith showed him a cunning smile. "I believe you may be correct, Lord Dreier."

"*Lord* Dreier!" Richard said. "You have got to be kidding me. Why didn't you just skip right to *Emperor* Dreier?"

The man's intense focus turned to Richard. He moved closer. "An excellent suggestion, now that you mention it. I like the sound of that. Ah, but first I have work to do before that day comes."

"What kind of work?" Richard asked before he remembered that he had planned on remaining silent.

"Well, you see, Hannis Arc has awakened the spirit king—with the aid of your gifted blood, no less—and that has made things more . . . chaotic, more complicated. I am going to need to use prophecy to help me overcome the obstacle of that remarkable event and such powerful men." He held up a finger as he leaned closer. "But I assure you, I will."

"You don't have a clue as to what you're up against," Richard said as he glared.

Ludwig Dreier smiled as if it were a joke only he understood. "Actually, I do."

"And what is it you want from us?" Richard asked.

The man flicked a hand as he walked on to Kahlan. "Many things. All in due time. We will start on that tomorrow. Tonight you can stand there as you wait until after I've had a good night's sleep. I want to be well rested so that I can fully enjoy overseeing what is to come."

He lifted Kahlan's chin. When he withdrew his hand, Kahlan's head flopped back down. Richard could see it reopen the wound across the front of her throat where the iron collar was cutting into her flesh from the weight of her head.

"Erika, be a dear and wake her for me, would you please?"

For the first time, the Mord-Sith, standing in front of Richard, staring at him the way Mord-Sith liked to do to intimidate a helpless victim, smiled. He understood all too well the meaning in that smile. She was telling him that she knew that she was really hurting him more than she could ever hurt Kahlan.

Erika finally looked away from Richard as she turned. "With pleasure, Lord Dreier."

The sound of the woman's boots striking the stone floor as she strode over to Kahlan echoed around the dusty dungeon. Richard remembered that steady, deliberate sound all too well. Mord-Sith didn't like to hurry in their work.

Without ceremony, Erika gritted her teeth and with a grunt of effort rammed her Agiel into Kahlan's midsection.

Kahlan's eyes and mouth opened wide as she woke with a shocked gasp of agony. She screamed, then, trying to back away, but she was already against the wall. She could do nothing as she hung defenseless. Richard could see not only the pain, but the bewildered shock of it on the face of the woman he loved more than his own life.

His growl of effort echoed around the room as he

tried with all his might to rip the chains from the wall. The iron cut into his flesh, but the restraints did not budge.

The Mord-Sith finally withdrew her Agiel. Kahlan dropped, knees bent, as she hung in the collar and manacles. She gasped, trying to draw in a breath, unable to put weight on her legs. Her desperate, choking gasps were horrifying to hear. Blood mixed with saliva dripped in long strings from her chin.

The fact that she wasn't unconscious from the poison inside, but rather from whatever occult powers Ludwig Dreier had used, was in a small way reassuring. But on the other hand, the poison had apparently weakened Kahlan more than him.

When she finally regained control, caught her breath, and managed to put some weight on her feet to take the pressure off the collar and manacles, Kahlan lifted her head to glare at the Mord-Sith.

"Erika."

"Mistress Erika," the Mord-Sith said with a smile. "You need to learn to address me properly."

When Kahlan didn't answer, Erika again rammed her Agiel into Kahlan's midsection. Kahlan shook as she cried out in agony.

She slumped when Erika withdrew the weapon and hung for a time, gasping for air, her whole body trembling. It was longer the second time before she began to recover from the pain enough to draw a breath. Richard would have traded his life at that moment to be able to kill the Mord-Sith.

Ludwig Dreier lifted a hand to stay Erika from using her Agiel a third time.

"Well, Mother Confessor," he said, stepping closer, "it looks like we have you back with us again."

Kahlan spit out blood to the side and then glared at the man. "You do know, don't you, Abbot, that I'm going to kill you?"

"Well, I do know that wizards keep their promises, but I don't believe that the same certitude applies to the promises of Confessors."

"In this case it does," Kahlan said with venom. "You are already dead. You just don't know it yet."

"Yes, yes, threat given, fine. Consider me suitably terrified, if it makes you happy, but it's late and as enjoyable as this is, I don't feel like any more chitchat tonight."

Ludwig lifted her chin to make her look into his eyes. Richard hoped that Kahlan had enough sense not to spit in his face. He knew that when she was angry she would do just about anything, and she was angry. Thankfully, she only glared.

"You and I have unfinished business," he told her as he smiled in a way that sent a chill through Richard. "You see, I firmly believe that a Confessor will be able to bring forth remarkable prophecy, prophecy more important than even sorceresses, prophecy unlike any other living person would be able to give. I have never before had such an opportunity, but at last I do, and I intend to exploit it to the fullest possible extent. I have practiced my special craft for many years, for just such an occasion as you will provide."

"'Special craft'? That's a pathetic excuse for torture. The simple truth is you get sick pleasure out of crippling and maiming people. Deep down inside you know that everyone thinks of you as nothing more than a sadistic pervert, so you try to justify it, give it a cause that you pretend is noble. But you are fooling no one. Everyone knows the truth."

He lifted a hand, gesturing dismissively. "I admit, it's true that I do find a . . . unique satisfaction in taking people to that place, where the pain is so intense that they can actually look over to the other side as they beg for release. It is then, through my special ability, that they are able to pull prophecy from the eternity of the underworld.

"Yes, I enjoy my calling, but who doesn't enjoy being able to do well what they were born to do? Don't you enjoy using your power as it was intended, Mother Confessor? Of course you do—I can see in your eyes how much you long to use it right now. How sad for you that you can't call upon it any longer.

"So yes, I enjoy using my special abilities. I do love to watch less important people as they are on the cusp, quivering and trembling as the tears flow. You see, pain opens recognition, and agony begets redemption through prophecy.

"Over the years, I have learned that gifted people give the most noteworthy prophecy. I believe, however, that a Confessor may very well give the most remarkable prophecy yet, truly unique and useful prophecy. After I've finished with the sorceresses, of course. I want you to 'marinate' in terror, for a while, first."

He patted the side of her face, the way a doting master might pat the head of a dog. "I do admit, I am going to enjoy immensely seeing the look on your husband's face as I pull your intestines out and wind them on a stick while you scream and cry and shudder and shake. So you see, no excuse is needed. I simply do so much enjoy my work.

"Maybe your disagreeable attitude will improve, then, when only I can help you. Maybe then, when only I can offer you your final release, you will be more respectful of those who are smarter and better than you."

Kahlan glared openly. "You are a pathetic freak of nature."

Richard knew by the look in her eyes that if she had suffered a moment of weakness, and wanted to leave the world to fend for itself, that moment was past. In that moment, he saw that there was no way she was going to quit. She wanted nothing more than to fight.

Richard saw a look of raw hatred in Dreier's eyes, a hatred fueled by rage at anything good and wholesome, a hatred that wanted only to destroy for the sake of destroying.

"If you only knew what I have in store for you. . . ."

"Enjoy the deluded dream," Kahlan said with calm authority only the Mother Confessor could invoke, "because I am going to kill you."

Ludwig Dreier straightened with an angry glare.

"Would you like me to begin on her now?" Erika asked.

He considered but finally waved a hand. "No, it's been a long day, making plans, and standing behind that sheet while we waited for them to arrive."

He turned a smile on Richard. "You see, Lord Rahl, the value of prophecy? I value and respect prophecy. Knowing prophecy, understanding it, knowing how to use it put you there, in chains, and me about to retire to a nice, comfortable bed with agreeable company to bring me pleasures and delights."

He turned back from the doorway. "Enjoy your night, all. Tomorrow we begin. Come along Erika. Oh, and take the torches. They have no need of light. Let them be in the dark. After all, they have been the whole time up until now."

The Mord-Sith pulled both torches out of the brackets and took them, giving Richard and Kahlan one last, icy look. The door slammed shut, leaving the four of them suddenly alone in the pitch-black cell. He heard the key turn in the rusty lock. The bolt finally clanged into place.

"Kahlan," he whispered, "no matter what is to come, just remember that I love you. He can't ever take that away."

That, Richard thought, was why the man hated them so passionately. People like him hated that others could value such simple happiness in life. That was what they wanted most to destroy.

"I know, Richard. I love you, too."

"Don't worry," Nicci said. "We're going to get out of here."

"What makes you think so?" Richard asked.

"We have to," she said with simple conviction. "The Mother Confessor has vowed to kill him, and I believe her."

"That's the toasted toad's truth," Kahlan said in the darkness.

Despite everything, Richard smiled.

77

Several hours after Ludwig Dreier and Erika had left, Richard heard people out in the hall talking in low, muffled voices. He lifted his head and looked off across the room, even though in the pitch black he couldn't see anything at all. The blackness was oppressive, making him feel blind, making him feel that he was sinking into the darkness within him.

"Do you hear that?" Kahlan whispered.

"I hear it," Samantha whispered back. "It's someone talking."

"It sounds like a woman's voice," Richard said as he tried to make out the words, but couldn't.

"Probably that Mord-Sith, Erika," Nicci said, "come to give us a good-night kiss with her Agiel."

Richard didn't know how long they had been unconscious while being hung up in the chains pinned to the stone wall, but he was pretty sure it was still a long way from morning, so he didn't think that it was Ludwig Dreier returning this soon.

But knowing Mord-Sith the way he did, it wouldn't surprise Richard one bit if Nicci was right.

He heard a key turning the rusty lock until the bolt clanged back. The sound echoed around in the darkness, dying out after a long moment. The iron door squealed in protest as it was finally pulled open, the sound echoing in the stone dungeon.

Richard squinted in the bright shafts of flickering torchlight suddenly thrown into the room through the open door. After being in total darkness for so long, the light seemed impossibly bright. After a moment, his eyes began to adjust.

Still squinting, he saw three figures enter. They brought two torches. He was surprised to see that it was three Mord-Sith, all in black leather. A fourth person remained back in the darkness of the stone corridor just outside the doorway.

The Mord-Sith placed the pair of torches in the iron wall brackets. Three Mord-Sith were more than enough to handle four helpless prisoners. Richard couldn't stand the thought of Samantha or Nicci being hurt by those women, but the thought of Kahlan being hurt by them caused his anger to ignite yet again.

Being in the shackles, he couldn't reach his sword, but it was still on his hip. They had probably left it there because it helped remind him of how helpless he was. People like Dreier liked to make people feel helpless.

If ever there was an argument as to why he couldn't quit the struggle, this was it—innocent people helpless against brutality. The sword was a reminder that while others were often helpless, he had the ability to act on their behalf. Except right at that moment he couldn't reach his sword to help himself, much less anyone else.

But having the sword on his hip did keep the anger close. Every time his anger flared, the sword's anger rose expectantly. He could feel it seething to be let loose.

The tallest of the three women stepped confidently to him. Like the others, she was blond, muscular, and wore the traditional long, single braid that all Mord-Sith wore. He found the black leather, though, to be less impressive than the red. The red had a purpose that, because of its practical aspect, actually made Mord-Sith look all the more intimidating. It was meant to mask the presence of large quantities of blood, so the red leather thereby emphasized the unsettling purpose of Mord-Sith. The black was a crude and graceless attempt by the man who made them wear it to create something more menacing. Richard suspected that Ludwig Dreier thought he could make death more frightening than the Keeper himself.

Rather than the other two going to the women chained to the wall, they stayed close behind the one looking into Richard's eyes.

"I am Cassia," she finally said. She briefly lifted a hand back to the other two. "This is Laurin and Vale."

Richard thought that maybe he could focus their cruel attention on him, and make them forget the others.

"Out for an evening stroll, are we?" he asked.

Cassia smiled crookedly with one side of her mouth. "I had heard that you had a sense of humor. Strange quality for a man in your position."

Richard braced himself for her Agiel, but it didn't come.

She shook her head, instead. "No. We have come to ask you some questions."

Although Richard heard no hostility in her voice, he groaned inwardly. He knew all too well what it meant for a Mord-Sith to ask questions. What he found a bit odd was her informal tone. It wasn't the icy voice Mord-Sith typically used when they meant to torture answers out of a person.

"What is it you want to know?"

"We have heard rumors about you. We want to know if they are true. If you lie to us . . . well, I think you know what will happen if you lie to us."

"Yes. Denna taught me."

That gave all three pause. The two behind Cassia shared a look. Richard wondered how they knew Denna, yet came to be here.

"You knew Denna?" Cassia asked. "Is that the truth?"

"Yes. Darken Rahl had her capture me. She had me for a long time, and in that time she taught me a lot of things."

Cassia nodded with an intent expression. "I knew Denna. I knew her well at one time." Her brow twitched with a puzzled look. "If Denna had you, and was training you, then how is it that you got away from her? Darken Rahl would have sent Denna for only one reason. People did not get away from Denna."

Richard didn't shy away from Cassia's steady, blue-eyed gaze. "I did. Now, what is it you want to know?"

"Answer the question I asked, first, and this will be a lot easier—for all of us."

Richard's whole body ached from being restrained

and unable to sit or lie down. His legs hurt, his back hurt, and his head pounded. He didn't know what kind of occult powers Ludwig Dreier had used to subdue them, but the aftermath was painful.

"I killed her," Richard said as he looked Cassia in the eye. "That's how I got away. I killed her. I don't wish to talk about it. Despite what she did to me, she was only doing what she did because she had been broken."

Cassia nodded, seeming to understand. Richard didn't quite know what to think of that. This woman was not reacting the way a Mord-Sith typically acted when she was intent on getting answers, or when she had been sent to torture a victim.

He decided to be a little less hostile in his answers.

"What is it you came to ask, Cassia?"

He deliberately did not address her as "Mistress."

Cassia, looking down in thought, finally lifted her head. "I have heard a rumor that you presided over the marriage of a Mord-Sith."

Out of the corner of his eye, Richard shared a look with Kahlan. The two behind Cassia were intently focused on him.

"Yes, that's right, Cara."

"Cara? Cara married?" Cassia looked astonished and incredulous all at once. "Cara is as resolute and formidable as they come."

"Cara was our protector, but she came to be more than simply a protector to the Lord Rahl. She had become a close friend to the Mother Confessor and me."

Cassia looked over at Kahlan. "Is that true?"

"Yes," Kahlan said without hesitation. "Cara was as hard as nails, but she also had a good heart. We loved her."

The three seemed mystified by that, as if they didn't know what to think.

"Then where is she now?" the one named Vale asked from behind. "If she is your protector, and your friend, then why isn't she here protecting you? Did she die in her service to you?"

"No," Richard said with a deep sigh. "It's a long story."

"Make it short," Cassia said. "We don't have a lot of time."

Richard looked at the intent expressions of the two behind before looking back at Cassia. He wondered what she meant about not having a lot of time, but went ahead and answered anyway.

"Kahlan and I were captured by Jit, a Hedge Maid. Jit infected us with a kind of deadly poison. Cara and others came to help us. In the meantime, the barrier to the third kingdom failed. Hannis Arc called the long-dead Emperor Sulachan back from the world of the dead in part by using my blood. The half people— people without souls—captured Cara, her husband, and all of our other friends. Kahlan and I were unconscious, so Cara hid us before the attack. Because of that, the half people didn't take us with the others. We later went in there and got them out. As we were escaping, Cara's husband was killed."

"I see," Cassia said. "So what happened to Cara? Why isn't she still with you?"

As the painful memory came flooding back, Richard had to pause. It was a long moment before he answered.

"Cara asked to be released from her service to me."

The room was silent but for the hissing torches as the Mord-Sith tried to take in an act that he knew must be incomprehensible to them.

"What is it you really want to know?" Richard finally asked.

"You are called Lord Rahl. Darken Rahl was the Lord Rahl. Darken Rahl was our master." Cassia lifted her chin while looking him in the eye. "Did you kill him?"

That was the question he had been afraid they were going to ask. Nonetheless he answered it with straightforward, plain honesty.

"Yes."

Cassia, Laurin, and Vale stared at him for a long, silent, uncomfortable moment.

Richard decided that maybe he should elaborate on his reasons, so that they would not mistakenly think it was by chance, or accident. He wanted them to know the truth.

"Darken Rahl was an evil man who caused untold suffering and death. I sent him to the underworld so that he couldn't harm anyone else and I would do it all over again."

"So then, how is it that you became the Lord Rahl?"

"He raped my mother. That makes me his offspring. I inherited the gift from him.

"At the time I wasn't interested in being the Lord Rahl, or even willing to accept the fact that I had the gift, but I came to see that I could use my ability, and the bond between the Lord Rahl and the people of D'Hara, to fight for something worthwhile—freedom.

Freedom to live our lives without the boot of tyranny on all of our necks. Freedom to live in a just world. Many wanted a chance for that and helped in the struggle. Cara was but one of them.

"She and the other Mord-Sith who have joined in that struggle are not weak for wanting freedom. They are stronger for it. I have held Mord-Sith in my arms as they died for our shared cause. I have worn the Agiel of Mord-Sith who have given their lives fighting for our beliefs.

"Those people, like those Mord-Sith, who want the same things in life that I want, are the reason I fight. I fight on behalf of all of them. There have been times when I have been weary and wanted to give up that struggle and leave the fighting to others."

He glanced briefly at Kahlan. "But the Mother Confessor, who is the one who came to ask for my help in the first place, is my strength, and it is for her, and all those like her, that I fight. I will fight for what is right to the very end. I will fight with my dying breath if need be.

"That, Cassia, Laurin, Vale, is why I killed Darken Rahl. He needed killing and I was the only one who could do it. That is why I am and must be the Lord Rahl."

Kahlan gave Richard her special smile. He was heartened to see it, even if it ended up being for the last time.

Cassia abruptly turned to Nicci. "I have heard that you were once a Sister of the Dark, but no longer. Why not?"

Nicci was straightforward and simple in her answer. "Richard showed me a better way. He is a good man. Kahlan is a good woman. I wanted to live life the way they showed me I could, if I chose to."

Cassia nodded in thought. She looked down as she rolled her Agiel in her fingers for a time, carefully considering her next words. Richard knew the agonizing pain caused by holding that weapon. Mord-Sith were taught to endure and ignore pain. In the madness these women had been cast into, pain was a refuge.

"The pain of the Agiel helps you to think," he said. "It's familiar, ever-present, comforting."

She looked up in wonder. "I guess Denna really did teach you many things."

"She taught me that people who had been ripped from everything good they knew in life, and were made to suffer for no reason but to turn them into monsters who could be used to serve the cause of evil, could still find their way back."

"Not all of them," she said with quiet remorse.

"No, not all of them. Some have been severed from their souls, and can never come back to humanity. But some still can."

Cassia let her Agiel drop to dangle on the fine gold chain on her right wrist, as if suddenly not wanting to be reminded of the pain.

"We served under Darken Rahl." She gestured back at the other two. "The three of us. He was everything you say. I would venture to say that we know that better than you ever could."

Richard nodded. "I understand. I know some of what was done to you by that man, but I'm sure I could never know it all."

The truth of his words ghosted across her face.

"We finally found a way to leave him," Cassia said. "Bishop Arc offered us refuge by using his powers to take up our bond. We thought it would be better.

"We found life with Hannis Arc to be little different, except that his schemes for evil were even more grandiose than Darken Rahl's had been. Once bonded to him, we only then learned that one of our own, Alice, had tricked us—betrayed her sisters of the Agiel." A dark look settled into her features. "She had delivered us to him in exchange for favors for herself.

"Then, just days ago, Lord Dreier arrived and enslaved us in service to him by using his occult powers to link our bond to him instead, as if we were property he could walk in and seize. In many ways, personal ways, he has proven to be more than a match for the savagery of Darken Rahl or Bishop Arc.

"Those two used torture as a means to an end. Lord Dreier, though, gets pleasure from the things he does to people. Sick pleasure.

"There were four of us he put into bondage to him when he arrived here. Like Darken Rahl, he took us to his bed as a form of domination, to show us our place as his property, to let us know that he can use us as he wishes, however he wishes.

"One night, he took Janel to his bed. He was fascinated—captivated—by her beauty. In the morning, he decided that because she was Mord-Sith and he found her so achingly beautiful, she would be the perfect one to use in his effort to obtain prophecy from the other side of the veil."

"He tortured her?" Richard asked. "One of his own Mord-Sith?"

Cassia nodded. "He and Erika commanded the three of us to watch it being done, to show us, he said, the tremendous value and importance of the work he does.

"There was no value in what he did to Janel. There was no point to it other than his desire to watch her naked body break. He got no prophecy in exchange for her life. He shrugged it off as a 'worthy attempt.'"

When she fell silent, Richard said, "Believe me, Cassia, I share your revulsion at all three of the men who enslaved you. That's why I fight against them and those who help them."

She nodded, looking down, rolling the red leather weapon in her fingers again as she considered. She spoke as she watched her Agiel turn first one way and then the other.

"Our lives have been in service to brutes, each worse than the last. We have never had any say in it. It was always framed as a choice but it was never really any choice at all. We have been the chattel of evil men, property, weapons they used for their ends, weapons they used to intimidate and harm others. Some Mord-Sith came to embrace that role. Some did not."

The other two silently watched Cassia speaking for them. Richard didn't say anything, giving her the space to find her own words.

"What we have come to ask," she finally said in a quiet voice, "is if you will take us back, if we can serve as your Mord-Sith. If you will be our Lord Rahl."

Richard shared a look with Kahlan.

Cassia still hadn't looked up into his eyes.

Richard spoke softly. "I can't do that to you, Cassia."

Finally she looked up, a tear rolling down her cheek. "May I know why not?"

Richard nodded—as best he could in the iron collar. "Cassia, I'm dying. We came here because we thought there was a containment field here where Nicci could heal us. But there isn't. With this sickness inside me and Kahlan, our abilities are cut off from us. If I were to take you up on your offer, I would only put your lives in mortal danger because I can't power the bond, and without that bond, your Agiel wouldn't work.

"Worse, it's now only a matter of days at most until this poison kills me and Kahlan. Then, you would be defenseless against a man who would want to extract revenge.

"The ancient bond the people of D'Hara have with the Lord Rahl is meant to be balanced. It does not mean you are merely in service to the Lord Rahl; it means he is also in service to you. You are his protector, but he in turn is yours. The people are the steel against steel so that he can be the magic against magic.

"I'm dying. I can't do my part to protect you.

"I admire your choice, I sincerely do, but I can't fulfill my duty not only as your leader, but to be the magic against magic for you. So you see, I can't accept your offer of service because it would be a fatal disservice to you."

Cassia smiled, then. It was a beautiful, warm, wonderful, sad smile. Another tear ran down her cheek.

"That, Lord Rahl, was the right answer."

With that, all three Mord-Sith went to their knees and bowed forward, putting their foreheads to the ground.

Together, with one voice, they recited the devotion, the bond, they had learned as young women, as did all D'Harans.

"*Master Rahl, guide us,*" they said with reverence. "*Master Rahl, teach us. Master Rahl, protect us. In your light we thrive. In your mercy we are sheltered.*

In your wisdom we are humbled. We live only to serve. Our lives are yours."

When they finished, *Our lives are yours* echoed around the dungeon, dying out slowly.

When that echo had whispered away, they remained where they were, foreheads to the floor, and then together recited it a second time, and when the echo had again died out, they recited it a third time, as was the tradition.

Finally, when they had finished, they returned to their feet, sharing a last look among themselves. Laurin and Vale gave Cassia a nod for her to speak for them.

"Lord Rahl," Cassia said for them all, "we would rather our lives end today, in service to you as our Lord Rahl, than to live another hundred years in service to monsters, as slaves to tyrants, as instruments of evil. To live only one day as we wish, as we choose, for our own purpose, for something good, is better than to live an entire life as slaves to hate.

"Please, Lord Rahl, we beg of you, accept our service, our bond to you. Be our Lord Rahl, even if it is only for your last day of life. It would honor us to uphold our side of the bond, even though you are unable to fulfill your part of it. To have your bond to us in your heart alone, even if you can do nothing to uphold it, is enough for us. It is everything to us."

The three women pressed their right fists to their hearts and bowed their heads, awaiting his decision.

Richard swallowed back the lump in his throat. This was why he couldn't quit. This was what he was fighting for—for those who needed hope, who needed to live for something good, who hungered for ideals in life, instead of living in savagery and hate.

"I accept," he said, fearing to test his voice more than that.

All three women broke into wide grins. The smiles sparkled in their wet eyes.

The one in back, Vale, immediately ran to the door and ushered the shadowed figure into the room.

As he shuffled in, Richard recognized that it was Mohler, the old scribe.

"Lord Rahl," the man said, "I feel the same. I have worked here my entire life. I have known Hannis Arc since he was but a boy. I have watched as he grew into a man driven by bitterness and envy. Now, Ludwig Dreier has taken his place, and he is no different. Like these women, I no longer wish to stand by and watch their kind destroy everything good in order to impose their will on everyone.

"I have known these four—now three—Mord-Sith, since they have been in servitude here at the citadel. We have all been enslaved by tyrants. I told them what I knew of you, what I have learned. I told them that I decided to help you, and I asked them to join me. I, too, Lord Rahl, am in your service."

Without further word, he shuffled forward with a big ring of keys, the right one already selected. He undid the lock on the collar first, then the manacles.

When he was free, Richard collapsed to his knees, unable to stand. As Cassia and Vale helped lift him to his feet, Mohler immediately went to Kahlan, to unlock her restraints.

Richard was there for Kahlan when she was finally free. She fell into his arms and hugged him with all her strength.

"Thank you for not giving up on any of us," she whispered in his ear.

"Never," he said.

79

D o any of you know where the others are?" Richard asked the three Mord Sith and the scribe, Mohler. "All the soldiers of the First File? There were a lot of men."

"And my mother," Samantha added.

"They are all down in the dungeons," Mohler said.

"The dungeons?" Richard asked.

"Dreier used his occult ability to render everyone unconscious—like he did to you," Laurin said. "There are only shackles for four people in here, so the citadel guard brought you four in here and carried all the others down to the lower cells in the other dungeons."

Richard looked around at the stone room. It was shielded and secure. "But I thought this was the dungeon."

Cassia shook her head. "This is only the upper dungeon area of the citadel, and by far the smallest. The citadel has an extensive dungeon complex—three full floors below us, with dozens and dozens of individual rooms. Some cells are only large enough to hold one person, but most are a great deal larger than this one. They could easily house hundreds of prisoners at a time down there."

Richard frowned at the three Mord-Sith. "Why would they hold so many people?"

Cassia pulled a finger across her throat. "To await execution."

Vale nodded. "There is an execution room on each floor below. Drains are cut into the stone for all the blood running from the blocks where the beheadings were done. Each execution room has a number of stations with well-worn blocks."

Cassia gestured downward. "The way it looks, they probably only used the cells to house people temporarily until they could be executed. From what I've seen of those rooms down below, it doesn't look like the dungeons and execution rooms have been in use for ages, but there is plenty of evidence that they were once in heavy use.

"The bodies were thrown in pits below the dungeons. One pit contains only skulls. The bones in others are a jumble—the bodies likely thrown in and left to rot. I have no idea how deep the layers of bones might be."

"We have to get my mother out of there," Samantha insisted, sounding on the verge of panic. "We have to get her out now."

Richard put a hand on her shoulder as he thought it through. "We will, Samantha, we will."

"She would get me out," she insisted.

Richard looked back up at the Mord-Sith and the scribe. "I don't understand. Why are there so many prison cells here? Do any of you know? I mean, this is a pretty small city for so many dungeon cells, to say nothing of all the executions."

"From old accounts I've seen," Mohler said, "the citadel has long been a prison for the Dark Lands, a place to confine the most dangerous people, such as those with occult powers, until they could be executed."

It was suddenly making sense to Richard.

"The barrier to the third kingdom was in this general area of the Dark Lands," he said. "The people back in the time of the first Confessor, the time of the great war, knew that the seals of the barrier would begin to fail one day and that occult powers confined there would begin to seep out. They left people in Stroyza to watch for the barrier to fail completely, but more than that, they built the citadel to collect and confine anyone with dangerous occult powers that from time to time had leaked out from beyond the barrier. People like Jit."

"Unfortunately, those powers apparently also settled into Hannis Arc and Ludwig Dreier," Kahlan said.

Nicci gestured in frustration. "Great. So a man with those occult abilities came to be the very one running the prison meant to confine him."

"More likely to execute him," Kahlan said.

Richard looked back at the shackles pinned to the wall. He was beginning to get an idea. He just needed time to think it through. But there was no time. He needed to act before it was too late.

"I know that look," Kahlan said. "What are you thinking? Get everyone out from below and do a lightning-quick attack?"

Richard's mind was filled with the flow and form of the dance with death, the way of a war wizard.

He was lost in that dance he had come to know so well.

"The threat we face is not one that will be helped with soldiers. For the moment, we need to leave them down there, out of the way. We need everyone in the citadel to think we are all still locked up and under control."

Samantha's hands fisted. "My mother is gifted. We need to get her out. She can help."

"Samantha, calm down. I know how much you want to get her out, but I know what I'm talking about. We will get her out, I promise, but we first have to make it safe to do so. You need to trust me in this. You wouldn't want to get her out only to have her killed because we failed to recognize the full extent of what we face, would you?"

"Well, no, I guess not, but—"

"But nothing. Dreier possesses occult abilities. He has already proven that he can cut any gifted person down in a heartbeat. He put all of us and the men down before any of us knew what hit us. Your mother has no chance against him. None of us do."

A devious smile spread on Nicci's face. "I have some ideas."

Richard was sure she did. Nicci was experienced at this sort of thing, at using her head rather than brawn. She also knew better than to try to use what they knew wouldn't work.

"We need to act with surprise, swiftness, and violence," Richard told all of them. "Capturing Dreier is the priority."

Kahlan's expression suddenly took an angry set. "Capture him! Richard, we can't risk capturing him! And what would be the point? The best thing to do is what you said. Surprise, swiftness, and violence. We need to kill the bastard before he has a chance to strike back. With his abilities he could kill us all. We wouldn't stand a chance of stopping him. We need to kill him, not capture him. Now we have the chance to surprise him and end the threat."

"The threat from Dreier," Richard said, "but what about the rest of it?"

"What about it?" Kahlan lifted her hands and let them flop down at her sides. "What can we do, Richard? We're going to be dead from Jit's poison before we have a chance to do anything else. We can at least kill Ludwig Dreier before we die. To be able to do anything else we would have to be cured."

"Exactly."

Richard smiled as he drew his sword. The ring of steel echoed around the stone dungeon.

Everyone looked puzzled as he turned. With a mighty swing, he struck the chain holding the collar that had been around his neck. As it cleaved the chain away at the wall, the blade sent hot fragments of steel flying through the room, some skittering along the floor, some rebounding off walls.

When the collar clattered to the floor, Richard picked it up by its short length of chain and held it up before the others. "This is a collar meant to contain the powers of the gifted."

"Dreier has occult powers," Kahlan pointed out. "Those are even more powerful than his gifted abilities."

A grin spread on Nicci's face. "But this place was made specifically to confine those with occult powers, not merely the gifted."

"Right," Richard said. "With this, we can capture Ludwig Dreier and keep him from using his power against us."

Kahlan folded her arms, interested, but not yet convinced. "Why? It would be easier to kill him. What's the point of going to the trouble of capturing him?"

"What kind of poison do we have in us?" he asked her.

Kahlan shrugged. "The call of death, from Jit."

"Which is . . . ?" Richard prompted.

Her eyes widened with understanding. "Caused by an occult power."

"That's right. Jit had occult powers. That's what is infecting us."

Nicci was smiling. "And Ludwig Dreier has occult powers. So, if we can capture him alive and hold him in that collar, maybe we can find out if there is a way to cure you two of that occult poison without a containment field."

"It's our only chance," Richard said. "We have to try."

"Even if you somehow get him in the collar," Kahlan said, "how are you going to get him to cooperate?"

Cassia leaned in as she smiled in the chilling way that only Mord-Sith could smile. "You leave that part to us, Mother Confessor. We are Lord Rahl's Mord-Sith now. We will get Dreier to cooperate."

"With this sickness in me, my bond doesn't work to power your Agiel," Richard reminded them.

"No," she agreed, the smile still in place, "but Dreier said that his occult abilities power our Agiel now, and the bond that powers them can't be broken as long as he's alive."

"So," Vale said, "we can use his own ability against him."

"We're going to do whatever it takes to protect

Lord Rahl's life," Laurin added. "That is what Mord-Sith do. We will get him to talk. If there is a cure, he will tell us what he knows."

Kahlan looked at the determination in their eyes. "Just leave him alive when you're done so I can kill him."

"You've got it, Mother Confessor," Laurin said.

"He's yours to kill," Cassia agreed.

"But until then, he is ours," Vale said with a gleam of menace in her eyes.

"Do any of you know where he sleeps?" Richard asked the three Mord-Sith.

They all shared a look.

"Oh yes, we know," Cassia said. "It's up on the third floor."

"Lead the way," Richard told her. "I'll explain the plan on the way."

"Gladly."

"Is there a back way up to his bedroom?" he asked.

"Yes," Cassia said. "Some of the doors are kept locked, though."

Mohler held up the big ring of keys he carried. "Not a problem."

"He has soldiers guarding his bedroom," Laurin said. "Tonight he has Erika entertaining him, rather than one of us. He was eager to get to bed, so I doubt he will be asleep."

"That means he will be distracted," Richard said. "But this is still going to require stealth. All of you will need to do exactly as I say. Along the way I'm going to need some of you to stay behind to guard our backs. I don't want any questioning or second-guessing. There won't be time to explain or argue. We can't have that if we are going to succeed and then get the others out of the dungeon. You will all need to do exactly as I say, when I say it, if this is going to work."

He was directing his comments mostly at Samantha without looking at her because he didn't want to sound like he was accusing her of something before she was guilty of it. But he also knew how she could be. He knew that he could count on the rest of them to follow instructions.

"If any of you have a problem with that, then you need to wait down here, otherwise you can come with me. Agreed?"

Everyone nodded.

80

A t an intersection of corridors, Richard took a quick look around the corner. He didn't see anyone before quickly pulling back behind cover. The corridors, dimly lit by reflector lamps hung at regular intervals, were interior passageways, so there weren't any windows.

Cassia had told him that the bedroom had windows. Since it was still night, they wouldn't provide any light, but they were a possible escape route. Richard doubted, though, that if things went bad, Dreier would jump from the third floor.

"How much farther?" he asked.

Cassia took a careful look. "At the end of the corridor, the halls go to either the right or the left. The bedroom is to the right, at the end, but it's not far. Like I explained, at the end of the hall that corridor opens up into a small rotunda right outside the bedroom. He keeps at least two soldiers there all the time. Sometimes more. Sometimes he stations eight or ten in the rotunda to stand guard. We won't know for sure until we make the final turn toward the bedroom."

"With Erika in the room with him," Nicci said, "he might not feel the need for more."

Mohler shook his head. "They aren't for protection. The abbot is sufficiently powerful to handle any threat himself. I think he likes to have the men there for show—as a display of his importance."

Cassia made a sour face. "He has them there because they can overhear what is going on in the bedroom. Dreier commands the women he takes in there to be noisy so that the soldiers outside the door will hear. He knows they will gossip about what they heard. He thinks it makes for an impressive image among the soldiers."

Vale was nodding. "He's a pig."

"All right, Mohler, Samantha, Laurin, Vale, and Kahlan, you five wait here." Richard pointed at the two Mord-Sith and Samantha. "You three protect the Mother Confessor. I'm counting on you. If for some reason Dreier gets past us, this is his likely way out. You will have to stop him and protect Kahlan if he comes this way. Mohler, do you have the collar ready?"

They all nodded. The scribe held up the collar by the chain, as if he were holding up a dead varmint by its tail. Richard took the collar in his left hand, balling up most of the chain in his fist to keep it from making any noise.

"You ready for this, Cassia?"

She flashed him a cunning smile. "You have no idea."

Kahlan caught his arm. "Richard, are you sure about this? It seems too simple."

"Sometimes simple is the best approach to a fight. Complicated plans have more to go wrong. We will only have one chance before he uses his powers. Simplicity, speed, and violence of action is our best chance."

Kahlan leaned forward and gave him a quick kiss on the cheek. "If anyone can do it, you three can."

"All right, let's go," Richard said to Nicci and Cassia. "Keep it quiet. You both know what to do."

Richard already had his sword out so that he wouldn't have to draw it anywhere near the bedroom. He knew that the ringing sound of pulling the blade would carry in the confines of the corridors. He didn't know how good the guards were, if they were really listening for the sound of any threat in the halls, or if they were instead listening to the sounds from the bedroom, but he didn't want to take any chances with making an unnecessary noise. They had to remain undetected until the last instant.

Around the corner, the hallway was empty. The long, dark blue carpet running down the length of the hall muffled the sounds of their footsteps as they moved swiftly along the hall. The three of them slipped carefully around a long table against the wall that held two empty glass bowls. Small tapestries hung in several places, further helping to quiet any sound they made.

When they reached the end of the corridor before the intersection, Richard squatted down with the other two. When he gave her the signal, Cassia lay down on her belly and carefully crawled to the corner. She stretched her neck so that she was just able to peek around the edge.

She pulled back and held up two fingers.

Richard let out a sigh of relief. That made it easier

for Nicci to do the first part. Once they started, they needed to be quick. Nicci set down what she had been carrying.

Cassia backed away from the corner and stood. She unfastened buttons and the black leather straps, turned away from Richard, and then pulled the top of her outfit down to her waist. She looked over her bare shoulder and gave him a nod that she was ready.

With two fingers, Richard signaled for her to go.

Cassia boldly walked around the corner and off toward the bedroom. All the guards knew the three Mord-Sith, and knew that they frequently went to Ludwig Dreier's bedroom to be with him. She walked deliberately, as if she had been summoned.

When Richard and Nicci heard Cassia tell the guards "Lord Dreier sent for me," Nicci stepped around the corner.

Without pause, the sorceress thrust both arms out, palms facing outward.

When Richard heard the two thumps, he knew that Nicci had stopped their hearts and both men were dead. Death was so swift they hadn't cried out. They probably hadn't even seen Nicci.

Richard handed her what she had brought. Nicci leaned out around the corner again and with her gift sent it silently floating down the hall, the way Richard had seen Zedd float rocks through the air. He hoped she would have enough control to keep it from hitting a wall, to say nothing of holding it stationary for a time and then at last hitting the target. Nicci had acted like it was a foolish question, but he didn't know how to use his gift to do such a thing so he would have no way of judging the difficulty.

He had to trust that Nicci knew what she was talking about.

Richard heard Cassia knock on the bedroom door.

The corridor remained silent. Richard took a quick peek. The two soldiers were slumped dead on the floor to either side of the white, double door. A number of reflector lamps lit the rotunda. Cassia stood facing the door, her breasts exposed to get Dreier's immediate attention, as they had the guards'. They needed him to keep his eyes on Cassia, and not look to the side.

Cassia knocked again.

Richard heard the door open.

"What is it?" It was Dreier's voice. "Oh——"

Nicci immediately sent the stone block sailing in at him.

The instant Richard heard the sound of stone hitting the man's skull, he was around the corner, racing the rest of the distance.

As he ran in at full speed, sword in one hand, collar in the other, Richard kicked the round table in the middle of the room aside. The table crashed against the wall and shattered.

Dreier was on his knees, bent forward, his head almost touching the floor. He was naked. Both hands clutched his bloody head as he moaned, sounding dazed and confused. The heavy stone block Nicci had sent flying in at him lay off to the side.

Richard slid to a stop on his knees just as Cassia threw a leg around Dreier to straddle his back. She grabbed his thick hair in a fist and pulled up on his head. His hands fell to his sides. Blood pouring from a long gash back across his scalp ran down the side of his head, turning an ear and his neck red.

As soon as Cassia had pulled Dreier's head up, Richard pushed the collar around his neck and slammed it closed. It made a clang that echoed through the hall.

Dreier was so groggy from the blow to his head that he didn't even know what had happened. He was like a rag doll, and offered no resistance.

The other two Mord-Sith, having heard the sound of the stone hitting the man's skull and the clang of the metal collar locking closed, came around the corner at a dead run.

Erika, also naked but for the Agiel in her fist, ran out toward the hall and skidded to a halt before she ran into Dreier, still slumped on the floor, now holding the loose flap of scalp up onto his head to cover the wound.

Sword in hand, Richard stood. Erika smiled at him over the top of her stricken master. Richard knew that she expected him to try to use the sword against her and then she could capture him by capturing its magic.

Richard instead slid the sword back in its sheath. "Sorry, but I've done that dance before. I'm not going to do it again."

Vale and Laurin came up on either side of her. They had their Agiel in their fists as well.

"Your choice," Richard said. "Surrender, or tangle with my Mord-Sith."

Her brow twitched. "Your Mord-Sith? Who do you think—"

Laurin jabbed her Agiel into Erika's kidney. The woman cried out as she dropped to a knee.

"If you would like, we can take turns doing this to you all night," Laurin said. "I suggest you get dressed instead, Erika."

Cassia held out her hand. "Give me your Agiel, first."

Erika reluctantly handed it over before going back into the room. Richard followed her in to get Dreier's clothes. He found them thrown over the back of a chair.

When he picked up the purple robes Dreier had been wearing, Richard felt an odd lump. He groped the robes and found a concealed pocket on the inside at the waist. With a finger, he fished out something small and flat.

He was surprised to see a journey book. He opened the black leather cover to see what it said.

Nicci looked as surprised as Richard. "Well?" she asked.

"Nothing in it," he told her. "Wiped clean."

She nodded. "A lot of the Sisters wiped theirs clean as a precaution. Others liked to preserve the messages in case they needed confirmation of instructions, or to remember certain things, or even as proof that they were acting on orders."

Richard sighed as he slipped the blank journey book into his pocket. "Unfortunately, this one tells us nothing."

Nicci gave him a meaningful look. "I'd sure like to check its twin."

"Me too," he said. "But I have no idea who might have it."

When he came out of the bedroom carrying the robes, he found Kahlan glaring down at the stuporous prisoner on the floor. "He had better prove useful."

"Nicci may need to heal him first," Richard said. "I think she might have cracked his skull."

Samantha briefly stared down at the naked man.

"Can we please go get my mother out of that dungeon, now?"

"Of course," Richard said. "We need to get Commander Fister and the men out as well. They need to get the citadel guard under control or we will soon have trouble."

"I can handle any who cause trouble," Nicci said. "Samantha or her mother could as well."

"They have archers," Richard reminded her. "An arrow in the back and you would be just as dead as if a sorceress stopped your heart."

Nicci sighed. "I suppose so."

"Can we go chain this pig up in the dungeon, now?" Cassia asked as she fastened the sides of her leather top back in place.

"Good idea." Richard smiled at the three Mord-Sith. "You did good. All of you. I'm proud of you. We just captured a dangerous man with powerful occult abilities and none of us were hurt."

"I got the idea from Samantha," Nicci said, smiling down at her. "If you can't use magic to stop those with occult abilities, just drop rocks on their heads."

Samantha looked proud as she watched the Mord-Sith haul a profusely bleeding, groggy Ludwig Dreier to his feet.

81

Once the men of the First File had been freed from the dungeons down in the lower levels of the citadel, they had raced up the stairwells into the grand greeting room and spread out through the gallery. As they had poured out among the columns, surprised citadel guards drew their weapons. These citadel guards had been the ones who had carried the unconscious men of the First File down into the lower dungeons and locked them in.

Commander Fister, at the head of his men as he led them into the grand meeting hall, without ceremony cut down the first two men who rushed in at him with swords. It was as shockingly swift as it was decisive. He hadn't even bothered to loose his men on the soldiers, as if the defenders were a mere pesky annoyance he could deal with himself.

Almost as soon as the two soldiers hit the ground, dead, and lay bleeding out on the rich carpet, the rest of the men had dropped their weapons and raised their hands in surrender.

Until it was decided what to do with the citadel guard, they had all been locked in the dungeons.

Ludwig Dreier, too, had been chained in the dungeon, right where Richard had been chained, with the shields to the collar and the room itself containing both his gift and his occult powers, as they had been meant to do by those in ancient times who had built the citadel, the same people who had once built the barrier to the third kingdom. Erika had been chained up beside him, where Nicci had been restrained.

As Nicci was seeing to the abbot's wounds to make sure he lived long enough to be of help, Cassia returned and said that she had found Richard and Kahlan a secluded bedroom to use while they waited for Nicci to finish. Richard had figured that after the ordeal of being chained down in the dungeon, he and Kahlan could at least get a couple of hours of sleep. With the way the sickness was wearing them down they couldn't afford to let exhaustion pull them into unconsciousness before Nicci was able to get answers and they could finally, hopefully, be healed.

Dreier was now their only remaining hope.

As he and Kahlan followed Cassia through the complex of halls on the way to the bedroom, Richard tried to think of some other solution, some other chance, some other way for them to escape the grip of the poison, but he could think of nothing.

Irena, rushing up one of the side hallways, spotted them out ahead and called out Richard's name. When Richard turned and saw her back down the hall, she hurried all the more to rush around the corner and catch up with them.

Richard knew that the woman was always trying

to find a way to place herself close to him. He saw the looks Kahlan gave the woman when she giggled and fawned over him. Richard disliked it even more than Kahlan, but he wasn't exactly sure what to do about it. He didn't want to be rude, but more than that, she was Samantha's mother, after all. He figured that the least he could do was to be polite.

"Richard! There you are," Irena called out, lifting a hand to keep his attention. "I've finally been freed from that terrible place down below. It was awful! I thought I would never get out of there. I was so relieved to hear that you escaped as well. Are you all right? Were you hurt? Is there anything I can do to help?"

Richard and Kahlan shared a look of silent resignation. Cassia stopped between two reflector lamps a short distance farther up the corridor, waiting for them to speak to Irena.

"We're fine," Richard said without elaborating.

As Irena cut around the intersection, rushing toward them, her hip bumped the edge of a table she hadn't seen against the wall just around the corner. When her hip hit the table, something dark fell out of her dress and dropped onto the gold and blue carpet. She cursed the table under her breath for being in her way as she snatched up the skirts of her dress in order to hurry to catch up with them.

She didn't notice that something had fallen out of her dress.

"Nicci told me that she told you to get some rest for now," Irena said. "You need to rest, Richard."

"That's where we're headed right now," Kahlan said, hoping to get the woman to go away.

Instead of getting the hint, Irena gestured with a flick of her hand. "I told the soldiers to take up their

posts back there, and that I would watch over you
and Kahlan to make sure that you rested in peace. I
told them to set up stations a good distance back up
the halls to keep anyone from bothering you. It's important that you not be disturbed for now, and you
know how noisy they can be."

Richard was about to tell her that he, and not she,
would be the one to give orders to the men and that
she had no business making such presumptions, when
he was stopped in his tracks by what he saw lying
on the gold and blue carpet.

The small dark thing that had fallen out of her
dress was a journey book.

He froze for an instant, his gaze locked on it.

Before she could notice him looking at the journey book lying on the floor behind her, Richard put a
hand on Irena's back and guided her forward toward
Kahlan. "Good, Irena, we would be thankful for your
help. In fact, Kahlan was just saying that she wanted
to ask you about something you could do for me,
and, well, here you are."

He shot Kahlan a look over the top of Irena's head.
Kahlan, knowing him as well as she did, got the message and said, "Yes, I was wondering . . . if you could
help us."

Irena twined her fingers together as she gazed expectantly at Kahlan. "With what? What kind of help
do you need?"

While she was focused on Kahlan, Richard slipped
unnoticed behind her and snatched the journey book
off the carpet. He held it up high behind Irena's back
to show Kahlan what it was, then rolled his hand,
letting her know that he needed her to keep Irena's
attention. Kahlan understood.

He turned his back in case Irena should happen to

look around behind her. The journey book was filled
with page after page of writing. He was sure that this
was the twin to the one they had taken out of Dreier's robes, but that didn't make a lot of sense. Why
would Irena have the twin to his?

He had to find confirmation, one way or another.
It was possible that this one had an entirely different twin. There could be a perfectly logical explanation as to what she was doing with a journey book
and why she had kept it a secret from them.

"Well," Kahlan said in a drawl to drag it out longer, "we were hoping you could help with Richard's
headaches. Nicci is busy at the moment and I was
hoping you could come to our room with us and see
if you might be able to do something for him—you
know, with your gift. Put your hands on him and do
some small healing to ease his pain and help him
sleep, something like that. You are so talented that I
thought if anyone could do it, it would be you."

Irena touched her fingers to her neck, cooing with
satisfaction at the flattery. "I would love to."

Irena droned on, asking Kahlan specific questions
about the nature of his pain. Richard didn't even hear
what Kahlan was saying to the woman as he focused
on reading the messages back and forth between the
journey book Irena had and its twin.

A sudden, icy sensation flashed through him when
he saw what he had been looking for.

His heart hammered over what he was seeing in
the journey book.

Irena had been communicating with Ludwig Dreier
all along.

82

The book was filled with messages. She hadn't erased any of them. All the messages back and forth for more than a year were still there.

There were messages from Ludwig Dreier telling Irena the specifics of what he wanted her to do for him, along with promises of rewards for her loyalty and service to him. There was even a message Dreier had written from the People's Palace, telling her about the wedding of a Mord-Sith that he was attending. By the conversational tone of the messages and comments going back and forth, it was easy to see that the two were like-minded and quite at ease with each other.

Richard quickly came to see that Irena's handwriting was neater and more legible than Dreier's. He spotted an account where she told Dreier that she had let herself be captured by Hannis Arc so that she would be closer to him in order to report on what he was doing to raise the spirit king from the dead.

She recounted to Dreier how Richard had "rescued" her and the things he had done to escape with them from the caves and how he had been able to defeat the half people holding his friends prisoner. She had subsequently used the opportunity to join and travel with Richard and Kahlan's group.

Ludwig Dreier in turn advised her on how she should react and behave, and the things he wanted her to find out. He told her to be especially careful not to let anyone know of her occult abilities.

Irena had been right under their noses the whole time, watching and reporting everything they were doing to fight and escape the half people coming after them.

Irena had been a traitor the entire time.

There was far too much in the journey book to read it all right then. With the way his heart pounded at the betrayal and his mind raced trying to piece together all that had been compromised, Richard was having trouble focusing enough to read. He flipped over a few more pages, skipping ahead, and spotted the passage where she told Dreier that Richard and Kahlan needed a containment field in order to be healed.

She told him that she recognized it as an opportunity to finally offer an excuse to get them to the citadel, where Dreier would be able to capture them.

Richard trembled in shock as he read Dreier's message back, telling Irena how pleased he was that she had found a way to convince them to come to the citadel. He described where he wanted her to say the containment field was located within the citadel, and how to get down there, in order to get them to a place where he could take them by surprise.

She reported to him their progress along the way,

keeping him abreast of when they thought they would arrive at the citadel.

Richard felt shame and rage that he had been so completely fooled by her story.

When he quickly flipped back to the beginning, as he suspected, he spotted Irena's report to Dreier that she had killed her sister Martha and Martha's husband when they had gone to see if the reports about Jit were true. She had then dumped their bodies in the swamp. She and Dreier discussed how they couldn't risk any of the gifted in Stroyza learning that the barrier was failing. Dreier said he would send soldiers to collect her other sister, Millicent, and her husband, Gyles, and take them to the abbey to make sure they couldn't interfere, either.

Richard could hardly believe she had killed her own sisters and their husbands, and was shocked to see Irena's report that her husband had started asking too many questions, so when an opportunity presented itself, she had killed him. The casual manner in which she reported killing her husband was shocking.

Dreier told her that if her daughter ever became suspicious, Irena would need to eliminate her as well. Richard was horrified to see Irena's reply that once Richard and the others were taken prisoner at the citadel, he was welcome to take care of Samantha if he wished so that she would cease to be a potential problem.

And then he saw it.

The passage read, "The old wizard was getting suspicious. Tonight I cast a concealing spell to make it appear I was in my bedroll so that I could go off to report to you. He somehow followed me and caught me writing in my journey book. Fortunately, he thought me merely a sorceress and was unaware of the occult side of my abilities. When he used his gift to try to restrain me and take my journey book, I was happy to finally have the opportunity and I beheaded the troublesome old man. He will no longer be a problem."

Richard's vision went red.

He turned and with a scream of rage rammed into the woman, catching her completely by surprise. Richard had both hands around her throat before she knew what hit her.

He slammed her up against the wall hard enough for her head and shoulders to break the plaster. Her hands snatched desperately at his wrists. He smashed her head into the wall again before she had a chance to summon her occult abilities. The sound of the powerful blow echoed through the hall. Blood splattered across the whitewashed plaster wall. Stunned, her eyes rolling, she fought to remain conscious. Her face glowed beet-red as she struggled in vain to get air.

Irena's feet kicked above the floor as Richard pinned her up against the wall, crushing her windpipe.

He was in a blind rage, screaming the whole time. Nothing else mattered to him but choking to death this traitorous woman who had killed Zedd.

As he strangled her, her face went from red to dark red to blue. Her wide eyes bulged. Her limbs hung lifeless, swinging from side to side as he repeatedly bashed her head against the wall.

"Richard, what is it?" Kahlan cried out. "What's going on?"

He realized that Kahlan had been asking the question over and over. She had been screaming it at him.

He was panting so rapidly he could hardly speak. "She killed Zedd!"

Kahlan's eyes widened. "What?"

Richard's lethal focus remained riveted on the woman he was strangling, on her blue skin, her dead eyes staring at him as his big hands shook with the effort of crushing her throat.

"She's been a traitor among us the whole time—working to sabotage us—to make sure we were captured—to see us all murdered by Dreier." Richard gritted his teeth in rage. Tears ran down his face. "She killed Zedd!"

With a growl of fury, he slammed her lifeless body up against the wall yet again. He kept choking her, even though he knew she was dead. He wanted to kill her a thousand times over.

His grandfather, the man who had raised him, the best, the smartest, the kindest, the wisest man Richard had ever known, had been murdered in cold blood by this evil, conniving traitor.

Kahlan gently pulled on his arm. "Richard . . . it's over."

He finally dropped her in a lifeless heap, her limbs flopping out to the sides as he stood over her panting.

It was then that he realized Samantha had just come around the corner.

She stood frozen in shock. Her dark eyes were as wide as they would go. Her face stood out white against her black hair.

Frozen in horror, Samantha stared down at her dead mother for a moment. And then she ran toward Richard, screaming, her fists flying.

"What have you done! You monster! What have you done!"

"Samantha," Kahlan said, trying to pull the young woman back away from Richard, or at least to catch her furiously flying fists, "you don't understand."

"I understand perfectly well!" she screamed. "He killed my mother! He killed her! I saw it!"

"Samantha!" Richard yelled back. "You don't understand—"

"I do too understand! I understand that you've taken everything from me! I hate you! You killed her! She was all I had left in the world and you killed her! You took her from me! You took everything from me!"

Down the hall, Richard could hear the sound of

boots as men raced at a dead run toward the shrill screams.

Nicci ran in around the corner. "What's going on?"

"Samantha!" Kahlan yelled as she again tried to pull the young woman away. "Listen to us!"

Nicci skidded to a stop when she saw the crumpled body of Irena on the floor. "What happened?"

"Richard killed her!" Samantha screamed.

Cassia reached for the young woman to help Kahlan try to contain her. Samantha jerked away from them, moving back out of reach, her hands fisted at her sides, her teeth clenched, tears streaming down her face.

"Samantha," Richard said, "you don't understand. You need to listen to me. I'm so sorry, but your mother was working with Dreier against us the whole time. She murdered Zedd. She helped Dreier capture us so the two of them could—"

"Liar! You're a liar! You didn't like her so you killed her! Now you're just making excuses! She loved us all! You're a liar!"

"Samantha," Richard said, trying to find a way to get the young woman to calm down and listen, "your mother killed your aunts to help Dreier—"

"That's a lie! That's not true! You're lying! You're lying!"

"Samantha, listen to us," Kahlan put in. "She murdered your father as well. We can show you—"

"Liars! You all only pretended to like us! You're liars! I hate you all!"

Kahlan took a step toward her. "Samantha, please, you have to listen to us."

"You took what I loved most. I hate you!" she screamed at Richard. "You took what I loved most in life!"

Men running up the halls from every direction raced toward the sounds of trouble.

Samantha thrust her arms to either side, driving them back with powerful fists of air that tumbled the men back.

"You took what I loved most," she said with venom to Richard. "Now I'm taking what you love most!"

She reached out and snatched the knife from Kahlan's belt.

Richard shot toward the girl.

Before he could reach her, Samantha spun, whipping around in an arc, and slammed the knife in her fist hilt-deep into the center of Kahlan's chest.

The impact made a sickening sound.

In shock, Richard saw Kahlan's eyes go wide as she tried to pull a breath. Her eyes rolled up in her head as she collapsed.

Richard was too late to try to stop what had already happened. Samantha had already dodged back out of reach.

Kahlan was dead when she hit the floor.

Samantha darted to an intersection in the hall and turned back, fists at her sides, glaring at Richard. "I hate you! We are enemies from now on!"

As men reached to grab her, she swept an arm out. The power she released sent the men flying, slamming into walls, smashing tables as they tumbled back down the corridor.

Samantha gave Richard a last glare and then took off running.

Richard didn't give any thought to going after her. He was instead already on his knees and bent over Kahlan's lifeless form.

Her dead eyes stared at nothing.

"No!" he screamed. "No!"

Nicci pushed at him, but couldn't budge him. He didn't even feel her trying to shove him aside. He was lost in numb panic.

"Get him back," Nicci said to Cassia.

She tugged at his arm as Laurin and Vale came racing into the hall, leaping over men still down on the floor and groaning in pain.

Both Mord-Sith came to a dead stop when they saw Irena's lifeless body in a heap, and then Kahlan, dead on the floor, the knife buried in the center of her chest.

Richard needed to do something. He needed to stop what was happening. He needed to make it all right. He tried to think of how to undo what had already happened, but he couldn't seem to form thoughts.

"Get him back," Nicci growled, tears running down her face, as she urgently tried to get Richard back away from Kahlan, tried to get his hands off her shoulders so she could see if there was anything she could do.

Richard didn't want to let go of Kahlan. He couldn't let go. He was in a dreamworld where everything was happening so slow he couldn't make sense of the echoing voices. He didn't even know what they were saying. None of it seemed real.

He couldn't allow this to happen. He had to stop it.

He couldn't comprehend the sight of only the handle of Kahlan's long knife jutting up from the center of her chest.

She wasn't breathing. Her eyes stared at nothing.

"No!" he cried out again as the three Mord-Sith pulled at him, trying to get him back.

Richard had seen more than enough dead people

to know that Kahlan was dead, and yet he couldn't seem to make sense of it. It couldn't be real. He knew it couldn't be real. Not Kahlan.

"Richard!" Nicci screamed at him as tears streamed down her face. "Please, let me see what I can do! Please, Richard, get back!"

The three Mord-Sith trying to pull him back were no match for his muscle.

"Lord Rahl," Cassia said, putting her face right in front of his, blocking his view of Kahlan. "Lord Rahl, her only chance is Nicci. You have to let Nicci help the Mother Confessor."

Richard blinked. That made sense. Nicci could help her. Shaking uncontrollably, he finally moved back with the help of the three Mord-Sith pulling urgently at him.

He reached a hand out toward Nicci. "Do something!"

She ignored him as she bent over Kahlan and worked swiftly to try to fix the unfixable.

The men had recovered and collected a ways back down the halls, standing in silent shock, watching.

"You have to heal her," Richard said. "Nicci, you have to. Don't let her die. Please, Nicci, don't let her die."

Nicci stared up at him briefly, then swallowed back her emotion as she turned to the Mord-Sith. "Get her into the bedroom. Put her on the bed. Don't touch the knife."

Richard wrenched himself away from the three trying to restrain him and rushed back in to scoop Kahlan's limp form up in his arms.

"I'll do it."

84

The walls of the room Cassia had found for them were creamy stone. One of the walls displayed a large, thick tapestry depicting a dark forest scene. It reminded Richard of the place in Hartland where he had first met Kahlan.

The room's one window let in the darkness from out in the Dark Lands. Raindrops pattered softly against the diamond-shaped pieces of leaded glass. Dark, rust-colored carpet muted the sound of the rain and low rumble of thunder.

The canopy bed was covered with dark blue-green fabric embroidered with gold edging. Heavy draping of the same blue-green fabric was gathered with ties around the posts at each corner, making the bed look like a holy shrine.

Now, Kahlan lay dead on that bed as if she were lying in state.

Richard stood numb and silent as he watched Nicci frantically trying everything she could do. Even as he watched, even as he hoped, even as he tried to tell himself that Nicci would be able to save Kahlan, he knew better.

The sorceress had slowly withdrawn the knife, sensing the nature of the damage every inch of the way as she had drawn it out. Richard couldn't believe how long the blade was. He couldn't believe how much steel had been plunged through her heart.

Richard had sharpened Kahlan's knife for her, so he knew that it was razor sharp. It was sharp enough for even that skinny girl to drive it right through Kahlan's breastbone.

When Nicci had finally withdrawn the entire length of the bloody blade, she had looked at it a moment, not knowing what to do with it. She had finally returned it to its sheath, where it belonged, probably so that no one would accidentally get cut on it.

The three Mord-Sith quietly guarded the doors, making sure that no one could come in. They hadn't known Kahlan very long at all, yet they had known her long enough that tears ran down the faces of all three as they stood silent watch.

Richard had given Commander Fister orders to have the men kill Samantha on sight if she came at them, but otherwise not to go after her. She had abilities they had no defense against.

He would have gone after Samantha himself, except he didn't want to leave Kahlan. But Samantha didn't really matter, now. No matter what he did to Samantha, it couldn't undo what she had done.

Kahlan's body heaved several times with a sudden jolt from Nicci's power. It was a desperate attempt to bring life back to Kahlan's lifeless form. It didn't do any good. There was no movement, no life in her.

Richard stared at the terrifying stillness of the

woman he loved more than life itself. Nicci had closed Kahlan's eyelids so her beautiful green eyes wouldn't be staring up at nothing.

Richard had never imagined how terrifying those eyes would look without a soul behind them, without her life in them, without Kahlan in them.

He would do anything if he could trade places with her, if she would just draw breath again, look at him again. Smile with her special smile for him again.

After a time, Nicci pushed herself up and slowly, reluctantly turned.

"Richard, we need to talk."

"So talk."

Nicci rose and stepped closer to lightly grasp his arm. "Richard, she's gone."

"No, she's not. She can't be gone. You need to heal her."

Nicci looked away from his eyes as she pressed her fingers to her brow. "Richard, the knife went right through her heart. Her chest is full of blood—"

"My chest was full of blood, one time, and you healed me, remember?"

Nicci nodded. "I remember."

"You used Subtractive Magic to take the blood out and Additive to repair the damage. Do that now for her."

"Richard," she said as patiently as possible, "you were alive when I did that, and that arrow had gone through your lung, not your heart."

"Do it," he repeated.

Nicci stared at him.

Richard gritted his teeth. "Do it, Nicci. Repair all the damage. Use your gift to put her back the way she was."

Nicci licked her lips. "Richard, her soul is gone.

That knife did more than pierce her heart. It severed her soul from her worldly form. She's gone. The same as Zedd is gone. I can't heal death."

Richard was losing his patience. "Nicci, I know some things about the world of life and the world of death. I have both in me. So does she. My soul, her soul, carry both."

"And what good is that going to do? What can you hope to accomplish by having her dead body put back the way it was when she was alive?"

"Do it. Do it now and be quick about it. We don't have much time."

Nicci stared at him.

"Do it!"

Nicci flinched. Finally, she nodded with a look of sympathetic understanding. She sat on the edge of the bed beside Kahlan and immediately went back to work, placing both hands around the bloody wound as she closed her eyes. Richard watched as Kahlan's chest compressed with the pressure of Nicci's hands.

The sorceress gritted her teeth.

Outside, lightning flickered and thunder rumbled through the mountains.

Inside, the room crackled with threads of lightning that lit the stony faces of the Mord-Sith. The lamps dimmed, not because their flames went down, but because the air itself grew thick with what Richard recognized as Subtractive Magic, the magic of the underworld itself.

The realm where Kahlan had gone.

Ropes of black lightning arced and crackled around the bed. Blinding threads of lightning threaded themselves around it, spiraling and twisting, jumping from one place to another. The sound it all made—especially when the white and black lightning touched—was at times deafening.

Several times Richard saw Kahlan draw a breath under Nicci's hands, but he knew that it wasn't Kahlan breathing, it was Nicci trying to pull life back into her. She was doing everything she knew to try to bring Kahlan back.

Finally the sound and fury died away.

Nicci stood and stared down at Kahlan for a time. The blood was gone, wiped out of existence by the Subtractive Magic while the Additive had knitted tissues back together and made her still heart whole again.

Nicci took a deep breath. She looked exhausted. She looked defeated.

"I'm sorry, Richard," she whispered, unable to look up at him. "I repaired everything that was damaged. She is again as she was before. It is not enough."

Richard stared at Kahlan's still, lifeless body. "Thank you, Nicci. You cannot imagine how much I appreciate what you've done for us."

"Richard, I've done nothing of any real use. Her life is gone. Her spirit has already crossed over through the veil. Her soul is already on that journey along the lines of the Grace. She is gone beyond, now."

"I know that, Nicci," Richard said, holding himself together for what was to come.

"Now, I need you to do one more thing for me."

Nicci frowned suspiciously. "What one other thing do you need me to do?"

Without answering, Richard walked to the door, to the Mord-Sith standing silent guard. He touched the cheek of each one of them in turn.

"Thank you for reminding me why I fight for life."

A little puzzled, they nodded.

"Thank you for giving us ours back, Lord Rahl," Cassia said.

He smiled, as best he could. It was forced. "Now, I need you all to wait outside, please."

The three shared looks with one another, uncertain what he had in mind.

"Lord Rahl," Cassia said, "we . . ."

"I know," he said. "Now, please wait outside."

They nodded tearfully and then, reluctantly, quietly left, closing the door behind themselves.

Richard went back to the side of the bed. His heart

pounded so hard that he rocked slightly with each beat as he stared down at Kahlan.

"We have to hurry."

Nicci's head came up. "What?"

"Every moment counts. I need you to do one last thing for me. We have to hurry."

Nicci stared suspiciously up into his eyes. "What do you want me to do, Richard?"

He swallowed. "I need you to stop my heart."

She did not look surprised. "I can't do that, Richard."

"You can, and you must. You healed her body. Now, I have to go beyond the veil and retrieve her spirit before it travels too far along the lines of the Grace and she is lost forever to the underworld."

"Richard, that's . . . Richard, I understand how you feel, I swear I do, but that's just not—"

"I have the touch of death inside me."

"And so you want to hurry it along?"

Richard's gaze turned from Kahlan back to Nicci's haunted blue eyes. "When Hannis Arc captured all of you, he kept you trapped in chambers behind a veil to the underworld. I stepped through that veil and into the underworld to come and get you out. Remember?"

"We weren't dead, Richard."

"In the third kingdom, both worlds existed together at the same time in the same place. Because I have death inside me, I am part of that third kingdom. I'm not only alive, I also carry death inside.

"I passed through the world of the dead to get you out of that prison. I was there briefly, in the underworld, and I made it through. I know a great deal about the underworld."

"Richard, this is different. You can't go to the world

of the dead and retrieve a soul that has crossed over. You can't do such a thing."

"Ordinarily, no, but Kahlan has that same touch of death in her that I do. That means that in this world, the call of death we have in us has been slowly stealing life away from us. But Kahlan and I are of that third kingdom, with both death and life in us, together, at the same time.

"That means that right now, in that place, Kahlan has the call of life still in her. She carries both worlds until the spark of life still attached to her soul extinguishes in that dark place.

"I have to go get her before that happens. I'm dead anyway. This poison is killing me."

"But we may be able to get Ludwig Dreier to show us how to heal you."

"Only after I bring Kahlan back. Then you can heal us. But before we try to heal that touch of death, I need to use it."

"Richard, it isn't so simple as you—"

"Nicci, you were a Sister of the Dark. You know that there is more to it all than most people can begin to understand. You must stop my heart and send me beyond the veil. You must."

Nicci shook her head. "No. Richard, I can't do that." Tears started coursing down her face. "I can't do that to you. I can't. Please, don't ask such a thing of me."

Richard gripped her shoulders and made her look back at him. "I am asking it."

She started sobbing in earnest. "I can't, Richard."

"Would you die for me?" he asked.

Surprised by the question, she looked up into his eyes. "Yes."

"Then you understand that sometimes those we

love are worth dying for. If you care about me, if you love me, you will grant me this."

"Richard, it just won't work," Nicci sobbed. "She's gone. You can't change that. It would be for nothing."

"Don't you see? If I can't bring her spirit back, then I want to be with her. Please, Nicci, don't deny me this. Kahlan needs me right now. She needs what only I can do. There is no one else with the kind of chance I have. I have to do it now, before it's too late. Let me go. Let me be with her.

"Don't hold me a captive in the world of life when you have the power to send me beyond the veil. Don't make me do it myself and damage my body so that I don't have a chance to return. You have to do it now, while the spark of life is still in her soul and before her spirit travels too far into that darkness for me to find her. Every second counts. Every second allows Kahlan's soul to slip farther and farther away into the depths of the underworld where the winged demons wait for her."

Nicci shook as she sobbed, hardly able to look at him through the tears. "They are waiting for you, too."

Richard drew his sword. If he had to, he could do it himself with the sword. If he had to, he would.

"I have my sword."

"Are you crazy?" she asked in fury through her tears. "The sword is of this world. It can't cross over with you."

With the hilt in his hand, his anger had been ignited. It powered him, gave him strength to do what he needed to do.

"Its anger will. The blade is bonded to me. That bond will cross over with me, even if the blade itself won't."

Richard lay down on the bed beside Kahlan's still, lifeless form. He had never imagined that he would lie next to her when she was dead. He had to partition his mind to be able to function, to be able to think at all, or the grief would claim him and then he had no chance.

He laid the blade of the sword down the length of his body, holding the hilt over his heart, feeling the word "TRUTH" pressing into his palm as Nicci stood beside the bed crying.

Only the rage of the sword kept him from losing control and screaming in agonizing grief.

"Hurry, Nicci. It must be now."

Her teeth gritted, her hands fisted, she leaned closer. "Richard, I don't want to lose you. We can't lose you. We all need you."

"Why do you need me?" he asked, looking up into her wet, blue eyes.

"Because you are the one. You always have been. You always know what to do to save us. You always do the right thing."

"That's what I'm doing, now." He smiled. "You know that you are far more than special to me. You have saved my life more times and in more ways than I can count.

"Now, you must take it."

"How can I?" she asked.

"It's all right, Nicci. This is what I want."

As he stared into her eyes, as she wept nearly uncontrollably, she leaned over, her long blond hair falling forward over her shoulders as she placed her hands to either side of the hilt of the sword over his heart.

Richard didn't tell Nicci that while he thought he had a chance to return Kahlan's spirit to her body in the world of life, he knew that he had no chance to return.

There could be no one with both life and death in them, no one with the knowledge and experience of having been to the underworld, who could come after him.

He believed that he had a chance—a slim chance, but a chance—to capture Kahlan's spirit in time and let it return to the world of life, to her healed body.

But he knew that, for him, it was a one-way journey.

This time, there was no way he could come back.

He was terrified of dying, of giving up the only life he would ever have, but he was more terrified of living without Kahlan.

He was fully committed to what he had to do. He had made his decision. Nothing was going to deter him.

He knew full well that this was the last time he would cross through the veil.

86

Nicci's power slammed into him like a bolt of lightning, compressing his chest. In an instant his heart was stilled.

Richard's eyes squeezed closed under the unrelenting pressure. With desperate effort, he gasped a breath under the enormous weight of pain pressing in on him.

He was all too aware that it was the last breath he would ever draw.

His muscles went rigid against the searing pain. Pain burned through the nerves of his jaw, down his arms, and into his back.

Things were happening too fast, spinning out of control. He felt himself suffocating as he was unable to get any air.

Time stretched until it became meaningless. Gradually, the agonizingly pain began to become more and more distant. The pain seemed to recede in his awareness as darkness increasingly seeped in around him to take its place.

He felt as if he was trying to hold back the night, but the weight of it was overwhelming.

At some point, he lost track of what the pain had felt like. It no longer seemed important.

But in place of the pain came something far worse: a kind of blind panic at the sensation of slipping away from the world of life.

It was happening too fast.

He felt icy-cold fear as he fully grasped that he was dying, felt the finality of it, and tried desperately to cling to the slender thread of life he still had left as light and images flashed through his mind. He saw people he remembered, places he had been. The colors were vivid and bright and real. He heard distant laughter. It was him, when he was a boy, laughing as he ran from Zedd. Zedd was laughing as he chased after Richard.

Mostly, though, through it all, there was Kahlan. He saw glimpses of her gazing at him with love, her whole face radiant with it, as she smiled with her special smile that she gave no one but him.

Then that, too, faded away as his mind descended into ever-gathering darkness, a kind of heavy, thick darkness unlike any other.

He could smell sulfur.

There was no up, no down. There were no boundaries of any kind, only a black void.

He focused on what he had to do, on why he had done this.

That overpowering need became all.

In that eternity of darkness, he had to find the one person he loved more than life itself.

He had to find his soul mate.

With that thought, the thought of how Kahlan was the one, the only one that he could ever love in the way he loved her, in the way that only one soul mate could love another, he began to have a sense of a track of light in the forever of darkness. It wasn't light, though, the way the sun created light.

This was a kind of spiritual light, the kind of glow that he would expect to see from the good spirits. It seemed to be everywhere, and nowhere. It was a feeling, a presence of spirit.

He recognized that it was the right one, the right spirit.

He thought that the light was beginning to coalesce, but then he realized that it really wasn't. Rather, it was that he was traveling along the trail left by that spirit he knew so well, and as he did, he was moving along a line, a pathway that it formed moving through the eternity of darkness.

He knew, then, that he was actually seeing the glowing line of the gift within the Grace itself.

And then he spotted the glow of her spirit moving ever onward, farther and farther away, sinking ever downward.

He was confused. It felt wrong. He didn't understand why it was spiraling downward.

And then he saw them.

The demons.

They were so dark they blended with the eternal blackness. They were darkness itself, the way a night stone was dark beyond simply black. And yet, he could see them, see their shape when they writhed and tumbled and twisted downward.

The dark ones had enveloped Kahlan's spirit and were taking her with them as they descended ever deeper toward the darkest depths of eternity, taking her where they could smother her spirit and keep it forever from the light, even as they smothered the light of her spirit so that only the glow of the trail it left was visible to Richard.

A snarl of glistening black fangs turned to him. With menacing, fluid grace they spread their wings wide.

Rather than resist, Richard used the rage from the sword to propel himself toward them. It felt like he had jumped from a cliff, falling through bottomless space that was not even space, but merely a black emptiness as he traveled ever farther from any light. Even Kahlan's spirit was dimming as it was being suffocated under the weight of dark wings wrapped around her, pulling her downward.

Richard shot through that dark tangle of wings and reached Kahlan, embraced her, joining with her soul to do what he needed to do.

In that instant, for a glorious, singular spark in time, he joined with his soul mate and they were one.

He knew that that brief, singular connection when they were alone and together in the darkness would have to last him—would have to last both of them—for eternity.

And yet in the underworld, there was no time. He knew that in the brief spark of time when they were joined, he had forever to do what he needed to do, even if it might be only a fleeting second back in the world of life.

But here, time was his.

Once it was done, Richard used all his will to leave her and streak past the demons, running from them, drawing that overwhelming, uncontrollable, predatory need to chase. Hungry for his soul, driven to chase, they all turned and then suddenly swept through the darkness to go after him.

They drew ever closer as he streaked away. Black fangs glistened in the darkness as they growled and snapped at him, eager, hungry for his soul. Richard let their claws hook into him, sinking ever deeper so they could pull him in until they were close enough for their black wings to wrap around him and capture him. Even as they did, he let the rage power him so that he could keep racing away from Kahlan's spirit, keep their fury and their attention on him.

And then, claws firmly gripping him, wings enfolding him, the dark ones dragged him downward, tumbling ever downward with him, suffocating the light of his soul.

But in doing so, in coming after him as he raced away, they had abandoned Kahlan's spirit, her soul.

In that infinite span of time he had been with her spirit, he had accomplished what he needed to accomplish.

He had given her the chance she needed to live.

Suddenly freed from the weight of the dark demons, the light of her essence, that spirit, that soul, still carrying the buoyant spark of life from being part of the third kingdom—part of both worlds fused together—began to ascend, ever faster all the time, ever higher, escaping the forever of darkness.

Richard saw her glowing arms open, reaching for him as she was pulled ever upward toward life. She tried to reach out to touch him, to draw him to her, to bring him with her, but she no longer could because as she rose he was sinking with ever-increasing speed under the weight of the demons that had cocooned their inky black wings tightly around him.

The last thing he saw was her spark in the darkness high above him as it winked out, and then she was gone.

He was suddenly alone with the dark ones, alone with them in an eternity of blackness under the dead weight of oblivion where there was nothing, where even his soul would be crushed under the pressure of darkness until it ceased to exist.

His last thought was one of joy that he had been able to save Kahlan from that fate, that he had been able to give Kahlan the gift of her life, that he had done what he had always said he would willingly do.

He had traded his life for hers, so that she might live.

In so doing he had also been able to draw all the demons with him into the dark eternity below. They could no longer shadow her in death. When it was her time, she would rest forever in the Light.

Even as he felt his own spirit become insubstantial as it faded away into an eternity of darkness, he felt joy.

It had been worth it to him.

Kahlan would live.

Kahlan gasped as she sat bolt upright, her eyes wide. She desperately gasped again, trying to get enough air.

Nicci cried out, jumping back as if she had seen a ghost.

Kahlan was only dimly aware of the warm colors of the strange room, the rust-colored carpeting, the heavy, blue-green fabric draped overhead and down around the bedposts. Almost her entire focus was on urgently drawing life and air into her lungs.

On desperately drawing her severed soul back into her worldly self.

None of it really made any sense. Everything was a jumble. She couldn't quite put all the images and events together into a coherent concept.

"Kahlan!" Nicci cried out as she rushed in close to take up Kahlan's hand. "You're alive!"

Kahlan looked down at her own hand in Nicci's. It did not look to her the way she thought it should look. It didn't look like it belonged to her, or like it could possibly be hers.

It should be light, luminescent.

It should be without form. It should be insubstantial.

But this was substantial. It had form. It was not made of light. It was flesh and bone. She could feel blood pumping through her, she could feel life coursing through her, she could feel weight, touch. She could feel herself whole again.

She still gasped for air, still struggled to get enough, to catch her breath, but she was beginning to feel like she was finally getting it under control.

"Where am I?" she asked, gulping for air.

Nicci was crying for some reason. "In one of the bedrooms in the citadel."

"No, I mean where am I?"

Nicci frowned through her tears. "I don't understand."

"Is this . . . death? It's all wrong. It doesn't make sense. Something isn't right. Where am I?"

"You died," Nicci said through her tears. "You were murdered. But you have both life and death in you, and that life sustained you for a bit while you were in the underworld.

"But now you are back, Kahlan. You're alive. Dear spirits, you're alive."

Kahlan felt euphoric. She had been murdered, but now she was alive. She understood what it meant that she was going to live. Life, wonderful life, wasn't over. She couldn't stop smiling as she looked around. She was going to live.

"Where's Richard?"

Nicci's face went ashen.

Kahlan followed the woman's stricken gaze and saw that someone lay beside her.

It was Richard.

Her heart jumped with a flash of joy at seeing him.

But as soon as she saw him, she knew that something was terribly wrong.

He was too still.

He wasn't breathing.

He stared up at nothing with dead eyes.

Kahlan screamed when she realized the awful truth.

The instantaneous joy she had felt at seeing him, turned to horror.

She fell on him, throwing an arm over his chest, over his sword's hilt clutched in his fists resting over his heart.

"No! Dear spirits, no! Don't bring me back to this! Please, don't do this to me!"

Nicci rushed to draw Kahlan back, pulling her arms from him, turning her away from Richard to take her up in her arms.

"What's happening?" Kahlan wept against Nicci's shoulder.

Nicci swallowed back her own sobs. "I'm so sorry, Kahlan. Richard gave up his life to go after you, to bring you back to life. He has only been gone a moment."

Kahlan looked over at the horrifyingly still body of the man she loved, her everything. "But why isn't he here? If I was able to return because I still had that third kingdom spark of life in me, then why didn't he . . ."

She remembered, then.

It all flooded back in like a terrible, dark, profoundly troubling dream seeping back into your memory after you woke, a dream that left a sickening feeling behind in you that you couldn't escape no matter how hard you tried.

"What?" Nicci asked, seeing the look on Kahlan's face. "Do you remember?"

Kahlan nodded. "Richard's spirit found me. In all that darkness, in all that eternity of nothing, Richard found me. I was lost in darkness and yet he found me."

"Then what?" Nicci asked when Kahlan fell silent, staring off into the nightmare.

"Then he pulled the dark ones off me, drawing them away to chase after him, instead. I tried to stop him—I didn't want him to do that to himself—but he was stronger and tore them away from me. He somehow pushed me back into the glowing lines of the Grace. I had no control. I wanted to stay with him, but I couldn't. Those glowing lines pulled me back. I don't know how."

"Because you still had life in you," Nicci said. "The Grace was healing itself, putting you back to where you belonged on that line of the gift coming from Creation."

Kahlan gazed at Nicci in desperation. "Then why didn't it do the same for Richard? Why didn't he return with me?"

"He couldn't. He went there to save you from Sulachan's dark demons, and he did. He did what only Richard could do. He pushed you back toward life. But now, there is no one to save him, no one to help him get back to the light, to his lifeline."

Kahlan looked over at him lying next to where she had lain. He had his sword clutched in his dead hands. His eyes no longer saw the world of life. Now, he was lost in a world of darkness.

To see Richard so still, without life in him, was beyond any kind of agony she had ever known.

"How did he die?" Her own voice sounded like someone else asking the unimaginable.

She looked back at Nicci when she heard the sorceress softly sobbing.

"Nicci, how did he die? What happened?"

She finally looked up with torment in her blue eyes.

"He asked me to stop his heart."

Kahlan's eyes widened. "You killed Richard?"

Nicci nodded, but couldn't find the words as she wept with the horror at what she had done. It was a torture she would always have to bear.

"Nicci, how could you kill Richard? How could you possibly do such a thing? You, of all people. After all he has done for you, how could you have done such a thing to him?"

Nicci sniffled to get herself under control so that she could explain.

"Because not to have done so, not to have let him have his deepest wish to go after you to try to save you, would have been worse. It would have been saving his life but killing his soul."

It was obvious what such a burden was doing to the woman. She looked ready to end her own life.

Kahlan reached out and cupped Nicci's face. "Dear spirits, I understand. I'm so sorry, Nicci, that it had to be you to do such a thing. You, of all people."

"I'm so sorry, Kahlan," Nicci wept. "I'm so sorry."

A spark of an idea, a spark of hope, came to her, then.

"Nicci, you stopped his heart. Can't you start it again? You said you did it only a moment ago. Can't you start his heart and let life come back into him, the way it came back into me?"

"No."

That single word had a world of finality to it.

Kahlan touched her chest where she remembered the knife slamming into her. She remembered the pain, the helpless terror.

"But I was stabbed through my heart. How is it working now? I don't understand. Why can't you do that for him?"

"Richard had me heal the damage to you before he went . . . But I couldn't bring back your life, and I can't bring back his. I don't have the power. Your heart started spontaneously when your soul returned, when Richard sent you back. Even if I could start his heart beating again, there is no soul there, nothing to keep it going. I can't pull his soul back from the world of the dead."

Tears ran down Kahlan's face as she stared at Richard lying there still as stone. She had fought countless battles, seen death more times than she cared to contemplate. She recognized that terrible stillness that existed only in death, when, after the last breath of life had faded away, the soul had left the body to journey beyond the veil.

It was a kind of stillness that was beyond redemption.

Richard was gone. It didn't seem like it could be real, and yet, she knew it was.

Kahlan lay down against Richard's dead body as she gave in to the agony and lost control.

All she could think was that he had come for her, traded places with her in death, and now there was no one to save him.

E ven as she wept against Richard's body, the words kept echoing around in her mind. *No one to save him.*

Kahlan sat up suddenly. She sucked back the sobs and wiped the tears back from her face as she scooted to the edge of the bed and hopped down onto the floor.

"Where are Cassia, Laurin, and Vale?"

Nicci gestured. "Standing watch outside the doors."

Kahlan raced to the doors and flung them open. The three Mord-Sith turned and gasped when they saw her.

"Mother Confessor!" Cassia cried. "How—I mean—I don't—"

"Richard traded places with me in the world of the dead so he could send me back," she said in a rush.

Their eyes widened, stricken with horror. "Lord Rahl is dead?" Vale asked in a shaky whisper.

"I'll explain it later. Listen to me. Cassia, go get Commander Fister."

She pointed to a hallway branching off not far down the corridor. "He is waiting right down there, not far but out of the way, along with a number of the men."

"Good. Tell him to bring a few dozen men. At least half of them archers. Laurin, Vale, you two go down in the dungeon and get Dreier. That collar he is wearing keeps his powers contained, so you will be able to handle him."

Although shocked to see her alive and at a loss to understand what she could be thinking, they nodded earnestly.

"What do you want me to do?" Cassia asked. "I mean, after I give the commander your instructions?"

"I want you to go get Mohler and bring him back here. We need his keys."

They looked confused. Or maybe it was just that they thought she might be a ghost, or a good spirit.

"Go! Hurry!" Kahlan said. "If we are to have any chance of saving Richard's life, we have to hurry!"

Cassia blinked. "You mean, there is a chance to save his life?"

"Yes!"

All three turned and raced away to do as they had been asked.

Kahlan rushed back inside. She thought there was a chance. She had to believe that there was. She forced her grief aside so that she could act. Now was not the time to grieve. Richard would tell her to think of the solution.

"Dreier has abilities we can't even imagine," she told Nicci.

Nicci turned away from staring at Richard's lifeless corpse stretched out on the bed. "What of it?"

"What if he could bring life back into Richard?"

Nicci wiped back her tears as she frowned. "Bring back life? What are you talking about? What do you mean, bring life back into him? You can't do such a thing to—"

She closed her mouth. She looked like she had been about to say "to the dead." She didn't want to refer to Richard that way.

"Sulachan and Hannis Arc can," Kahlan said. "Even those half-people soul trackers could wake the dead, remember?"

A horrified look twisted Nicci's face. "You want to ... what? Have Ludwig Dreier turn Richard into one of those walking dead? You want the man to use his power to reanimate Richard's dead body? Kahlan, you can't, you wouldn't. He wouldn't really be alive. He would just be another of those monstrous corpses that moves, but he wouldn't be alive. It wouldn't be Richard.

"Kahlan, Richard is gone. His life force, his spirit, his soul has left him and gone beyond the veil."

Kahlan paced for a moment, thinking, refusing to allow herself to give up. "Nicci, I'm just trying to think of how to do what he did."

"What he did? What do you mean?"

"Richard had you heal my body—the wound and my heart—so that my body would be ready for my spirit to return."

Nicci was frowning at her. "So you are suggesting that we get Dreier to make his body alive again, like some kind of mutant half person without a soul?"

Kahlan paced to the window and back along the

thick, rust-colored carpet. "No—I don't know. I'm just trying to think of a way to help him. We have to help him."

Nicci cocked her head. "Help him . . . what?"

"Well, you remember when he saw those people who snuck up on him—back right before all those half-people spirit trackers attacked us."

"Yes, I remember. But they weren't there. They vanished, somehow."

Kahlan nodded. "Richard said that the souls of the half people Sulachan created were ripped from them, and also that in order to animate the dead, part of that process involved ripping the dead person's spirit from the underworld—disconnecting them from where they belonged. Those spirits were lost, they were severed souls."

Nicci folded her arms, frowning as she tried to follow what Kahlan was getting at. "All right. . . ."

"What did Richard say they said to him? 'Bring us our dead.' He said that they expected him to reunite them with their dead bodies."

Nicci rubbed her eyes for a moment. "You mean, you think that maybe Richard's spirit could be reunited with his dead body? How?"

Kahlan lifted her arms in a gesture of frustration. "I don't know, Nicci. All I'm saying is that if there is any chance for Richard to ever return, it has to be soon, and he has to have his body ready for his soul to return to."

"Like Richard wanted your heart healed so that when he went to get you, your soul could return to your body, because there was a home for it after I fixed it. So you think that maybe Richard's spirit will find a way back to his body?"

Kahlan shook her head in frustration. "I don't

know, Nicci. I'm just trying to think of something— anything. I can't accept that Richard is really dead. The way he crossed over and came back before makes me think there has to be hope. Richard has gone to the Temple of the Winds in the underworld. He is of the third kingdom and so he went through the world of the dead to rescue you and the others.

"This is Richard we're talking about. He's done it before. He has gone to the underworld before and re- turned."

Nicci gently grasped Kahlan's shoulders, then, and looked into her eyes. "Kahlan, Richard made sense, after a fashion. A crazy, wild, Richard kind of sense, but sense. This is different. This is . . . I don't know, this sounds to me like you are just trying to wish something into being true because you're des- perate."

Kahlan stared back. Hopelessness clawed its way back into her. "Maybe I am, but don't you think we should try? Do you want to let him go without trying? We have to try."

"Kahlan, look at him." Nicci turned Kahlan's chin to make her look past her toward the still body lying on the bed. "Look at him. Kahlan, Richard is dead."

Kahlan looked back into Nicci's eyes. "So was I."

Nicci wiped a trembling hand back over her fore- head. "Yes, and you had Richard to go to the under- world itself to bring you back. Who is going to bring him back?"

Kahlan felt the terrible weight of despair crushing her. "I don't know, Nicci, but we can try, can't we? Please, Nicci? We can try every last crazy thing, can't we?"

Nicci took a deep breath, then. "Yes, of course we can. You're right. We have to try."

Kahlan and Nicci were standing beside the bed, waiting, when there was at last a knock on the door. Without waiting for an answer, Cassia opened the door and stuck her head in.

"Mother Confessor, we have him."

Kahlan gestured impatiently. "Bring him in."

She put on her Confessor face, the expression her mother had taught her, the countenance that showed nothing of what she felt. She was dying inside, terrified and in agony inside, but none of it showed on her face.

She was again the Mother Confessor.

The doors opened and the three Mord-Sith led Ludwig Dreier in. They gave him a last, rough shove so that he stumbled into the room. He wore filthy, old groundskeeper clothes they had found for him. He missed a step, balking when he saw what was waiting for him in the room.

Commander Fister stood near the foot of the bed, behind Kahlan and Nicci. The room was ringed with over a dozen archers, all with arrows nocked, holding them in place, the strings with tension on them but not yet drawn fully tight. There were also men with swords out, as well as men with axes in hand, and others with pikes. It was the archers, though, that Kahlan could tell worried Dreier the most.

When he had rendered them all unconscious with his occult ability, they had not had time to do much about it. A man with a sword, no matter how swift, still took a brief bit of time to reach his target.

But an arrow could be released in an instant.

"Well, well, Mother Confessor," Dreier said as he straightened, "it seems you have me at a disadvantage."

"I'm glad that you recognize the reality of the situation."

He looked around at the room. "I know you said you intended to kill me, but this seems an odd place for an execution."

Kahlan stepped aside so he could see Richard's body on the bed. He frowned when he realized who it was.

"Is he actually dead?" he asked, his astonishment overcoming his fear.

"I stopped his heart," Nicci said.

His frown deepened. "Not that I object, but why would you do that?"

"Here's the thing," Kahlan said. "We want you to do something to keep him alive for now."

He scratched an eyebrow. "What?"

"Use your occult abilities to keep him alive," she said.

He stared at her a long moment, looked over at Richard, and then back at Kahlan. "He's dead. You must realize that. I can see from here that he's dead."

"We know his condition," Nicci said. "It was necessary to stop his heart, but I don't have the ability to restart it. We need you to do that."

His frown grew even more incredulous. "He is dead."

"We didn't bring you up here to tell us what we already know," Nicci said, heat increasingly coming into her tone. "If you want, we can take you back down to your cell, chain you back up, lock the door, and throw away the key. Or, maybe we can have these three fine young ladies convince you of the benefits of not being tortured by a Mord-Sith."

Cassia briefly jammed her Agiel into the small of his back. He grunted with a cry of pain as he dropped to one knee. She motioned with her Agiel in front of his face for him to get up.

He stared at the weapon with open fear as he rose. "What is it, exactly, that you want me to do for the corpse of Richard Rahl?"

Kahlan hated the way he was referring to Richard, but she maintained the Confessor face. She had more important matters on her mind. She needed to stay focused, despite her inner anguish.

"We know that occult powers can do some remarkable things with creating the likes of half people and reanimating the dead, but beyond that, we don't know if you can do anything that would convince us not to have you tortured to death. So, you tell us. What can you do to keep him alive?"

He tilted his head to look past them. "May I get a closer look?"

Kahlan nodded and the Mord-Sith walked him

closer to the bed. He reached out and touched Richard's face, then his neck.

"What's in it for me?" he asked as he looked back.

"Depends on what service you can provide," Kahlan said.

"Well, I can't really be of any use to you at all with this collar around my neck. It prevents my ability from functioning."

"If we take the collar off, what can you do? You don't need it off to tell us."

He checked the resolve in her eyes before again studying Richard more closely from the side of the bed.

"Well, not a lot. I may be talented, and may have a great many skills, but I can't revive the dead."

"Then I guess you will soon find yourself in the same condition," Kahlan said. "Dead. I guess this conversation is over."

He put a finger under the collar, trying to ease the discomfort of it. Kahlan could see his hands trembling slightly.

"Well, there are things I can do with occult abilities that suspend the death process."

"What does that mean, exactly?" Nicci asked.

He gestured toward Richard. "If he stays like that, he will soon go all stiff, then begin to decompose and rot, just like any corpse. With my occult abilities, I can suspend that process before it starts so that the body stays viable, after a fashion."

"How does that work?" the sorceress asked.

"It's complex to explain to someone not schooled in the use of occult abilities."

"Make it simple for me while you still have the ability to talk."

He swallowed at the look in her eyes before again

glancing over at Richard. "Well, you were a Sister of the Dark. You must know some of the basics about the underworld."

"I do."

"Then you know that time means nothing there, in the eternity of the underworld. What I can do is create a bridge to link some of that timelessness of the underworld to his body."

"And what would that do?" Kahlan asked.

He shrugged. "I'm not positive. I've never done it before, never had cause. But it's the basic concept behind using occult powers to enliven corpses or to create half people. The half people, for example, live for long periods of time because they carry a link to the underworld. That timeless link keeps them from aging like normal people. Keeps time from working on their living body the way it ordinarily would. By using a link like that, I can keep his body the same as it was the moment he died. With time moving slower for him, he will remain in that state for quite some time."

Nicci rubbed her arms as she glanced over at Kahlan. "The Palace of the Prophets was like that," she admitted. "Nathan Rahl lived there for close to a thousand years because the spell around the palace was linked to the underworld."

"Exactly," Dreier said, lifting a finger to make the point. "It can't bring back the dead, but it keeps the body in the state it was in when he was alive, doesn't let it age the way the dead ordinarily would, and thus not decompose."

"Then how do we bring him back to life?" Kahlan asked.

"I never said you could. I only said that I could keep him viable. I can't make the dead come back to life. I can animate corpses, but they aren't actually alive."

"So what good would this do him?" Nicci asked.

Dreier lifted his hands in frustration. "None, as far as I can see. He's dead. His life force is gone. His spirit is in the underworld. You asked what I could do. That's the closest I can come. I can link his remains to the underworld to halt the process his body would go through after dying."

"So that would preserve him for now," Kahlan said, "until we can figure out how to bring his life force, his spirit, back into his body."

Dreier made a face. "Preserve him for a time, yes. Bring his spirit back into that preserved body? That can't be done. He is dead, ladies. Dead, dead, dead. I don't know how to bring the dead back to life. But if you do, then I suppose this would keep him from deteriorating until you bring him back from the dead.

"I can do a great many things with my abilities, but there are limits to how far one can bend the laws of nature. One of those limits is the Grace itself. It defines life and death. It can't reverse death."

Kahlan wondered if the man was telling the truth—if she could trust him to tell her the truth. She looked from Dreier's eyes to the still form of the man she loved. The man she desperately wanted back.

Kahlan knew that Richard hadn't actually, technically, reversed her death. He had used the spark of life still in her soul. That spark was what had brought her back.

Richard had that same spark of life in his soul. At least, she hoped he still did. In the underworld it would fade rapidly.

It was the balance to the poison Jit had infected them with. She had put death into them when they were still alive. That death had been extinguishing their life force, but for a time life and death existed together. They were part dead, yet part alive.

"All right," she said. "Do it. If that's the best we can do for now, do it."

Dreier waggled a finger. "Not so fast. What's in it for me?"

"What do you want?"

"I want you to let me and Erika go."

Kahlan, still wearing her Confessor face, stared into Dreier's eyes. Her entire life had been devoted to uncovering truth. She weighed what to do, what she dared to do. Everything hung in the balance, and on the choice she made. The right choice did not mean success, but if she made the wrong choice, all would certainly be lost.

In that brief instant, she weighed his words, the risks, and made her decision.

Kahlan gave him a single nod. "Done. You do what you said to keep Richard's body viable, and we will let you go."

Nicci took hold of Kahlan's arm. "Mother Confessor, I don't think that's such a good idea. What he is proposing to do, when it comes right down to it, is of virtually no value. And for that we would be giving him his freedom? So that he could plot his revenge? So that he could use those occult powers against us on another day? If he could start Richard's heart, maybe, but just to keep him the way he is . . . ?"

Kahlan stared at Dreier for a long time. It was his occult powers she was considering. Finally, she turned and paced to the bed. The big men all around the room looked grim and despondent. They had lost their Lord Rahl. It was unthinkable. What was to become of them all without Richard?

"When I was young," Kahlan said, "there was a boy I knew of who lived there in Aydindril. One day, in late winter, he fell through the ice on a lake. He was under the ice for hours before they were able to get his body out. He was dead, of course—drowned under the ice. They wrapped him up, preparing to bury him, when he revived.

"I don't know much about such things, but I saw it with my own eyes. Who are we to say when the soul has actually crossed over for good, when that veil has closed? If there is a way to keep Richard on ice, so to speak, to give him a chance to return back through that veil, then I want to take it."

Nicci regarded her with an understanding look. "If you say so, then I agree."

Kahlan gave the signal. All around the room, the archers drew back their bowstrings.

"Take off his collar," she said to the scribe standing quietly back against the wall.

Mohler shuffled forward with his keys.

"You make one wrong twitch," Kahlan told Dreier as Mohler unlocked the collar, "and you will have a dozen arrows through you from every which way."

He nodded. "And do I have your word as the Mother Confessor that if I do this, you will let me go?"

Kahlan glanced at the sorceress a moment, then to Dreier.

"You have my word as the Mother Confessor. If you keep your end, we will let you go."

In unison, the archers tracked Dreier's every step.

He kept a wary eye on them as he went to the bed where Richard lay.

He gestured over the body. "Can you remove that sword, please? It interferes with what I have to do."

Kahlan lifted the weapon and slid it back into the scabbard at Richard's hip. Being that close again, touching his cold flesh, seeing him that still, almost made her panic, almost made her lose control of her Confessor's face.

Kahlan finally stepped back. "All right, go ahead."

They all watched as Dreier wasted no time in laying his hands on Richard's chest. He closed his eyes a moment, then placed one hand on Richard's forehead. The air in the room began to hum. The sound built until the glass in the window rattled. A momentary glow came to Richard's body as the room darkened.

Dreier lifted his hands back.

"It is done."

Kahlan stood by the bed and stared at Richard for a moment. "I don't see anything different."

"I told you, the man is dead. Nothing is going to change that." He gestured in frustration at Richard. "I did what I told you I would do. He will be preserved for now. He will not go stiff in death and decompose. He will stay as he was when alive. You will be able to tell for yourself when in a short time he does not get stiff as the dead always do."

Kahlan went to the window set back in the thick stone wall, looking out at the dawn of the gray day. She put a hand over her stomach. She felt like she might be sick. She leaned under the arch and opened the window to get some fresh air on her face.

She had never thought she would see another day. Now, she didn't care if she did.

"You may go," she said without looking back over her shoulder to Dreier. "Commander, see that he has safe passage out of the citadel. I want him out of here, and I want him out now."

As they all watched and waited on her, Kahlan took a breath to steady her voice.

"But I gave my word as the Mother Confessor. Don't you or any of your men do anything to break my word. Get him out of the citadel and let him go. Do it at once."

Commander Fister reluctantly clapped a fist to his heart. "Of course, Mother Confessor." He gestured to his sergeant. "Take some of the archers and see to getting him out."

Kahlan didn't look back. "Laurin, Vale, please go with them to make sure the abbot is promptly sent out and on his way."

Dreier was eager to leave before she could change her mind. In a moment they were gone. The commander fidgeted for a time after the door closed as she stared out the window.

"Kahlan," Nicci finally asked in a quiet voice, "do you really think what Dreier did was of any use? Do you really think that it gives us any hope at all?"

Kahlan was silent for a time, staring out the window without seeing anything, as tears ran down her face and dripped off her jaw.

"No," she finally said in a frail voice as she stared out at nothing. "Richard is gone. He took my place in the underworld. I saw the winged demons take him down into the depths of darkness. He is lost to us."

Nicci stepped closer. "You saw that?" she asked in a soft, fearful voice. She had been a Sister of the Dark and knew full well what such a thing meant. "You saw the dark ones take him down?"

Kahlan nodded without looking back.

"Dear spirits . . ." Nicci whispered. She covered her mouth with a hand, holding back a cry of anguish at having sent him to that fate.

"Mother Confessor," Commander Fister said, "there must be some small hope that Lord Rahl will somehow . . ."

"Come back from the dead?" Kahlan slowly shook her head, tears streaming down her face. "I would love to believe it. I would hold out hope if I could. For a brief time I thought I could. I tried. But my whole life I have been devoted to the truth, no matter how harsh and cold the truth may be. I am the Mother Confessor and I can't believe in something I know isn't true."

The room behind her fell silent again as she stared out the window.

Kahlan wiped tears from her cheek as she turned to one of the men. "May I have your bow, please?"

Puzzled, he handed it over. Nicci, wondering what Kahlan was doing, went to the window beside her.

Kahlan nocked the arrow and drew the string to her cheek. She settled herself and called the target to her the way Richard had taught her.

Nothing else existed.

Time slowed.

She didn't even feel herself release the bowstring. Like a breath of breeze, the arrow was away.

Kahlan watched its flight, watched it going exactly where she had envisioned it to fly.

The arrow hit Ludwig Dreier square in the back of his head on the left side, exiting his right eye socket. Dreier dropped, dead before he hit the road leading away from the citadel.

"Beautiful shot, Mother Confessor," the archer said, sounding sincerely impressed when she handed him back his bow.

"Richard taught me to shoot. You wouldn't believe how good he is . . . was . . ." she said, her voice trailing off.

Nicci arched an eyebrow. "Not that I object, but you broke your word. You said you would let him go in exchange for what he did."

Kahlan met Nicci's gaze with an iron look. "I kept my word. I told him I would let him go. I never said how far." She gestured out the window. "I didn't tell him that that was as far as I ever intended on letting him go."

Some of the men smiled just a little. That was the Mother Confessor they knew, the Mother Confessor they had fought beside. The Mother Confessor with an iron will and an unwavering sense of justice.

Kahlan softly asked everyone to leave, then. She wanted to be alone with Richard.

She sat on the edge of the bed beside him, looking down at him, as everyone started quietly filing out.

Nicci shared a silent, tearful, sympathetic look with Kahlan before gently closing the doors behind her as she left.

Kahlan didn't know how she was going to go on, or what she was going to do.

She was lost.

Everything was lost.

She understood how Cara felt.

After crying in desolate solitude for hours as she lay beside Richard's body, desperately wanting more than anything to have him reach out and hold her in his arms, after being certain that she would die of inconsolable grief, after wishing she could die and have the suffering end, Kahlan finally wiped her tears, straightened her clothes, and emerged from the bedroom.

Nicci, a number of soldiers of the First File, and the three Mord-Sith were standing silent vigil outside the bedroom, but down the hallway a respectful distance, not wanting to appear to be standing by the door, listening to her cry. When Kahlan started off in silence down the corridor to go speak with Commander Fister, they all followed behind her. They were thoughtful enough, though, to give her plenty of space to be alone in her grief. Even Nicci hung back with the others. She could tell that it would be best to give Kahlan some privacy and not ask any questions.

There was no comforting such inner agony and they all knew it. They were grieving, too, but Kahlan's grief was different.

She had lost her entire world.

She had lost her soul mate.

As she came around a corner, Erika suddenly appeared from a dark doorway right in front of her.

The Mord-Sith again had on her black leather outfit. Gripping her Agiel in a tight fist, she was considerably closer to Kahlan than any of the people back down the hall following behind. And the Mord-Sith was already moving at a dead run as she emerged from the doorway. Kahlan had fought in the war with Cara enough to recognize the way Erika was holding her weapon. It was a killing stance, meant to deliver a single strike to stop the heart of an enemy.

Erika's eyes were filled with hate.

Instinctively, Kahlan had already raised her hand as Erika flew toward her.

Kahlan's fingers just began to contact the center of the woman's chest, just below her throat.

In that instant, time became hers.

The contact of her fingers was still ever so slight, barely more than that of a lover's warm breath on a cheek.

Time was hers. Kahlan could have counted every hair at the hairline on Erika's forehead and then every eyelash.

Although Erika's face was filled with hate, Kahlan felt no hate. She felt no pity, no rage, no anger, no sorrow. There was no mercy in Erika's eyes, and there was none in Kahlan's, either.

In that infinitesimal spark of time, Kahlan's mind

was without emotion, filled only with the all-consuming rush of time suspended.

As she watched Erika before her, frozen in time in the midst of rushing in for the kill, Kahlan knew that the woman had no chance.

None.

She was already dead. That fact simply hadn't caught up with her yet. Kahlan could see in the woman's eyes that she did not yet comprehend what was about to happen. She still thought that she was in control of what was about to happen.

She was not.

The cold ferocity of Kahlan's power slipping its bounds was breathtaking. She felt it welling up from that deep core within her, obediently inundating every fiber of her being in its onward rush.

In that instant in time, her power was all.

As Kahlan had done countless times before, she released her restraint on that wave of power just as it was cresting through her.

Erika's mind, who she was, who she had been, every desire she had ever had, was already gone.

In a timeless instant of pristine violence, thunder without sound jolted the air of the hallway.

Glass chimneys on the nearby lamps shattered. A window exploded outward. The floor and walls shook from the concussion. Nearby doors blew open. The ripple of power lifted the carpet, rolling it in a wave racing away in both directions. The terrible shock of it cracked the plaster of the walls all up and down the hall.

Behind her, people were thrown to the ground. Those closest felt the searing pain of it the most.

Screaming, Erika collapsed. Her arms and legs twitched as they began pulling in, drawing her up into a ball as she screamed. Bones snapped. Flesh ripped. The woman could do nothing to stop the pain of her body coming apart as the lethal result of her Mord-Sith ability absorbed the unleashed power of a Confessor.

As the woman in black leather writhed in agony, the men, who had finally recovered and scrambled to their feet, came rushing forward to make sure the threat was subdued. The threat had been subdued before they had even seen the woman.

The threat had been ended the instant Kahlan had seen her.

Cassia, Laurin, and Vale, all in red leather, closed in beside Kahlan, looking down at the result of a Confessor unleashing her power on a Mord-Sith.

This time, there would be no begging to carry out the wishes of the Confessor who had touched her. It was different when a Mord-Sith was touched by a Confessor's power. For a Mord-Sith, such a touch meant a long and agonizing death.

"Pick her up and take her down to the dungeons," Kahlan said to the men. "Leave her down there where her screams won't bother anyone. No need to lock her in. She won't be going anywhere, but she will be the rest of the day and probably the entire night dying."

"I had heard the stories," Cassia said in a whisper as she watched the men picking up the twisting, screaming woman dripping a trail of blood as they carried her down the hallway. "The truth is a lot worse than the rumors."

Kahlan nodded. "She chose her own fate the day she eagerly swore allegiance in her heart to Ludwig Dreier."

As the men vanished down the hall, carrying the

screaming Erika away, Nicci took Kahlan by the arm and pulled her close.

"Kahlan, the poison you carry in you, Jit's touch of death, cut you off from your power, preventing you from using your ability. So how did you do that?"

"I no longer carry Jit's poisonous touch of death in me."

Nicci blinked in surprise. "What?"

"When I was in the underworld, Richard removed it. Because we were in the world of the dead, the touch of death could cause no harm when it was pulled out of me, the way it would have here in the world of life. The world of the dead is, in effect, a containment field for death. The veil keeps death on that side. Thanks to Richard, Jit's touch of death was left in the world of the dead where it belonged."

Nicci put a hand to her heart as she let out an audible sigh. "That's wonderful. Dear spirits, that's wonderful."

Kahlan nodded. "A good spirit healed me. Richard's spirit."

Cassia brightened. "Then you aren't going to die?"

Kahlan shook her head. "No, but I have nothing to live for, now. Ironic that when I was dying, I wanted to live, and now that I'm going to live, I only want to die."

Nicci put her arms around Kahlan, giving her a silent hug in sympathy.

When they parted, Nicci's expression turned suspicious. "If you could use your power, then why wouldn't you have used it on Dreier? You could have simply taken him with your power and not have had to go through all that."

"It's not as simple as it sounds."

"Maybe not," Nicci said, "but still, had you taken

him with your power you would have been certain
that you had gotten the truth out of him."

"I did get the truth out of him. I've spent my life
getting the truth out of people like him. I don't always need to unleash my power. He told us the truth.
That was all he could do for us—for Richard."

Nicci gestured back toward the bedroom. "He
wouldn't have been able to pose a threat had you
touched him and he might have also been a valuable
source of information."

Kahlan shook her head. "I made a calculated decision."

"What do you mean?"

"Other than animating corpses, they couldn't really bring the dead back to life. I don't think there
was much of anything he could have told us that
would have been worth the risk of trying to use my
power on him."

Nicci flicked a hand toward the blood on the floor.
"What risk? You took Erika with your power."

Kahlan gave Nicci a look. "Erika didn't have occult powers."

Nicci straightened. "Oh. I guess there is that."

"Indeed there is. I've never used my Confessor ability on someone with occult powers. We know that
regular Additive Magic doesn't work on those with
such power. My ability is partially Additive Magic.
Even Zedd couldn't stop those like Dreier with powerful occult abilities."

"So it might not have worked?" Cassia guessed.

"Having it not work would have been the least of
it. My power doesn't work the same on everyone.
Mord-Sith, for example, can capture a person's magic
when the person tries to use it on them, yet when they

try to capture a Confessor's power it turns deadly, as you saw with Erika.

"It is entirely possible that had I tried to use my Confessor power on Dreier, he could have turned it back on me in a similar way and used the opportunity to have us all. It could easily have been a fatal mistake for all of us. The risk was too great, and besides, I believe we got all we could from him, so there was no point. That was the calculated decision I made."

Nicci nodded with a sigh. "I should have known you would have thought it through."

Kahlan stared off into her thoughts. "Richard taught me to think of the solution, not the problem. That's what I was trying to do."

W hat are we going to do, now," Commander Fister asked when Nicci and
Kahlan parted and the hallway fell silent
again.

Kahlan swallowed. "Richard isn't coming back.
We need to face that. I was only fooling myself. The
awful truth is that Richard is dead.

"We know what he had wanted done with Zedd's
remains. He would want us to do the same for him.
He is gone now, lost to those of us left behind in this
world. We owe it to him to take care of his worldly
remains. We are going to have to prepare a funeral
pyre and say our good-byes."

Tears slowly ran down the faces of all three Mord-
Sith.

"Kahlan, are you sure?" Nicci asked. "What Ludwig Dreier did used occult power. We don't know if
there might still be hope."

"Hope?" Kahlan asked. She shook her head as she

swallowed at the painful agony of the memory she still couldn't get out of her mind. "You didn't see what I saw. Those dark, winged demons chased him, caught him, hooked their claws into him so he couldn't get away, and then wrapped their black wings around him to smother his soul as they carried him down into oblivion."

Everyone stared in silent horror.

"There must be some hope," Nicci finally said in a weak voice. "Richard would want us to have hope."

Kahlan felt empty. The world of life was dead to her.

"Hope? Hannis Arc and Emperor Sulachan are headed for the People's Palace. Sulachan wants to break the world of life. He wants to loose the world of the dead on all of us.

"The only one named in prophecy who had a chance to stop that was Richard. Prophecy has named Richard every step of the way, in everything he did, as the pebble in the pond, as the only one who had a chance to set things right.

"Prophecy says that the only hope to stop this threat from the third kingdom being set free on us all is for Richard to end prophecy. He is the only one with a chance.

"Now, he is dead. We have no hope without Richard. In a way, since there was so much prophecy involving him, since he was so tightly woven into so much of prophecy, since he was *fuer grissa ost drauka,* that means that with him dead, prophecy, too, has ended. It died with Richard. After all, what can it say about him now that he is gone? He was the one, and now he is gone.

"In a very real way, by dying Richard has ended prophecy.

"There is no one else who can stop evil from

darkening the world. Time and hope has run out for life.

"To tell you the truth, I can't think of a reason to care."

"Kahlan," Nicci said in a comforting manner, "Richard wouldn't let that happen. The people of D'Hara need him. Richard would return from the dead to protect them. He is the Lord Rahl. He is bonded to them and they to him. He would come back from the world of the dead to protect them."

Kahlan swallowed back the grief, trying to hold back the tears by trying to maintain a Confessor face.

"I understand the sentiment, Nicci, and the words are very noble—they really are—but they are just words. It takes more than wishes and words. You know in your heart as well as I do that there is no way for him to return, that he is gone."

Kahlan thought that maybe she should be the one unwilling to accept the reality of Richard's death, that she should be the one saying that he would return and hoping against hope for some miracle to come out of thin air.

But she was a Confessor, and as a Confessor Kahlan's entire life had been devoted to truth. She couldn't deny the truth because it was painful.

Even in this, she could not deny truth.

Cassia rolled her Agiel in her fingers. "Mother Confessor, I was without hope. I found my way back."

Kahlan gestured to the woman's Agiel. "And does your Agiel work, now that Dreier is dead and Richard is . . . gone?"

"No," Cassia said with a sad smile. "But is it so bad that I don't feel the pain? At least for a time?"

"I guess not," Kahlan said as she put a consoling hand on the woman's shoulder. "But not feeling the pain means that Richard is gone, and the bond to the Lord Rahl is dissolved. I guess, though, that not feeling the pain of that link is a small consolation."

She knew that, for her, the pain had only just begun.

"What about Lord Rahl's sword?" the commander asked. "I mean, do we leave it with him, when we . . . prepare his funeral pyre?"

Kahlan knew what she had to do. "No. With Zedd gone, and Richard gone, the sword now falls to me. Bring it to me."

He silently tapped his fist to his heart.

Talking about it, having to face the reality, was crushing her soul. Kahlan felt faint with the grief twisting in on her. Her knees almost buckled. Nicci caught her arm and helped her over to a window where she hurriedly unlatched it and swung it open.

"I think you need a little fresh air," the sorceress said.

The thought of Richard lying dead and all alone back in that room was making Kahlan feel hot and dizzy. She couldn't get the image out of her mind. She couldn't think of anything else. Richard seemed so alive, and yet, her mind could bring forth only the image of his worldly form lying lifeless on the bed as his severed soul was being carried down into eternal darkness. Even though part of her could think of him only as alive, he was already receding back into the realm of memories.

Kahlan wanted to scream, to cry, to turn things back to the way they had been. For some reason, she couldn't cry. She thought she might pass out instead. Her hands shook. Her whole body trembled.

"Kahlan," Nicci said in urgent, but soft, compassion, "you need some air. Breathe. Come on, take a deep breath. It will do you good."

Kahlan leaned on her hands on the stone sill, breathing in the cooler air. She felt a tear roll down her cheek and drip off her jaw.

How was she going to go on?

What was she going to do?

She just wanted Richard. She ached for him to be there by her. Somehow, none of it seemed real, and yet it seemed more real than anything had ever felt.

She had wanted so badly for Richard to have a life with her, a life they could share and enjoy away from conflict. A time to live for just themselves. That chance had slipped away from them. Now, they would never have a life together.

As she gazed out across the grounds and to the forest not far beyond, she spotted a creature at the edge of the woods, sitting on its haunches, watching her.

It was Hunter.

As he sat there, silently looking up at her, Kahlan thought that he almost looked like he had come to offer his condolences. More likely, Red had sent him in a gesture offering hers.

Red had known. Red had told her. Had Kahlan listened to Red's warning and done as the witch woman wanted, Kahlan would be the one who was dead, and Richard would be alive.

She looked over at the sorceress. Of course, Nicci would be dead, too.

Prophecy rarely turned out the way it seemed.

In this case, events had turned out exactly as Red had predicted, but in ways that Kahlan could never have imagined.

And yet, the prophecy had been precisely correct.

Kahlan hadn't listened.

Now, like Richard, prophecy, too, was dead.